PALACE SECRET

**A Tale of Love, Adventure and the Quest
for the Secret Behind the Door.**

The Thrilling Sequel to "Valley of the Queen"

William Diebold

ISBN: 0692874666
ISBN: 9780692874660

To my grandchildren, Coco and Weston.
May they enjoy reading as much as I do.

Chapter 1

$$\daleth \lrcorner \sqrt{}^{L^r} = -\mathsf{V}\mathsf{I}^{\circ^{(\mathsf{F})}} \daleth \lrcorner \sqrt{}^{L^r} + \frac{\ell}{\daleth \lrcorner \sqrt{}^{L^r}}\ \ \daleth \lrcorner \sqrt{}^{L^r} + \sqrt{}^{L^r} (\daleth\negthinspace\lrcorner) \ \daleth \lrcorner \sqrt{}^{L^r} \ \lrcorner \angle\daleth \sqrt{}^{L^r} (\daleth\negthinspace\lrcorner)$$

Prehistoric Earth

Ngocan, the chief scientist, and leader of the Ferrens, checked his calculations once more and compared them against his recent readings from the glowing oval-shaped portal nearby. The portal was an access to an inter-galactic wormhole, which could transport the Ferrens back to their home world, Ferrenxis, a system several light years away. It was comparable to walking from one room to another, but in reality was from one planet to another over great distances within a burst of focused magnetic energy. This method of transport from this planet to theirs was only available for a short period about once every ten thousand years when the stars were properly aligned to allow it. On his desk, he pondered an intricate chart of galactic magnetic fields in the form of a series of concentric circles once again. He entered all of his calculations in his logbook, which he always kept with him, and noted there looked to be less than one day remaining before the wormhole would destabilize, and no longer be able to transport them home.

When the Ferrens arrived on this planet called Geb from Ferrenxis they had high expectations because Geb physically resembled their world. It was the third planet from the star of this system, and its atmosphere and surface features appeared perfect for them. Their arrival in a single craft was timed for the construction and inception of a wormhole event that would connect them with Ferrenxis. Because of the complexity of the interstellar alignment of planets necessary for the wormhole, they had a very limited time

1

to determine the plausibility of maintaining a colony on this world. After an initial battery of tests confirmed their calculations that the environment and atmosphere could support them, they made a quick decision and brought ten thousand scientists, engineers and workers through the wormhole to begin a colony. Unfortunately, their initial testing failed to detect the intense level of gamma rays from the star that proved deadly to the ultra-sensitive Ferrens. In the first one hundred years they lost half of their population. They were forced to construct large habitats underground to live and survive until the next wormhole event opened to their home planet.

Their greatest problem initially was the supply of food and since they were a colony of scientists they approached the problem with a pragmatic concern for the survival of their people. They devised a ready solution by choosing among the species inhabiting Geb one that closely resembled their own, and they altered the DNA of these creatures to give them more intelligence, which was necessary for their work. As a result, they cultivated an entire species they called Champas (sh-ampas) who were devoted to them and labored daily to supply food for their Ferren masters.

The scientists all agreed there was little chance for the Champas, with their limited intelligence, to survive after the Ferrens departed. The Champas were only just now developing a language beyond grunts and clicking sounds. They had no sense of preparing for the seasons and were given little chance to endure the harsh cold weather predicted in the immediate future. Besides, they had not evolved into semi-intelligent beings according to the natural order, and systems of this world. Nature would again take its course, and return this planet to its existing processes of evolution.

Most of the surviving nine hundred Ferrens departed early during the wormhole event, and there remained only a small group whose responsibility was to manage the creatures on the surface. That group was now making its way through the portal.

Next to the doorway, leading to the transport chamber, stood two of the Champa creatures. Physically they looked very similar to Ferrens and wore identical bodysuits to the ones commonly worn by them. Their eyes roamed the room, but they stood rigidly straight as commanded by their Ferren master, even though they had been in the same position for two hours. The super-oxygenated air of the closed lower chamber made them a bit cheerful and light-headed. Ngocan considered them as with any creature experiment and noted that if they had tails, they would be wagging.

Ngocan looked up from his calculations as his wife Delane entered, and sat beside him before the large console where he worked. "Any sign of her?" he asked. He did not physically speak for they could communicate among their species by willing their thoughts outward. It was something they could not do with the Champas they had developed as the Champa mind was still too primitive.

Their daughter, Anh, had gone to the antechamber to say goodbye to the Champas she managed and had not returned. Ngocan was very proud of his daughter who was principally responsible for the recent successes in the continued cultivation and mental progress of the Champas. A large section of Ngocan's logbook was a section written by Anh who followed in her father's footsteps as a scientist. Anh like a few others among the Ferrens was not sensitive to the star's harmful rays and thrived in the surface environment much like the Champas she managed. She had filled her father's logbook with observations while she studied this phenomenon in hopes of determining why she was not adversely affected by the star's rays like most of the Ferrens. Her personal theory was that she was many generations separated from those who first arrived on the planet thousands of years ago and they as a species were gradually adapting to the environment on Geb. But the final decision to depart Geb was made long before this most recent wormhole event. Her research was disregarded as no longer relevant and filed away with a mountain of data gleaned from centuries of research and experimentation on Geb.

Along with their training, the Ferrens had inbred in the Champas a compelling devotion to serve and obey them. This form of DNA experimentation and alteration was strictly forbidden by law on their home world. But here, with creatures of less intelligence and bearing it was deemed acceptable and even necessary for the survival of the Ferren colony. Ngocan had cautioned Anh not to get too familiar or attached to these Geb creatures that deceptively and closely resembled Ferrens. He believed she would continue her experiments after they returned to Ferrenxis as they demonstrated great promise as a willing servant class for their Ferren masters.

Delane shook her head no and replied, "I am concerned. The last few days, as we were preparing to depart, she has been acting strange. She wouldn't deliberately stay behind, would she? It makes no sense. All of her friends left through the portal early on in the process. She would be alone here."

"I'm sure it is nothing. You know how she is with those Champas of hers," replied Ngocan. "Her experiments cultivating, breeding, and training them have been brilliant, and something for which she can be very proud. I knew it would be sad for her to leave them, particularly since she insists on treating them like peers, talking with them the way she does in that strange language they have developed. I find it amusing that she thinks they can understand all that babble that comes out of their mouths. She seems to think the one she named Rush is cuddly and cute. She asked if she could take it back with us. I told her no because it was not the best specimen, and besides, she would not want to see it dissected and examined. That ended that discussion summarily," he mused.

Three hours later, Ngocan and Delane guided the two Champa specimens through the portal and stood nervously waiting, as the window to depart grew short. They were now the very last to go, and Anh had still not returned from the surface. Ngocan, with his logbook firmly in hand, had already determined the portal would close soon based on his calculations which were at best only estimates. He was growing anxious as the power indicators wavered slightly.

"We can wait no longer, Delane," he said. "We must go now."

"I won't leave her," she replied. "I won't leave my daughter here alone."

Just at that moment, Anh rushed in. Being of eighteen Geb years with dark hair, and an oval face, she wore a body suit of a pale maroon color similar to her parents. Just behind her, wearing only a small animal skin loincloth, and looking around the large room with a bewildered expression, was her Champa pet Rush. "Mother! Father! I am here. I hoped I could catch you to properly say goodbye before you left," she declared, nervously. "I love you both and will miss you very much."

They looked at her in surprise. "Nonsense," said Ngocan. "You are going with us, and you are just in time. Come along. The portal will close very soon. We mustn't waste another minute."

"I'm not going, father. My place is here with my Rush," Anh replied.

"You listen to me, young lady…"

"I am with child, father!" she shouted, interrupting him.

Both of her parents stopped short and stood frozen in place, looking at her. The timing could not have been worse. Their minds reeled with questions, but in the end, her mother spoke first.

"Who of your friends is the father?" Delane asked.

"Oh, mother, don't you see?" she begged. "My Rush is the father. I love him! I am staying here with him."

There followed a momentary silence as both shocked parents gaped at her, marshaling their reactions to this surprising news. Slowly Ngocan's demeanor turned to rage, and he started toward her shaking so violently he dropped his logbook. But Rush who was a head taller, and a much more formidable figure physically, put himself bravely between Ngocan, and his daughter.

Ngocan raised his hand to strike but then paused in the face of their mutual defiance. Instead, he turned abruptly in anger wanting nothing more to do with them, and advanced toward the portal hurriedly.

"Come, Delane," he ordered, loudly.

"No!" she pleaded. "Please! No!"

He grabbed her arm firmly and led her toward the portal. Delane looked back at her daughter through tears and held her hand out in a desperate appeal. But before she could call to her again, they were through the portal and disappeared.

Before Anh could say anything, the bright portal abruptly went dark, leaving the room in a loud silence. They were gone from her forever. Rush recoiled and went to his knees at the sight of this miracle. Anh joined Rush on the floor to hold and comfort him. He was trembling and afraid, and suddenly, for the first time, so was Anh.

Seven months later, Anh had a baby girl. They called her Nagani, after a legendary wise, and benevolent ruler she had always loved.

Chapter 2

1992   Over Northern Cambodia

Hoa Cuc (hoe-a cook)
Champa (sh-ampa)

The white helicopter raced across the jungles, and rugged terrain of Northern Cambodia, as if on a combat mission. This was not lost on Jack Largent as he gazed out the window on the familiar landscape with some anxiety.

He had flown over the jungles of Vietnam and Laos during the Vietnam War. But the Sikorsky 76 luxury helicopter he was a passenger in this time was very different from the Huey UH-1, which was his common means of transportation back then. Dirty, and often bloodstained canvas seats, were replaced by a plush, off-white interior with comfortable, embossed leather throughout. The inside of the helicopter was quiet enough for easy conversation between passengers in contrast to the loud, ear-pounding noise Jack had been accustomed to during the war.

As a note of further concern, Jack and his Asian wife Mai were moving their family from Chicago to take up residence in the same remote jungle valley where they had both barely escaped with their lives two years earlier. During that perilous experience it was discovered that Mai was the long-lost queen and true heir to the throne of the Champa people. They were returning in triumph to Siem Kulea, the paradise valley and traditional center of the Champa world. There she would be welcomed and reunite with her people as they re-consecrated the valley that was their hallowed ground and celebrate the rebirth of the Champa nation.

Jack is forty-four, with sandy hair, brown eyes, and a square chin. He has a slim build, like his friend Daniel Vega, who is piloting the helicopter. Both were dressed similarly in tan slacks and loose brightly flowered native shirts.

It has been over twenty years since Jack was a photographer in Vietnam. Since then, he built a very successful business as an advertising photographer in Chicago, with major clients in the food, and product industry. This journey marked a major change from that business routine, but one that he welcomed because in spite of his success, his work toward the end seemed repetitive, and though he would not admit it to anyone, even boring. The fact is, that with all of the excitement in these jungles two years ago the focus of their lives had been irrevocably altered from a typical young Chicago family to one considerably more complicated.

There were five passengers in the cabin of the fast moving and comfortable helicopter that morning. Jack Largent and his wife, Queen Maisong Sambath Largent, sat together on one side of the cabin. Opposite them, sat Kelly Ryan, a close friend, and former assistant to Jack in his advertising photography business in Chicago. Beside her, sat Jasmine Ngo, Jack's present photo assistant, who was moving with them to Siem Kulea. On her lap, sat Jack and Mai's three-year-old daughter Devearney, examining an illustrated children's book about pigs that can fly.

Jasmine is of medium height with a focused take-care-of-business alpha personality. She is Asian, being of the Champa faith and heritage like Queen Mai. Her features give a hint of her rock hard body, and the martial arts training that has become a lot more than a hobby for her. Her loyalty to Queen Mai is absolute, and her feelings toward Jack have evolved partly from that. Her devotion to protecting both of them is paramount and deeply embedded according to her Champa faith.

Kelly Ryan Marsh is five-five, buxom with reddish brown hair, and a bubbly personality to match. She was, for many years, Jack's stellar photo assistant, and surprised him five years earlier by coming out as lesbian with her partner Catherine Marsh. But Jack was even more surprised when they asked him to father their child. Now they are the parents of a four-year-old, Charlie Marsh, who is presently back in Chicago with his nanny.

Catherine, her partner, is a billionaire several times over. Part of that was inherited, and part was due to the success of her production company

NearNorth Productions, a television news entity, with channels on cable and local television. It was her investigation while writing a story on an Asian despot by the name of Colonel Minh that brought the four Chicago friends to Vietnam and Cambodia two years ago. Since then, she has published two best selling books related to their adventures. But Catherine would be the first to say a large part of her financial success was the result of the exceptional talent and expertise of Mai, who as a vice president of her multi-national conglomerate runs the separate financial division along with the CFO, Brad Martin. Catherine, Kelly, and Mai are very close, and often refer to themselves as the three musketeers.

Jack shuffled in his seat and rested his hand on Mai's. She took it up into her lap with a smile and squeezed it firmly. Mai, Queen Maisong Sombath Largent, is petite and alluring with jet-black hair, dark glasz eyes, and full lips. She is very friendly with most people, completely approachable, and comfortable in that regard. In reality, she is anything but common, being partly alien having descended from a long line of alien queens dating back to pre-historic times. The mother ancestor of her lineage was a pure alien from another planet, who mated with a human producing the first queen called Nagani. Within the Champa culture, this first queen is historically symbolized by a seven-headed snake, called 'Nagani' in her honor. It also represents the maleficent bearing of this complicated queen.

Mai, however, embraces the other, more benevolent side of the ancient queen of legend represented by the Hoa Cuc, a flower common in that area of the world that has become the symbol of her ancestral family. As with the Champa queens before her, and because of the unique circumstance of the original part-alien birth, she self-reproduced her daughter and heir, Devearney, just as her predecessors have done, once each generation. These are important details about her physical self, which she only recently discovered. She has yet to share this information with Jack because she was cautiously uncertain of his reaction.

Dressed similarly to the other women that day, she chose for the trip to wear white linen slacks and a tasteful loose-fitting blouse against the March heat in Southeast Asia. Perhaps demonstrating some nervousness on her part, her gold-sandaled foot bounced to an unheard beat as she sat.

Jasmine was attentive to Jack's moods as his talented assistant. She noted from across the cabin his anxiety and that his feelings seemed reflected in Queen Mai.

She leaned over and whispered to Kelly sitting in the seat next to her, "Wow, they both look uptight all of a sudden. Where did that come from? An hour ago, they were elated about returning to the valley. Is there something going on I don't know about?"

Kelly replied, "They're probably remembering the final moments of their escape from the Siem Kulea valley. It was pretty messed up. Cat and I only got involved afterward when they were safely many miles away in a helicopter flown by Daniel."

Jasmine looked surprised and pointed with big eyes and a nod of her head toward Daniel Vega who was the pilot that morning in the cockpit flying them to Siem Kulea.

"Yes, that's him. He helped them get away from Colonel Minh back then. His mind is probably going through lots of memories too. He met his wife Su Ling who saved their lives during that escape. It is quite a story no matter which version of it you hear," said Kelly. "The helicopter they escaped in was full of bullet holes when we found them. It was trashed. We left it there in the jungle and flew away in the one Catherine, and I chartered.

"The whole thing started because Catherine in her role as a cable news online reporter was investigating a man named Colonel Minh because she believed he had stolen a large amount of Vietnamese gold when South Vietnam fell. She soon learned the story was much bigger than she ever expected. Colonel Minh's ambition was to rule all of Southeast Asia. He got his chance when he discovered that there were thousands, maybe millions, of indigenous Champa faithful intermingled among the nations and cultures living in Southeast Asia that were compelled by their beliefs and traditions to serve and obey their queen. The interesting thing about it and what became a problem for him was that their queen had been missing for a thousand years. He realized that if he could find this missing queen, he might have a super-motivated, ready army to lead in a rebellion to overthrow the existing governments in the area.

"Mai worked for Catherine at the time and was helping with her investigation. In the process, she met Su Ling who worked for Colonel Minh and was in charge of marketing his many antiquities purloined from ancient sites in the area. One day, as they were discussing Asian art, Mai asked about the hoa cuc, an Asian flower she saw on a vase she was admiring. When Mai told Su Ling she had a birthmark similar to this flower on her lower right hip, Su Ling became excited. Upon further discussion, Su Ling determined that Mai was the long-lost queen who the Champa faithful were compelled to serve and obey. Further complicating the situation, Su Ling discovered the same Colonel Minh had killed Mai's parents when she was a little girl. Mai was enraged when she learned this and became obsessed with killing Colonel Minh, and gaining revenge for the death of her parents. As part of her plan she arranged to return to Vietnam with Catherine to assist her in her investigation. While there, Mai allowed herself to be kidnapped by Colonel Minh to get close to him so she could kill him and have her revenge. But she was unexpectedly drugged in the process and used by him for a time as the long-lost Queen Dau Te Po to gain the support of the Champa faithful and organize them as a rebel army. Jack tried to rescue her but was also captured by the insanely ambitious despot. In the end, Mai got her revenge, and they escaped, but not before Jack was put in great peril and even tortured and branded."

Jasmine's expression showed her surprise. "Oh, they both could have been killed! No wonder they have some anxiety. I would be having fits. Thanks for explaining. I wanted to know what I got myself into by following them over from Chicago, although I truly had no choice."

"Yes, I think I heard about that. You are Champa too, aren't you? Did Mai, as your queen order you to go with them to Siem Kulea? I heard if she tells you to do something, you have to obey her," said Kelly now curious herself.

"Yes, we are compelled by our beliefs and faith to do so," replied Jasmine. "But honestly, it's not like it sounds at all. We want and are even happy to obey and serve our queen. We Champas have been waiting many centuries for the return of our queen so that in serving her we may find the fulfillment in life we seek. Serving our queen is what we live for. I am not sure if I can fully explain to you what that means to us. As a people we were always left with an empty feeling no matter how successful we became. She changed all that when she revealed herself to us. 'We were lost and now we are found' has become our mantra, and our call to serve. She said it would be nice if I continued to assist Jack in Siem Kulea. It wasn't that she told me to. She left me an out. But I wanted to go and was even honored she chose me. Now, seeing how nervous both of them are, I'm not sure what is really going on, and I want to help if I can."

"I don't think you have to worry about anything. To start with Siem Kulea is fully restored, and even modernized in many subtle ways. You will not believe how beautiful it is. It appears as a jungle paradise replete with exotic flora of every variety and is surrounded by protective mountains. There are no signs of any war or destruction from when the Vietnamese army came in and destroyed everything at the same time Mai and Jack were escaping. That's all gone. I had a lot of fun working on that project with Su Ling. She is Mai's closest friend in Asia. She took charge. In fact, after I felt comfortable with her management style, which was pretty demanding, I saw that she was doing what we wanted with matchless perfection. You are going to love living there," Kelly assured her.

Kelly glanced across the plush interior of the cabin, and made eye contact with Mai who gave her a slight nod. Mai couldn't physically hear their soft conversation from across the cabin, but she could sense what they were saying, and even communicate with Kelly, through a method Mai called Mindspeak. It was an ability to interact with others using only thought processes, and she wasn't always successful with everyone. Mai recently experienced a reconnection with her ancestors, and with that, discovered she possessed some unique capabilities. This was all new to her and she was having fun learning to use them. In this instance, she was aware they were talking about her and Jack. So she took the opportunity to test her new skills and listen in.

Kelly wasn't Champa, but she felt a devotion to Mai that was similar, because of an earlier incident between them that bound her feelings toward Mai forever. Upon discovering this newfound skill, Mai started communicating her thoughts back and forth with her dear friend as an experiment. Kelly opened up her mind to Mai as a willing and fascinated partner in the exercise.

Kelly continued with her narrative to Jasmine. "Of course, before all that happened at a temple near Thap Cham, Vietnam, where Jack, Catherine, and Mai had gone to investigate Colonel Minh, Mai discovered the long-lost Champa royal treasure hidden there by the ancient Champa Queen

Dau Te Po. That legendary Champa Queen had been forced to hide it there when she was fleeing the Dai Viet forces overtaking the Champa kingdom around the year 1000 AD.

"Mai became an instant hero to the Vietnamese people, who honored her with their highest award. In Vietnam, she is still a celebrity, and quite famous. But more importantly, she fulfilled the prophecy of the Champa people that the true queen and heir would restore the wealth, and heritage of the Champa people. It was just after that, she let Colonel Minh's people kidnap her, and he took her to his base camp where he had set up his head-quarters in the remote Siem Kulea valley.

Kelly was curious about one thing peculiar to the Champa culture and decided to mention it to Jasmine to see how she reacted. "You probably know this already, but I have heard that only a Champa man can marry their queen, but as an alternative with her mark of ownership on an outsider, he would be accepted by the Champa people. Thus, in their eyes, he would be her slave-consort. That's why she branded Jack just before they escaped from Colonel Minh."

Seeing Jasmine nonchalantly nod an affirmation and approval of this outlandish and barbarous practice, Kelly was momentarily surprised but continued with her comment. "But it's kind of funny in a way. If you ask me, Jack is just the opposite of being her consort. She does whatever Jack wishes. I see it every time we're together. She adores him. She is as devoted to Jack as her people are to her."

"So what happened to Colonel Minh?" asked Jasmine, still focused on the narrative.

"Mai killed him brutally with the same branding iron she used on Jack, and they got away in the helicopter with Daniel piloting."

"Oh, I see!" said Jasmine. "And that was when I believe you said the Vietnamese attacked and destroyed Colonel Minh's palace headquarters. That was lucky timing for them."

"Yes," said Kelly nodding before she continued. "After we had been back for a year, or so, we saw that Mai was growing restless, and more unhappy with each month she stayed in Chicago. She sensed an obligation to her people as their queen, and she felt that she was responsible for the chaos in their lives that resulted from her actions back then. She was anxious to return to the valley so she could help them find the peace and happiness she wanted for them. Catherine and I decided we would surprise her by restoring Siem Kulea, the traditional residence of the Champa queen. Since the funds already existed to gain ownership and restore the grounds we moved ahead with our plan and restored the palace. Mai still has not seen it, but it is pretty amazing now."

"We Champas believe the ancients who we venerate speak through Queen Mai," said Jasmine. "That is why we honor her in the same manner."

"Yep, and I know about the ring."

"What about the ring? Do you mean the one she always wears?" asked Jasmine, looking at the large-ruby ring on Mai's right hand resting on her lap.

Kelly took a big breath, and continued, "When she found the Champa treasure, it turned out that the remains of the ancient and legendary Champa Queen, Dau Te Po, were also there in that cave. You probably already know Queen Dau Te Po had taken her own life allowing herself to be entombed alive with the treasure to save her people. Her spirit wandered the universe without a home until Mai found and reopened the cave. Queen Po spent the next few months trying to contact Mai in her thoughts, and dreams, which had become quite vivid for Mai while under the influence of the drugs of Colonel Minh. Later on, when Mai finally reached into one of the chests and plucked out that special ring that belonged to Queen Po, and put it on, they joined together as one in mind, body, and spirit. Queen Po protects her but is also teaching her all she knows like speaking in thoughts as she sometimes does with me. She calls it Mindspeak. This is not something she shares with others. I can do it with Mai because she taught me how, and my mind is an open book to her."

Suddenly, they both heard a voice from within their thoughts that said, "That was a very good, and succinct narrative, Kelly. What do you think, Jasmine? Do you believe we can converse in thoughts?"

Kelly smiled, and looked over at Mai who was watching them with an amused look on her face. But this Mindspeak experience was something entirely new to Jasmine, and she jumped at first putting her hands up to her head in response. But in the next moment, she realized her cell phone ear buds were in her lap. She looked at Kelly, and then across the cabin at Mai with big eyes. Her mouth hung open in surprise. Almost at once, she bowed her head toward her queen truly astonished at this sign of her hidden abilities.

The voice continued, "Jasmine I have a high regard for your talents. I specifically hoped you would decide to come with us because you are Champa, loyal to me, and are suited perfectly for my purposes. I intended to sit down and discuss this with you before we left Chicago, but things got hectic, and it didn't get done."

She further explained, "My husband is very talented as you are aware, but I know he can be very reckless with little thought for his safety. Through you, I can keep an eye on him all the time, and your martial arts training will be an added benefit. You and I will be lending our thoughts back and forth using this technique. I want to train with you for that. It takes some practice, and I am still pretty new and working to master it."

Jasmine at first started to speak, but then sat back, and concentrated. She was intrigued by the possibility, and thought, "Thank you, my lady. I am honored that you put so much trust in me." She glanced over at Mai respectfully across the cabin and was surprised to see her nod with a warm affirming smile.

"I have no doubt you are ready to give your life protecting my husband, Jasmine. I think I have judged you well, and that is my charge to you. Protect Jack with your life. Don't let anything happen to him."

Jasmine bowed her head. "Of course, my lady. I am honored to be of service. But if you will allow me. I don't understand why you just don't tap into Jack's mind as you are doing ours right now?"

"Queen Po asked me the same question when we joined together, and I will tell you what I told her. To put it in simple terms, Jack is off limits. I will not ever enter into his mind for any reason, and I will not allow Queen Po to do so either. That is our agreement. The only other person I have allowed the same latitude is Lady Su Ling because she is the most wonderful person in the world. I trust her implicitly, and I owe my life to her."

Mai paused briefly and then smiled at her daughter, Princess Devi, pointing in her book, and relating her version of the story to whoever would listen. "Please bring Devi to me," she commanded.

Jasmine unbuckled, picked up Devi, and brought her over to Mai. She sat her down between Mai and Jack on the leather bench seat.

"Wook, daddy, the pig can fwy like us," Devi said.

Jack chuckled, and said, "Can you imagine a helicopter that looks like a pig?"

Jasmine sat back down, turned to Kelly almost immediately, and whispered, "I am bewildered by my queen. It is like she has superpowers, or something. That was amazing what she just did. I had no idea she could do that."

The voice came back in their heads again. "Jasmine and Kelly stop talking about me now. It is distracting."

But after a moment, the voice again spoke within their minds. "Look, Jasmine, I have always had a superior mind than most, but with Queen Po joining herself with me, I can access and use much more of my brain than other humans. I found it a bit bewildering at first, and now I just go with it. I have only recently been able to explore what I can do with that. Queen Po is very good at it. Not much escapes her, and thus me. I confess sometimes her abilities even amaze me. Let's leave it at that, and move on shall we? Jasmine, there are very few who are aware of my ability to do this. You will discuss this with no one."

Jasmine bowed her head and nodded in response.

Kelly looked at Mai seriously, and said in Mindspeak, "Please, my lady, while we are talking thus, may I ask, did you get a chance to tell Jack about the Nagani? You have discussed this with Catherine and me, and I know you were worried about telling Jack."

Mai sighed, and answered her in thought, "No, Kelly. I just don't know how to tell him and I am afraid of his reaction. I don't want to have him think I am some kind of freak, and lose him. I don't know what to do. I feel so uncommonly helpless in this."

"Do you want me to drug him until after the ceremony as was proposed?" asked Kelly. "That was one alternative we considered that under the circumstances might be practical. I don't personally like it, but you mentioned it might be the safest way to get through this opening ceremony without an incident. I believe you even said when it got to the second part in the late evening, the induction ritual, it could get pretty bizarre, and Jack is going in blind. I have to admit Cat and I are very excited to see it. But I don't think that is anything Jack would like. I just don't know. If the drug will make him docile, and obedient until you are ready to deal with it, it is one less thing you have to worry about."

This was a surprising observation coming from Kelly because without a doubt, as Jack's former assistant, she and Jack had a close, but non-romantic relationship. She was always protective of him much like Jasmine. With the unpredictability of the Champa people's reaction to Jack, Mai was considering it might be the safest thing to do. The Champa people are an ancient, sophisticate, and very intelligent people. But they can border on barbaric when it comes to dealing with outsiders. During ritual, they go into a group halluci-nogenic state during which there is simply no telling how they will react. It is a time when they are most devout, and immersed in their ancient beliefs.

"Let's just see what happens, Kelly," replied Mai. "This is Jack we are talking about and the idea of drugging him repulses me. At the moment, I can't imagine doing that. If it becomes necessary to go that route, you will know. Protect Jack. I depend on you, Cat, and Jasmine to take care of that for me. Do not let there be a scene."

They both looked across to Mai and nodded.

Jack looking back from the window into the cabin, noticed this, and remarked, "What? Am I missing something?" Mai's anxiety as they approached the Siem Kulea valley continued to surprise him because she was usually pretty cool-headed in stressful situations.

Mai and Jack were eager to return three months earlier when Kelly announced that the reconstruction was complete, but Su Ling begged Mai to wait awhile for her people to bring the area back to the familiar daily routine practiced in the rural valley in past centuries. Thus, when Mai returned as their queen, they would all feel that the people and the valley were as perfect as Mai would wish them to be.

In spite of the general secrecy, knowledge of the return of Queen Maisong who many considered to be the reincarnated legendary Champa Queen Dau Te Po, quickly carried by word-of-mouth among the indigenous Champa people throughout Southeast Asia. There were many thousands of devoted applicants following the Champa beliefs who wished to live in the valley and serve their queen. Su Ling carefully screened them down to the three thousand devoted followers that presently reside in the restored valley paradise. But those not chosen did not return to their former countries. Instead, they were provided farms and lands for free, and they settled on the other side of the mountains that surrounded the valley. These numbered in many thousands forming a protective buffer of devoted followers for Queen Maisong for many miles in every direction.

Mai broke away from staring out of the window for a moment and took a deep breath. She watched as little Devi narrated each page of her book, and looked up at her daddy often to make sure he was listening. Devi was like a matched miniature copy of her mother, and the resemblance was remarkable. Perhaps the only variation in their look was that Devi had her jet-black hair in bangs and Mai did not.

As they got closer, Mai's thoughts turned to her dear friend, Su Ling. Mai had not seen her in over two years. But she had spoken with her, and had heard many reports in the last few months of her efforts to restore Siem Kulea on her behalf. She loved Su Ling more than anyone, after Jack and Devearney. Su Ling was the most amazing woman in the world. She was kind, thoughtful, and Mai trusted her implicitly. She was looking forward to being with her again, and that thought brought a smile to her face.

Mai took Jack's hand, pressed it to her lips, and then held it tightly in her lap.

Chapter 3

March 1992   Siem Kulea, Cambodia

L ady Su Ling regarded her reflection in the full-length mirror with approval. She ran her hands down the length of her tight silk dress, turned sideways, and lifted her head in a proud pose. Her beauty and intelligence were matched by her ambition and arrogance, which were considerable.

She was wearing a teal, embroidered gown with a flowered bodice that accented her almond eyes, and delicate Asian features. But the exquisite jewels she wore, and judged with her dress, were what dominated her attention at the moment.

Queen Maisong had a fortune in jewels perhaps matchless anywhere in the world, which she had taken with her when she last escaped from Siem Kulea. They were the collected jewels of the many Champa queens who had lived in Siem Kulea over many centuries. The previous month, the jewels were brought to Siem Kulea, and were now kept in a secret vault known only to a few. Su Ling had personally supervised the storage of the treasure, and had in private tried on every piece of jewelry that she fantasized as her own. At that very moment, she was admiring a set of emerald earrings, and a matching necklace, that accentuated her bare-shoulder silk dress perfectly. She looked very much like the beautiful queen she imagined herself to be.

With a sigh, she ordered one of her maids to remove them. The maid moved quickly to obey for it was not a good idea to show any hesitation fulfilling the wishes of Lady Su Ling who was already ramped up with anxiety over preparations for the arrival of Queen Maisong. These particular maids were carefully chosen by Su Ling, and were not Champa. They were blindly devoted to her rather than the Champa queen. The same was true of several others she chose to live in the valley posing as loyal members of the Champa faithful.

The maid replaced the necklace with one given her by Queen Maisong as a reward for saving her life. It was of less quality, but it was still a very exquisite necklace of gold with seven dark red rubies hanging from it.

She admired herself again for a moment, but then said, "No, not this one either. Bring something of a more simple and plain design, more appropriate for daytime. This one is too dressy."

For a long time, she had been conflicted between her well-feigned Champa devotion for her queen, and her now driving ambition to replace her as the ruler of Siem Kulea. Perhaps her loyalty had been turned because she had known Queen Mai from the beginning, and in some ways felt she had made her who she is. Su Ling was jealous of the Champa peoples' devotion for Queen Mai. *Didn't they know that it was I, Lady Su Ling, who had brought them together, and made all of this happen?*

She felt Mai was never suited for the position as queen of the Champa people. Mai was easily one of the wealthiest women in the world, but she never acted like she was anything more than a common mud-foot native. Mai made herself approachable to everyone and even seemed embarrassed at times by their devotion. Su Ling had no trouble demanding the respect, and obedience of these people who she considered boorish and inferior. She had a royal, entitled mentality, and thus was perfect when it came to restoring the white palace to its former glory. She drove the workers relentlessly with her constant demands for detailed perfection. She reminded them again, and again, that only the best would do, both in product and effort. She was so demanding, and controlling, that everyone began to bow in her presence whether out of respect, or fear. Her whims became commands, and Su Ling could not get enough of it.

She delayed the return of Queen Maisong by three months because she wanted to live as a queen in the valley that she came to think of as hers. It was, after all, because of her hard work, and talent, that the valley was restored better than before. She saw to the careful selection of the people in the valley, many of whom showed her their honest regard, and gratitude for picking them from all of the others. She set up their comfortable living, and working conditions in the valley, and they were grateful to her for that. Su Ling demanded their respect, obedience, and deference, and they were eager to comply; even thankful for her demands on them. They needed to serve, and she filled that void nicely.

When she was called on to help restore the Siem Kulea valley, she became positive it was indeed her destiny to have and rule over it. She firmly believed things were meant to happen, and the gods were in the process of giving her what was rightfully her due.

It has been just over year since she and Daniel arrived to begin reconstruction of the valley at Siem Kulea. Under Kelly's overall supervision, they were in charge of the process with Su Ling supervising the restoration and Daniel handling the logistics. They found it in ruins, and overgrown by the surrounding jungle. Su Ling performed brilliantly while managing the reconstruction, and it was not long before the valley began to look like its former self and even better. The White Palace was appropriately ostentatious while bearing a sophisticated Asian presence. The living quarters still had the original amenities but in addition featured modern bath areas.

There were literally thousands of loyal Champas who came to the valley once it became known their queen was returning. They all wanted to live there with their queen but Su Ling decided to limit the number to three thousand persons actually living in the valley. She devised a test to discover which among them were truly loyal to Queen Maisong. She put up a full size portrait of Queen Mai on one end of one of the rooms within the palace. In the portrait Mai was wearing the formal crown and jewels of the Champa queen. Her gown was hung low on her waist revealing the Hoa Cuc birthmark that was on her lower right hip and was the formal sign of the rightful queen of the Champa people. Each applicant was taken to this room for a moment on the way to where they would fill out their application to live in the valley. If they entered the room and honored the portrait in any manner, it was noted in their paperwork. Most of the applicants upon seeing the portrait went right to the ground in adoration. Even Su Ling was amazed at their devotion.

The native Champas lived in comparatively simple housing, but with modern bathrooms, and water systems, they considered themselves living in luxury. Su Ling brought modern irrigation to the valley while still insisting on traditional methods of planting and harvesting of crops. She was honestly pleased with the results, and it inspired her to push everyone to work hard to make the valley perfect for their queen. But of course, they did not know she was speaking of herself.

She could not say when exactly, but people began to kneel in her presence as if she were the queen. She was Lady Su Ling given the royal title by Queen Maisong in gratitude for her efforts on her behalf. Moreover, she was in charge of the reconstruction process, and in command of the valley at least for a time. Perhaps for any or all of those reasons they knelt before her, and bowed their heads, and Su Ling had never experienced anything like that before. She gave a command, and it was instantly obeyed by everyone, and without question. It was an addicting elixir gleaned from the bottle of ambitious jealousy that she drank from more, and more often.

Unlike Queen Maisong, Su Ling embraced the darker side of the Champa traditions, and heritage. She was not the Hoa Cuc, the flower. If she ruled, she would be the Nagani, the symbolic, dark snake of the Champas, both in spirit, and deed. She was a shape-shifter of a kind in that she could be the sweet, innocent friend, and loyal servant in one setting, and the demonic-cruel ambitious viper in another.

Ritual excited her, and she had already conducted many rehearsals for the erotic dance of the serpent goddess that would be performed for the first time in several hundred years that very night. She was positive that only she could emulate the sensuous timbre of the dance, and properly project its subliminal inducements in a way to make all of the Champa people embrace the Nagani with her. If she danced, she was convinced the Champa people would bond with her and she wanted them to become addicted like her to the dark side. When she took over the valley in triumph, it would be the catalyst that motivated them to follow her.

She had been trying to convince Queen Maisong to let her stand in for her during the dance and ritual. *"Who better?"* she asked herself. She reminded Queen Maisong that she closely resembled her, was the same size, and would be wearing the traditional mask of the snake so that no one would know it was not the real queen.

In ancient times, the same ritual ceremony was much more brutal, and captive slaves were sacrificed to this snake goddess. Now it is a fatted calf but still quite vivid in its symbolism as it is traditional for all participants to mark themselves with the blood of the sacrifice so that they were all one during that dark side ritual in honor of the ancients.

None of this appealed to Mai. The Hoa Cuc flower that symbolized Queen Maisong fit her perfectly. She possessed a pure and free spirit always seeking the best, most altruistic path forward. She tried to see the good in everyone, and ignore their common faults. She was not naïve, just a person blessed with a positive attitude. She had a love for her people that grew daily, and she was ready to do anything to assure their peace and happiness.

Su Ling had recently joined forces with an old friend and lover; a former ward of hers from when she was still working for Colonel Minh. They had first met when he was sixteen, and she was twenty-one. He was the brilliant adopted son of Colonel Minh, Hinsu Yameda. She was appointed as his mentor because of her background and intelligence. But they soon discovered as he came of age that they both entertained healthy fantasies for the dark side, and that sealed their bond forever as lovers.

He was now the head of Asian World Investments, Colonel Minh's former empire, and he conspired with her eagerly when he found out that she was in charge of restoring the White Palace and Siem Kulea. Su Ling only had a trace of Champa ancestry in her background, which made her compulsion to serve Queen Maisong little more than a pretense. On the other hand, Hinsu Yameda was pure Champa, but even so, he also did not possess a compulsion to serve Queen Maisong as was common in most Champas. This was curious and his ambition extended a lot farther than the peaceful valley of Siem Kulea. He believed that to realize his ambitious goals he needed to know what he suspected Queen Maisong might know about the ancient aliens who were regarded as gods by the Champas.

There was a secret connected with the Champa people that dated back to the time of the ancients. According to legend, the ancients had a power that allowed them to control the Earth for a time. But not only did anyone not know what this secret was, they did not know where it was, and Hinsu Yameda was convinced the secret lay within the environs of Siem Kulea.

He spent a week during the reconstruction at Siem Kulea in the guise of a construction consultant. During that time he and Su Ling reinvigorated their strong romantic and sexual appetite for one another. Su Ling's husband, Daniel, was never around after the first few months because his far-ranging, and successful cargo business made constant demands on his time. He had been in charge of the logistical side of construction and his part was completed by then. Thus, it was easy for Su Ling to arrange a consultant visit for a week when Daniel would be far away.

Su Ling made sure Yameda watched the very erotic dance rehearsals for the ritual celebration, and each session ended in wild and abandoned sex for the two of them afterward. It was a love affair conjured in the darkest pit of their twisted minds. They spent every night in the new luxurious quarters Su Ling had built for herself adjacent to the restored Palace. Su Ling's screams of passion could be heard by all of her personal servants, but they were handpicked, fiercely loyal to her by that time, and would never say a word to anyone of her betrayal. The two conspirators fell deeply in love as they searched for the secret they believed would make them as gods to everyone around them.

Toward the end of his scheduled one-week visit, they discovered a chamber beneath the palace basement undisturbed since the time of Colonel Minh. There were many ancient parchments, and writings, within the chamber in a language that Su Ling could not read, and were left untouched by Colonel Minh. Yameda was particularly interested in them, and seemed to have some limited success interpreting their logograms. He photographed, and took copies of a few of them but the number of parchments was enormous, and in the end he added it to his list of things to address when he took over the valley.

Their main reason for accessing that hidden underground chamber was to investigate a unique door hidden behind a large wall sculpture that Su Ling remembered and showed to Yameda. The door behind the stone sculpture was bizarre, and Su Ling recalled the time when Colonel Minh found and tried to open it. But while the sculpture swung out of the way with little difficulty, the door behind it was solidly sealed, and in spite of concentrated efforts, no one could find a way to open it. At one point Colonel Minh had tried blasting his way through, but it and the chamber within were made of a material that was impervious even to explosives. The door bared not the slightest mark as a result of anything he tried.

The design of the metal door made it particularly interesting while at the same time ominous in nature. Mixed into the unique design were a series of concentric circles, Hoa Cuc flowers, and foreboding snakes that Yameda called Nagas. Further begging an answer was that the door had no handle, but there was a hole representing a place to put one, should it be found.

But almost as soon as they discovered the chamber with the door, Ramadi and Fetu, the former and very loyal guards of Queen Mai who were given responsibility for security in the valley, closed access to the chamber awaiting further instructions from their queen. Hired by Kelly, they were cognizant of Su Ling's disloyalty and ambition, and dedicated themselves to protecting the interests of Queen Maisong during her absence.

Rather than make any further attempt at accessing the door, Su Ling and Yameda decided to leave things as they were to avoid any further suspicion. Su Ling would continue as a devoted loyal friend, and servant to Queen Maisong while Yameda would investigate the secret of the Champas, and try to find the answer to the mystery. They both believed that the answer might lie beyond the door, but then the problem was how to open it.

Interrupting her thoughts her loyal servant Hata arrived in the chambers where Su Ling was admiring herself in the mirror, and bowed low before her. "My lady, you look magnificent," she remarked.

"Thank you, Hata," said Su Ling, agreeing with her. "Did I hear the helicopter just now?"

"Yes, my lady, security reports the helicopter is over the valley. Queen Maisong will arrive very soon."

Su Ling clapped her hands demanding to be attended. She took one last look in the mirror, straightened her simple gold necklace, and then hurried out the door with her entourage in tow.

Chapter 4

March 1992   Siem Kulea, Cambodia

Mai had Devi on her lap as Jack moved over right next to her on the leather seat to share the moment. She was unconsciously stroking Jack's hand letting her nerves show. He smiled at that, and said to her, "We're almost there. I think these are the mountains surrounding Siem Kulea. I confess, I'm a bit nervous."

"Mmm…me too," she replied, "and very happy. I don't think I've ever been happier. Po is telling me about the first time she came to Siem Kulea, still a little girl, but already their queen. She says she was really nervous too, but the people accepted her immediately, and she felt as one with them from the start. I hope they accept me like that."

"Don't be silly," said Jack. "Every one of them is hoping to be accepted by you, Queen Maisong. They are wondering if they will measure up, and if you will find them worthy. Take a deep breath, and relax, darling. I'm sure, this is going to be great fun and, a very wonderful experience for everyone."

As the helicopter began descending into the valley paradise, Mai gave a start, and then her eyes began to well as she saw the seven gold gleaming spires of the palace in the distance through the trees and lush jungle foliage. "Oh, Jack," she cried, "It's so beautiful! It's exactly as I remember. I can't believe this is really happening."

The palace at Siem Kulea is painted white with seven pointed gold towers that reach high above the surrounding jungle. It is by far the largest structure in the valley with a small village supporting it. Beyond it there are many acres of tilled fields, rice paddies and miles of rich thick jungle stretching up to the mountain foothills in every direction. From high above, they could see a waiting multitude of thousands of loyal Champa faithful near the vicinity of the palace where Queen Mai was to greet them in the early afternoon. They were all looking up to the sky at the white helicopter carrying their queen and cheering loudly. From the air it looked very colorful and festive.

Daniel Vega called back from the pilot's seat, "OK, we're set to land. Are you all ready back there, or do you want me to go once around the valley?"

Jack felt Mai's hand crushing his, and replied, "Daniel take us once around the valley, and let Mai get a look at the restoration, please. I think she needs a moment to collect herself."

Mai leaned over quickly, and kissed him on the cheek happily. "You know me too well, Jack Largent. Thank you, my darling."

"I think I saw Su Ling and Catherine down there. At least I won't be alone while you are busy being worshipped," he joked.

Mai gave him a playful punch in the shoulder. "You mean like you worship me every night, GI?" she countered, playfully.

Mai did not for a moment believe she was any kind of a real goddess. She knew her imperfections only too well. But her people believed in her, and she would never do anything to mock that. She envied and respected their faith and deep devotion, which was the product of thousands of years of history and tradition. Her connection to the ancients, who were as gods to the Champa faithful, and the belief that the ancients spoke through Queen Maisong, were the reasons they revered her. Mai knew only that she had an exceptional mind that was capable of extraordinary things. She was at times as surprised as everyone else when her intellect revealed something that spoke to her brilliance. Considering everything she discovered in the last two years after joining her mind, and spirit, with Queen Dau Te Po, Mai was well grounded. Her close Chicago friends kept her that way. She treasured their commonality with her at the same time she was being served, worshipped, and obeyed by her devoted followers. She definitely liked the commonality more.

Jack looked out the window beyond Mai at the thousands of people surrounding the palace. He quickly calculated there must be a hundred thousand of her followers down there. In spite of his joking with Mai, the huge crowd reminded him of how devoted the Champa people were to their queen, and their beliefs.

Daniel called out again, "How about it, ready to go in? I bet Su Ling is getting anxious. I don't like to keep the wife waiting. She will make me pay for it later."

Jack looked to Mai, and she nodded, smiling eagerly. "Yes, Daniel. Take us home, please!" he said.

The large white helicopter swept around, and came to a soft landing on the helipad behind the palace, away from the huge crowd, and where they were greeted by the palace staff.

After setting down, and as the rotors were winding down, the side door opened, and Mai turned to look out. The first persons she saw were Ramadi and Fetu, her former personal bodyguards under Colonel Minh. They were bowing before the door, and dressed in the traditional palace tight silk pants and loose shirt top similar to what they had worn two years ago when she had last seen them. Mai broke into an eager ear-to-ear smile upon seeing them again, and handed Devi to Jack as she prepared to get out.

The two huge, handsome, and fit Samoan men had risked their lives helping Mai and Jack escape and were severely wounded in the process. Mai thought they had been killed and she was deeply saddened for a time by the assumed loss. Mai counted them more as protective brothers than guards and had come to rely on them when she was still being held by Colonel Minh. During that dangerous time, she only felt safe when they were with her.

Kelly had come upon them early during reconstruction amidst a very long line of loyal followers applying to serve Queen Maisong and live in the valley. She knew of their story and showed her gratitude for what they had done by offering the two men financial backing anywhere in the world they wanted to go with their futures assured. They refused the offer, and said they only wished to serve Queen Maisong again in Siem Kulea. They were made head of security for the valley right away, and that decision proved prescient over the following year.

Ramadi reached up, carefully lifted Queen Maisong down from the door of the helicopter with little effort, and then knelt with head bowed before her.

"My dear friends Ramadi and Fetu," she said, freely displaying her happiness, "I would tell you to stand but then you would be too tall for me to kiss, you wonderful, magnificent men."

She placed a meaningful kiss on the cheek of Ramadi and then Fetu followed by a meaningful hug for each of them. Finally, she held both of their hands while she just enjoyed the moment. "I have missed you both more than you can imagine, and it gives me great pleasure to know we will be working together again in our valley. I truly love you both."

From behind in the helicopter Daniel leaned back to Jack who was watching, and joked, "Jack, aren't you jealous?"

"Hell no, Daniel, I will compete with Mai for who has the most gratitude for them saving Mai's life."

Jack held Devi in his arms in the cabin doorway as they watched Mai share the special moment with her former guards. Beyond them twenty or more of the palace staff all dressed in colorful Champa styled clothes of bright flowered designs, were bowed with their heads pressed to the ground worshipping their Queen Maisong.

Devi seeing this, touched Jack's face, and asked, "What's wrong, daddy? Are those people sick?"

"No, darling. They are Champa people, and your mommy is their queen," he explained. "They are bowing down before her to show how much they love her."

"Oh!" she said. "Mommy says I'm a princess. Will they bow like that for me too?"

"Most likely, Devi darling. Everyone loves you. Let's watch and see what happens," he said, kissing the top of her head gently.

Mai spotted Catherine kneeling with bowed head like the rest along the path leading to the back of the palace. Noting that Catherine is her best friend, a famous television personality and very wealthy, the sight of her kneeling before her on the ground was very amusing to Mai. She went to stand over her and questioned, "Really?"

Catherine looked up at her with a big over-sized grin, and motioned to the many kneeling and prostrated servants between Mai and the back door of the palace, and said, "When in Rome…"

Kelly who had descended from the other side of the helicopter walked up beside Mai to greet her partner.

"Come on...get up," said Mai, shaking her head, and smiling back at her. "You and Kelly go stand over there out of the way where you can observe. Be very quiet, and invisible. We have lots to talk about. But later–go!" she commanded, slapping her behind as Catherine and Kelly rushed to get out of the way.

Standing impatiently on the left side of the gathered staff, Su Ling finally pushed forward, to formally announce the arrival of their queen and welcome her properly. She clapped her hands and commanded, "I call on all present to bow down before Dau Te Maisong, descendant of the ancients, living goddess and rightful queen of the Champa nation." Incense burners began consecrating the air around them as the assembled staff bowed, knelt up, and chanted a mantra of devotion solemnly. Su Ling clapped her hands, and all present again bowed to the ground in silence.

The silence was so pervasive that Mai heard Catherine standing in the back to one side say to Kelly, "Looks like I got out of there just in time!"

Mai was not amused, and looked at her sharply.

Catherine ran a finger across her lips, and signaled she would be extra quiet with an embarrassed, apologetic expression of guilt.

Again Su Ling clapped her hands, and the ritual was repeated, and that was followed by another, the third and last time.

It was not but a few seconds before Mai said to the group, "Please rise."

Su Ling, remained on her knees, and said, "Your Majesty, welcome home. Welcome to Siem Kulea. We are blessed by your presence. Please accept this palace, which we have prepared as your home; this valley, which we have prepared according to our heritage; and ourselves as your devoted and obedient subjects ready to serve and obey you."

Mai put out her hand, and allowed Su Ling to kiss it, and then drew her up, and kissed her on the lips followed by a big warm and enduring hug.

Still holding her in her arms, Mai said, "I have missed you very much, Su Ling. I look forward to spending a great deal of time with you. You are the most amazing woman in the world, you are always right, and I trust you implicitly."

Su Ling was surprised and secretly elated by her greeting. *She is still mine! She just repeated the post-hypnotic suggestion I gave her when she was in my power under Colonel Minh. I could not have hoped for more.* But then she wondered how much influence she actually had over her. She sensed something different about Mai and she remembered she felt the same way the last time she was with her. There was an aura about her as if something was protecting her now. She would have to be careful not to expose her true feelings.

"I too have missed you, my lady. I am pleased to know we will share much more of our time together now that you are back in Siem Kulea," she said.

Daniel was just climbing out of the helicopter as Jack said, "Well, Daniel, now we both get to be jealous."

Daniel looked over, and said, "Yeah, those two have been carrying on like that for a long time. I don't much care for it. How 'bout you?"

"Please take no offense, but I never understood the whole deal with your wife, Su Ling, even if she did save our lives. Mai really likes her, so I just go along with it. But you're right. It's getting old."

Breaking away from their embrace, Mai turned back toward Jack, Daniel, and Jasmine, who were now standing by the helicopter, and said, "Jack, darling, you remember Lady Su Ling. Bring Devi, please, I want Lady Su Ling to meet her.

Jack stepped forward holding Devi in his arms. Su Ling with a warm smile, said to her, "Good morning, Princess Devearney. I am Lady Su Ling. My life is dedicated to serving you, and your mother."

Devi replied in a toddler voice, "I'm Princess Devi. Will you bow to me?"

They all laughed at the surprising comment. Su Ling bowed from the waist formally before saying, "You are my Princess Devearney who I love, serve, and will care for as you grow up. Welcome to your new home in the valley of our Champa heritage, Princess." This proved delightful to the little princess who giggled.

Su Ling turned, and nodded to two handmaidens who walked forward, and bowed. "May I introduce Princess Devearney's handmaidens, Uri and Iris," she said. The young Asian ladies were dressed in formal pantaloons with silk shirts. Uri reached out, and took Devi in her arms. Devi gave a big smile, and seemed to like them immediately as if they were old, and familiar companions.

Mai said, "You of course know Jack, and this is Jasmine, Jack's assistant. Can you see that she has proper quarters in the palace?"

A lady of middle age with a friendly smile stepped forward, bowed and said to Su Ling, "My lady, may I suggest one of the smaller quarters by the pool we have reserved for guests?"

"Ah, a good suggestion," said Su Ling. "Queen Maisong, may I introduce Chu who manages the staff, and the affairs of the palace."

Chu knelt and bowed formally and held it for an extended moment, a sign of her focused devotion to Queen Maisong. Mai said to her, "Greetings to you, Chu. I am sure we will get to know each other very well."

Su Ling said to Chu, "Can you take care of that for me?" And then, "Jasmine, if you will go with Chu, she will see that you are properly settled, if my lady approves."

"Yes, of course. Thank you," said Mai, smiling.

Su Ling turned to Mai and said, "Your Majesty, please follow me into your palace where you can freshen up before I give you a tour of our reconstruction efforts around the palace grounds."

The group entered the back door of the palace. Just inside was a sizable rear entrance area where there were two portals, and a hallway leading off on the right. On the left, was a large double-door made of polished bronze. On the door mounted in two halves was a large ornate sculpture bearing a series of concentric circles in a design surrounded by a menacing seven-headed snake sprinkled amongst Hoa Cuc flowers. It was the kind of unique artwork you could admire for its intricate detail and craftsmanship, or find it completely out of character in a place many regarded as a paradise.

Su Ling said, "The door is beautiful isn't it, Your Majesty? It has so much meaning for you."

Mai turned instantly, and looked at the door as if obeying a command.

"You like it," said Su Ling studying her reaction.

"Holey moley, what's that all about?" exclaimed Jack, in real surprise upon seeing the foreboding bronze snakes on the door.

But Mai only gazed in wonder at the large ornate sculpture that covered both halves of the nine-foot high doorway. She continued to ignore Jack's reaction, and instead walked over and laid her head against the doors affectionately. Admiring the sculpture, she ran her hands over it gently. After a moment she kissed the sculpture, and turned around to the group delighted with a huge smile on her face. "Su Ling you're right. It is beautiful. How did you know? This was not here before, and it bears so much meaning for me and the Champa people."

"During the restoration, Your Majesty, a door leading to chambers below the palace was discovered. There was a large room there with a many old artifacts and drawings. Among them were a number of sketches and designs for the palace, and one of them revealed the original design for this doorway to the queen's chambers. We had a Champa artist do the sculpture. I planned it as a surprise for you. I hope Your Majesty is pleased," she said.

"I am very pleased, Su Ling. I love it. I honestly do not know what to say. The sculpture design is most beautiful and perfect for the doors to my rooms," said Mai.

"What's going on?" asked Jack, not understanding at all, and feeling no empathy.

"Darling, this is the symbol of the Nagani," explained Mai, gently. "It is one of the legends of our beliefs. She is very important in our faith, and traditions. She represents the beginning of us all, the queen mother. Look upon her as the balance, or malefic side to the Hoa Cuc, the flower that represents our family and me," she said, taking his arm affectionately. "She is the Nagani, the one who demands obedience."

"It's a freaking snake, Mai! You can't be serious!" he exclaimed, loudly. Bewildered, and confused by what he saw, he pulled from her grasp and gestured toward the door displaying his exasperation. "I will not have that door in my home," he declared. "These doors need to be removed if we are to live here. At the very least it will terrify Devi. Heck, it terrifies me!"

But Devi, secure in Uri's arms only regarded the massive door with a look of childish wonder, and pointed at it playfully.

Mai shook her head, and looked at him with a charging anger that he had seen only once before in their entire tumultuous relationship. "That is not your decision to make. This is my palace made with love for me by my people. This is our culture, Jack, and you had better learn to live with it."

Mai was suddenly self-conscious, frustrated, and embarrassed by his outburst in front of Ramadi, Fetu, Su Ling and her handmaidens. Staring blankly at him with pulsing eyes and too angry to find further words, she abruptly turned away from him, and said to Su Ling, "Devi and I will enter my chambers now, and freshen up."

Su Ling went to the doors, and pushed one of them open revealing the rich, and lush interior of the queen's quarters. She stepped back, and said, bowing, "Your Majesty…"

Mai marched into her chambers, and the two handmaidens with Devi followed. Jack started to follow, but Su Ling stepped in front of him and said, "I'm sorry, Mr. Largent, but no males are allowed in the queen's chambers without her express permission. We have separate quarters for you."

She gestured toward a male servant who was waiting on the side. "If you will follow Jobi, he will make sure you have everything you need."

Jack looked at her for an extended moment demonstrating his own frustration, and then at the open door of the queen's chambers. Su Ling did not hide her feelings on the matter. She gave him a proud smirk daring Jack to resist her instructions. He entertained the thought of going after Mai but seeing Ramadi and Fetu standing at the door tense in response to the situation, he thought better of it. Not wanting to make a further scene, he sighed, and said, "OK, I guess. Jobi, please lead the way."

Kelly, who watched this sudden turn of events while standing next to Catherine, took Jack's arm and said, "Boss, I think it's time you had a history lesson. Let me join you, and let's talk. I suspect Mai did not tell you everything about Champa traditions. OK?"

Jack recovering from his outburst, was relieved to hear a friendly, and understanding voice. He found a smile from somewhere, and replied, "Sure Kel. I never had breakfast this morning and I could use a bite. It looks like I'm eating alone anyway. I could use a drink too, after that. Wow, did you see the look on Mai's face? I've rarely seen that side of her. I don't get what's going on. How about you?"

Kelly smiled, and replied, "Jack, they have the most amazing drink here. It is called a Black Orchid. Wait till you taste one! It will make your day go better. We can have a bite, and get you ready for the induction ceremony later."

"Induction ceremony? What does that have to do with me?" he asked.

"Come on, boss...let's have a drink together," she said, leading him behind Jobi through the middle doors into the family chambers prepared for him.

Su Ling turned, smiled, and gestured for Catherine to go with her into the queen's chambers to join Mai.

Catherine rushed in, and went straight to Mai. "Hey, are you OK?" she asked. "That was awkward."

Mai had one hand to her face nursing a worried expression as she pondered what had just happened. "This is not going well," she replied. "I hope he's going to be OK. It will get really ugly if he shows any kind of attitude during the ceremony."

She glanced to the side, and saw little Devi being introduced by Iris and Uri to her mother's six handmaidens. As she came to each of them, they bowed, and kissed Devi's offered hand. Devi gave a cute little-girl giggle, and twisted her face in laughter as each handmaiden reverently kissed her hand.

On a signal from Su Ling, Uri who knelt beside Princess Devi, stood up, took her hand, and said, "Come, my lady, let me show you your special princess quarters. You are going to love it. It has lots of flowers, and cuddly pets to entertain you."

When they were gone, Catherine turned to Mai and asked, "Didn't you tell him about any of this, Mai?"

Mai looked at her sadly and shook her head. "I was too afraid he wouldn't come, and then what would I do? I'm not complete without Jack. Damn, I don't know what to do. The Champa rituals can seem very bizarre to outsiders, and you just saw good evidence of that at the door to my chambers."

"Well, don't worry," said Catherine. "Kelly and I have talked about this extensively, and she is just the right person to explain it all to Jack. He trusts her, and they have a bond not shared by most. Forget about it, and have your day. Don't let anything interfere. I am sure everything is going to be OK," she said, trying to encourage Mai.

Mai considered her words as Su Ling stood back, and gestured toward the six kneeling young ladies who had just finished meeting Princess Devi. "Your Majesty, would you like to meet your handmaidens now? There were over three hundred applicants and these were the six that were chosen to serve you."

Mai instead allowed her attention to be momentarily diverted to the royal chambers as she turned around. "Su Ling I am amazed. This room is exactly as it was except for the bed, and door. I love the additions to those although Jack will take some time getting used to it."

The queen's chamber was large, airy, and opened to a garden on one side. The walls were done brightly in maroon and gold, but most impressive was the ornate bronze bed. The headpiece was made up of Hoa Cuc flowers festooned over many concentric circles. But right in the center was another smaller sculpture of the Nagani, but this time the central head of the seven-headed serpent evolved into a female human form in the middle.

"The bed is magnificent. But I am worried about Jack's reaction to the sculpture," Mai said.

"My lady, tonight is induction," said Su Ling. "He will become Champa. It is a great honor for most, but it might be too much of a shock for your husband Jack revealing all of this at once. You and I have discussed this situation before. What is your decision? What would you like us to do with him?" Su Ling asked, hoping to drug Jack, and keep him passively in control for a time.

"I think Kelly has already decided for us," commented Catherine, with one raised eyebrow. "As she led him into the family chambers she was telling him about the Black Orchid drink. I think Jack will be passive, obedient throughout the ceremony, and not a problem. Tonight when you culminate your new relationship, he will be a perfect lover."

Mai turned sharply around toward Catherine, and looked at her, the anguish on her face apparent as she processed what Catherine said. Then she quickly clapped her hands toward Su Ling, and commanded, "Take me to him. Now!"

Su Ling led them hurriedly through a side door that led through room size closets to the family quarters beyond. Jack and Kelly sat at a small table off to one side with a view of the grounds and mountains beyond. Drinks were just being served. Jack reached for his drink while in friendly conversation with Kelly. "OK, let's see what's so special about this Black Orchid drink," he said, as he lifted it toward his lips.

"Stop!" exclaimed Mai, walking quickly toward him. "Jack, don't drink that!"

Jack turned around surprised, and smiled upon seeing Mai. He put down the drink quickly, got up, and rushed to her. "Mai, you needn't be concerned. I'm sorry for my outburst. I just got a little excited out there. This is all new to me, but not to worry. This is your day, my love. I won't make any more stupid scenes. I promise," he said, smiling sincerely.

Catherine who had followed Mai into the family quarters remarked, "Mai was worried about you, Jack."

Mai shook her head at the others, clapped her hands, and ordered, "All of you please leave. I wish to be alone with my husband. Leave us!" She gave the black orchid drink to Jobi who hurried out taking it with him.

Catherine took Kelly's arm, and followed Su ling and a handmaiden, closing the door behind them.

Mai took Jack's hand, and led him to a small chaise lounge on one side of the luxurious interior of the family room. "Darling, sit with me. I have something to tell you, and I've been remiss in not sharing it with you sooner." She was shaking nervously and her eyes watered. "You have a right to know, and make your own decision about what is about to happen today. But please remember no matter what happens I love you very, very much. Please never forget that."

Jack's began to show some concern. "Mai, you know I love you. Nothing you say could ever change that. You don't have to worry about me. I accept you as you are whatever queenly version you come in."

Mai sighed, and brought his hand to her lips, kissed it, and ran his hand against her cheek. Then she held his hand tightly in her lap, and took a deep breath. "Jack, I am the Nagani. I am descended from the ancients, the Nagani. That is why the Champa people worship me. The birthmark on my hip, the Hoa Cuc, is the symbol of the Nagani. There can only be one each generation. Each Nagani makes their heir, their successor."

"Darling you know that doesn't matter to me..." Jack protested.

"Jack, stop. Please listen. There is more. Oh, my love, please forgive me for not telling you sooner. I did not know any of this before, and I only found out after joining with Queen Po. I love you so much. Please listen to me and try to understand."

"But I am telling you it doesn't matter. I love you, Mai. I love Devi my daughter of my own flesh and blood. Nothing you say will change that. We three are bonded for all eternity," he replied.

"That's the other thing I have to explain to you. Devi is not of your flesh and blood. She is Nagani also," said Mai, with real concern showing in her rapidly darting and fearful eyes.

Jack slowly pulled back his hand as he processed the words she had just spoken. "Are you saying you had an affair with another man, and let me believe she was mine? Tell me you're not saying that."

Mai begged him with her eyes to understand as she shook her head.

"No, no, Jack. There was no affair. I am the Nagani. I reproduce without male sperm. I swear it is true. I am of alien descent. My DNA is slightly different than human. You must believe me. I can prove it to you but right now you will have to just accept my word. Please, Jack. Please trust me. I love you so much."

Jack got up from the couch abruptly and exploded. "Devi is not my daughter? My own flesh and blood?" He began pacing back and forth at this surprising, and shocking news. His face showed his bewilderment. He turned suddenly toward her, "It's all a lie. We've been living a lie."

Mai pleaded, "No, Jack. No lie...my love for you is not a lie. I can only reproduce if I feel the emotions, and passions, that come with a true love for someone. It starts the necessary hormonal reactions within me that make the self-reproductive sperm leading to my heir. Without my love for you I could not have made Devi. She is as much your daughter as mine."

"I am not sure I can believe that or anything you say. First you tell me my child is not mine, and then you tell me you had something like a virgin birth? Do you know how crazy you sound?"

Jack was pacing as Mai watched, not sure how to respond. But then he had a thought. "Wait, that snake on the door, you called it "The Nagani". You don't mean you are descended from a snake, Mai? You can't believe that."

He stood there looking at her shaking his head. "This is crazy! You're all crazy! I need to think," he said as he began pacing again. "I can't make any sense of this. This is all so wrong? Where did all of this come from?"

He turned suddenly on her, very angry and shook his head with his hands out, but then dropped them to his side despairing, and said, "Please go. Just go! Go to your *people*, and leave me alone. I will be getting out of here as soon as I can. I don't want anything to do with any part of this."

"Jack, please, I love you. You don't understand." Mai pleaded as he turned his back on her, and walked away.

But then he turned around once more, and said, "I don't know what's worse: hoping that you're lying to me, you're crazy nuts, or that you're telling the truth, and have been deceiving me all along. Go! I am done with this. I don't want to see you ever again," he yelled from the other side of the room. "Get out of my life! I don't even want to look at you. Who are you? What the hell are you?"

Kelly had been listening at the door outside the family quarters, and hurried back through the large closet into the queen's chambers before Mai found her eavesdropping on their conversation.

Catherine and Su Ling came to her immediately.

"How is it going?" Catherine asked.

"I could have handled it better. You know how Mai is; all honest and straightforward. It was too much for Jack. He got really angry. He just told her to get out. He said he was leaving. He yelled at her. I have never seen him do that that, Cat," Kelly explained.

"Here she comes," Kelly said, as they resumed places around the room.

Mai entered passively, as if in a daze, and stood in the center of the room, her body rigid with her eyes staring into nowhere. She slowly walked over to a large high-backed pillowed chair and sat, slumping back in thought. Her handmaidens came over, and gently began to tend to her. Their love and concern for her was obvious as they removed her jewelry, and began attending to her hands and feet. Answering to gentle prodding Mai moved forward passively in the chair and they took her hair down letting it fall over her shoulders. She accepted a drink of ice water, but all the while she was far away in thought.

Catherine and Kelly sat in chairs opposite her and waited quietly. They knew Mai well enough to know this was not a time for conversation. But in fact, they didn't know what to do because they had never seen Mai like this. She seemed to be lost, almost robot-like and holding her feelings within.

Back in the family quarters Jack was upset, and still pacing when Daniel came into the room. "Jobi said you wanted to see me, Jack. What's up?"

"I want to leave right away, Daniel. I have to get out of here. I have to. Can you fly me?" Jack asked, looking determined, and confused.

Daniel went over to the drink table, and poured two fingers of single malt scotch from a decanter over a couple of cubes. He offered it to Jack.

"Here. You look like you could use a drink. What's this all about, Jack? Want to talk about it?"

"She lied to me, Daniel." Jack protested as he sat down. "She's not real, not even human if you believe her story." He laughed somewhat hysterically throwing up his hands. "She told me she is descended from a snake. A snake! How can someone so intelligent believe something as ridiculous as that? But then she tells me that Devi is not even my daughter. That was it for me. I can't handle this place, Daniel. It's all lies and superstition. This valley is pure evil, and I have to get out of here. I never should have come back. What was I thinking?"

Daniel sat down opposite him, and said, "I know about all of that, Jack and the legend of the Nagani. I think I believe it's true. Su Ling told me about this a year ago after a phone conversation with Mai. I'm surprised it took Mai this long to tell you. I think you're overreacting. Mai is still Mai, and Devi is still your daughter. Nothing has changed really."

"You knew? You can't mean you believe that bizarre story. It's crazy, Daniel. Surely you must see that. How can you believe such fantastic stupidity?"

"Jack, you misunderstood…about the snake at least. Look, calm down, and let me explain. That's the problem with you. You get your head going sideways sometimes. You go off half-cocked, and don't really hear what people are saying."

But Jack was having none of it. He was proving Daniel's point even then by ignoring him while he was thinking at that very moment about what Mai told him. Finally, after Daniel called to him several times, he turned abruptly, and said, "What? WHAT?"

"OK, look," said Daniel. "Here is what I know of the legend. The snake is symbolic. It represents the power of the Nagani. She was the first queen, a female child that was of part human and part alien when conceived. She looked human but had a few alien characteristics; one being a superior mind, and another that she could self-reproduce. They named her Nagani, and after that every Champa queen was called the Nagani and considered a living goddess."

"That's crazy, and you believe it? What about the snake?" said Jack shaking his head.

"That is a symbol of the Nagani. It doesn't mean she's descended from snakes. Su Ling thinks the ancients lived underground, and took on the snake as their symbol to bring respect, and fear to the people who served them above ground. The snakes of the region self reproduced so that added to the legend. They are extinct now like the aliens if they ever existed. That's all.

"Jack, remember I am married to Su Ling and she is also of Champa heritage and very close to Mai. If you think about it, the story is not any crazier than some of the stuff you read in the bible. But check the facts you can verify. The Naga legend in Southeast Asia is of a snake god that came from the ocean. That could just as easily have been aliens coming from another world. Su Ling told me she believes the mother alien mated with a human and created the first Nagani.

"It's crazy," repeated Jack.

"It's not crazy, Jack. Just different, and most importantly, it's possible."

"It's all crazy," said Jack again.

"Any more crazy than Mai having an amazing IQ, or the spirit of Queen Dau Te Po joined with her?" Daniel asked. "Or how about finding the ancient Champa treasure by the temple at Thap Cham when no one else could, and fulfilling that legend?"

"Yeah, well, I have seen good evidence proving all of that," said Jack.

"Then why would you doubt her word now? She is still the same Mai who loves you, and Devi is your daughter you love more than life itself.

In the next few minutes Daniel watched silently as Jack stubbornly repacked his luggage without folding anything. He was acting again as if he was no longer listening to Daniel.

Finally he turned to Daniel and said, "I was a fool to ever come here. I want to leave now, Daniel. Is the helicopter fueled up?"

"Well yeah, Jack, it is," Daniel answered. "But can't we talk about it some more before you go off half-cocked?"

"Talk. Yeah. That's the problem. You've all been talking and laughing at me behind my back. Everyone knows about my freaky wife and this evil place but me. How could you let me go on like this? Are you going to fly me out of here, or not?

"Well sure, Jack. But where here do you want to go?"

Mai was still staring lost in thought when Su Ling brought her the news that Jack had sent for Daniel. Not a minute later, Mai heard the helicopter take off from the rear of the palace. She leaped up from her chair, and ran out into the garden to see the helicopter leaving the valley. "Oh no!" she cried. "Oh please, God, no! Jack, don't leave me. I love you so much!"

Mai stood, and watched the helicopter get further away until she could see it no more. She suddenly felt empty, lonely, and tears ran down her face.

She walked slowly back into her chambers despondent, and broken. Everyone was standing wanting to help her in any way they could. All at once, Mai could not hold back her feelings any longer, and she began wailing in long heavy sobs. She went to the bed, and laid across it crying as if the world had ended for her.

The room turned ominously dark as a thick cloud hindered the sun outside bringing the palace into shadow. Catherine and Kelly at first went to her and tried their best to comfort Mai unsuccessfully. She only yelled at them and demanded they go away. They sat back down looking at each other sadly, and feeling quite helpless under the circumstances.

Su Ling left to be sure that Princess Devi was kept in her quarters until things were resolved with her mother. When she returned, she sat opposite Kelly and Catherine secretly enjoying the drama between Jack and Mai. She did not like Jack, and felt Mai's feelings for him were a threat to her control. This could not have worked out better if she had planned it.

The six handmaidens knelt by the bed all in a row, all ready to help if only they could find a way. Everyone waited through a silence only broken by Mai's heartfelt weeping.

After crying for an hour, Mai turned over on the bed staring straight up at the ornate gold leaf ceiling. Several minutes later she sat up straight.

Immediately, two handmaidens attended her with tissues, and water, which Mai quickly drank. She looked at the first handmaiden who she remembered. "I know you. You are Ceva?" she asked, as she wiped her eyes.

"Yes, my lady. You are correct. I served you when you were here two years ago and have been honored to be chosen as your first of handmaidens if it is your will."

Mai held her hands for a moment in recognition and then nodded. "Get me ready for the introduction, and reunion. I bet I look awful. I feel awful. Come on. Let's get this going. We don't have a lot of time and I've been wasting it. Su ling was right. I should have listened to her. Jack will never understand our ways. I should have let Kelly drug him. I will be better off without him around."

Kelly came over, and hugged Mai gently. "You don't mean that, Mai. We all love Jack. It was hard for Catherine and I to accept what you have told us of the Champa ancient history. Even you only learned about it after joining with Queen Dau Te Po. In any case, now is not the time to consider such things. We have a lot to do if we are going to get through this day. Let's get this consecration done, and then we can worry about what to do with Jack."

Mai pushed back, wiped her face, and smiled a weak smile. "You're always the one with the proper perspective, and wise counsel, Kelly. Yes, let's get done what we came to do this day."

"Su Ling, can you show me the Nagani outfit for the midnight ritual service?" Mai asked as her handmaidens began to attend to her.

"Just a moment, my lady, I will model it for you," replied Su Ling, running out of the room.

The handmaidens had repaired Mai's makeup, and were putting on her a floor length tight skirt of a light gold embroidered silk material, when Su Ling reappeared, and presented herself before Mai in the ritual gown Mai was to wear later in the evening for the sacred Nagani snake ritual. Su Ling and Mai were a very close match in size, and the dark erotic snakeskin outfit Su Ling wore would surely fit the same on Mai. The proof was the gold tight skirt with matching halter top Mai presently wore that she would greet her people with first that day. Su Ling was fitted for that garment in preparation for Mai wearing it during the afternoon introduction and consecration festivities.

The ritual snake gown worn by Su Ling was a long skirt cut just below her navel with a bustier top of gold and black snakeskin. Su Ling's breasts were mostly exposed, and presented in an intricately weaved gold braid design which lifted, and supported them provocatively. There was a tight hood that completely encased her head in the same material. She wore a magnificent necklace of gold with emeralds that glowed against the color of the gown and lay exquisitely between Su Ling's noticeably enhanced cleavage.

"Wow, Su Ling. You look amazing," observed Mai honestly. But Mai could not see herself wearing that outfit with her breasts so exposed, and appearing in public for any reason, even here in Siem Kulea.

"I chose this necklace from your collection, my lady," said Su Ling. "I think it goes well with the outfit. Don't you agree?"

"Yes, and particularly on you it works well," agreed Mai.

"Now for the last part, my lady," said Su Ling, as a snake mask of black, and gold was placed on her head concealing her face and forming a crown. Su Ling clapped her hands and erotic music played from somewhere in the garden outside. She began to dance as she had rehearsed in a very seductive, and erotic manner before Mai.

Mai stopped what she was doing, and watched her. She had to admit Su Ling's dance was thought provoking but not in a way she was receptive to at the moment. She glanced over at Kelly and Catherine who seemed fixated with big smiles on their attentive faces. They were obviously enjoying Su Ling's dance. That made Mai smile, but at their reaction to Su Ling's performance not her actual dance. She rolled her eyes, and clapped her hands firmly bringing the dance to an end.

"My lady, is something wrong?" asked Su Ling, genuinely concerned. "Don't you like the gown I have prepared for you tonight?"

Mai turned to Catherine and Kelly. "I think you ladies need to get ready for this afternoon's celebration."

"Uups, that's our cue, Kel," said Catherine. "We will catch up with you later, Mai. Good luck, and remember we are here for you. You're not doing this alone."

After they left, Mai dismissed her handmaidens, approached Su Ling, and kissed her on the cheek. With a serious face she remarked, "I have rehearsed that dance in Chicago, and I think I learned it well. But I confess I dreaded performing it. You are marvelously talented, and perfect for the ritual dance, and you have confided in me that you wished you could perform it. Honestly, I'm not up to it, especially after what's just transpired. So, I've made a decision, Su Ling. You will dance in my place tonight. We look very much alike, and no one will know it's not me."

"My lady?" questioned Su Ling, in pretended surprise.

"I can't wear that gown, Su Ling," said Mai. "I am barely able to make an appearance before my people, much less carry out the ritual ceremony in that erotic, and revealing gown. When it comes to that tonight, you will stand in for me. I insist. Tell your maids who learn of this to keep it to themselves, or they will suffer dire consequences."

Su Ling bowed, and said, "Yes, my lady. It will be my honor to stand in for you." She smiled to herself because things were falling into place just as she hoped, and everything was proceeding according to her plan.

Chapter 5

March 1992   Siem Kulea, Cambodia

When Queen Maisong was finally ready to appear before the thousands of gathered followers, she was an hour late. Even so, the festive throng that had been waiting for several days did not notice. The crowd filled and spread far beyond the vast green lawn extending from the side of the palace. They were festive and in high spirits on this glorious day of the rebirth of their Champa nation. The bright, colorful clothes they wore added to the carefree atmosphere and were reflected in the exotic flowers that festooned the streets, doors, and houses. The air was filled with smoke of many colors, and the smell of incense was pervasive. As their anticipation grew, not one person was sitting. Everyone wanted to be close enough to see their queen. When the time came, and they finally saw Queen Maisong appear, a gong sounded three times, followed by a thunderous cheer that rang out in the valley. At first, it was just a roar of adulation, but then it evolved into a deafening chant of, "Hoa Cuc," over, and over.

She stood on an extended open platform at the top of the steps leading up to the side of the palace. The entire area was decorated beautifully with exotic flowers of every color gathered from the surrounding jungle. In the center of the platform stood a throne of bronze. Fashioned at the back toward the top of it was a sculpted Hoa Cuc flower in gold. On the steps leading up to the throne stood her six handmaidens, three on either side. There were six Champa palace guards in ancient costumes standing at the base of the steps. Behind Queen Maisong, just off to the sides, stood Lady Su Ling on her right, and Uri and Iris, holding Princess Devearney on her left. To either side of the throne just behind them stood Ramadi and Fetu dressed appropriately as guards from one thousand years ago. They were beaming with pride.

Mai let her devoted followers cheer her until it seemed they were never going to stop. Su Ling said there were more than one hundred thousand followers in attendance for the formal consecration, introduction, and reunion ritual. But the crowd looked to be twice that size as their numbers went off to the horizon. Mai noted that dressed in the bright, and colorful, Champa silks and linens, the crowd appeared as a field of flowers from a distance.

Mai wore a floor-length cape of cashmere golden silk, embroidered with gold Hoa Cuc flowers, and clasped at her neck. Her hair was up, and wound in gold ribbon. On her head, she wore the Champa crown of gold with red rubies that she had saved from the ancient Champa treasure at Thap Cham.

Iris walked Princess Devi forward beside her mother. The princess had her hair up with a small tiara and wore a small gold cape like her mother. She seemed a bit intimidated by the boisterous crowd in front of them, and held Iris's hand tightly as she looked out on the multitude of joyous, cheering people.

Kelly and Catherine were watching from one side dressed formally in long beautiful evening gowns of teal and sequined blue styled by Ferrani of Milan. They stood on Mai's left about twenty feet away at their table in the shade on the verandah that wrapped around the outside of the palace.

"That's our girl," said Kelly.

"Yep," added Catherine.

Mai put up her hand, and a gong sounded three times bringing the crowd of devoted followers to instant silence. She did not smile and didn't feel like smiling in spite of the fact she was with so many who truly loved and were devoted to her. Looking out at the very festive and unexpectedly large gathering she felt lonelier than she had ever been her entire life. Earlier she heard the helicopter leave like a hammer pounding on the roof of her chambers. She knew that Jack was on it, and her heart stopped beating as the sound of the rotors faded into the distance. She was deeply wounded, and all this celebration as a consequence held no purpose or meaning for her. She was going through the motions only for the benefit of her people. Mai stood there in a daze as her mind drifted to the memory of Jack, and their happy life back in Chicago. She was having second thoughts about continuing and seemed lost as the silence extended awkwardly.

"Your Majesty?" whispered Su Ling from the side.

With that, Mai remembered where she was, and shaking off the almost overwhelming gloom she felt, reached up, and removed the clasp at her neck allowing her flowing silk cape to fall to two kneeling, and attending handmaidens revealing her magnificent royal gown. The top was a halter of gold cashmere silk embroidered with Hoa Cuc flowers that framed an elaborate necklace from which hung six large red rubies matching her crown.

Her midriff was bare, and she wore a matching cashmere silk embroidered material that hung low on her waist as a tight skirt with a slit down the left side allowing her to walk comfortably. She portrayed the embodiment of the Hoa Cuc legend. What had everyone's attention, in spite of the gold and rubies, was the Hoa Cuc, the flowered birthmark, on her lower right hip just above the skirt. It was the sacred sign of their true queen. This crowd of Champa faithful had come to bear witness, and declare their undying loyalty and devotion to their goddess queen. Iris, kneeling beside Princess Devi on the platform, assisted her in dropping her little cape so that she was identical to her mother, except that she had gold silk low waist pants instead of a tight skirt.

As the crowd observed that Princess Devi also had the Hoa Cuc on her hip, a roar even louder than the previous cheer heralded, and the impromptu chanting of "Hoa Cuc" began once again. People began to dance, and sing amongst the cheers creating great, and spontaneous merriment. They continued to cheer as Mai sat down on the throne, and Iris placed Devi in her lap. Mai watched passively as the celebration continued for several minutes. She felt little happiness as a result of their reverie on her behalf.

Su Ling gave a signal and dozens of acolytes in white began circulating with censers of smoking colored incense among the kneeling throng. A hundred young girls followed them with baskets filled with Hoa Cuc flowers that they tossed among the joyous devoted followers of Queen Maisong. After a time, the gong sounded three times again, and the crowd grew silent. Su Ling read a long declaration commemorating the day and led the crowd of Champa faithful in adoration of their queen.

Mai, representing the icon of their veneration, formally declared, "I, Queen Maisong, together with all Champa faithful here, and around the world, consecrate this valley as our sacred Champa homeland, now and forever; the sacred and protected land of the Champa people."

A gong sounded three times, and the entire crowd bowed down with their heads to the ground in worship of their goddess queen. The gong sounded once, and they rose to their knees as Su Ling declared. "Your Majesty, we declare our eternal devotion and loyalty to you. We are honored and grateful that you have returned to us. We were lost, and now we are found. We bow and pledge our lives in service to you."

The gong sounded three times once more and the entire crowd bowed down to the ground again. They remained just so until Mai nodded and said, "You may rise and celebrate the birth of our Champa nation once more."

There rose once more a loud, jubilant cheering of "Hoa Cuc" in time with drums that grew so deafening, Princess Devi put her hand over her ears. People danced to the beat, and it seemed the cheering would continue forever. Mai felt a love for them far greater than she had imagined but it did little to alleviate her sadness.

But then unexpectedly the cheering stopped as confusion spread amongst the loyal followers. The crowd began to murmur, and protest in bewildered surprise. Their confusion turned to feelings of disgust, with yelled taunts, and expressions of hate toward the stage. Many of them remembered the time of Colonel Minh who had abused and taken advantage of their faith for his evil agenda.

Kelly who enjoyed watching the crowd celebrate and honor Mai was surprised at their sudden change of attitude. She was alarmed until she looked toward Mai and saw that a man had walked forward on the stage near the throne. He was standing with his head bowed near the throne wearing tuxedo pants only with no shirt or shoes.

Kelly jostled Catherine's arm in surprise and stood up at their table excited. "Cat, look, he's here! He didn't leave!" she said, pointing to Jack standing to the side of Mai's throne on the platform. His hands were clasped behind his back just as Jobi had coached him.

Daniel arrived just at that time dressed in a formal black tuxedo and sat down at the table next to Kelly and Catherine to watch.

"I thought you left with Jack," said Kelly surprised. "I heard the helicopter leave."

He reached over and sipped from her glass of wine before he explained, "Oh, that was some of the kitchen staff making a supply run. It seems the crowd is much larger than anyone anticipated, and it has taken them this long to figure out they were going to need more food and a whole lot more booze. Hell, I could have told them that last week," he explained, with a shake of his head. "What did I miss?"

Mai at first couldn't comprehend why the adoring crowd had turned on her so suddenly. With this confusion, she was shocked from her doldrums, and when she looked around to her left and saw Jack she exploded in a bright smile at the sight of him. She bounced in her seat, and involuntarily clapped with happiness. He came forward acting very humble for the crowd and knelt down like the attending handmaidens to the side of the throne on the platform. The crowd responded with an abrupt silence as their feelings changed upon seeing him kneel before their queen.

When she saw him, Princess Devi broke into a big-eyed smile and wiggled out of her mother's lap down to the platform. She ran over to Jack, yelling gleefully, "Daddy!"

She jumped into his arms, and Jack held her close and kissed her little head again, and again, while still on his knees. Jack cried as he told her, "I love you," over, and over.

Princess Devi looked up at Iris who had run after her, and said, "This is my daddy, my daddy!"

Iris was at first confused and unsure what to do about the antics of the princess. But when she glanced at Queen Mai and saw her wondrous smile of approval, she relaxed. She stayed by the princess protectively while watching her hug her father.

Princess Devi hopped down from Jack's arms, took his hand, and started pulling him toward the imposing throne saying, "Come on, Daddy. Come sit with us."

"I am not sure what is proper here, Princess," he answered, looking over at Mai cautiously.

But Mai was done with that. She got up, and hurried over to Jack. She bent toward him, kissed him on the forehead, and said, "Stand up, my love. We are breaking tradition right now, and if they don't like it, they can go find another queen. We are one family and will stay as one, Devi, you, and I forever. Without you, nothing matters to me, queen, or no."

Jack stood up, and Mai kissed him meaningfully on the lips for everyone to see. During that long and enduring kiss, they were alone, just the two of them, oblivious to the thousands that witnessed their love in silence. Nothing else mattered as they journeyed deep within their feelings for one another. After a minute, they stopped and held each marking the moment. Then, still holding his arm, Mai turned and faced the crowd.

There were microphones, and a sound system set up, but Mai ignored them, and said in a natural voice, speaking in the traditional Champa language, "I am your rightful queen and heir to the Champa throne."

It was a part of the legend of the Champa queen that when she talked thus to her people, every true Champa could hear her. For her voice was not only carried on waves of sound, but also it was of the mind as if coming from within them as was their embedded faith.

She declared, "I am the Hoa Cuc, the Nagani." A roar went up from the front to the back of the crowd in affirmation of her declaration.

"You are charged with obeying me in all things. If you believe in me, follow me. I will bring you my love, my peace, and happiness.

She turned directly to look at Su Ling because it was Su Ling who had told her it was necessary by tradition for Jack to be branded, or the people would not accept him.

"I have followed the sacred traditions dating back thousands of years. Look, and see my mark." She turned Jack, so his bare right shoulder showed the Hoa Cuc brand, which she had burned into his shoulder two years before. "I have branded this man as my slave, and consort, according to our laws, and traditions, though it broke my heart to do so."

She paused for effect, and then turned to the crowd and continued, "I love you all very much. But hear me now, when I say that I, the Hoa Cuc, the Nagani, am ready to leave this place, and you behind. I will go away with my family and leave this valley forever to live where we are *all* welcome, if you do not accept this man I love as one of us. That is the truth I tell you now. He is found more worthy in my eyes than the best of you. I say now that if you turn away, and shun him, it is you who are found wanting, and unworthy in the eyes of the Hoa Cuc. And I will not live with people of such narrow, and backward minds."

Once again amidst a very uneasy and worried silence, she paused and then continued as she stepped forward to emphasize the importance of what she was about to say, "This man is my husband who I love with all my heart, mind and soul. Why you may ask would I, the Nagani, love this one man so? I will tell you although it is your duty to obey me regardless. My husband Jack is the kindest man I have ever known. He is sensitive, creative, and compassionate, and he has proven his love for my daughter, and me many times over even to risking his life to save me. He is patient with me in my many moods and listens to me. He brightens my spirit at all times. When I am with him, I am whole. When he is gone from me, I am incomplete."

She paused once again, and the crowd listened intently and dwelt on her every word. She turned back, and held her hand out for Jack to come forward. He reached down, picked up Princess Devi, and then joined her in front of the throne.

She continued, "This is my husband, Jack. He will not be your king, nor rule over you. But he will not be my slave either, nor my consort. You will accept him as the most honored man in our world, the man I love. You will bring him into your hearts, and your homes as the friend he truly wants to be with you. You will learn to love him as you do your queen and princess. That is all I ask of you this day," she said, pausing afterward.

The valley was quiet as she finished, and at first, Mai was not sure of their reaction. After a moment, she inquired of them, "What say you? Will you serve and obey me, and welcome my husband Jack into your hearts as one of us?"

The cheer went up instantly in answer to her question and became a very resounding outcry of affirmation.

After a moment, Mai, with tears in her eyes, and a smile on her face, put up her hand bringing them to silence once more, and said, "Thank you, my beloved people. You have made me proud to be your queen this day. Let the festivities begin!"

As the celebration began in earnest, Mai turned and led Jack over to the side behind the throne. She kissed Devi and gave her to Iris to hold. Then she kissed Jack warmly and wiped away tears from her face. "Thank you, my darling, my love. I do not have words for the happiness I feel at this moment. I truly thought you had left, and my life was over. I heard the helicopter leave. What happened?"

"It was one of my more pig-headed moments, Mai. I was being selfish and narrow-minded, and I wouldn't even listen to Daniel who was doing his darndest to reason with me and convince me to stay. But then he asked me one simple question, 'Where do you want to go?'

"It stopped me cold because I couldn't think of an answer. I realized there was nowhere on Earth I would rather be than with you and Devi. I was insanely foolish, and I'm sorry. I don't know what got into me. Please forgive me. I love you and Devi more than you can imagine."

She kissed him, took a deep breath, and said, smiling through tears of happiness, "I love you more. Go find the rest of your tux, handsome, and join Kelly, Catherine, and Daniel on the verandah. I will catch up with you as often as I can. I am sure I will need a lot of grounding before my people are done honoring me this day. Once again, I am complete. I love you, Jack Largent."

Chapter 6

March 1992   Siem Kulea, Cambodia

For a time at the very beginning, Mai sat on the throne with Princess Devi on her lap. As Devi became more restless within the first hour, Mai commanded Uri and Iris to take her inside and to entertain her during this process for safety reasons, and so that she would not have to worry about her.

For another hour each family came forward in a long line to present themselves before Queen Maisong. Mai wanted to go down to the crowd, but Su Ling said it was impossible for security reasons. It soon became apparent that there was no way most of the very large assembly of Champa faithful were going to be able to get closer to their queen. Mai looked out at the impossibly long line and suddenly beckoned Ramadi and Fetu to attend her as she made her way down the stairs, and waded into the crowd before anyone could voice an objection. Her handmaidens stayed by her forming a small circle, and Ramadi, Fetu, and six guards positioned themselves in between the handmaidens widening the circle a bit. But there was not the slightest incident. The Champa people went to their knees respectfully as she approached, and she went to as many as she could, and greeted them personally. After meeting her, they backed away respectfully and allowed others to greet her. It was an instantaneous and orderly process born out of respect, love and a bond they all shared with their queen.

Jack returned fully dressed in his tux and sat at the table with Kelly, Catherine, and Daniel. He watched Su Ling for a moment still standing on the verandah, on the opposite side of the throne. She was visibly annoyed by Mai's impromptu performance, and tapped her foot in protest. At first, Jack assumed she was concerned for Mai's safety, but then he thought he detected something else in her demeanor. Standing not far from their table was the lady who was called Chu, and Jack got up to try to talk with her.

"Do you speak English?" he asked her.

"Yes, a little, Mr. Largent. I am not as good at it as I should be. I will work on it so I can be better," she said.

"Hah! That sounds pretty good to me," he said. "Call me Jack, would you? I am not big on formalities, and I would be more comfortable if in conversation with me you tossed them aside. I know you have been waiting a long time to be formal, and respectful when dealing with Queen Maisong, and I understand that completely. But please, I would like to be able for you and me to just talk as friends, Chu. May I call you Chu?"

"Of course, Jack. You honor me. As you may imagine this is a great day for the Champa people. Queen Maisong has fulfilled our dreams and assured a bright future for us all. You do realize she is more than just a queen to us."

They watched for a moment as Mai greeted family after family, each kneeling before her as she came to them. Mai smiled, bent to them, and held their hands, and talked with them happily. She did not lay a hand on them, or propose to bless them formally, but greeted them as fellow Champas sharing the joyous celebration. Still, many after she passed, backed away respectfully, and then finding a space went with their heads to the ground to worship her. Jack wondered what they would think if they knew that a week ago she sat on the floor of their townhouse with Devi and painted faces on her toenails for fun.

Chu studied Jack's reaction while he watched the devotion of her people toward Queen Maisong.

After a moment, he replied to her question, "Yes, and I admit it is somewhat awkward for me. But I have enough respect for you and your people to honor those beliefs. I think I envy the passion that your people have for their faith. That is an area I can use some work. My character is naturally skeptical of most religions. That is, I was before I met Mai. I have seen her do some astonishing things, and it is not difficult for me to understand why your people worship her."

"But you do not," suggested Chu.

"Oh, but you are wrong, Chu. We all have particular ways we worship Queen Maisong. My way is to be myself as I am with her. I love her dearly, and we have both nearly died for each other. We share our love as hand-held adventurers exploring our world and universe. It is a great ride, and I love sharing it with her."

Chu watched, as afternoon pastry was served at the tables on the veranda. Thinking of one more item to check she started to walk away, but turned back a moment and said, "I can see why she loves you, Jack. I have to say, I will look forward to talking with you. Now, I have to run and make sure things keep progressing, as they should. That is how I best worship and serve our queen. Please come to me if you need anything, or have any suggestions for better serving Queen Maisong."

"I do have one question," said Jack.

"Yes, what would that be?" asked Chu.

"How is Lady Su Ling doing? I am not one of her fans, but my wife cares about her a great deal," he said.

Chu's expression changed, and at first she did not answer him. But then she said softly and close to his ear, "You would do well to keep an eye on her, Jack. Appearances can be deceiving."

For the next hour, Mai wandered the crowd, meeting as many people as she could in her own way. There were so many she had hardly made a dent when at last she took a break and made her way back up to the verandah to share some time with Jack, Catherine, and Kelly.

Su Ling kept insisting she go inside, and rest a bit, and at last, Mai accommodated her. She headed for her quarters with Su Ling following closely behind. But just outside the palace doorway, she stopped and put her hand up blocking Su Ling. Turning toward Jack, she took his hand and led him quickly into the palace, down the hallway, and into her private chambers. Before Su Ling or anyone could follow, she closed the door leaving her and Jack alone, with a command they were not to be disturbed.

"What about the festivities?" asked Jack genuinely happy to have her to himself.

"We're going to have our own festivities, GI," whispered Mai. "You go boom-boom me now, GI!" she exclaimed, using the silly Vietnamese bargirl vernacular that held a special meaning for them. She added, with a crooked grin, "Wait till you see the bed!"

After making love to each other like newlyweds, or two people who were truly grateful to be in each other's arms once more, Jack and Mai lay silently content. Jack chuckled, and Mai asked, "What? What's so funny, GI?"

He laughed again as he traced a hand down her belly, and around her navel. "This bed is over the top, don't you think. It's as big as a yacht, but I have to say I think I'm growing to like the snake thing. That headpiece with the snake evolving into a woman is rather inspiring in its own way. It's very erotic and what's more, I believe she looks like you, Mai! This whole thing is over the top for me but I think I see why everyone is so excited outside."

"Yes, they are feeling fulfilled after a very long time without hope of doing so, Jack, and I am feeling much the same. I am satisfied and complete on the opposite side of that paradigm, and that is expressed in everything I do especially the sensual stuff. And you get to reap the benefits, GI," she said turning and smothering him happily with kisses. "I promise never to tell you again that I believe there is something important I have to do. I have found it, my love and I am most pleased you are here to share it with me. I love these people, Jack. I truly love them. As I walked among them today, I could feel a bond stronger than anything I could ever imagine. I will do anything it takes to ensure they live happy, peaceful, and fulfilling lives."

She pulled back and got serious for a moment. "But I have to warn you, darling. Tonight at midnight this place will dissolve into one large love fest. The gong will ring three times signaling the beginning of the serpent ritual. Everyone will be masked, and all men and women will be dressed in erotic outfits. Anyone can make consensual love to anyone, and traditionally, I am supposed to be among them. The Serpent Ritual is a fertility rite during which the goddess goes among her people and joins with them in celebrating the time we were honored when the gods lived with us on Earth. It will last for three hours until the gong rings three times once more. That is why the gong always rings three times when we draw everyone's attention. It is a reminder that we are all one in spirit serving the ancient gods who once dwelt among us."

But Jack hadn't heard much of what she said after she mentioned she was supposed to be among them.

"Oh come on! So you're going to make love to several men, and women, later tonight? Is that what you are telling me, Mai?"

"No, Jack, not tonight, and not ever. You are the only man with whom I will ever make love. That is ours, and ours alone, my darling. Su Ling is stepping in for me. She will wear the outfit I would normally wear, and sit on the throne pretending to be me as the people worship her and perform the sacrifice to her. Then she will dance the most erotic dance you've ever seen. After that, she will whip you, and then drag you off to make love. That will start the free love fest until the gong sounds three times again."

"Oh, I get it," said Jack, "and with the mask, no one will know it isn't you. Whoa, that's a relief. But wait, did you say she is going to whip me?" Jack was getting that not so good feeling again.

"Yes, but only symbolically. Don't worry. It's part of the induction routine for you to become an official Champa. She will strike you three times. Then you are supposed to fall to the ground before her, in worship position just as my people do. Then the gong will sound three times again, announcing the beginning of the Nakahi Atua…the serpent's time. It is a time of fertility when all Champa women demand the service of their men. I have seen it several times, or I should say Queen Po has, and it is quite extraordinary. It is not long before only the masks are left, and that is by tradition and law. Any man or woman, who removes their mask or shows their face is shunned, put in the stocks, naked, and disgraced. Thus, everyone has an excuse to give themselves up entirely to the serpent anonymously," explained Mai. "I am sure there was a time this ritual was observed for practical purposes such as to increase the size of the Champa workforce, but later it became one of our fondest traditions. It is celebrated every twenty years, once each new generation. Babies conceived during ritual are especially honored and privileged their entire lives."

"Su Ling will act out this part also, careful to not reveal her real identity. She loves this kind of thing as much as I do not. I am fortunate that she resembles me so closely. With the mask I am confident that no one will suspect the subterfuge," explained Mai.

"I am sure I would be able to tell it isn't you," said Jack.

"Well, no, darling, that is the other thing. You will not have any control over yourself. At the beginning of the ritual everyone drinks of the Nakahi Parata. It's an ancient traditional drink that enhances the receptors in an area of the brain that reacts to the senses. The effect is a group hallucinogenic state that will probably make you wildly erotic like the others. Your senses will be running on overdrive. You will want to make love to anything that walks especially the serpent queen."

Jack chuckled.

"You're laughing?" Mai pushed herself up with straight arms from the bed to get a better look at his face. "You *are* laughing. I have to admit I did not expect that would be your reaction. I thought you would be appalled by all of this. Now I don't know what to think," confessed Mai, with a curious expression on her face.

"Well, you just told me I was going to lose all my inhibitions, and it was OK to do what I feel with anyone. I mean, that is a blank check to erotic happiness on a scale I could never imagine normally. So, yes, I am smiling. What do Kelly and Catherine think about all of this?" he asked.

"Oh! Now I see, GI!" she joked punching him in the arm playfully. "So you think you are going to mix it up with Kelly and Catherine again, huh? Isn't one baby with them enough?"

"Well, as Catherine said, "When in Rome..." he quipped, with a big smile.

"Hah! This isn't Rome, or Vegas either. Don't you worry, handsome. I may not be there in person, but I will have my eyes on you. So don't forget who feathers your nest," she said, kissing him again.

She continued, "I think myself, Fetu, Ramadi and our security team, will be the only sane ones in the valley tonight, and we will have our hands full to be sure no one gets hurt. The children will all be several miles away having a private celebration.

"And in answer to your question, if it was a question," continued Mai, "Catherine and Kelly are prepared, and even eager to do the Nakahi Atua ritual. I have seen their outfits, and they are awesome. The ritual hasn't happened for hundreds of years and Catherine and Kelly have been talking about it since I mentioned it to them. It's a free pass for everyone, Jack. Who knew?"

But Jack was thinking about something else and got serious for a moment. "Do you trust Su Ling, Mai? I'm not sure I do, and I don't think she likes me very much. It's just a feeling, but I get bad vibes from her."

"Yes, I trust Su Ling. Thank god for Su Ling. She is a perfect double for me. I love that woman, Jack. She is the most amazing woman in the world, and I trust her implicitly. Don't be surprised if you hear about her in my bed sometimes when you're away. Old habits are hard to break. She means a lot to me."

Jack kissed her gently. "OK, I suppose I get that. She saved our lives, and I love her too for that. But she is different now somehow. She's changed."

Mai laid back on her pillow not wanting to hear his opinion of Su Ling after all she had done to get Siem Kulea ready for her and saving her life before that.

Jack read her body language and changed the subject with a gentle kiss on her cheek. "Before I go stupid again, I want someone to tell me what this tradition is all about. I have figured out that you are not descended from snakes, or even believe that, and that it is a symbol of your power and ancestry instead…I think."

Mai kissed him back, turned toward him, and snuggled in close and told him, "There is much that even I don't know, and there is a lot that's just handed down tradition. Here is the short version of what I know, for now."

Mai spent the next few minutes relating what she knew of her ancestors and the legend of the ancients being careful this time not to leave anything out.

"How do you know all this, Mai?" asked Jack when she finished.

"Well, that's the thing. I didn't before joining with Queen Po. After that, I just knew it."

"Like the self-reproductive thing," he said.

"Yes, darling. That should not matter to you one iota. Devi is yours, and in many ways more yours than mine," she said.

"I think that's true, Mai," he said. "We have always had an unusual bond. But the self-reproduction explains why Devi looks like a miniature you."

She nodded, and kissed him, "It's complicated. But it is, what it is."

Ceva knocked softly at the door and begged entrance. Mai told her to come, and she entered, bowed and said, "Your Majesty, Lady Su Ling said to remind you the banquet starts at five. It will break at ten for people to prepare for ritual, and then ritual is at midnight. Does Your Majesty require anything?"

Mai grabbed Jack's arm and looked at the time on his watch. Oh, crap! We've been making out like school kids for two hours, Jack. It's a quarter to five! Let's go, my love, party time again!"

She clapped her hands, and her handmaidens appeared instantly ready to attend her. She bounced naked out of bed, and let them hurry her into her bath. Jack watched with pleasure as she began talking with them in earnest ignoring him as she walked away. At twenty-nine she was in her prime mentally, and, as he noted just then, physically too. He never got enough of seeing her naked.

He threw off the covers and sat on the edge of the bed stretching his muscles in earnest. As he opened his eyes and looked up, two of Mai's handmaidens were standing nearby with their heads bowed. "Our Mistress has ordered us to attend you, Master Jack," one of them said with a slight smile. "We are ordered to show you to your bath, and bathe you if you wish."

Jack noted he was sitting completely naked before them, and it was too late to be embarrassed. Instead, he told them, "You tell your Mistress that I am quite capable of bathing myself, and I know where my shower is. Tell her, that I will meet her here to go to dinner in thirty minutes."

"Yes, master Jack," one of them said bowing. "But may I advise you that Her Majesty will not be ready for an hour, or more, so you may take your time. If you get hungry before that, Jobi is ready to bring you something."

Jack nodded, got up, and gathered his perfectly folded clothes. *When did that happen?* He headed for the family quarters. Suddenly a nap seemed the most important item on his list, and finding his bed, he laid down and quickly went to sleep.

Chapter 7

1992   Siem Kulea Northern Cambodia

Later that same night around eleven, Mai lounged on a divan dressed in a comfortable blue silk áo dài with white pants and sipped a glass of wine as she enjoyed the show performing before her. She watched Jack dressed only in a loincloth holding his arms out to the sides while her handmaidens oiled him down from head to foot. Fortunately, he had spent a week on the beach in Florida on his last photo shoot as an advertising photographer and that had given him a dark tan, which had not quite worn off. At forty-two he was still in good shape from working in the studio on sets and playing power volleyball in the gym three nights a week.

Jack was enjoying this routine now, but an hour ago he was embarrassed when Mai told him to strip in front of her handmaidens so they could prepare him properly for the ritual event.

He told them he would prepare himself, but on a signal from Mai, Ceva stepped forward and insisted, "No, master Jack. For the next hour, you do what we say so you look right for tonight." She pointed her finger at him sternly signaling she would not take no for an answer. "Is important. Must be perfect. You take off your clothes, and stand here."

Jack looked to Mai for help, but she was too busy laughing at his predicament while peeking her eyes over the edge of a pillow. She came up for air and said, "You better obey her, Jack. She is responsible for you looking like a proper slave for your queen tonight. It's her neck if you don't look right. Don't make her have to get Ramadi and Fetu in here."

Jack gave up, and went with it. After a while, he was having fun and Mai was laughing with him, "Hey, baby, we're not in Chicago anymore."

"You missed a spot over here," he directed the handmaidens oiling him down. "Now I know what Seabiscuit must have felt like as they got him ready for the Kentucky Derby," he quipped.

"Hah! You wish," Mai answered, smiling. "On the other hand maybe I could make some money putting you out to stud." She tapped her cheek as if pondering such an option. "You seem to have made a good account of yourself so far."

Ceva made one last inspection and then motioned the ladies to step back. Mai sat up straight and judged their work for a moment. "Good job, ladies. He looks great."

Then she nodded to Ceva who dismissed the rest of the handmaidens in the room ordering them to return to their chambers, and to remain there waiting in the event any emergencies arose throughout the evening. They were given orders not to leave unless summoned.

Just at that moment Hata, Su Ling's handmaiden, entered and knelt before Mai while sneaking glances of Jack still posing after being oiled down for the night's festivities.

"Your Majesty, Lady Su Ling has confided in me concerning your switch with her tonight for the ritual. I assure Your Majesty, that your secret is safe with me. She sent me to fetch your husband, Jack, for the ritual tonight," Hata said.

"What do you think, Hata? Does he look like a proper slave ready for induction?" Mai said still enjoying the situation.

But Hata did not realize she was joking and regarded Jack with unfettered contempt. "Yes, my lady. My mistress will be most pleased to take the whip to this one for induction tonight. She is almost ready, and that is why she sent me to check on him."

"You go back, and tell Lady Su Ling that Ceva will bring him out to the verandah by the path to the ritual celebration when we are done here. I want to inspect him first," Mai said. "We will only be a few more minutes."

"Yes, my lady," said Hata, giving Jack one last look as Ceva put an orange headband on him.

After she left, Jack quipped, "Wow, I'm glad she isn't the one with the whip. If looks could kill, I was just mortally wounded! I wonder what her problem is."

"Come on, babe. She was probably thinking of something else. You know how demanding Su Ling can be," Mai assured him as Ceva left through a different doorway.

Ceva returned shortly, leading another man by the hand who was dressed identical to Jack and of the same physical appearance. He even had his hair styled like Jack's, and he was wearing an identical orange headband. She stood him beside Jack who gaped at the man with his mouth wide open in surprise.

"I think I can still tell the difference," said Mai, getting up for a closer inspection. "Turn around, boys," she ordered, as she walked over from her lounge.

Jack and the other man both turned around, baring their naked behinds for Mai's review.

"Jack, darling," Mai said, running her hand over his backside. "I never realized what a fantastic ass you have, but then I never compared it to the competition.

"My lady, remember it will be dark, and the air will be full of incense and smoke," offered Ceva with a smirk, amused by Queen Mai's comment.

"You want to explain what is going on?" demanded Jack, a bit put-off about being treated like an object of comparison with another man. "I thought you were preparing me for this ritual thing. Who's this guy?" he asked, pointing to the man next to him.

Mai ignored him playfully as she sat back down, and ordered, "Turn them around and put on their masks."

Ceva directed Jack and the other man around facing Mai and put on a mask covering the top part of both of their faces.

"Yes, that makes a huge difference. He will pass nicely I think," said Mai. "Turn them sideways so I can compare brands," she ordered.

Jack turned to his side as the other man was directed to do the same showing the Hoa Cuc brand on his shoulder like Jack's.

"Oh, come on, Mai. Enough is enough! He's branded too? When did that happen?" asked Jack.

Just at that moment Ramadi rushed in, and said, "My lady, I'm sorry I'm late. I was rechecking the security at the ritual event, and you were correct. I will be sure to pick up the camera afterward."

Gesturing toward the man, he said, "Was I right? Is he acceptable?"

"Yes, great job, Ramadi. I am amazed. The brand is almost identical. What did you do, dye his hair, or something?" Mai asked.

"Yes, but that was a minor thing. I was fairly positive he could pass for Jack when you expressed your concern to me four weeks ago," he said.

Mai motioned for Jack to sit beside her, patting the lounge with her hand, and motioned for Ramadi and Jack's double to join them opposite.

She kissed Jack quickly explaining it was for putting up with her antics, and then she further explained, "Darling I already told you this ritual tonight is pretty wild. It is very possible someone might get carried away, and hurt you. I have been worried about that for a while now, and have been talking with Ramadi about the situation It was just a feeling, but I didn't want to take any chances. He has gone through his Champa guards who are all exceptional, loyal, and devoted men. He found one that resembled you enough that with a few alterations he thought he could pass for you. His man was happy to do this and even honored to wear my brand like Ramadi and Fetu. His name is 'Cavil'. Say hello to your stand-in tonight, my love," she said.

Jack shook hands with his double sitting opposite him and exchanged a few friendly words.

He turned to Mai. "So no ritual for me?"

"Oh don't look so disappointed, GI," she said. "You and I are going to be busy enough. Nope, sorry. We're sitting this one out."

Jack let out a breath of relief. "Thank god. But you could've told me, Mai."

"We had to keep it a big secret, Jack," she explained. "This is not a game. This is very real for my people, and not to be taken lightly. You will notice that except for Ceva, even my handmaidens don't know. I couldn't take any chance of word getting out, so I made sure to tell no one, but the very few I needed to carry out my plan."

Ceva approached and knelt before her queen. "My lady, we should hurry. Lady Su Ling will be waiting," she said.

"Yes, of course. OK, Jack, listen carefully. Here is what you have to do…"

Ceva led Jack, masked and in his loincloth, out to the verandah. Lady Su Ling met them there dressed and masked as Queen Maisong, along with six guards. There was a small crowd at the bottom of the steps waiting to escort them to the ritual. Erotic music was playing in the distance to pounding drums designed to get the large crowd in the proper mood. It signaled a call for everyone to embrace the moment, and let their passions run free. It was the beginning of a long, and lively night for the Champa people.

Upon seeing Jack, Su Ling, wearing her mask, and looking every bit like Queen Mai, circled and inspected him. She ran her hand over his backside possessively and then gave him a sharp strike with her whip. "Well, Jack, are you ready to give yourself formally to me tonight?"

Jack was surprised how much she actually looked like Mai and he had to admit she looked spectacular in the snake-dress she was wearing. He replied, "Yes, my love. I am this night all yours to do with as you please."

In a lower voice, he whispered to her, "I just want to get this over with."

She bit his ear, gave him a peck on the cheek, and said, "I am going to enjoy this very much."

But just as she started to lead him down the steps to join the ritual procession, Jack said, "U-up, hold it. I'd better make one last pit stop, or we'll both regret it later. Sorry, I'll be fast, I promise. Do you mind, my darling?" he asked, loudly so everyone could hear.

Su Ling was a bit irritated, but said, "Make it fast, GI," for all to hear, mimicking Mai's well-known nickname for him.

Jack hurried off, and a minute later his perfect stand-in returned. Su Ling took his arm possessively, and led him away.

Chapter 8

March 1992   Siem Kulea, Cambodia

The next morning there was a beautiful sunrise marking the beginning of a new era for the Champa people in the Siem Kulea valley. On average days, most of them would be up and heading for the fields, or tending to livestock. But on this morning most were still in bed, not having had but a few hours sleep, if any, the night before.

One young boy was awake and returning home early from the children's encampment. His route joined and followed the path to the White Palace at one point before breaking off toward the village, and his home. He played a soccer ball with dexterous feet as he came down the path guiding it skillfully along its way. Suddenly, he stopped and stood straight, not sure what he was seeing. Moving slowly closer, he realized it was a man, naked and bloody, lying face down in the middle of the path.

The boy ran to the village, and straight to his home. After much effort, he woke his father and brought him out to the path where he found the body. The father examined the man who was still wearing the ritual mask. He bore Queen Maisong's brand and looked like her new husband. He felt for a pulse, but the man was dead. The many bloody whip marks on his body gave evidence he had been whipped severely and apparently beaten to death. The father sent the boy home admonishing him he must tell no one, and he hurriedly went to the palace to report what he found.

The father was brought into Queen Maisong's sitting room and was questioned immediately by Ramadi and Fetu. He was told to wait. Then just as quick, Ramadi and Fetu hurried out, and examined the body. It was Cavil, and he was dead. They quickly retrieved the body, wrapped him in heavy burlap before anyone else could see him, and buried him secretly in an area behind the palace near a maintenance shed where a ditch for irrigation had been already prepared the previous day. The entire process took less than thirty minutes.

Immediately thereafter, Queen Maisong and her husband, Jack, greeted the father in her sitting room. He looked at Jack surprised, but then realized he must have made a mistake when he thought it was Jack on the path. With Ramadi and Fetu present, Queen Mai told the man that for the sake of continued peace in the valley he must make an oath, and swear never to tell what he saw that morning to anyone. The man went to his knees before Queen Maisong and made a solemn vow that he would do as she commanded. He was rewarded with a handsome sum and most importantly the good favor, and confidence of his queen for his effort and loyalty.

Later that morning, Jack dressed in white Khakis and flowered shirt found Mai sitting alone in the garden off of her quarters in meditation. He sat down, put an arm around her, and asked, "Are you OK?"

"No, I am not," she said, worrying her hands. "We were very lucky, Jack. That was supposed to be you. I don't know what I would've done if that were you."

"You knew it might happen, Mai. You knew. But how did you know?

"It was just a feeling, Jack. I get feelings when my universe is out of order. I have had them off and on since Queen Po joined up with me. I have had feelings about this for over a month now. I can't explain it. It just is."

"Mai, I know you don't want to hear it. But Su Ling has to be involved in Cavil's death. I am almost positive, and if not her, then that maid of hers, Hata most certainly is involved. There is something wrong with those two."

"You're right, Jack," she said. "I don't want to hear that. Su Ling is my friend, and she would never do anything to hurt you. As it is, we can't do much to look into it without revealing what we found, and I think that it is better laid to rest for now. Any exposure would destroy the positive beginning we have made for our Champa people.

"Look, handsome," continued Mai trying to hide her concern, "we will be eating shortly, and Su Ling will be joining us. Be careful what you say.

Remember, everyone thinks you were there. Only I know you were not. Don't give it away under any circumstances."

Jack pulled her close. "I'll be good. I promise. But you have to promise me to not keep secrets. In the end, I think it will help for you to talk things over with me."

"You are the one person I try to share everything with, Jack. Right now I'm honestly surprised about what happened. It seems our perfect paradise isn't so perfect after all," she said. "I can't make sense of it. I can't reason this out like I usually do. I don't understand it. I can't gather my thoughts about it. I get so far, and I hit a wall every time usually resulting in a headache. I forget what I was thinking, and I have to start again. It is as if this matter is blocked in my mind."

"Maybe that is your wonderful mind telling you it's wasted energy, Mai."

"Maybe," she said taking his hand and heading inside for breakfast.

But Jack thought it might be something else entirely. He focused on the words of the palace manager Chu concerning Su Ling. "Appearances may not be what they seem."

Mai wearing one of her favorite áo dàis sat down with her friends for brunch hoping to find some relief from the stress she felt after that morning's events. Sitting around the table on the verandah were Mai, Jack, Catherine, Kelly, and Jasmine who Jack invited at the last minute because she had worked through the night with Ramadi and Fetu. Their particular assignment was to keep an eye on Kelly and Catherine and protect them without them knowing. Daniel had left early the previous evening to take care of a problem with a damaged shipment in Bangkok.

Catherine and Kelly talked incessantly from the moment they sat down like young teenage chatterboxes and were eager to relate their adventures the night before at the ritual. They professed to have an extraordinary time but finally admitted that when it came to details, it was a foggy haze of mixed but mostly gratifying episodes for most of it. They both agreed they felt unusually good and remembered the night as a pleasurable experience. They were somewhat successful in distracting Mai from what had just happened that morning. She relaxed a bit as they lifted her spirits. They talked about the costumes, people, and the outrageous things some of them did, and soon had her laughing along with them.

"I don't think we will recognize anyone from the ritual," said Catherine. "I'm pretty sure we stood out, but with masks on, they all looked too similar. Kelly and I were quickly joined by other ladies even at the beginning," said Catherine smiling. "It was like a smorgasbord of delights and I'm positive my darling and I grazed freely."

"I remember the guy in the donkey mask," said Kelly as Catherine laughed beside her. "He started the night with no pants and for obvious reasons. I didn't think that was possible."

Su Ling was late. They gave their orders and were served by the time she arrived. Jack rose courteously upon her arrival. He came around to hold her chair for her, and said loud enough for everyone to hear, "Su Ling, it was indeed an honor to bring you so much satisfaction last night."

But then he whispered surreptitiously in her ear, "What the fuck was that all about? I'm on to you, you bitch! I've got my eye on you." He gave her chair an extra shove and sat down again. Jack had no doubts she was involved in the death of Cavil in spite of what Mai thought.

Catherine and Kelly had their antennas up and on full with what they heard Jack say to her. They remembered Mai whipping Jack and unexpectedly hard at the beginning of the ritual, but then the rest of the night they realized they hadn't seen her again and they didn't remember seeing Su Ling at all. But there had been so many people and everyone was masked so that was not unusual, and then they all drank the kool-aid.

Su Ling looked over at Mai who was smiling, or was she laughing at her? Jack was also smiling and in particularly good spirits for one she knew was whipped severely the night before. She had taken great satisfaction in that at the time. She became confused and concerned as she settled in, and allowed servants to pour her coffee and orange juice. A maid stood by awaiting her breakfast order. Su Ling kept glancing at Jack, as her confusion grew and she considered what to order. Kelly had an omelet, and Su Ling finally said, "I'll have what she is having."

"What, Su Ling, no Num Banh Chok, this morning? I thought you loved that stuff," said Mai in friendly conversation. But then she made a point of taking Jack's hand on the table, kissing it, and covering it with both of her hands. Su Ling read that as more body language pointed at her.

"I guess I am going Western this morning, my lady. Thank you for asking," she replied nervously. "Jack, you look like you weathered the ritual nicely," she commented, not knowing what else to say as she straightened the napkin in her lap.

"Well, you did make it interesting," he returned. " I have a few stripes on my back but it was the least I could do for the woman I love. I didn't mind a bit. But I thought you were only supposed to pretend to whip me."

Mai kicked Jack under the table because he was getting into a problem area without realizing it.

Su Ling fidgeted nervously with her napkin staring down at her plate before deciding how to answer.

"Jack, I'm sorry," she said quickly while glancing at Mai anxiously. "My lady, I guess I got carried away. Please forgive my overzealousness. The ritual can be disorienting especially with the drugs. Jack, are you OK? I was worried about you," she said as her anxiety built.

"Did you whip Jack?" asked Kelly, surprised.

"Yes, she got in a few licks early on," explained Mai quickly bridging the awkward moment. "It was nothing, Su Ling, not to worry. Jack is only having fun with you," said Mai. "He is fine and had a good time. As it was, I left early, and Su Ling made sure Jack was well taken care of last night in my absence. I was called away to the children's camp, and missed the whole thing because one of the young girl's broke her arm when she fell off of a pony."

Jack realized for the first time that Kelly and Catherine did not know Su Ling had stood in for Mai and that this conversation was getting complicated. *Ooops.*

Mai tried to help by changing the subject, "From what I hear it was quite an event. Too bad no one filmed it," she said pointedly.

Kelly and Catherine made awkward glances toward each other because Catherine had done exactly that, and secretly without Mai knowing.

Just then, Su Ling looked at her watch and jumped up. "Oh! My lady, I must apologize. I got a late start and I just remembered I have an interview in Bangkok this morning. I set it up before we arranged this. Please forgive me. I have to run. My transportation is probably wondering where I am."

As Su Ling came over and kissed Mai on the cheek, Mai said, "Of course. Make it fast so we can spend some time together. I want to catch up on everything."

After she departed, Kelly said, "Well that was a phony exit if I ever saw one. I wonder what's on her mind?"

Jack leaned over and whispered to Mai closely, "What do you think?"

"I think she was fooled last night," Mai whispered back. "She has no doubt it was you at the ritual."

"No," said Jack. "I mean do you think she killed Cavil thinking it was me?'

"No, Jack," whispered Mai, bothered by his question, "I told you, she wouldn't have done that. She loves me. She is the most amazing woman in the world, and I trust her implicitly. No, it was probably some Champas who got carried away. We'll probably never know." She gave a sigh as they straightened up at the table.

"And as for you two," Mai said in an accusatory voice aimed directly at Kelly and Catherine. "I'm surprised at you. That was some of the most decadent, perverted sex I've ever seen."

"What are you talking about, Mai?" asked Catherine, surprised.

"Don't play innocent with me. I have your video," said Mai, having fun with them, "and I am going to keep it. Did you really think you could film the sacred Champa Serpent ritual without me knowing?"

The two very accomplished alpha-women looked like guilty children in the principal's office. After a moment, Catherine put down her fork and said, "We're sorry, Mai. But it was such an opportunity. Stuff like that never happens anymore. I mean you have to go back…"

"A thousand years?" said Mai interrupting.

Catherine smiled, "Yep, even further I think."

They were all silent for a moment, but then Kelly asked, "What exactly did we do? I don't remember much after the first thirty minutes, and we already told you about that. I don't even remember how we got back to our suite. But thankfully we woke up alone with just the two of us."

"That stays here. What happens in Siem Kulea stays in Siem Kulea," Mai said, enjoying their discomfort. "I'm going to keep that video for when I need some amusement. Maybe if your nice, I will share it with you over drinks sometime. You won't believe what you did."

"We know how to keep a secret," added Jack, joking. "You two gals were something else though. No offense to Mai, but Catherine, I think that might have been the best sex I've ever had. I'm glad I went. We just might have made a brother for young Charlie, and Kelly, well I all I can say is, 'Whew!'

I'll tell you a secret I'm keeping," he continued. "You both said the same thing when you climaxed. Do you remember what it was?"

Both Catherine and Kelly with huge eyes and their mouths open, flushed bright red instantly and looked at Jack as if begging him not to tell.

Mai kicked Jack under the table again, but inside she was laughing, and thanking him for coming up with that bit of humor when she needed it most. *"I love you, Jack Largent."*

Chapter 9

1997   Ban Kongmi, Southern Laos

There are not many structures in this small village snuggled between two mountain ranges amid dense jungle. But there is a bar, and it has been around for as long as anyone can remember. The building is rustic and weathered on the outside with holes in the roof that defy repair.

A man came through town once in an old French Citroen truck and convinced Lee, the owner, he could put a roof on his bar that would last a lifetime. Lee paid the man, and for a week he worked on the roof during the day and drank Lee's rice whiskey at night. When he moved on, Lee took the opportunity to update the bar with new windows to replace the broken ones he had never bothered fixing. But the following May when the rains came, his roof leaked as always, and he hasn't bothered fixing anything since.

All that happened many years ago and Lee has since reasoned that his regular patrons like the place because it never changes. But perhaps it was also because the inside of the bar was dark, musty, and seasoned like they are.

As he has done for countless afternoons, Lee likes to busy himself with washing glasses and wiping down his bar. He wears a wrap-around, white apron over his midweek shirt of yellow cotton, and loose white pants, with an oversize belt to corral his ample belly. His ever-friendly face shows only a few lines considering his age, and this day displays a two-day beard. He has discerning eyes that are suspicious of strangers, and beyond his affable demeanor is a calculating mind that has guided him safely through the constant schemes of rogues, and vagabonds.

This once boisterous village is a lot quieter now broken up only by the happenstance of a lost tour bus. The new highway was built off to the north, and not many end up going on the remote jungle road that winds through this village. Lee doesn't mind. He only speaks the native Lao tongue and doesn't understand most of the sightseers. It frustrates him when he can't share stories. He prefers this peace to the caustic banter of tourists, and his wife's family in Ban Na.

But today offered something different. His old friend Martinez showed up in the middle of the night. He was ragged, dirty, and looked to Lee worse than he had ever seen him. He liked Martinez because he was not like the others. Most of the time he seemed as if he were playing a part in a movie. He was like a chameleon and changed character readily as it suited him. Lee had seen him do this many times right there in his bar. His favorite role was one of a poor unrefined Latino that most judged him to be at first sight. It was his preferred assumed persona especially when he was trolling for information. But Lee knew that Martinez was a learned man and could be quite articulate. Once, he confessed to Lee that he had a college degree from a school in the United States, but he left all of that behind to escape the draft. His role-playing friend amused Lee, and it was something they laughed about many times over drinks.

When he showed up at the bar after all these years, Lee took him in and offered him a shower, fresh clothes, and a few drinks before his friend collapsed in sleep. An hour ago he had woken up and sat at the far end of the bar. He has been drinking quietly there ever since.

Once he and Martinez were as close as brothers. Together they had shared many stories and adventures. But when Lee wanted to give up that life to manage this same bar twenty years ago, Martinez took the other path. Lee was surprised that Martinez was still alive, and he was elated to see his old friend. Mercenaries like Martinez who followed Colonel Minh used to frequent this area, until the time when the Vietnamese came and killed most of them.

Lee guessed Martinez's age must be close to fifty, but his face looked younger. His was a rugged, darkly, handsome face with a full head of wavy black hair, and just a hint of grey at the temples. If fate had not taken him elsewhere, he might have ended up on the big screen. Like his personality, his face could change instantly to what Martinez wanted you to know. If he liked you, his face would show it, but if he did not, most people avoided him.

Martinez smiled at his old friend, and finding a memory etched into the bar, he asked in Lee's native Lao tongue, "Hey Lee, what of Phu Banh? Wasn't he married to that bargirl of yours? What's her name?"

Lee wandered down and began straightening up the bar near Martinez although nothing had moved there in many days. "Yeah, Taili married him, and then one night they robbed my cash box and left. I haven't seen either of them since.

After Martinez only nodded, Lee asked, "Eddie, what happened to you these many years? Do you want to tell me about it now? Last night you were weak, so I didn't bother. You know, my friend, I am always here for you. You know?"

"Yeah, Lee. I know," affirmed Martinez, nodding.

"I will always owe you a debt for what you did, and I can never repay that fully. I missed you, my friend. I confess I thought you were dead like the others," he said, waiting for Martinez to fill in the time since they were last together.

But Martinez instead remembered back when Lee first started working at the bar. He met a pretty Lao girl and wanted to settle down. At first, Martinez was upset because guys don't just quit their compadres over a woman. But as Martinez got to know her, he could understand. Her name was Belah, but Martinez called her Belita. Her charms won Martinez over too, and he grew to envy Lee for her love of him.

One night, about a week after she announced she was pregnant, three particularly bad men unfamiliar to Lee or Martinez came into the bar and wanted Lee's money. They did not hide that they had plans for Belah too. They waved guns around threatening everyone even pistol-whipping one man who stood up to them. There were murmurs, and grumbles from the sultry crowd, but they just sat and watched as the three men cleaned out Lee's cash box.

Martinez was out back taking his time in the little outhouse that serviced the bar and missed the arrival of these bad men. Just as he returned through the back entrance, one of them grabbed Belah and began forcing kisses on her. Before Lee could react, Martinez erupted in a wild rage and charged the biggest of the three. The man raised his gun in a surprised panic, and shot Martinez nicking him in the top left shoulder. But even wounded, Martinez did not waver and landed on the man throwing him backward to the hardwood floor. He continued pummeling him with fists to the face even after the man was unconscious.

Lee, meanwhile, grabbed the gun he kept hidden under the counter by the cash box and shot another of the three men dropping him dead on the other side of the bar. The remaining man seeing his friends overcome, held Belah with one arm around her waist and a knife pressed against her throat. He faced Lee who had his gun pointed at him and threatened to kill her if he did not drop the gun. But before a bad situation could get worse, Martinez leaped quickly from the floor, grabbed the man from behind, and held his arm holding the knife away from Belah in a show of his unusual strength. He twisted the man around, and then broke his arm over the edge of the bar freeing Belah as the knife fell on the bar at the same time. In the next instant, he picked up the knife, grabbed the man, and slit his throat in a bloody line from one side to the other letting him fall lifeless to the floor.

Belah ran to Lee, and held him tightly in her arms, crying. Martinez looked to the other man not moving on the floor where he had beaten his face to be unrecognizable and decided he must be dead too. He dropped the knife and looked toward his friend who nodded to him in thanks. But when Martinez looked at Belah she shrank from him like he was a monster. She was horrified by what he had done even in saving her. It was out of feelings for her that Martinez had been enraged to act in the first place. But he saw in her eyes that she feared him now as much as the dead men on the floor. He knew then that any feelings she had for him were gone forever, and he knew it was time to leave.

The next day with his wound treated, and wrapped in a bandage, he left without saying goodbye. His amorous fantasy eventually faded away drowned in the promises of too many women in too many places. His life unfolded mostly responding to his misdeeds. His adventures led him through endless camps, and villages, and facing death with so many faces he questioned why it was he was still living. But Martinez was a survivor, even in the worst of times, like a rat that scurries across the pitted floor knowing when to run away, and when to eat from the lifeless carcass.

Lee leaned in close because he did not want the others in the bar to hear him. "I think since you are back, you might want to stay a while, my friend. There is a reward out for you; about five year's profit of what this bar makes. You know, you are safe here, but nothing lasts. One of these cockroaches will tell someone eventually, and they will come looking for you here. If you don't want to talk about it, it is OK with me. But I think you might like to talk because sometimes it helps. This I think is true."

Martinez smiled at his friend and nodded. "Where is Belita, Lee? Is she still around?"

"Yes, of course. I almost forgot. I have another place now farther west in Ban Na. Belita's family lives there, and she opened a little restaurant on the river. She got her whole family involved. I am proud of her, she is quite the business-woman," Lee explained. "She speaks three languages, and the tourists love her."

"I am not surprised, Lee," said Martinez. "She was one of the few women I could talk to about worldly things. She has quite a mind. I confess I think I loved her for a moment, my friend. I apologize for that."

"Well, she runs Lee pretty well too," Lee said, joking. "I come here to this old bar to get away sometimes from her and her family. She wants me to close this place but I will not. I love this old bar. It has lots of memories. I'm sure you understand."

Martinez nodded, and as Lee poured him another shot into a well-used whiskey glass, he told Lee what happened to him. As he began telling his story, Lee leaned in even closer.

Martinez explained that he continued his mercenary ways as a hired gun after the fall of Colonel Minh, and for a time had such a reputation that he was always busy. No matter the assignment, those who hired him knew that Martinez would get the job done. He spoke proudly of that. Things were different now. For the last year, he was smuggling drugs out of Laos into Thailand. He didn't like the people he worked with. He didn't trust them, and for good reason. That job ended seven days ago when Thai police am-bushed the shipment they were sneaking across the border in two trucks. They seized the drugs hidden in the bottom of feed barrels worth millions of dollars. Everyone was killed but Martinez, and he might as well be dead. If either side found him, they would kill him. This remote village and bar was the one place he felt safe at least for the moment.

"Do you ever think of going home; you know, back to the United States? I wonder why you never mention it?" Lee asked.

Martinez looked at him for a moment, and replied, "There's blood on the field, and blood on the foam, and blood on the body, when a man goes home."

"What are you talking about now?" asked Lee shaking his head.

"That's an old poem I never forgot, my friend, and I never dreamed it would ever apply to me, but now it does. I can't go home," said Martinez. "I've changed too much. That door is closed to me."

"I have plenty of money now. Belah has made us successful. I could lend you some if you need it. Why don't you just go, and start all over again?" Lee asked.

Martinez shook his head. "I have been here so long surviving amongst the worst that life has to offer that I've become the worst that life has to offer."

Martinez looked around at the few men sitting within the shadows at tables in silent conversation, but he did not know them. He looked at Lee and wondered how he too had survived. There were lots of guns, and bullets flying most nights in the old days, and always a fight about nothing. But the next day, those same men were compatriots raiding remote plantations or ambushing government shipments, and most of them were ready to die for each other.

A stranger who entered called Lee to the other end of the bar. Martinez continued to stare at the names scratched into the surface of the bar like a book with many chapters. He had known many of them, too many. They were all dead or gone now. People in his line of work did not live long by the manner of their lifestyles. They worked, played for real stakes, and were hard men. Martinez was one of the hardest.

At the other end of the long bar the man threw his backpack valise on the counter. He began trying to talk to Lee in English, and the man was getting nowhere. *Another fucking tourist* thought Martinez as he watched the pantomimed attempt at communication between them. The tourist silhouetted by the open door behind him looked ridiculous in a brand new Jungle Jim outfit probably purchased at one of those fancy and expensive, camping supply places in some big city far away from here. He even wore a safari hat. Now he was trying French on Lee, and that wouldn't have been a bad idea except in this remote village. It was remote for a reason, and if the stranger took a moment to look around at the ghostly figures at some of the tables, he would know he wasn't welcome.

Lee came over and refreshed Martinez's drink, and the stranger took the opportunity to follow Lee down the bar. Martinez was in a bad mood and stared down at the bar while getting angrier at the stranger for no real reason. He noted the stranger landed on a stool next to him and was ordering a drink for himself, but still Martinez ignored him as best he could. The man even smelled like a woman, like sweet soap, or something. It was an insult. This jungle pompadour didn't even know better than to fear to make his acquaintance. There was a time when a stranger would not have dared approach Martinez for fear that he might get his throat cut for the effort. That was a part he played many times. In reality, it was just a façade he used to ward away trouble, especially from the kind of men he frequented.

Now the man was eagerly attempting to talk to him. Martinez ignored him hoping he would go away, but the man persisted until finally Martinez turned and faced him directly. He gave him his best mean look.

"What do you want? Huh? What the fuck is your problem, senor?" challenged Martinez, trying to look foreboding in the light peach tropical shirt that Lee had lent him that morning. But he realized too late as he spoke to the man in English, it was probably hard to look mean and dangerous wearing a light peach tropical shirt.

Chapter 10

1997   Ban Kongmi, Southern Laos

The stranger became visibly excited. "Oh, OH!" he replied, smiling broadly. "You speak English. All the better! I was having a terrible time trying to communicate with the bartender here. I just can't get the hang of the local language. I should, you know. I should do better. I'm an archeologist. Marty Wenabe is my name. I'm a professor at John Hopkins University," he said, holding out his hand. "May I buy you a drink?"

In spite of his preconceived notions, Martinez looked at the amiable, and insistent, young man beside him, and nodded. He was just not familiar with our ways thought Martinez as he sized up the stranger. Wenabe was not yet thirty and had a handsome face, and curly hair. To Martinez he seemed a bit plump perhaps exaggerated by the ridiculous outfit he was wearing, and his smile and manner were engaging. Martinez decided he wanted to know more, and besides, it was not his policy to turn down a free drink.

"Of course," he replied. "My name is Martinez. You are not from around here I think. And you are in luck because I do speak English, something very rare in these parts. I also speak Spanish, Vietnamese, Cambodian and of course Lao. Perhaps you are looking for a guide," Martinez suggested, seizing on an opportunity after noting his empty pockets.

Wenabe called Lee over, and drinks were filled once again. "I managed to find a ride across the border from Vietnam," he said. "I want to get to Siem Kulea. Do you know it? It is a valley on the other side of the mountains in Northern Cambodia. Strangely, it does not seem to appear on any of the printed maps of the area, yet I am told it is real, and it is there. Funny thing just now. I tried to convey my wishes to the bartender, and every time I said, 'Siem Kulea' he pointed toward you. Do you know what he meant by that?"

Martinez only gave a sad smile and raised his glass in an unspoken toast with the stranger. He turned away and drank slowly, the alcohol a comforting friend finding a welcome path down his throat as he remembered. Siem Kulea and Colonel Minh: that was the last good time before everything changed, before the world went to shit. That was the life. There was plenty of money and women then. The memories made his eyes water, or maybe it was the drink. Now they were all gone. All dead. Colonel Minh too. Now there were only the tourists.

"Why do you want to know about Siem Kulea?" asked Martinez. "No one asks about that place. I think you are making a mistake. No one knows about that place."

"It appears you do, sir," said Wenabe in moderate protest. He paused for a moment hoping Martinez would continue, and when he didn't, he said, "Well, as I said, I'm an archeologist, so naturally I might be interested in such a place as that. I mean it is rather old isn't it?"

Still, Martinez said nothing, so Wenabe suggested, "Say, how about we sit over there at a table and talk a bit. Would you mind? I think we both would be more comfortable if our conversation were a bit quieter and more private."

When Wenabe asked Lee if he had any better wine for them, Martinez nodded to Lee in a rehearsed conspiracy from the old days. Lee gave a big smile and nodded eagerly as he hurried off.

As they sat down at a table across the room away from any of the other patrons, Lee again appeared, and he produced a surprisingly good vintage French pinot noir to offer for inspection.

"Well, now we're talking!" said Wenabe. "Go ahead, and open that, please. I've been starved for a good wine since I left Boston. How do you suppose he came to have such an excellent wine in a place like this?" asked Wenabe of Martinez.

Martinez did not answer but had no doubt the wine was one of many cases looted from French rubber plantations in Cambodia. He might have stolen that one himself. Lee poured the wine, and Wenabe swirled the liquid in his glass, sniffed, and took a drink. Then he nodded and smiled an approval toward Lee.

Martinez had seen this before: all the sniffing and swirling of the wine. It reminded him of another world, and another time, when he too would treat a good wine like a beautiful woman; caressing and teasing it before partaking of its charms. Here he thought it was out of place, and made such men look like women, and this was not the place to look weak. He nodded toward Lee, and after Lee poured him a glass, he drank down almost half of it in one long gulp, wiping his mouth with his forearm afterward true to the character he was playing. It amused him to see Wenabe's expression.

"Hey, that is good!" Martinez exclaimed, after offering a loud belch. "Lee, get us another bottle of this wine. The professor is buying, no?" he suggested. He repeated the instructions in Lao, but Lee already knew he was going to make a lot of money selling wine that afternoon if Martinez kept the stranger talking.

"Yes, I'm happy to buy if you can help me, and answer a few of my questions," he said. "I am eager to hear what you know about Siem Kulea." he commented.

Martinez was now engaged. Enjoying good wine and conversation was one thing he liked to do and he had plenty of good stories to tell. His recent misfortunes, and the price on his head forgotten for the moment, he pointed at Wenabe, and began.

"You're in luck, my friend, because you have happened on one of the foremost authorities in the area, and by your good fortune, Siem Kulea too. Yes, I know all about Siem Kulea. I used to run...supplies back, and forth, through this area in the old days when Colonel Minh controlled everything. Nothing happened without his approval. He was a great leader, and the people loved him. You know about Colonel Minh?" asked Martinez.

"Uh, no," Wenabe lied. "I have not heard of him before this. Was he a kind of warlord, or something?"

"Ah, yes, warlord," said Martinez. "He was a man like me. War for us was an opportunity to make money. You know what he did? He stole the Vietnamese government gold right from under their noses and got away to Thailand when Vietnam fell. Colonel Minh was very resourceful and he controlled the area all the way up to the Chinese border. That was after the Americans left Vietnam. He was like a king, and all the people loved him."

Wenabe took a sip and reminded himself he heard from others quite the opposite story about this Colonel Minh. Still, in every untruth there dwells a glimpse of reality. He urged Martinez to continue.

Martinez wrapped himself into his latest persona as a native tourist guide. "Well, about fifteen years ago he buys Siem Kulea, and makes it his base of operations. It's a perfect location because it is a valley surrounded on all sides by mountains. You will not believe it even when you see it. It's like a paradise. So, the Colonel appoints me as one of his prime lieutenants to secure the area, and my men and I make sure he can live like a king without worrying about outsiders. You understand, he lives like a king, but he is not a king. But at the same time, he finds a queen and she is a real queen. She is from the Champa people like many of the natives around here, but she is special. She is beautiful and has great personal charm that captures you without you even knowing. The people go crazy for her and follow her. They will do anything she wants, and that is fine with Colonel Minh because he decides to arm them, take over Cambodia, and maybe even Vietnam. For a time, it was working perfectly according to his plan. He thought up the whole thing. He brought great prosperity to everyone. You would have loved it. It was like—I don't know. It was the good time."

"That sounds wonderful," said Wenabe, "and you were a big part of it. I can see where those sorts of conditions might appeal to a resourceful man. It must have been exciting for you back then."

"Yes, and I was just thinking of it when I saw you there in your fancy jungle outfit," said Martinez. "I was thinking that now all my compadres are gone, and replaced with tourists, like you."

"Oh, yes, my outfit is a bit too much, isn't it?" commented Wenabe, candidly. "I lost my baggage at the airport when I came into Ho Chi Minh City, and I had to find something I could wear in the field. I was heading out on a junket north the next morning, so my options were limited. Unfortunately, this was all I could find that fit well in the short time allotted me. I look like a bit of a clown, don't I."

Martinez was surprised at his candor. "A clown," he laughed, heartily, "Yes, a clown! Exactly. But you do not fool Martinez, my friend. You are very intelligent, and playing a part, I think, and you hope to get something from me for nothing. You think to get me talking, and find out all I know," he said, tapping his finger on the table."

"I think we are both playing parts, Mr. Martinez," said Wenabe, perceptively. Let's see. I believe you're playing Eli Wallach's part in 'The Good, the Bad, and the Ugly'. Do you know of it? I have to say our present surroundings fit that persona very well. I expect to see Clint Eastwood come through that door any second."

Martinez stared at him for a moment processing the image. Then he gave Wenabe a shrug and threw it away with his hand as if it was unimportant, but he knew Wenabe had his character dead-on. This man was indeed as intelligent as he first thought.

"I assure you I am not a clown," continued Wenabe, "and you are not simple-minded as you wish me to think you are. In the end, no matter what façade we present to others, our intelligence is betrayed with our eyes if one cares to really look. We both have something the other wants, so let's be straight with each other and get to it, shall we? What say you? Will you tell me what you know of Siem Kulea?"

Martinez picked up his wine glass, and swirled it a bit to aerate the wine and held it up to the dim candlelight to judge. "Good legs, don't you think? I suspect we can get drunk on this wine. I confess Lee overcharges for his fine wine, and he will no doubt overcharge you, my friend." He sniffed the wine, and then took a sip.

Wenabe smiled but was still waiting for an answer.

It had been a long time since Martinez had anyone challenge him in conversation like this man, and he liked him for that. "I will make a deal with you, my friend, but first let's get another bottle, just so we can enjoy the conversation, no?" asked Martinez.

Wenabe looked sideways at Martinez still playing his role.

"I'm afraid the simple Latino is the role I assume most of the time with strangers. Please forgive me," said Martinez. "It's like an old coat that hides my imperfections and I am most comfortable wearing."

"No need. It's quite charming on you," said Wenabe, putting his fat wallet on the table in front of him.

Martinez began sizing up Wenabe, looking for where the money was for him. There was money to be had here; he was sure, just not sure how much. As if on cue, Wenabe opened his wallet, and Martinez felt he was whole again watching him place a few bills on the table.

"I will make a deal with you," Martinez said. "As compensation for my valuable time, I will agree to tell you what I know for a few dollars as you are suggesting. You know, it is hard to find qualified and informed experts such as me in this area about this particular subject. This kind of information is certainly worth more than that fancy jungle suit you wear, no? Much more I think. So, you make this deal?" asked Martinez.

"Yes, deal," agreed Wenabe, pushing the money on the table toward him. "Now tell me more about this queen you spoke of. Why is she so special?"

But Martinez only smiled, shrugged his shoulders, and waited. It took Wenabe a few seconds to understand, and then he began removing more bills from his wallet. When Martinez was satisfied with the amount on the table, he nodded and began again.

"Special, yes, this queen is very special, and she is beautiful. She is beautiful like no other, I think. It is kind of strange because there is something more. She has an effect on you when you see her. I don't know how to describe it. It was just a feeling for me back then when I saw her. I will tell you what I have told no other. She is the only woman I have ever loved. She looked right into my eyes one day. Only once, and I was hers forever. Es una pasada! I swear it is true," he said, nodding sincerely. "She was perfect for that place, and that time. The people loved her. I loved her. Everybody loved her, but Colonel Minh. I tell you a secret. I think he liked boys, but he tells no one.

"Still Colonel Minh was very smart, and he needed her to be his queen so he could control the people. But in the end, she brought him down. She brought us all down. Too much of a good thing, I think, like this wine we are drinking. It can deceive you, and make you want more while it slowly takes possession of you, even controlling your mind, and blinding you to what is really happening," said Martinez. He paused a moment remembering once again that afternoon when the helicopters came many years ago.

"In the end, the Vietnamese with their helicopters, and rockets, came and killed Colonel Minh, and destroyed this palace and all the buildings. It was all left in ruins, and then they went away," he said, pausing again to remember.

He looked at Wenabe. "Now your turn," said Martinez. "Why are you asking about Siem Kulea? Perhaps you tell me, and I will remember more."

It was getting darker in the bar as the sun set outside, and the lone fluorescent light on the ceiling was across the room. There was a used candle in a bottle on the table between them. Lee replaced it with a new one, which he lit and it gave them better light. Wenabe reached over to his backpack and pulled out a drawing on a piece of paper. He laid it out on the table showing it to Martinez.

Martinez squinted at it and reached into his pocket. He retrieved a pair of wire-framed glasses and put them on. They were scratched in some places, and the lenses were dirty but Martinez seemed not to notice. "I cannot see so well after dark, and sometimes I wear these. I do not think they make me look attractive for the ladies," he confessed.

But Wenabe's prior assessment of Martinez found proof as the glasses gave him a professorial look and prompted a passing thought for the archeologist. *This man Martinez has many layers to him.*

Martinez studied the design of eight concentric, and intertwined circles drawn on the paper as Wenabe asked, "Have you seen anything like this design at Siem Kulea?"

Martinez understood, but then said, "Maybe, but I cannot remember where. Let me think on this a moment. I am sure I have seen this before."

They continued their conversation as Martinez told Wenabe about how he came to Southeast Asia. A few minutes passed, and then all of a sudden Martinez exclaimed, "Yes! I have it! I know where I saw this design. Tell me first what it means, this design."

"Mr. Martinez, have you ever heard stories of an ancient people living in this area a long time ago?" asked Wenabe.

"Yes, of course. Everyone knows that. A long time ago there were ancient people, gods even, living here. It is what all the people around here believe. I am a practical man, and I'm not so sure. I think it is a story like many stories, just made up by someone mostly out of old-time ignorance and myths. I don't think I believe."

"I told you I am an archeologist. Do you know what that is?" asked Wenabe.

"You study old ruins of buildings and cultures," said Martinez.

"Yes, exactly, and in my research, I have seen these rings in other places around the world, and I think they are significant, perhaps as a sign of the ancients. Now, where did you see these rings at Siem Kulea?" asked Wenabe.

Martinez was nodding as Wenabe explained, and then with his question, he shrugged his shoulders once more waiting for Wenabe to put more bills from his wallet into play.

After an equal amount was put on the table as before, Martinez answered again, pointing at Wenabe again as he started, "One time when I was working with Colonel Minh we were carrying heavy crates into the white palace. That is where Colonel Minh lived. He rebuilt it on the ruins of the old palace that had been there for centuries, and he made it look like the original one I think. Anyway, we carried in lots of crates and took them down into a chamber beneath the palace. It was the deepest part, below the basement even. It was dark down there and was lit by candles on the wall because there was no electricity. The chamber was all stone, but different, it looked to be carved out of the mountain. At one end was a big sculpture of a woman standing among many snakes that went all the way to the ceiling like I have seen at some temples in Cambodia. As big as it was, it had been pulled away from the wall, and behind it was a massive door maybe ten feet high made of bronze, or maybe gold. I know this because I saw the torches reflecting in it. It looked very imposing and heavy. I remembered wondering at first if the Colonel kept his gold behind the door like a bank or something, but later I did not think so."

"What made you think that?" asked Wenabe.

"It was more of a feeling, you know. I thought it, but for no reason really. The door was different than any door I have ever seen. It had no handle only a hole where the handle should be. It was a very strange door," explained Martinez. "I don't think Colonel Minh put it there."

"You think the door was already there," said Wenabe excitedly. "I understand. Where did you see these markings, the circles?" asked Wenabe, listening intently.

Martinez put down his glass and looked at Wenabe directly. "That was the amazing thing that I remembered just now. The circles were on the door. I had not remembered about that before you showed me this drawing."

"You're sure?" asked Wenabe, not believing entirely what he had just been told.

"Yes, because I had a chance between carrying crates to take a candle and look closely at it," said Martinez. "But it was different than this design. It was like this but in the corner on the border around the circles was the Hoa Cuc, you know, the flower of the Champa people. I remembered the flower, not the circles. But there was something else that made me cross myself with the holy sign of when I was an altar boy."

Professor Wenabe had not a clue what he was talking about, but then Martinez did a cross on his forehead, and lips, and heart before he continued. "There were snakes on that door, evil looking snakes that made you afraid to touch the door. They were not like the ones of stone on the other sculpture. They were very real looking, except in metal like they would come alive and strike at you. The snakeheads had open mouths with fangs, and eyes of jewels that seemed to watch you. After I saw it, I wanted to get out of that basement, and I never went down there again. I forgot about the circles until just now when you asked me."

"I can't wait to see it," said Wenabe.

"Oh no, you can't go there! No outsider can go there. You have to be invited. It is very dangerous if you try to go there without permission," said Martinez.

"Surely there are many trails into, and out of that valley," protested Wenabe.

"No, only one or two now and they will know when you get within twenty miles of that valley. All around on the outside of the mountains now live only Champa people. They don't like outsiders. Their queen has returned to them, and they will protect their queen with their lives if they have to," explained Martinez. "Word will travel fast. They will capture you, and you will die. There are many stories of those who have gone there, and never returned," said Martinez. "I have never been back. I've seen the power of that queen and the blind devotion of her people."

"But I don't understand. I thought it was all in ruins. I thought you said everything was destroyed when Colonel Minh was killed by the Vietnamese forces," said Wenabe, confused.

"Yes, but two years later, she came back, and rebuilt it all again. Then from among thousands of people, the queen picked some to live with her in the valley, and the rest settled on the other side of the mountains. It is like a wall that protects her in every direction," Martinez said. "You cannot go there unless you are invited. I mean that most sincerely, my friend. They kill strangers who try to enter the valley."

Martinez studied the design on the paper and suddenly got an idea. Fate had handed him some information that could save his life, and he knew just who would want to know about it.

"Do you really think there is something important behind that door?" he asked.

"Yes, my friend, I am certain of it," affirmed professor Wenabe.

Chapter 11

1997 Ubon, Thailand

Hinsu Yameda prided himself on being a man of great patience. An unapologetic narcissist, he considered himself superior to everyone around him with perhaps one exception, and since the demise of Colonel Minh, he has been the head of the Asian World Investment Corporation. He led his company back from the brink of disaster that accompanied the death of Colonel Minh, the destruction of his military forces, and his ambitious agenda. Now, seven years later, the corporation was stronger than ever with assets and working capital that in most cases surpassed their rivals.

His close circle of confidants thought he would seek some revenge for what Queen Maisong Sambath had done to their former leader, and at first he considered several of their schemes.

In the end, he saw they only invited trouble, and his judgment then has been vindicated since. There was another reason he did not entertain the idea of revenge for the death of Colonel Minh. He needed Queen Maisong, and what he thought she knew about the ancients to fulfill his own goals for the future. Working with Su Ling, he gained a great deal of knowledge about Siem Kulea, the Champa heritage, and the legend behind Queen Maisong Sambath. Su Ling knew Queen Maisong possibly better than anyone, even her husband who Yameda considered little more than a minor distraction he would deal with at the proper time.

Very handsome, with sculpted features, bold chin, and dark eyes, Yameda is considered a wunderkind of Asian industry because of his age, and superior intellect. He is the adopted son of Colonel Minh, and when his stepbrother and sister died under mysterious circumstances in a plane crash many years ago, he became the sole heir to the vast fortune accumulated by Colonel Minh.

Now he micromanages and oversees every part of his vast Asian empire. No significant decision is made without consulting him first. He works autonomously except for Su Ling and she is the only other person he cares about or listens to. His marriage to the daughter of a wealthy and powerful, Thai politician increased his status in Thailand. But his wife and two sons are immaterial to his ultimate ambition, and he sees them rarely by mutual agreement. They are not even allowed access to his mountain retreat from where he runs his financial empire.

At that very moment, he was pondering a painting, which hung over the fireplace in his ultra-modern office. It had been painted by one of the most familiar of the impressionists. The Dutch artist had copied a Japanese painting that had greatly influenced the valued impressionist at the onset of his career. That Asian artist was now relatively unknown compared to the Dutch painter. Yameda prized the painting as a constant reminder of how European countries had spent centuries raping Asia of its monetary wealth and culture. It was his ambition to retaliate in a way that would make these once powerful European nations bow in subservience to their Asian masters. He was worse than any despot who had ever lived because he was diabolically clever and infinitely patient, letting his machinations play out in invisible strategies that seduced most into believing him harmless or ignoring him altogether. His devices unfolded in a financial game of the highest stakes, except the other players did not even know they were playing until they had lost. It was almost too easy for him as bit-by-bit, he methodically accumulated control of major western corporations. His latest objective was a data mining company Le Beaulieu Financière Mondiale of France. They were number one in the world in their field, and thus, an excellent target for his corporate quests.

He nodded to himself as his intercom buzzed from the offices downstairs. His secretary and personal assistant informed him that the man named Martinez had been deposited as instructed in a chamber in the depths below his large, imposing, fortress villa and that Su Ling had just arrived, and was freshening up in her suite.

Su Ling's arrival was expected even as the man Martinez was not. His attraction for Su Ling was mutual on many levels, but the one that interested him the most was her sadistic and cruel side, of which few people were aware. They shared that bond discretely, and could not be away from each other for any significant amount of time because of it. With Martinez now being trussed up in a chamber below, he smiled to himself at the hapless victim's unfortunate sense of timing. He was going to enjoy this immensely.

He knew there was a price on Martinez's head for leading a large heroin shipment coming from Laos into a police ambush. The Laotian drug lords blamed Martinez as the lone survivor, and Yameda gladly promoted that claim and put a bounty on his head. But Yameda knew the truth was very different. It was he who informed the Thai police where to ambush the drug shipment. It was retribution for a particular drug lord who secretly sold outside of traditional circles and cut Yameda out of the profit. Yameda split the drugs with the police and made a nice return from it.

Now he was ready to dispose of Martinez, and end this chapter with the deception complete, and largely in his favor. Yameda was a sociopath who took great pleasure in the misery of others. He believed it was his right as a superior being to control those around him. Su Ling was the exception and the only one who could talk with him on the same level. She helped him recover, and even profit, from the disaster of Colonel Minh while at the same time she pretended her love for her husband, Daniel Vega. She brought Yameda inside information on financial markets stolen right from Queen Mai's personally trained, and very talented analysts. She had her own loyal operative working there with access to everything. Yameda used this information to make AWI one of the most powerful corporations in the world. Now they were in the middle phase of their extended plan. Su Ling would help him to control Queen Maisong and make use of her vast technical resources. For that, Su Ling wanted only one thing: to rule Siem Kulea herself one day.

He told his secretary to ask Su Ling to meet him outside the cell area downstairs.

When Yameda and Su Ling entered the special chamber below his villa that they used for their twisted games, the prisoner was already chained down in stocks that held his torso firmly in place. His neck and head were presented ominously two feet over a drain in the stone floor. When Martinez heard them enter, he began begging frantically in Spanish, and then English. Yameda spoke Thai, Chinese, and Japanese, and he ignored the frantic pleas of mercy as he decided which of his priceless antique Samurai swords he would use for the execution. Four of his favorites were mounted as a shrine on one end of the specially purposed playroom. After a moment, and with due reverence, he lifted one he named *Kochi* from its rack on the wall. He released it from its scabbard and bowed before kissing it on the sleek-sharp blade.

Su Ling walked over to observe the hapless victim who struggled, and pleaded for his life in frantic desperation. She and Yameda commonly liked to taunt and torture their victims before mercifully ending their torment. She found this most entertaining and stimulating on many levels. They were as gods to their victims hearing their hopeless pleas and deciding their fates. Yameda took his time enjoying the feel of his instrument of death and the havoc it was playing on Martinez who struggled against the stocks in help-less desperation.

But then he heard the words 'Maisong Sambath' from the victim's mouth, and he lowered the blade, turned slowly, and looked at Su Ling with a curious expression.

She smirked. She was sexually aroused by the scene before her: the victim straining without hope in his chains, and Yameda walking around him ritually wiping his blade, and preparing his instrument of death like an Asian grim reaper. It was pure theater, but it was also a demonstration of the perverse power, and superiority, they assumed over others, and that excited them both. She was leaning against a support column nearby with her arms folded, wearing high heels, an elegant blouse, and slacks suited more for shopping on the Avenue Montaigne, Paris than this foreboding dungeon.

She noticed Yameda's look, and deadpanned with a flutter of her hand, "He is begging for his life with a claim he has important information for you about the flowers, and snakes, at the white palace, my darling. He said something about concentric circles, and that they were important and meaningful. We have already talked about some of this. But on reflection, I think we should hear what this garbage has to say before we mercifully dispose of it. Who is this man anyway? What has he done to end up in our playground?"

"He is a drug smuggler of no importance. His name is Martinez."

"Martinez?" she asked, surprised, as she pushed away from the column to examine the victim more closely. "Is this perhaps the Martinez that used to work for Colonel Minh?"

"Well, yes, I suppose it could be. He goes back a long way," answered Yameda.

Su Ling walked over to the dirty, half-naked man on his knees. Her expensive heels clicked loudly on the stone floor as she approached. She bent down to get a closer look at the man locked down in the stocks firmly, with his head placed perfectly to begin its journey into the afterlife. He was sweating profusely and moving his head in odd angles trying to cheat death one more time. She took hold of his hair and jerked his head up to examine his face, and said, "Yes, this is the right Martinez. I remember this one well."

"You!" Martinez cried in surprise.

"Yes, it is I, and I would think you would remember me," she said, smirking.

"Madre de Dios! La Pequeña Serpiente. Please, I beg you. I have always remained loyal even over these many years. Please, mercy, mistress, please!" he pleaded through slobbered breaths.

She threw his head back, walked to Yameda, and kissed him. "Darling, you are so deliciously menacing sometimes. That is one of the things I admire about you the most. I would like to question this man further, and it may take a while. Why don't you relax upstairs, and I will be up when I finish with him," she said. "Surely, you can put off your fun until later," she suggested.

Yameda stared at her for a moment, then nodded, and turned away to admire the sword only minutes ago he was preparing to use. "Just so, yes," he said, with a sigh as he slid the Katana he was holding back into its scabbard, and placed it up on its wall mount. "Perhaps I was acting hastily, but I doubt that I am the most iniquitous between the two of us, and that's what I love about you the most. Be that as it may, he might have information that is useful. I am sure you will find out what he knows forthwith. Do you wish me to have my men fire up the hot coals for you?"

Su Ling stood over the prisoner. "No, my darling. That won't be necessary. I suspect this one is ready to reveal all its secrets to Su Ling and most eagerly," she said, running her hand through Martinez's hair possessively.

Yameda nodded, and he departed, saying as he left, "I will have your favorite wine chilled and ready for you upstairs. Remember mercy is not always the most satisfying path for the residue that throws itself at our feet, and it is a lot less stimulating."

"Yes, darling, I agree. But do me a favor. Send a glass of wine down here for me, would you? This might take a while."

Chapter 12

1997   Ubon, Thailand

After Yameda left, Su Ling ordered Martinez to be released and the two guards opened the stocks and freed him. Martinez rubbed his sore wrists as he counted his blessings. But then he realized this play was far from over, and the second act was just beginning. They placed his sweating and haggard body on his knees before Su Ling who was sitting in a comfortable chair near a round table on one side of the chamber. Her chilled glass of wine arrived and she took a sip while she considered her options. In contrast to the sophisticated, elegant, and relaxed demeanor of Su Ling, he fidgeted, in loose, dirty, and torn white pants. Everything else had been taken from him. The two guards took positions immediately behind him with their hands on his shoulder as a warning. He knelt before her nervously, unsure what was to come.

She regarded him a moment longer, and then said, "Would you agree that I have saved you from torture, and certain death?"

He nodded cautiously, his body glistening against the lights within the ominous space. "Yes, mistress Su Ling. Thank you, for that kindness. I am most grateful," he said, careful to use the appellation she preferred when he worked for her many years ago under Colonel Minh.

"It is our custom in this part of the world that your life belongs to me now. I like that. It is an ancient custom, but befitting our present circumstance, would you agree?"

"Yes, YES! That is indeed the custom. Yes, I like that custom. I remember the days I worked for you under Colonel Minh fondly," he responded eagerly. "When I was serving you, that was the last time I felt useful. Life held a purpose, and meaning for me then. I loved those times and loved working for you, mistress Su Ling.

"Since I was sent away, and became a mercenary, I have been on a downward spiral, and you see me now, and what I have become as a result. If you know anything about me, then you know I am loyal. I confess, I long for those times when I was serving you, mistress Su Ling," he said finding the words he thought she wanted to hear, even it was his personal reality.

Su Ling looked at the two guards and ordered, "Leave us!"

"But, my lady, Mr. Yameda gave…" said one guard, starting to object.

"Now!" she interrupted, clapping her hands.

The two guards departed closing the door behind them.

She collected herself and sighed. "You will this day resume your service to me, and dedicate your life to fulfilling my wishes," said Su Ling. "As it happens, I have a use for you, and your considerable talents. Does this sound like something you are ready to do: serve me, and obey me again without question?"

Martinez could not believe this sudden turn of fortune. He relished working with this woman when they were both working under Colonel Minh, and fate had put him once more in her hands. "Yes. I am ready to serve you in any manner you wish."

She motioned for him to sit in the chair opposite hers. "As much as I enjoy men kneeling before me, we have much to discuss, and I want your complete concentration. What is your given name? I am not sure I ever knew it," she commented."

"It is Eddie," he replied.

"Yes, Eddie. I remember now. That is much easier and so less formal. It has been a long time since you worked for me, Eddie," she continued after he sat down. "However, your memory does not fail you completely. I think you meant to refer to me before as the 'Little Viper'. That is what Colonel Minh affectionately called me; his 'Little Viper'."

"Yes, yes, I remember now," he said, smiling cautiously. "Little Viper, but you were never so little, I think, mistress. You were always one step ahead of everyone. I was your loyal servant then, and I am your loyal servant now. You will not be disappointed."

"Well, I admit I had to make you the scapegoat for the failure of our last mission together," said Su Ling. "That is why Colonel Minh sent you away, but it appears you landed on your feet as a mercenary. You always were a survivor, Eddie. With all that happened, you never betrayed me, and I haven't forgotten your loyalty. That is what saved you from torture and death this day. I'm most happy I found you, and to be working with you again. I'll get you set up, so we can make a proper use of your talents."

Martinez nodded eagerly seeing his future once more take a positive turn. It was enough to know they were ready to execute him moments before just for their amusement. The fact that she saved him, and valued his service gave him perversely a sense of belonging, and a purpose, however misguided, missing for many years.

The elegantly dressed, beautiful Asian woman sitting opposite him was more attractive than anyone he had ever known except for one beautiful queen. She was even approximately the same size and looked very much like her. But she was missing something, a soul perhaps. He had subsisted for many years living day-to-day without meaning as if just putting in time, and going through the motions waiting for death. With that, she easily contested the woman who had held his heart and was now little more than an exalted memory embellished by time.

"Please, tell Su Ling what you know about the circles and the snakes. Do not leave anything out because the most minute detail might be just the thing that will demonstrate your value to Hinsu and me when I barter for your life."

"There was a man who came to Ban Kongmi asking about Siem Kulea," he began, eagerly accepting his role as a loyal servant and co-conspirator.

"A man...what was his name?"

"Uh...uh, Marty Wenabe. He said he was an archeologist and a professor at a university. He wanted to go to Siem Kulea," he began.

Su Ling sat back and considered this information. "Tell Su Ling everything you know about this man. I want to hear all about this archeologist. Maybe he can be persuaded to serve me too."

An hour later, Su Ling walked into the spacious lounge of Yameda's villa that dominated his estate and overlooked the valley and the Mun River near

Ubon, Thailand. They exchanged a deeply sincere kiss, and then Yameda offered Su Ling a glass of her preferred wine.

"My chef is preparing your favorite meal, my sweet. I confess I have missed you these many days. It is not the same for me around here without you," he told her. "Did you leave the man in stocks downstairs for me to finish up?"

Su Ling gave him another warm kiss, accepted the glass, and took a sip. "Mmm, I love this wine." She smiled, and said "Actually no, Hinsu. I want you to spare his life."

She admired a full plate of appetizers, chose one, and took a bite enjoying the unusual mix of cheeses within.

She turned back toward him, and continued, "My darling, I know you wouldn't have him in your dungeon if there weren't a good reason, but please, hear me out. I know this man. We have a history working together under Colonel Minh, and he was, and continues to be very loyal to me. Besides, he has too much experience to simply toss away. At the very least he knows Siem Kulea, and the surrounding areas, like the back of his hand, and we may need that. I want you to repair his reputation. Spread the word that Martinez helped you find the real traitor, and that you have disposed of him in kind. You may even want to implicate one of your enemies. I know you have done that before to your advantage. Martinez serves me again now and I will make good use of him."

"You are still using those drugs on your subjects aren't you, my sweet?" Yameda said as he considered what she told him. "I am not sure this time it is in my best interest to follow your wishes on this, as much as I would like to."

"Yes, I use drug routines when it suits me and you reap the benefits. I think I'm even better at mind control than Dr. Minh was. I learned a lot from that old buzzard. I like it. I find it stimulating in a way to have others helplessly do my bidding.

"But I did not need to use those routines on Martinez. He is the sort of hard man that simply needs someone to be the focus of his loyalty. That is the advantage of perceived power to devoted underlings. It removes their inhibitions and gives them the unfettered freedom of blind loyalty and obedience. His recent experience and this situation today will allow me to mold him into an almost perfect disciple ready to obey me without question. As it is, I turned him over to your man Nate to clean him up and get him a wardrobe so he can perform on a corporate level."

"Martinez, a businessman?" asked Yameda, surprised. "I guess if he keeps his mouth shut he might pull that off. But it is hard to believe he can clean up at all. Why is this necessary, Su Ling?"

"Darling, we are a good team and have learned a lot from each other. You taught me patience and I have learned from you to plan my strategies with a perspective for the long game. Good operatives are always necessary in those operations. You are positively brilliant, and I love you dearly, but sometimes you are a poor judge of men. I knew this Martinez back when we all were with Colonel Minh. I worked closely with him often and saw his talent firsthand. He often went on difficult, special missions for Colonel Minh and me. Some of them required an agent with great sophistication, and he was always successful. He is cunning, skilled and deadly.

"Our last mission failed because I misjudged our adversaries, and I unknowingly led him into a trap. They were ruthless and tortured him, but he never gave up my name. He never betrayed me. Fortunately, he escaped that too and returned loyally ready to serve me again. But I had already closed that door. I told Colonel Minh it was his mistake that caused our plan to fail. It was a loss worth millions. Colonel Minh wanted to put him to death for it, and I agreed but secreted Martinez away with orders to make himself scarce until I could find a use for him again. He became a mercenary, I lost contact with him, and that has been his role ever since.

"He has fooled even you," Su Ling continued, "with that silly Latino peasant role he loves to play. Underneath, I assure you he is a well-educated and refined individual. I admit he does not look like much now. I have retrieved him from the lowest depths of existence where he learned to somehow thrive nonetheless. Bringing him back from such a life, and even torture and certain death makes him all the more grateful, obedient, and devoted to me.

"Most importantly, he is a survivor. He is the only one of Minh's mercenaries that has survived. That says something right there, and you have to admit he even survived your well-planned ambush, and betrayal of the drug shipment. He gets things done, and did you know he is an American? That will be most useful for my plans. He only left the United States to avoid the draft back during the Vietnam War. It is ironic, and our good fortune, that despite that he ended up in Southeast Asia.

She sat down on the small loveseat beside Yameda. "I am sending him with Nate, and two others, to search the office in the United States of a man Martinez met in Southern Laos just across the mountains from Siem Kulea. He is a professor of archeology at John Hopkins University in Maryland, and his name is Marty Wenabe. The interesting thing about him that my new, devoted servant Eddie Martinez told me was that he was asking a lot of questions about concentric circles. He said professor Wenabe had information from all over the world about them, and he wanted to follow up a theory of his about Siem Kulea. Nate is making a passport, false background, and credit cards right now for Martinez. They will leave as soon as they are done. I don't want to waste time on this. I am going to eventually set him up in Chicago as one of our agents there."

"Chicago? Why Chicago? Queen Maisong no longer lives in Chicago. Your schemes are beyond me sometimes, Su Ling. What do you have going on in your beautiful head right now?" asked Yameda,

"Siem Kulea is only one half of the equation when it comes to bringing down Queen Maisong. The other half is in Chicago. Mai may have left Chicago, but she is still a major part of Catherine Marsh's NearNorth Productions. We need to find out everything we can about them, where they live, and their daily routine. More importantly, we need to find out about their children. That is their Achilles heel. Mai has a daughter, and Catherine has a son. With all their security, and power, they will fall to us if we have those kids. They will do anything we want to get them back," she explained.

"The complexity of your planning always amazes me, my darling, and as you said, I have learned a lot from the way you work. But perhaps this time there is a more simple solution available to us. Why not use the trigger you said you planted in Queen Maisong that will make her obedient to you. You told me you planted it in her when she was in your charge while working at Siem Kulea with Dr. Minh. When you brought her out of the drugging he used on her and while she was still vulnerable, you reprogrammed your own trigger that could be used to control her," said Yameda. "She may have all the answers we need. Why don't you use that?"

A servant brought in a tray of warm wet linens for them to wipe their hands and announced that dinner would be served in ten minutes.

As they both took advantage of the towels to clean their hands, the view outside their windows captured their attention. The sun was setting beyond the river and the few boats still on the river caused the water to dance in an array of reflective colors.

Su Ling looked out the wall-size windows for a moment and then commented, "I love this place, Hinsu, almost as much as I love the Siem Kulea valley." She turned, held him in her arms, and kissed him gently. "I love you dearly, and I always look forward to our time together."

They embraced for a moment, and then she gave a sigh, and answered his question, "Queen Maisong Sambath Largent is different now, Hinsu. She is not the weak naïve little girl whose mind I enslaved at Dr. Minh's. She is strong, confident and powerful. Even though she still seems to be under the post-hypnotic suggestion I gave her regarding her feelings toward me, I can sense she may not be susceptible anymore to mind control. In fact, the situation might be just the opposite. I'm afraid to try anything lest she realizes I am not as loyal as she thinks, or worse, decides to go walking around in my head."

"What are you talking about...walking around in your head?" he asked.

"I am fairly certain she has gained an ability with some people to read their thoughts. She has not done it to me, but I have noticed she has with others. She has not mentioned it to me, and I don't think she knows that I am aware she can do it. But sometimes, when she is relaxed with me, she has said some things in passing without considering her words. That gave me clues that something was going on. I don't think she is very adept at it yet, but she is learning and working on it."

She turned to face him. "I've told you that the spirit of Queen Dau Te Po is within her. I think that old bitch protects her, Hinsu. I admit I'm afraid of that and becoming under her control. I have seen at least two instances where people wanted to strike her and instead fell helpless at her feet in adoration. I have to be satisfied that she cannot think anything wrong about me. When she thinks of me, she sees me only as a friend who can be trusted. That alone can be most useful as we move forward with our plans.

"I believe the secret of her new-found mental powers has something to do with the ring she wears," suggested Su Ling. "She did not have that when I knew her before. It seems to have a life of its own, and I think it protects her somehow. I have asked about it when I was with her, but she only says it was a ring she retrieved from the treasure she found at Thap Cham. She is very secretive about it with me, and never mentions it, but she never takes it off either. I think that has something to do with Queen Po's spirit joining with hers. I suspect that was Queen Po's ring. It glows at times, and I know Mai is always talking to herself. I think if we make her take off the ring, and come to us, we can take her, and then we can do what we want with her. It is something to consider."

Later, as they sat down beside each other for a candlelight dinner over-looking the river, they continued their discussion.

"I have been considering this matter," said Yameda. "I want to try that trigger you think is still planted in her subconscious. I am not sure but I believe she has knowledge of the ancients that will be useful to us."

"Hinsu, I can't do it. You will have to try that if you want to. I'm sorry. I am certain it would be disastrous for us if I tried to do it," she replied.

After a moment she continued, "On the other hand, I have no qualms about taking down any of those close to her. You should have seen me the night they had the Serpent Ritual celebration in the valley, the first one in hundreds of years. Acting as Queen Maisong, I was supposed to have her husband Jack brought to me in a loincloth as part of his induction into the Champa world. First, I made him kneel before me and I hand fed him the hallucinogen that made him docile and helplessly mine. I gave him an en-hanced dose so I could play him like a puppet on a string during the ritual. I led him to a post where I bound him while I danced in front of him. At one point, I pulled my knife, and removed his loincloth leaving him naked, and believe me, he was as excited, and into it as much as I was. All of the Champa people and I were as one as I danced the serpent dance and gave myself up to the dark side. You would have loved it. It was one of the most sensual mo-ments I have ever experienced.

"At the end of my dance the gong sounded three times, and everyone went into a frenzy of carnal abandon. They were by now fully under the power of the drug and gave themselves up to the sacred ritual. I admit I was caught up in it too, but I did not use or need the drug to take me to the next level. After a few strikes with my whip, I was supposed to release my new slave, Jack. But instead, I got lost in the moment and continued to beat him mercilessly with my whip until he passed out. I had him revived, and taken down, and I rode him to orgasm. I had him eating out of my hands. He was worshipping me, not Queen Maisong. He knew it was Su Ling he was making love to, and he worshipped and gave himself to me anyway. When I was done with him, I gave him to my servant Hata with instructions to deposit him on the trail back to the White Palace. I had conquered him. The last I saw of him that night he was beaten, bloody and being led away like a lamb."

"Just so," commented Yameda, "and did anything come of what you did to him?"

She turned to him with a curious expression on her face. "That's the thing, Hinsu. The next morning I was invited with Mai's close Chicago friends to breakfast on the verandah, and Jack was there. I was nervous about attending because I had gone over the top, and let my true feelings show when I beat him severely the night before. I went to that breakfast with those erotic memories still vivid in my mind. I was surprised to find him at breakfast sitting across the table. He looked fresh, and clean, and acted as if nothing had happened. He whispered a rebuke in my ear. "

"Maybe someone was standing in for him. You were standing in for Queen Maisong. Don't you think they would have had somebody stand in for him?" he suggested.

"No, it was Jack," replied Su Ling. "I have no doubt about it. I talked to him, and he even had the brand on his shoulder. My faithful maidservant Hata swears it was he too. She hates him more than I do because she is totally loyal to me and often proves it by amplifying my feelings to others. She told me on one occasion that she would kill him for me if given the opportunity. If she had noticed anything, she would have told me. I admit it took some of the satisfaction out of it seeing him the next morning and acting like nothing had happened."

"You seem disappointed," said Yameda.

"Well, yes, I guess I was at the time. I wanted control, especially when it came to Mai. I wanted him to know who was the boss between us; to conquer him, and I thought I had. But the next morning, he acted as if I was nothing. Even Mai seemed to be enjoying his lack of respect for me but at least I am sure she still loves me, and trusts me blindly."

"You must be careful, Su Ling. She is one of the smartest, most perceptive women you and I know. But we can use her trust in you when the time is right," said Yameda. "I think I will arrange a meeting with her. You can set that up…maybe a trip to Europe, or someplace where she will not suspect."

"What about Chicago?" asked Su Ling. "She goes there several times a year? We could arrange a meeting in Chicago easily."

"No…not Chicago. That is Catherine Marsh's home ground, and thus Queen Maisong's home ground. We need to get her away for a chance meeting where I can be alone with her. I will try a friendly approach first, and then if I have to, I will try that trigger of yours. Somewhere in Europe, I think," said Yameda.

"OK, I will work on that. But if that does not get what we want, I have some ideas that I will prepare for, just as a backup plan, of course."

"No rush, my love," said Yameda. "I'm not ready yet. The financial information you have been bringing me has been most productive. A few more years, and I will spring the trap, and have Ms. Marsh on her knees. Metaphorically, of course, but perhaps that is a third way to get what we want from Queen Maisong Sambath. I wonder what it would be like for a silver-spooned celebrity like Catherine Marsh to lose everything." He laughed loudly. "I would love to see that. With so many ways to achieve our objective, I don't think Queen Maisong's future looks very promising."

They got up and walked over to the banister overlooking the river.

Yameda smiled as he considered further what Su Ling had told him. After a moment, he said, "So you whipped Jack Largent? I would have loved to have seen that!"

Su Ling had a thought and smirked. "Darling, which of us is more jealous of Jack Largent? Hmmm?" she asked, with a playful nibble on his ear. "I am beginning to think you have another reason for wanting to meet with Queen Maisong away from everyone else."

"You see right through me, Su Ling. But really, my love, we share everything. Why not our own queenly concubine?"

Chapter 13

1998 Paris, France

For Mai, the Brise Tres Legere Hotel in the suburbs of Paris was a perfect place to stay. She did not care for congested cities, and shopping held no fascination for her with the possible exception of a few designer shows. This particular hotel on the outskirts of Paris promised privacy, seclusion, and most importantly discretion, when needed.

Mai was in Paris as a result of the persistent playful urging of Su Ling. But there was to be more to this outing than the friendly distraction of a shopping trip to Paris. Mai was aware through her watchful, and very protective security team at Siem Kulea, that Su Ling had arranged for her to meet Hinsu Yameda that very night for dinner. She was happily compliant with the charade because she was eager to spend some time discussing the ancients with him.

In an attempt to know her adversary well, Mai began to research Hinsu Yameda several years earlier. She became fascinated that they shared so many mutual interests. He was known for his involvement in Asian archeological efforts in general, and Champa history in particular. He spent a good deal of his time speaking on the subject at prominent gatherings while raising funds for worthy causes related to ancient Asian history and culture. He was particularly knowledgeable in that area, and she was more than willing to appear to be manipulated for the chance to engage in a conversation with an individual who could speak with some learned authority on that topic.

With so much in common, it was understandable that she became interested in meeting him. She went as far as attending a charitable fundraiser where Yameda was the featured speaker in Bangkok earlier that year and they exchanged a few friendly words. He was cordial and respectful and they pledged to get together some time soon in the future. She was testing the waters, but he left no doubt he was equally interested in meeting with her again, and to perhaps discuss more than ancient history.

For her part, the more information she gained concerning him, the more obsessive she became. She found herself unreasonably attracted to him on both a physical and intellectual level. The word irresistible came to mind. Admittedly, it intrigued her because she had no doubt there was a deeper reason for that attraction, and she was determined to discover why she felt about him the way she did. This man headed an organization to which she had brought great ruin, and yet she perceived he wanted to be her friend and more. She was certain of it, but she was not sure why.

Now on the night of the planned rendezvous, Mai was sitting alone at a table in the dining room of the very elegant hotel, and she was not enjoying herself in the least. Su Ling had told Mai she would be meeting her for dinner that night, just the two of them. But she told her to dress formally in her best with the promise of something very special she had planned for her afterward. Of course, Mai knew otherwise, but she didn't mind and was looking forward to the surprise meeting. The time came, and went, that her informants told her Yameda would make his appearance. While only glancing nervously at the impressive menu she held in front of her, she gazed around the dimly lit old-world atmosphere at the damask curtains, and muted, pastel-painted walls.

Though the muted lighting and décor left little room for recognition from one table to the next, Mai prayed her nervousness over meeting Hinsu Yameda alone did not show. She put down the large menu. Her fingers mindlessly tapped the tablecloth. With her hair up, and wearing the plunging neckline dress that was her only purchase the day before, she was stunning. Thus far, it was all wasted on the stuffy tuxedo-clad wait staff. Mai sipped her wine and pouted. She was suddenly unsure of herself, something foreign to her. She became self-conscious of how she was dressed. No doubt she was sending the wrong message. She picked back up the menu and began to peruse it once more, this time with her anxiety mounting. Queen Po was urging her from within to leave, and leave now! As those urgings by Queen Po grew stronger, Mai was having second thoughts.

But then she sensed someone sat down opposite her. Mai smiled to herself, and lowered the menu. She pretended bewilderment, but at the same time, she couldn't help being amused. "You?" she said. "So we meet again. Why am I not surprised?"

Oh god, what am I doing here she thought. *He is even more handsome in person than I remember.*

Hinsu Yameda smiled and reached for her hand. She let him take it, and kiss it gently before returning it to the table.

"I must confess, my impression of you at our last meeting in Bangkok was as one mesmerized by your charm, and beauty," he said, speaking very much what she had been thinking about him. "Are you pretending our meeting is not just another one of life's chance encounters between two people alone in this magical city?"

He was as handsome as Mai was beautiful and the room was warmed by their presence…a matched pair.

"Mr. Yameda, I know for a fact that this meeting is not by chance, but I came anyway. Indeed, sir, to be certain you understand this situation completely, I am not interested in anything more than a friendly discussion. I am married, and I love my husband very much," said Mai honestly. "I did not acquiesce to this meeting to trade flirtatious remarks with you."

"Why would you jump to such a conclusion as to my motives? But if you are afraid of me, then tell me to go away," he challenged, taking up her hand once again and squeezing it softly.

She paused. "You know I won't do that," she replied after a moment, not at all understanding why she said what she said. She pulled her hand back slowly.

"Yes, I do, and you know that we have much in common, and much to discuss including our mutual attraction for one another. You feel that don't you?" he suggested, gently.

Mai paused and studied her napkin, surprised at his blunt remark. She was suddenly very confused, and her anxiety returned. She looked up at him, and spoke honestly, "Yes, and it is not a comfortable feeling for me. But please, let's not play games. We're both here because we share a mutual interest in the ancients. I mean, that's all, right?"

"Mai, may I call you Mai? Queen Maisong seems so formal. Please, call me Hinsu. I feel like I know you very well although we have never really had a chance to sit down, and have a discussion as we are now. I have been infatuated with you for a very long time. In my own way, I have been protecting you, and your family from those who would see you harmed. Now that we are face-to-face once more, I have to say what I feel is no longer just infatuation, and what's more, I can sense you feel it too. No?"

Mai gently patted his hand, and said, "Hinsu, I would be lying if I said I did not feel something very strong for you. This is a happy occasion for me. I would like us to be friends. That is my hope in coming here. Anything else is out of the question. Please, let me be in that regard. I am very happy with my life," she protested, softly.

He nodded smiling and kissed her hand once more before returning it to the table. Then he abruptly changed demeanor and smiled broadly as if in acceptance of her rebuke. "OK, but lets at least share this meal, shall we? I too am content to spend this brief time having a discussion of the ancients with you."

A formally dressed waiter appeared from nowhere and showed a wine for approval. He poured a glass for Hinsu who tasted, nodded, and then watched as the waiter refilled Mai's empty glass. "I hope you don't mind. This is an excellent, dry white I found particularly inviting, and I took the opportunity to order it when I arranged the table for us."

"I know," replied Mai nodding.

"You know?"

"Yes, of course. I checked on the table and a wine beforehand, when I heard Su Ling and I were to meet here. As you can see, I already started. It is an excellent white that I am already familiar with."

"So, I suspect you are also entirely aware of my ruse to be alone with you. Please don't be angry with Su Ling for arranging this meeting. She only wished us to share this meal, and get to know each other better. She spoke of your interest in me, and my many causes in support of Asian history.

"Oh, I'm not angry with her. She always has my best interests in mind. I love her in my own way as…"

"As you love me…is that what you were going to say?" he teased.

"You are incorrigible! I told you I cannot have such feelings for you. I don't even want to think about it. Something else is going on here, and honestly I feel like I am being compelled against my will," she said.

"You are, but you must expect to be. You are being drawn to me because we are chosen to be together, Mai. We are destined to do great things. I think you and I are chosen to rule this world. There, I have said it. What do you think of that? You might have considered such a thing yourself," he insisted.

She laughed freely when she thought he was joking, but then, she realized he wasn't, and her demeanor changed accordingly. She straightened up in her chair and replied, "You *are* crazy. Only you could believe something so preposterous. You are living some sort of fantasy within a fairy tale. I am not a part of that, I assure you."

"The Hoa Cuc on my hip like the one on yours is the sign of our destiny, and the only proof I need," we said.

Mai dropped her napkin and stared at him. She was honestly stunned by this revelation, but she had time to think about it as the waiter again appeared. Mai insisted that Hinsu order first while she pondered what was happening.

He inquired about the Riff of Paella. What is in that?" he asked.

The waiter replied, "It is a Riff consisting of Lobster, Langoustines, Squid, Baby Clams and Cockles in a Saffron-spiked Shellfish Fumet."

"Yes, I will have that," said Yameda, and then he and the waiter both looked at Mai.

But Mai was lost in thought. It was as if this man who claimed to have the Hoa Cuc on his hip had some power to attract her, and compel her to want to make love to him. She had never heard of a male with the Hoa Cuc symbol and did not know what to make of it. She found herself staring at his lips, which with his other features were so inviting. But she shook her head away from such a thought because she didn't care about this man really.

But that was crazy because she did care. What the hell? She blinked slowly in thought wanting to know Queen Po's opinion concerning this most surprising information but found nothing where she usually found her counsel. Why wasn't she present when Mai needed her? She became nervous again, and conflicted, wanting to get away and stay at the same time. Damn!

"Mai?" Hinsu said.

She started as her thoughts found reality again. She looked up at the patient waiter, smiled, and said, "Yes, I'll have the same."

The waiter finished writing in his book, gave a head bow, gathered up the menus, and departed quietly.

Two small scented candles off to one side added to the ambiance of the private table. For any other couple, it would have provided a perfect romantic environment, but these two did not need romantic lighting to be attracted to one another. Hinsu was ready to go with it, but Mai would fight it until she no longer could. She had come for answers, not for sex, but his charms began working away at her once more.

"Why are you here alone?" Hinsu asked as he lit a cigarette. "Where is that photographer husband of yours, and your beautiful daughter? I have seen his work in a few of the books he has published. He really is very talented."

Mai sipped her wine grateful for the change in topic, and said, "Yes, Jack has an amazing eye whether he is photographing pizza, orchids, or artifacts. I suspect you already know he is photographing a new archeological site found in the state of Andhra Pradesh, India. Devi is back in Siem Kulea getting ready to go to Chicago. She didn't want to come to Paris again with her mom; just being a teenager."

"She will never be Queen, Mai. You know that, don't you?" he said. "The true heir can only come from our union."

"What? *WHAT*?" she said, shocked by his comment. She felt a sudden charging anger at his attack on her daughter, Devi. "That's what this is about? Now I see what you want with me. How can you say such a thing? Thank you for bringing me back to reality, Mr. Hinsu Ya-me-da. I do not know what this thing between us is, but I know in spite of what you think, it is not love. You and I are being compelled by some force, and I am going to fight it for the sake of my family. Oh, and by the way, Devi has the Hoa Cuc on her hip just like we do."

"She does?" Now it was his turn to be shocked. Yameda was not aware of that, and it momentarily stunned him because it definitely complicated his plans. He was surprised Su Ling had not mentioned something so vital to his objectives, but then he had never revealed wanting to have a child with Mai to her either. In all the years he had been conspiring with Su Ling, and all the times they mentioned Mai's daughter, he was never told she bore the Hoa Cuc symbol like her mother. Hinsu shook his head. How could he not know that?

"I guess I am not as smart as I think," he joked in retreat. "But your family are humans and, Mai, you and I are not like them. We are pureblood, and you know it."

"Devi has the Hoa Cuc, and that makes her as pure as us," Mai protested. "Even more pure than you certainly." There followed an extended pause while both of them allowed their thoughts to regroup.

After a moment, Mai resumed the conversation, "Come on, Hinsu. We don't know butkus about all of this. You and I don't really know what is going on here, only bits and pieces, and a lot of Champa traditional myths. What about your two sons? Do they have the Hao Cuc sign on them?"

He paused, crushed out his cigarette in an ashtray, shook his head, and said, "No, they do not, hence my surprise that your daughter does."

Mai shook her head, finally understanding the situation. "So it looks like my lineage is moving along, and yours stops with you, and *that* is why you are so hot to breed me!" said Mai, growing angrier by the minute.

"But Hinsu, I am sorry to inform you it doesn't work that way, and you have been sadly left ignorant as everyone is except for we queens on this particular subject. To put it bluntly, I don't need you to make an heir. I am the Nagani. We true queens *self*-reproduce and make our own heirs. It is not your destiny to rule anything. I am the Nagani as will be my daughter. We are of the purest blood descended from our ancestors while you only pretend to be. We rule our people, and you never will. That is a fact you will just have to accept.

"Furthermore, you leave my family out of this," she continued. "I swear to you now, If you ever lay a finger on them in any way, I and my people will come after you until we destroy you." she said throwing her napkin on the table, and getting up to leave.

Hinsu grabbed her hand, and said softly in quiet desperation, "OK, OK please...I'm sorry. It was exceedingly presumptuous of me. I beg you. Please, stay and forgive my foolishness. We have much to discuss, and what you just told me about your daughter changes everything for me. I will give up on that idea, I swear. It was not the main reason I wanted to talk personally with you anyway. I confess, I let my ego get away from me, and it distracted me from my real purpose for being here. Now, please, let's discuss what we both really want to talk about.

"Tell me what you know about the Ferrens," he continued, changing the subject. "Tell me what you know, and I will tell you what I know. There is a newly discovered archeological site in China, Mai. I have seen it, and it is vexing on many levels. I got a full tour, even of the areas the government won't talk about."

Mai sat down again because this was in fact why she came in the first place. The Chinese discovered an ancient site that remarkably had signs of being from the time of the Ferrens, her ancestors. Of this she was aware and she was very interested in what they might have found.

"The Chinese saw the same thing I did, and they know it is very old, and unlike anything ever seen before anywhere. That is really the reason I wanted to talk to you," he said. "They have teams of scientists working on what they found. They did not have my personal experience, knowledge, and background to draw from, so I am positive that I am years ahead of them in interpreting the many strange logogram-type drawings on the walls. I suspect only you, and I can interpret them, no?"

"What do you mean?" she asked. "You are referring to the site they found deep in the mountain while searching for rare minerals?"

"So, you know about that. Yes, exactly. An earthquake opened up a rift in a cavern that revealed the site. They are playing it up like it is an ancient Chinese site, but I talked with their top scientists, and they know better. It is without a doubt an ancient site at least ten thousand years old. Yet it is strangely modern and definitely not from this planet," he said.

"You mentioned the Ferrens. Hinsu, that is the first time anyone I know has actually spoken their name. I did not know anyone else knew that name but me. I certainly have not mentioned it to anyone. Do the Chinese know that name for the ancient ones?"

Their conversation was again interrupted as plates were set down in front of them and the rich smell of the cuisine wafted up at them. Just as quickly wine was poured once more, and the wait-staff departed leaving them alone. "This looks terrific, and I'm famished," said Mai. I think it's worth noting that you ordered what I was going to order exactly."

Mai suddenly had a thought; an intriguing and disturbing one that shocked her as she dropped her fork with a bang, and looked at Hinsu with aggressive eyes.

"What is it? Is something wrong?" he asked mid-bite.

"We're twins aren't we?" she demanded.

"Try the baby clams," he replied. "Some people believe they are an aphrodisiac."

"Answer me, Hinsu. Are we twins?" she asked, her anger at the inscrutable man opposite her returning with a vengeance.

"Yes, my dear, we are twins," he confessed, wiping his mouth, and pausing for a moment. "Colonel Minh killed our parents and raised me as his own. The silly old man never knew about you. You must have been somewhere else when he took me that night. We were both very young, and he never made the association when he discovered you through Su Ling. She never disclosed anything to him about your parents in Vietnam and Colonel Minh never knew who you really were when you conspired with Su Ling to kill him. I realized the possibility of a connection between us when I began researching your background. I always knew I was adopted but I never made the link, and I don't think Su Ling has ever deduced the relationship between us either. I am surprised you don't remember having a twin brother."

"It was a pretty traumatic time for me. I remembered having a brother vaguely, but I was never sure it was a real memory. We very young when they took our parents away, only three or four, and I never imagined having a twin," she explained as she again turned her thoughts back to that time long ago.

But then another entirely repulsive thought came to mind, "Oh, Hinsu! How could you? You want to have a child with me, and you knew all along that we are twins. That's sick!" she said. "You're sick like your twisted father and uncle."

"They were not my blood relatives. I was adopted remember? But now you understand your compulsion as I understand mine. It's the most basic form of preservation of the species. We are singularly different from the humans around us. We are superior in almost every way. I use a greater percentage of my brainpower and with utmost efficiency. I actually had myself fully tested. We are the same, and we are very special, superior to everyone around us, and we should rule over this world like our ancient ancestors did," he said.

"No Hinsu, we are not the same. You want to be a god, and I want to live life simply in peace as one with nature, my people, and the universe. We are not the same," she said.

"Your people know. Your Champa people worship you, Mai, and they are ready to die for you. Who between us is living as a goddess in her own private paradise?" he protested.

Mai tried to stare him down, but in the end, his logic hit home, and she fell silent in the face of his credible perspective. At times like this, she could count on the spirit of Queen Dau Te Po to advise her, but she had not been sharing her thoughts with Mai since Hinsu sat down at her table.

Positive he had won that point, and his plan was again moving forward he continued his theory of the ancients, their ancestors, and what had happened ten thousand years ago. As he talked, Mai quietly listened as many of her own ideas were proposed, or confirmed by Hinsu. He was positive once she saw their mutual connection to the ancients, which was their bond, she would forget about others and join with him.

He told Mai he was not sure why the ancients chose Earth, but it was probably because the atmosphere was closest to their own planet. In China, he had seen a wall that appeared to tell their history mixed with images and symbols. He could interpret some of it and that impressed the Chinese. They gave him full access as they became impressed with his insights and interpretations. They let him photograph some of the logograms in hopes that he would help them define the meaning of them.

"The aliens seemed to be able to travel great distances in space, but only when certain stars and planets were aligned." Yameda thought they might travel by some sort of magnetic energy.

"I think they changed the atmosphere on Earth to accommodate their own species. I also suspect they bred humans giving them a primitive intelligence," he said.

"I thought we all agreed that happened because of evolution over tens of thousands of years," Mai said knowing she already believed that they had bred some of the humans to serve them.

"Even so, where did that first spark come from?" asked Yameda. What if, in fact, the ancients accelerated the evolution of humans to accommodate their needs? They needed humans with primitive intelligence to raise crops, and make food for them."

"Like slaves," said Mai.

"Like devoted followers and worshippers of their gods, something again you know all about," said Hinsu once more striking home a point with Mai, and her present existence in Siem Kulea living as the queenly, living goddess of her people.

"One thing for sure," he continued, "is that the images showed the ancients living below the ground in huge chambers like the one we found inside the mountain in China. They were not shown as snakes as some have rumored them to be. As I have often suspected, that was a myth born out of a need to control and dominate humans. Fear is a powerful weapon.

"I believe they built these chambers in various places around the planet," he continued. "I think they lived below the ground because the atmosphere became un-potable for them in spite of their efforts to change it. So humans lived above ground and raised food for them, and the ancients lived below ground. We can assume that was not their intent when they came here.

"They changed the Earth while they were here in several ways, and it was kind of an experimental lab for them. Through their various devices around the globe, they could control the weather. So if they needed rain in one area of the world, they would just send it over. If humans didn't worship and obey them, they would make it really hot, or send storms to destroy them. With that kind of technology, you can easily understand why they were worshipped and obeyed.

"That's kind of funny in a way," said Mai. "Something as simple as controlling the weather can give you the power to rule the world.

"Was there any indication of what happened to them?" she asked.

"Yes, I think so. But I'm not positive my interpretation is correct. It appears the stars aligned in a certain way as needed about ten thousand years ago. They went home through some sort of portal that wasn't at the location in that mountain in China. They had to go then or wait for who knows how many years for the stars to align again. With having to live underground, I'm sure leaving was a much more desirable alternative for them.

"I don't think the device they used to control the weather was at that site in China, Mai. But I think you know where it is, don't you? Both the portal and the means to control the weather, I am betting you know where those devices are," he said.

He leaned forward closer to her. "Mai, I have a weird looking object. I stole it from the Chinese site without them knowing. I found it behind a hidden panel. They've not seen it or know that I have it. It is about eight inches long and looks like it is made of gold. But I don't think it is gold. There is something about it that is different. I haven't been able to find a way to test it yet. It has snakeskin-like texture on one side of it. It is strange looking, and I'm not sure what it is. What is it, Mai?" he asked hoping to move on to a discussion of the ornate and unusual door that he knew to be below the basement of the white palace.

"Hinsu, I really don't know what you're talking about. I don't have a clue what that object is that you have," she lied.

"Oh wait just a minute! That's how you think you can rule the world," said Mai, with a disdainful smirk. "You think you can control the weather like the ancients did. I was wrong! You are more of an ambitious megalomaniac than Colonel Minh ever was."

"No, I am infinitely more intelligent and patient than that stupid man. But you are pushing all of my buttons tonight, Mai. I want you like I have never wanted any other woman and I am determined to make love to you and make a true heir to the Champa throne."

He leaned in closer to her and looked right into her eyes as he said, "Queen Dau Te Po, isn't it a great day to be queen?"

Mai heard the phrase that once was as a lightening bolt to her free will. It was the same trigger that Dr. Minh had implanted in her subconscious to always have control of her when he wished. She knew immediately what it was and what he was trying to do. She slid her hand into her purse and released the safety on the Beretta she kept there to defend herself. She stared at him without moving. As the old feeling of being controlled and powerless began to come over her, she was not sure she could move or even wanted to. She felt her will to do anything wavering and dissolving and she felt herself wanting to give into it. She had not had that feeling in many years and did not believe it was possible for her to be taken in this way again especially after she joined with Queen Dau Te Po. She helplessly began to concentrate on his words and found herself wanting to go there and to be in that world of sublime obedient happiness once more.

He continued, "The time is right, and as much as you like to protest, you have been excited by my presence as much as I have been enthralled in yours, and neither you nor I, know what an amazing species will come of such a union. Only that if it comes from our genes it will be far superior to any human. I am taking you as mine, and you will obey me," he said looking directly into the eyes of the confused and bewildered Champa Queen.

"Why don't you ask Jack what he thinks about that," said the formally dressed handsome man now pulling up a chair to sit at their table.

"Daniel!" said Mai shaking her head, and snapping out of a momentary fog. She was surprised, and honestly relieved by the interruption to a conversation that was about to take a dangerous turn for her.

Yameda was surprised and frustrated by Daniel's sudden appearance. "My friend and I are having a private meal and a discussion that you have rudely interrupted. I must ask you to be on your way, sir." He snapped his fingers bringing two very fit bodyguards to his aid from the shadows of a nearby table.

Daniel put out his hand, "Daniel Vega, at your service, Mr. Yameda. Su Ling, your lover, is my wife. I have unfortunately heard a lot about you of late," he said, throwing his hand away when Yameda refused to shake it.

He continued with his timely interruption to Yameda's plans. "Mai, you haven't touched your food, and it looks delicious, mind if I have a taste?" he asked, smiling in an overly cordial manner.

"Where is Su Ling?" asked Mai pushing her bowl toward him.

"I saw her here at the hotel tonight from across the lobby. But she disappeared before I could talk to her. I haven't seen her otherwise in over a year. We've been separated for some time. Our marriage was never real I think; me with too much business to take care of, and her with Yameda," he said, letting his true feelings show through, and glaring at Yameda as he spoke.

Yameda's bodyguards stood right behind Daniel who ignored them much to Yameda's dismay.

"I must ask you again, sir, to leave, or my men will escort you out of here," he said.

"I can't imagine what Su Ling sees in you," said Daniel, continuing to ignore the threat. "A pompadour like you could not be a better lay. So what is it? What do you have that I don't?" asked Daniel, loudly.

"Daniel…" said Mai, startled by his aggressive tone.

Yameda put up his hand to interrupt her, "What we have, Mr. Vega, that you cannot ever give her is an intelligent, and sophisticated, mutual appreciation for the dark side. That is an unbreakable bond. She is under my power, or I am under hers. Honestly, I am never sure which. But she is mine, and you will never have her," he said proudly. "Now, leave us, or my men will see that you do, and I confess, I cannot control them once they get started."

"Oh yeah…about that," said Daniel waving his hand.

Instantly five men, including Ramadi and Fetu sprang from a table not far away. Tension filled the air of the elegant restaurant as Daniel continued eating calmly, and Yameda sat back stiff in his chair. Daniel swallowed his food, took a sip of wine and then looking up at the men patting down Yameda's bodyguards said, "Ramadi, I'm sorry. I promised you and Fetu a gourmet meal this evening, and we only got to the appetizers. Perhaps you will return after escorting these thugs out of here. I always enjoy your company."

Ramadi bowed slightly, and said, "My lady, please forgive this interruption but it appeared Mr. Vega needed our assistance." He watched as his men finished searching Yameda's two men, and signaled them toward the exit at the point of a gun.

Mai looked at Yameda who was red with anger, and she found herself amused at his dismay. "Hinsu, you look like a ripe pimple ready to pop. I'm sorry your plans didn't work out. But if you wish to continue our discussion, I'm willing. I am sure Daniel will find it interesting."

Daniel picked up Yameda's glass of wine and took a sip. "I have to say this wine is a bit too oaky tasting for me. I can make some suggestions for the next time you wish to attempt to seduce another man's wife."

That was enough for Yameda. Standing up abruptly, he said, "I believe I will be leaving now. Good evening, Mai. It has been enjoyable. Mr. Vega, we will meet again I'm sure."

Daniel shook his head, "You better hope we do not, you Asian psychopath. The only thing between my fist and your face at this moment is my desire to not embarrass Mai any further tonight."

Yameda ignored him. "Thank you again for a pleasant evening, Mai. I hope we can get together soon."

Mai replied, "Goodbye, *brother*. Go in peace. Always remember, I am not your enemy. Making me one will lead to your great misfortune, and we both would regret that."

As Yameda straightened his tuxedo and departed quickly for the entrance, Daniel said, "Mai, I'm sorry. I just couldn't stand by watching that ass continue to make passes at you."

"Oh, Daniel, I am not angry in the least. There is nothing to apologize for," she said, touching wine glasses with him.

Daniel moved over to take Hinsu's seat, and said, "Well I'm not proud, I would finish this whatever-it-is, but I really could use a big thick steak right now. Do you mind?" he asked, summoning the waiter.

As the waiter took his order and left, Mai remembered to set the safety once more on the Beretta in her purse. After collecting herself, and taking a deep breath, she exclaimed smiling, "Hah! Mind? Once again you swoop down in your helicopter and save me. I will confess, Daniel Vega, I was out of my league with Hinsu Yameda. He was moving too fast for me to think clearly. I think he even tried to access an old hypnotic trigger from my Colonel Minh days. I am surprised it still had any effect on me. It was the weirdest sensation. I could feel it attempting to come over me as if in slow motion. I could smother you in kisses right now."

"I can't say I would mind that at all," he admitted. "Would you really have betrayed Jack, and slept with that snake?" he asked.

"Not in a million years, Daniel, at least not willingly. But it was strange. The more I investigated him, the more I felt a compelling attraction. I wanted to be with him in a way I couldn't understand. I thought it was sexual, but in the end, it was something else entirely. I found out from him that we are twins.

"Really?"

"Really."

Daniel shook his head. "Mai, this is Daniel. We have been saving each other's bacon for many years now. You always tell everyone how reckless Jack is. But he has worked on a dozen archeological sites, and I have never heard of him doing one thing that is reckless. But you...this is reckless."

She sighed, and explained, "It didn't seem so reckless at the time, Daniel. I wanted to meet with Yameda because I wanted to discuss the ancients with him. I thought he might have information I didn't, and it turns out I was right...sort of, and frankly, Daniel, our future right now may very well depend on what Yameda knows or doesn't know."

Daniel shook his head. "Sometimes with you, I feel like I am reading a book of tall tales." He already knew enough about Mai to fill that book, and most of it was very strange indeed.

He took a sip of wine and continued, "There never is an end to your story, Mai. I have known you for a long time now. But if you will forgive me for suggesting it, sometimes I wonder if you shouldn't see a shrink."

They stared each other down for a moment and then Mai laughed heartily. "You're right, Daniel. Maybe I should have a long time ago, but I married Jack instead. Thank God for Jack. He is so patient with me. But sometimes I think I'm beyond help, and besides, it's all real, not just in my head."

"Pardon the pun?" commented Daniel.

After Mai gave him another look, he continued, "I find it a bit bizarre, even fascinating, that you have another person inside of you talking with you all the time. A psychiatrist would call that schizophrenia. That must be weird even for you with both of you sharing the same mind."

"Yes, and no, and it is. Queen Po within me is real, Daniel. You believe that don't you?" she asked, seriously.

As the waiter placed a perfectly grilled steak in front of him, he replied, "I have no doubt of that Mai. But I don't claim to understand it for a minute."

"It's like my thoughts except I know it's her when I think thoughts I never dreamed of. It happens all the time, and I don't even notice it anymore," she explained. "She is always commenting about everything, especially people we meet. She likes you by the way."

"Good to know," he said, through a bite of his steak.

"But when Hinsu was here it was strange," she continued. She fled my person because she sensed his mind was so similar she was being drawn to it. I believe if he had this ring he could bond with her. I always assumed she would protect me from ever being hypnotized again, but she wasn't there in this instance to protect our relationship. She is back now doing her best to comfort me. Hinsu and I being twins is singularly unique and she told me that even she was surprised because she has never heard of a male bearing the Hoa Cuc mark. In fact, she suggested that he was lying and didn't actually bare the mark. The implications of that are many, and warrant a lot of thought on the matter.

"Hinsu wants his own child, his own heir. He might even try to harm Devi to eliminate her as competition or even..." Mai had a sudden horrible thought as Queen Po amplified her considerations. Devi was now just as much of a candidate for his children in his mind as she was, and did having the Hoa Cuc make him an eligible ruler of the Champa people?

Mai considered that a moment and said, "We'll have to keep an eye on him."

"Yeah, well, maybe Su Ling can work on that. She seems to spend a lot of time with him lately," said Daniel.

Mai felt sorry for him, but stayed neutral, "Peas in a pod, those two. But you needn't worry about her. She won't harm me, or mine. I trust her, Daniel. I am sorry the two of you did not work out. When I see her next we will have a discussion about that, and Yameda.

"Don't trust her, Mai. I mean it," said Daniel.

"I have to, Daniel. She is my friend and would not do anything to hurt me. She is the most amazing woman in the world, and I trust her implicitly. Her judgment is always right. I love her, Daniel," she said.

Daniel stared at her for a moment. "Did you hear what you just said?" he asked.

"What?" she asked. "What did I say?"

Daniel wiped his mouth, put down his napkin and leaned in toward Mai across the table. "Mai, is it possible she has hypnotized you?" he asked. "You know, left you with a post-hypnotic suggestion of some kind. You were pretty much under her control back then."

"Don't be silly, Daniel," she protested. Su Ling is the most amazing woman in the world, and I trust her implicitly. She is always truthful with me and watches out for me. Her judgment is always right. I love ..."

She stopped before she finished the sentence and they just stared at each other.

He said again, "Mai, tell me about Su Ling."

She softly said, "Su Ling is the most amazing woman in the world, and I trust her implicitly. Her judgment is always right."

Her hand started to shake, and Daniel took it up and held it. "She's a snake, Mai, of the worst kind. Do not trust her."

Mai pulled back her hand, and said, "I'm getting a headache thinking about this and I am tired. I have to go. Thank you for being here for me this evening, Daniel. It is comforting to know that you, Ramadi, and Fetu, have my back."

"Actually this was all Jack's idea. He noted your sudden interest in Yameda and asked me to keep an eye on you while he was away. When you planned this trip to Paris, I recruited a few good men with a promise of a gourmet dinner."

Mai started to get up, but then sat back down again and looked at him seriously from across the table.

She took his hand in hers and said, "I may need you now more than ever, Daniel. Hinsu Yameda does not lose. He always wins, and we have just embarrassed him and thwarted his plans. He is going to come at us. I am sure he means to kill you and wound me in a way I will never forget. We have stepped on the tail of the snake when we should have crushed its head."

She gave his hand a final squeeze, leaned over the small table, and kissed him on the cheek. Then without another word, she got up and left.

Daniel watched her leave and saw Ramadi with two men join her at the door.

He sat back and thought about what she said. "I'm not in danger, Mai," he said, solemnly, to the empty chair. "I am only a pawn in this game, and he has already defeated me, and pushed me off the board when he claimed Su Ling.

"But he knows you are the only one who can challenge him now, and that makes you first on his list. You are right. He will come at you, and in a way you won't suspect."

Chapter 14

1998 Chicago

Once Su Ling explained her long-term plan to Hinsu Yameda, he embraced it as his own. He and Su Ling were of the same diabolical mind. Both, like master chess players could see the end game clearly with their first few moves on the board, and most importantly they knew the power of patience.

NearNorth Productions was a news outlet conglomerate that had recently developed their own television network with one station in prime time, and two on the cable system in Chicago. Catherine Marsh owned it, but Howard Landell, her personally chosen partner, was the boss and ran its day-to-day operations. The corporation was independently wealthy based on its financial division developed mostly through Mai's perceptive involvement, and who, for reasons of her own, still worked as a vice-president in the organization. That simple fact meant that if NNP never produced another successful news show on its promising prime time, and cable networks, it would still be one of the most profitable corporations in the world. That made it a very attractive target for Hinsu Yameda's schemes.

Eddie Martinez settled in Chicago and adapted easily. He quickly began catching up on the twenty-five years he was absent from the United States. He read news and entertainment magazines voraciously and spent most of his free time walking the streets and exploring Chicago neighborhoods. He was well funded and documented according to Su Ling's plan to set him up as in his new persona as an experienced security executive.

Martinez was eager to assume his new role. He was back in the game in a manner he could never have envisioned a few years ago. He did not regret the many years he spent in Southeast Asia. That experience gave him a tremendous confidence in his abilities. Beyond the many skills of which he was adept, Su Ling taught him perseverance, and that was a lesson well received. He was determined to prove to her that she made the right decision in whatever long-game she had planned.

The city of Chicago, nestled up against the southern tip of Lake Michigan, was a perfect fit for Eddie Martinez. The people were Midwest honest, and naively trusting in his view. A deal with the shake of a hand was a deal, and no one had their hands in your pocket looking to make an easy buck. This was refreshing after his last twenty years in Southeast Asia.

He went by the name of Eduardo Fuentes, keeping his first name, and using a similar Latino name for his second. Most people on the job just called him "Eddie" and it stuck.

He looked nothing like his persona in the jungles of Northern Cambodia. He was now in his late forties although he looked ten years younger, and had abandoned the felonious attitude that had marked his adventures overseas. He was no longer looking for the quick buck, or where the money was for him. He was happy to put that life and character behind him, as he became more upscale and sophisticated in his new role. He exchanged jungle fatigues and work boots, for Italian made suits, and with a refined vocabulary and polite demeanor, he got a chance to assume still another persona that fit him surprisingly well. On Su Ling's orders, he was even taking a course in German, although he had no idea what she had in mind for that.

He wisely took his time working for another prominent Chicago private security firm where his well conceived but phony resume easily got him hired. He settled in, worked hard, and learned their routine well before finding a way to work himself into the security department of NearNorth Productions. After three months, he initiated an impromptu meeting with Big Ben Washington, NearNorth Production's head of security at one of his favorite hangouts, a bar called Redman's on the Southside, just off of Maxwell Street. It was a blues bar, and Eddie became a regular there. He saw Big Ben several times before they actually met one night while ordering drinks at the bar.

When Ben found out Eddie had a background as a mercenary, he couldn't wait to tell him about his own experience many years ago when he was in Ubon, Thailand, protecting Catherine and Mai after her escape from Colonel Minh. Eddie was a good audience and seemed genuinely impressed by Ben's story. He told him a few stories in return but changed the location of his activities to South America so as not to get entangled where their stories might logically cross paths.

A month passed as the two became good friends and drinking buddies. Big Ben brought Eddie home to meet his wife and kids, and it was not long before he was a regular there too, especially on weekends when Ben would spend his Sundays smoking pork butt Memphis style on his backyard barbecue. Ben's wife had a girlfriend she introduced to Eddie, and soon she became a regular at those weekend get-togethers.

After a while, it became Big Ben's mission to try to entice Eddie to come work for NearNorth Productions, but Eddie claimed to be happy where he was and insisted that he didn't want work to interfere with their friendship. Big Ben persisted and inquired through industry sources about Eddie. When he heard nothing but superlatives about him, he decided to make it his mission to get him on board at NNP and he thought he knew how to make him an offer he wouldn't refuse.

Of course, Eddie didn't need convincing at all. He was just waiting for the right time to make his move. When Big Ben finally came to him with another offer, he jumped everyone in security at NearNorth Productions to a supervisorial position. He took to it readily and even suggested a few minor changes that had merit. Who better to do security than someone who was an expert at breaking it?

Right away Eddie was diagramming, and writing down everything as Su Ling had ordered. It was easy for him. All he did was plan ways to bring harm to NNP or steal secrets from its closely held operations particularly in the vastly successful financial department. He spent days watching even the most common of employees as he monitored the security of the large corporation, and it was not long before he had a good feel for its weaknesses. He found several and even uncovered an employee who was selling company secrets to a competitor. He reported her to Ben, casually saying he did not want to take the credit for it. Ben accommodated his wishes but felt his decision in hiring Eddie was vindicated.

In reality, Eddie felt conflicted with his intended mission and did not want it reported that he had strengthened the security at NearNorth Productions. That would just mean a lot of awkward questions from Su Ling. He was not sure why he continued to work at cross-purposes. After a while, he could no longer deny that his loyalty was changing in subtle ways and driven from within. It was as if something, or someone, was guiding his decisions. He at first reasoned that his actions helping to enhance the security of NNP were necessary for building up his reputation. But even after his reputation was solid, he continued to work against his assignment from Su Ling, and in the back of his mind, he knew something else was going on. The sum of his efforts was that he had again, and again, worked to enhance the security at NearNorth Productions, and not leave it vulnerable for whatever Su Ling and Yameda had in mind. He became confused about carrying out his mission, but he was certain of one thing. He genuinely liked the people he worked with, and who had embraced and befriended him as one of their own. In the end, he became protective of them.

In his position as supervisor, he had full access to everything in the building, except Catherine and Kelly's private condominium. Hence he did not know what to expect, and was surprised when he was summoned to Catherine's office one day on the thirtieth floor of their building.

When he arrived and was ushered in by her secretary, Big Ben was sitting in a chair next to Catherine's partner, Kelly, both of them to one side of Catherine's large glass-topped desk.

"How are you, Eddie?" Catherine began, cordially.

"I'm fine, Miss Marsh," he answered, smiling. "Thank you for asking, but I have to admit I'm a little nervous at the moment. I'm not in any kind of trouble am I?" he asked smiling.

"No, nothing like that. Please, sit down, Eddie," Catherine said. "We want to run something by you, and see what you think. You know my partner Kelly, and Ben, of course."

"Yes, nice to see you again, Miss Ryan," he said, nodding to her.

After Eddie was seated comfortably, Catherine began, "Eddie, Big Ben tells me that you have performed superbly since joining our security team here at NearNorth Productions. He says that you even found several faults with our security procedures, which have since been remedied."

Eddie looked at Big Ben and nodded. "Thank you, but I assure you it was not that big of a deal. Ben has always had a solid routine going, which probably was invulnerable in my opinion."

"Well, not from what he has told me. But here is why we asked you to join us today. We would like your thoughts on something. We are receiving an increasing amount of threats on our family, and friends, and we need a good man to make sure that we have the tightest security possible. Acting on Ben's suggestion, we are considering hiring a man to work independently of Ben with his own security team dedicated to my family, and my friends when they visit. We think you would be perfect for that job, Eddie. What do you think?" she asked.

In his wildest dreams, Eddie had never imagined this turn of events. The wolf was apparently being put in charge of the hen house, an error that would be fatal under most circumstances. He knew Su Ling would be pleased. "I am honored, Ms. Marsh," he said, and especially that you, and Ben, have such faith in me. It means a lot to me because I respect Ben very much, and of course you too, uh…"

Kelly laughed. "Eddie we want you to start right away, at least by the end of the week. Can you do that?" she asked.

"Yes, of course, Miss Ryan. But I will want to take a few days to look things over if you don't mind. This is Monday. I think I can have a team in place by Friday. Does that sound OK?" he asked.

"Friday would be fine, Eddie," Catherine said.

"I will need to meet with both of you on Friday morning to outline my security plan for your approval. Rather than hire unknown outsiders, I would like to take some of Ben's team and hire a few from the security firm where I formerly worked. Does that sound alright to you?" he asked them.

"That's your department," said Catherine. You get the people, and whatever else you need to ensure our safety." She quickly checked her calendar, and then said, "I will clear my calendar for ten on Friday morning."

"Well, OK then. Very well," Eddie said, nodding. "I guess I would like to get started if you will excuse me. I need to discuss some things with Ben, get a key, and access to the condominium. Perhaps he can show me around if he has the time."

Ben nodded, "My thoughts exactly. Let's get to it."

As he started to get up, Kelly said, "Eddie, you have not asked about your salary? Aren't you even curious?" she asked.

"I assumed it would be the same, Miss Ryan. Perhaps a small raise, but it's not important. The challenge of the new responsibility is all that really matters to me for the moment." He shrugged, and said, "In some ways your affirmation and trust in me is like getting paid."

Catherine nodded, and replied, "We can discuss salary on Friday when we see your plan, Eddie. OK?"

"Yes, of course. I will look forward to it," he said, as he departed smiling.

Eddie, after doing a security walk of the condominium with Ben, left the building and called Su Ling to give her the news. At the time, she seemed to be in thought, and this was confirmed later that same day when she contacted him in return. She requested that in about two weeks time, Eddie set up a way that one of her operatives could inspect Catherine's condominium. Eddie tried to ask her several questions, but she refused to answer, telling him it was better for everyone if he did not know more.

Reluctantly he set it up. He gave Su Ling notice when Catherine and Kelly were to be out of town, and Charlie was not around. The operative came, and went, although Eddie never saw any sign of him. Eddie spent a great deal of time afterward searching the condominium thoroughly, and found nothing: no bomb, no video, and no hidden devices of any kind. This bothered him a great deal because he was not sure what Su Ling was planning. He made a note to weekly search the condominium thoroughly just in case the mysterious operative returned unannounced and left a device of any sort. But as time passed, Su Ling never mentioned it again, and apparently nothing came of it.

Chapter 15

2001 Chicago

Three years passed with Eddie Martinez as head of Catherine's personal security in Chicago. During that entire time, he had carefully avoided being in the same room with Queen Maisong Sambath Largent. With his security plan in place, he could let his very capable subordinates take over, and he did. As it was, this was not a major problem because she did not travel to Chicago very often. With their superior technology in place, Mai met in cyberspace with Catherine and Kelly, and they usually elected to go to Siem Kulea for physical meetings, not the reverse. That said, Brad Martin insisted that Mai meet in Chicago once each quarter to discuss financial matters and Mai was fine with that arrangement.

Eddie was avoiding direct contact with Mai because he was not sure if she would recognize him on the one hand, or if that strange feeling he had upon meeting her many years ago on the trail at Siem Kulea would overtake him again. At that time, he was leading her husband Jack as a prisoner tied and on a rope leash down the mountain to turn in to Colonel Minh. Mai, who was Colonel Minh's version of Queen Dau Te Po at the time, rode up on her black stallion and intercepted their party. She ordered Martinez who was visibly enthralled with her to take the prisoner, up to the work farm and lock him in a cell. He never knew what to make of the instant grip she had on him, but he knew it was different from anything he had ever experienced with any other woman. It was an intense mesmerizing influence, and one he was never able to forget. While the effect her presence had on her Champa people was legendary, he did not doubt that the impact she had on him was at least the same, and perhaps even more pronounced. Thus he felt it was better to avoid direct contact under the awkward circumstances he presently found himself. Working as a spy for Su Ling while supervising security at NearNorth Productions was a delicate balance at best. He could not predict what his reaction would be if he physically met with Queen Maisong again, or worse, what her response would be toward him. He had no doubt that sooner or later Su Ling was going to call on him to do something of great harm to Queen Maisong, Catherine, her close friends, or family. The lingering devotion he still felt for Queen Maisong had gradually converted him into a counter-spy. He stayed on and worked hard at his job so when the time came he would be in a unique position to deal with any contrivance of Su Ling's and assure that no harm came to those he now cared about at NNP.

But then one day, quite by chance, he ran into Mai coming around a corner in the hallway near Catherine's office. She was visiting Catherine at the time but was scheduled to be across town meeting at the Financial Division. He was surprised and close enough to smell her perfume, and even though she only glanced at him for a second, the impact was remarkable. He remembered that second when their eyes met as if it were indelibly carved into his subconscious. The rest of the day he couldn't stop seeing those beautiful glasz eyes of hers. He was consumed with that image, and even he did not understand it. It was enough to bring back the old obsessive feelings he had for her years ago, and that was the reason he had not slept all night and was still pacing his apartment early the following morning.

The last few years in Chicago had been some of the best of his entire life. Queen Maisong and her friends whom he had been working with at NearNorth Productions represented the good in this world. He enjoyed his work and the trust and respect that people at NNP had for him. He lamented that he was not really a part of that life and was just playing a deceptive role designed in the end for nefarious, and maybe even ruinous purposes.

He sat down and stared out the window of his fifth-floor apartment as he considered his options. No matter how much he argued with himself he kept coming to the same conclusion. He would confess everything to Queen Maisong and put his fate in her hands. He realized finally that he was her servant, and had never stopped being so from the moment they met on that trail many years ago. Even in his present role working as an agent for Su Ling, he had not betrayed her. She was the center of his universe, and if she were truly the person he thought she was, he would be safe with her. She would know what to do next.

This realization meant he had to talk with Queen Maisong. But how to do it, he asked himself? Of course, he could just call down to his secretary and set up a meeting. As the one in charge of security, this would not be a problem. But no, he thought, there was that other problem that bothered him. Lately, he had become concerned that there was at least one other operative working for Su Ling embedded at NearNorth Productions. He did not know who it was, or in what division they were working. But this additional operative presence was apparent by some of the things that Su Ling had told him about NearNorth Productions during their last conversation, and that he had not revealed to her. Thus he resolved that the meeting with Queen Maisong must be kept secret from anyone at NNP.

He checked her schedule for that morning and saw she was meeting with Brad Martin, the firm's Chief Financial Officer, as she had been almost every day for the last week. His offices were in a high-rise just the other side of the river on Wacker Drive. That was a short cab ride from their building, and more importantly away from NearNorth Productions. He grabbed his cell phone, wallet, keys, and weapon and headed out the door.

Chapter 16

2001 Chicago

As it happened, after a week of rigorous workdays, Mai was at that same time making last minute preparations for leaving Chicago that very morning and getting back to her valley paradise in Siem Kulea. She decided to leave a day earlier than planned having finished her work on that quarter's overall financial strategy with Brad Martin to their mutual satisfaction the day before. She had already alerted her aircraft crew at Midway airport and was informed by her handmaiden, Ceva, who always traveled with her that she was packed and ready to go. She heard the doorbell to her suite, and Ceva came into the room soon after telling her the limousine was downstairs and a man was there to collect her bags.

She nodded, and Ceva led the man into the suite accompanied by a security guard. After the man gathered the seven large bags on a cart in the hallway, Ceva went with him downstairs.

Mai checked around to be sure she did not forget anything. Dressed casually in light slacks and blouse, she put on her matching topcoat. She had on minimal jewelry as was her custom in public, and wore gold sandals. Grabbing her handbag, she took one last look around and nodded to the security man standing by the door.

When she started to leave the suite, she all but ran into Catherine coming in the door. They hugged, and Mai said, "I am going to miss you. I wish I could stay longer, Cat. But my valley is calling me home. I am anxious to get back. Give Kelly a big hug and kiss for me, will you?"

"Give her one yourself," said Catherine. "We have a meeting with our lawyer Gerald Doyle, so we are dropping you off at Midway on the way."

"Oh, great! Well, we had better get going. I am thirty minutes late already," said Mai.

"Excuse me, Your Majesty," quipped Catherine, "but what good is it to be a queen, if you can't make people wait for you?"

"I agree completely, Cat," answered Mai. "But I don't think anyone else does, especially when it comes to airports. They are urging me to hurry, or we will be delayed taking off. At least we can load up in the private parking garage."

"Uh, well that was good for Ceva and the baggage, but actually this time we are going out the front," said Catherine. "Since we are going to Midway, it saves us twenty minutes through heavy traffic, so put on your armor. Security says there is a crowd including paparazzi and reporters. I think it has something to do with your interview on Oprah that aired yesterday. Sorry, but that's the price of being a celebrity, Mai."

Eddie by chance made a quick routine check of his security team and was stunned when he heard Mai was already leaving for the airport. He had not yet had the private conversation he was suddenly compelled to have with her. He quickly formulated a new plan, made a call, wrote a note, and hurried downstairs ostensibly to supervise the security outside the entrance to the building.

Kelly and Catherine exited the building first and quickly made it through the throng of reporters, and paparazzi to get into the waiting limousine. A moment later, Mai came out of the building to cheering crowds, reporters with questions, and paparazzi snapping photos. She at first acknowledged the crowd, but then began driving her way through them toward the limousine led by two security men in front and two behind.

Eddie positioned himself, and noted the security team of four were doing their job, and handling the crowd situation well. He was simply one of the crowd as Mai passed him and she did not take notice. But then, as luck would have it, she lost her footing, stumbled, and started to fall. Eddie who never took his eyes off her, was near enough to jump forward and grab her up before she actually found contact with the sidewalk. The security team immediately reacted. But then seeing it was their boss who caught her, they relaxed and resumed making a path for Mai.

As Mai collected herself, she said, without looking at him, "Thank you, kind sir. You have saved me from embarrassment or worse!" But then their eyes met as they had many years ago on that remote trail at Siem Kulea. Mai tilted her head and continued to stare into his eyes, and her smiling expression turned to one of curiosity, as she thought she recognized the man who so gallantly had broken her fall. She knew it mattered, but in that instance, she couldn't remember why, or where she had seen this man before.

"Please, think nothing of it, my lady," said Martinez politely. "I am happy to be of service, and in the right place at the right time." But with her touch, and looking directly into her eyes, she pummeled his heart, much as she had those many years ago. He swooned in spite of himself as their gaze held for an extended moment, but then he remembered and slipped the small note surreptitiously into her hand.

Just then, Mai was distracted by the driver standing at the door of the limousine urging her to get inside. "Please, Queen Maisong, we must hurry. I am afraid we are a running very late," he explained. "If we lose our window, you could be waiting on the tarmac to take off for an hour, or more."

Mai gave one last wave to the crowd and climbed into the back seat of the limousine. As she settled in she took the opportunity to look out the window once more for another view of the man who had broken her fall moments before. But he was not there anymore, and she could not find him in the crowd. With bags put away and everything in order, the limousine sped from the curb. They turned the corner quickly with their security following close behind, and headed toward Midway airport to rendezvous with Mai's waiting airplane.

As the city passed by outside the window, Mai could not stop thinking about the man who had broken her fall outside the building. She knew she had seen him before although it taxed her memory to recall where and when. She then realized he had given her something, and she opened her hand to find the small folded note.

While Kelly and Catherine debated over something ardently across from her, Mai read the note and quickly hid it away again. "Did either of you see the man who broke my fall when I stumbled just before entering the limo?" she asked.

"Yes," Kelly said. "That was Eddie Fuentes the head of our personal security. Those men protecting you all week work for him. I would have thought you met him already. Is there a problem?" she asked.

"No, he seems nice," Mai replied.

"Yes. He has done very well by us. We think he is one of the very best, Mai. I really thought you had been introduced. We will have to take care of that next time," said Catherine.

After thirty minutes they arrived at the private side entrance to Midway and drove to the hangar housing her aircraft. The crew were waiting at the bottom of the airstairs and were ready to take off as soon as she was aboard.

Catherine and Kelly did not even get out of the limousine but said their goodbyes to Mai inside with promises to see her in January in Siem Kulea. As soon as her bags were unloaded, they sped off with friendly waves.

The crew with Ceva and Mai's personal bodyguards gathered around Mai and waited respectfully as she stood at the bottom of the airstairs and watched the limousine leave until it was out of sight.

Then to Ramadi who was at the bottom of the stairs, she ordered, "Take two of your men and acquire another vehicle. Do so quickly. I have to go somewhere nearby. Tell no one of this meeting."

Then she turned abruptly to the co-pilot still waiting beside her, and said, "We will be delayed a couple of hours. I have to meet someone, and then I will return. It is important and confidential. Please inform the pilot. You will tell the tower only that we are delayed."

Ten minutes later they were in a town car heading across Chicago to the private, and very exclusive hotel written on the note. They did not stop at the front of the facility but drove around to the back to a single story secluded suite as instructed in the note. They disembarked near a short walkway leading to the door of the suite.

On the way, Mai briefed Ramadi on where they were going, and why. He insisted that she let him secure the premises before she got out of the car. Ramadi knocked on the door with his gun drawn, and ready. Eddie opened the door, stepped back, and put his hands up showing he meant no harm.

Ramadi knew him as head of Catherine's personal security but they rarely met. Under the circumstances he was compelled to be cautious. He turned him in place and put his hands up against the wall while he frisked him thoroughly. Finding nothing he told him to sit in one of the chairs at a round table and not move while he checked the room.

"My gun is on top of the dresser with two magazines next to my briefcase," said Martinez. "Look, I mean no harm to Queen Maisong. You know me. I care about Queen Maisong as much as you do, maybe even more."

Ramadi only nodded and circuited the room checking everything carefully. He returned to the door and signaled Mai it was OK to enter, not once taking his eyes off Martinez as he did.

She walked in with two bodyguards, inspected the finely appointed quarters, and then asked Ramadi to stay but instructed the two guards with him to wait outside.

"Do you know this man?" she asked Ramadi.

"Yes, but not well. He is the head of Ms. Marsh's personal security. I have had meetings with him two or three times over plans for your security, my lady. The last time was last year I think," he replied.

Mai walked over to stand in front of Martinez and have a good look at him.

Martinez audibly swooned a deep breath and found himself light-headed as he had been long ago on the trail at Siem Kulea.

But when he swooned Mai recognized him for who he was and it all came back to her. She silently stared at him as her anger grew. She removed her coat, and tossed it on the bed.

Ramadi tuned in to her feelings and moved directly behind Martinez holding his neck. She gathered her thoughts, turned to Martinez and asked, "Who are you?"

"I am Eddie Martinez, my lady. That is my real name. I was a mercenary for Colonel Minh back in the old days. We have met before on the trail coming into the valley. I had some prisoners…"

"My husband, Jack," Mai said, as she reached out and slapped him as hard as she could in focused anger. "You had my husband tied up on a leash like a dog, and I told you to take him to the slave farm, and put him in a cell to protect him. There he was brutally whipped and tortured instead. I cannot remember a time when I was angrier than that," she said. "That was unforgiveable."

Ramadi grabbed him by the neck and pushed him to the floor on his knees before her. Mai was livid and vented her anger freely as she slapped him again three more times while Ramadi held him helpless. But Eddie did not resist and offered his face for her gratification. She started to slap him again but then gained control of her anger, and sat down in a chair at the table instead. After a moment, she poured a glass of wine from the chilled bottle and took a sip as she tried to collect her emotions.

At last, she turned to him and said, "I have carried my unrequited anger for you these many years and I am not done. You have a lot of nerve showing up as you have. What do you have to say for yourself?"

"Yes, my lady, I heard later what had happened with the prisoner although at the time I did not know he was your husband, but that was not my doing. I make no excuses, but I delivered him safely and locked him in a cell. There were no guards present at the time, so I left clear written instructions tacked to the door that it was your wish he be kept in a cell, left alone, and well fed. I swear to you that is the truth. I have never disobeyed you, my lady. I hope I can convince you of that. I have been your servant since that day. Even now I do not know why you have had such an effect on me. But you have. You do something to me that makes me want to serve and protect you. I honestly don't understand my feelings for you. But they are undeniable and there always." With the last statement, he gave a sigh throwing out his hands at his sides.

"I remember that incident at the work camp, my lady," Ramadi commented from behind the kneeling Martinez. "Colonel Minh's guards could not read, and in their ignorance, they followed their normal procedures for new prisoners at the work camp. That is how Jack ended up getting whipped. I believe this man speaks the truth as to that."

Mai looked at Ramadi and said nothing as she considered his words. Martinez was a big man; fit, and imposing. He became a leader of mercenaries during his Minh days by being the worst of the worst. Yet here he was submitting to her like one of her devoted Champa people. She remembered he was much the same on the trail that day, and that was why she had put Jack in his hands for safekeeping. She realized now it was possible Queen Dau Te Po who also cared about Jack, took possession of Martinez that day on the trail to help protect him.

She knew from Kelly and Catherine that he was a very competent security man who was liked by everyone, and his clothing choices claimed a sophisticated mind. Yet before her, he was little more than a fumbling awkward little boy. If it was a performance, it was a humbling one and an academy award winner.

"I know my being at NearNorth Productions, and working as the head of the personal security for Catherine Marsh must be disconcerting for you," he continued. "But I can explain, and I want to assure you I have protected you, and yours, even though I was working for those who plot against you."

"Who would that be," she said, interrupting.

"I work directly for Su Ling, my lady and through her, Hinsu Yameda," he said.

Mai gasped in surprise. "I don't believe you," she said too quickly. "Su Ling is the most amazing woman in…" She stopped herself suddenly hearing her own words recited as they had been to Daniel Vega in Paris several years before. During the intervening time, she did not allow herself to question whether she was indeed programmed by Su Ling with a post-hypnotic suggestion governing her feelings. Every time she attempted to consider it, she got a headache and so, she didn't think about it.

"My lady?" said Ramadi watching her stare at Martinez silently.

"I assure you it is the truth, my lady," continued Martinez, after a moment of silence. "Although I am not sure how I can prove it to you. I confess, I am surprised you accepted my invitation to meet," he said, glancing nervously over his shoulder at Ramadi. "May I ask what persuaded you? It was a desperate last-minute ploy on my part born out of my concern for your safety and that of your family and friends."

Martinez continued to look very uneasy as she remained silent staring through him in thought.

He regarded her silence as a rejection and became despondent. "Oh god! You have to believe me," he said putting out his hands at his sides as he spoke in earnest. Ramadi grabbed him firmly in response to his sudden movement. "Ms. Marsh and Ms. Ryan may be in great danger. You, my lady, may be in great danger. I am sure they are plotting against you."

She looked up at Ramadi who stood aggressively behind Martinez with one hand firmly holding his neck as if he were a puppet. He looked ready to do the worst with him, and his face was asking for permission.

She shook her head ever so slightly toward Ramadi, and then said to Martinez, "Two things in your note persuaded me to meet with you. You addressed me respectfully as 'my lady', and you warned of other operatives within the organization that might be working against us. It was not something I could let pass without investigating. Now I have to convince myself that you speak the truth."

"I am willing to do anything to have you believe me, my lady," he said still kneeling before her. "Please tell me what I must do to convince you. You trust and acceptance means everything to me. I don't know why it is so important to me. It just is."

Mai nodded having seen much the same reaction in others.

"There is a way if you are truly willing to prove the truth of what you say to me. I have the ability to access your thoughts. But I cannot do it unless you open your mind to me, and give me your consent. Fair warning. I will know your every thought, and I will be able to control you from within your own mind after that forever. Are you willing to let me do that?" she asked.

He did not question what she told him but instead answered without hesitation, "Yes, I am an open book to you, my lady. But I have to tell you there are some beastly, and embarrassing things hiding in there. What do I have to do?" he asked.

"Come here on your knees before me, and lay your head on my lap," she commanded him, softly.

"My lady?"

"Kneel here, and rest your head on my lap," she repeated, patting her lap as she did.

Eddie awkwardly knelt forward, and carefully rested his head on her lap ending with a contented smile as he felt her hands rest on his head. He sensed he was home, and safe for the first time in a very long time. Almost as quickly he went into a deep sleep, and Mai went into the state of mind she used to concentrate and focus her abilities.

What she found within the mind of this complicated man was fascinating because it contradicted in many ways what she believed to be true, and yet there was no better evidence than what she found harbored within his memories. He was indeed a very bad man who had done some very bad things in his life. But his past actions were a mixed bag of good and evil born out of compromise and necessity. He was a survivor. He had never intentionally harmed an innocent person and had as he said protected Queen Maisong and those she cared about when given the opportunity. She focused on his time at NearNorth Productions and relived his conflicted mission, and his manner of resolving his differences in her favor. She was surprised as she considered his relationship with Su Ling that she did not get a headache as she had in the past when she tried to reason her own relationship with her. Su Ling's betrayal was laid out clearly before her. Once she had verified that part of his statement she went deeper into his past.

He was orphaned as a child, and like Mai never knew his parents. He struggled all his life, and yet earned a college degree in business. He never had anyone he felt he could trust, and never had anyone that he could call family. Now he was alone, and incomplete, like a discarded canvas longing for an artist to pick it up give it meaning.

Mai found herself surprisingly impressed and intrigued with the story revealed in his memory that was as he said an open book to her. She read his thoughts, and browsed through his memories for over an hour, and then she removed her hands and sat back in thought. Su Ling's betrayal was shocking. But Mai had no doubt now that it was true. In the short time, she had been examining this man she bonded with him, and trusted him. Ironically, as he wished her to save him, he was, in fact, saving Mai and her people. His loyalty to her was absolute, even matchless. She ran her hands gently over his face, and said, "Eddie, wake up please."

Eddie opened his eyes and knelt up quickly in surprise. He looked around showing his confusion. "I must have dozed off...I'm sorry, my lady. I must have been more tired than I thought."

Mai considered the boy-man who knelt before her wanting desperately to come home and to know that everything was going to be OK. She saw the similarity in the burden she undertook as Queen Maisong that her people had placed on her. All of them found in her the spiritual mother that represented their destiny, their reason for living, and their home. Through service to her they found fulfillment. At times it became overwhelming, and this was one of those times.

With the revelations of her mistaken judgment and trust in Su Ling after all these years, she felt her own personal need for reassurance, and to find her own place of refuge. Even as she was the center of the world for her devoted Champa people, Jack was the center of hers. Jack wherever he was represented home for her. More than anything right then she needed to talk to him.

She turned to Ramadi who had stayed patiently nearby for over an hour without a sound, and told him, "Thank you, Ramadi, my dear friend, for protecting me. You may relax. Eddie is one of us now. You needn't be concerned about him anymore. Please get yourself some refreshments, and order lunch for you and your men. Please notify the aircraft we will be delayed another hour or more."

"Sit here, Eddie" she said motioning to another chair at the table near her as Ramadi exited the room to meet with his men outside.

Eddie sat down, and Mai pushed a pitcher of water and an empty glass toward him. "Why don't you call room service. Order lunch for yourself, a small salad for me, and we will talk. Please attend to that while I make a personal phone call."

Mai heard an obedient, "Yes, my lady," as she opened her cell phone and called Jack who was in Egypt at the time recording a new discovery around the ancient Djoser pyramid site. It was a preliminary assignment as he was to return the following year when they were going to actually open the chamber they found nearby. Mai loved that no matter where Jack was in the world, they could talk instantly by phone and they did so several times each day.

With what she had learned from Martinez, she needed to talk to Jack to restore her judgment but surprisingly, when they connected, and he asked how her work was going, she didn't mention a thing about Martinez. She only wanted to hear his voice, as it was, in fact, her personal place where she found safety, and comfort. She felt complete, and whole again as she always did when talking with him.

After a short conversation she informed him, "I am on my way home. Baby, when will you be back in Seam Kulea? I miss you."

"I should be back by the end of the week," he replied. "We are wrapping things up here. I miss you too. Is everything OK? You sound different somehow. You're not coming down with something are you?"

"No, Jack, my health is fine, and everything is OK. I just needed to hear your voice. Ramadi is with me, and we are preparing to return soon. Hurry back, my love," she said.

"I will. Give Devi a great big whopping kiss for me, and tell her daddy will be home soon."

As she said goodbye and hung up, Mai sighed. Her once simple world had become very complicated, and while she welcomed that, and even thrived on it, she fondly remembered the simpler times when they lived that first year with Devi in Chicago before Thap Cham, Colonel Minh, Champas, and everything else that was her world today.

A few minutes later after lunch was delivered and they were settled again, Mai said, "Eddie, the most disturbing information I learned from you was about Su Ling. Tell me what you know about her. She saved my life, so I have never questioned her loyalty."

"Yes, she saved my life also, in a manner of speaking. She and Yameda were within minutes of lopping off my head for their amusement. They had me bound on a stand in a dungeon below Yameda's villa with my head positioned over a drain in the floor. When she ordered them to release me, I was so relieved and grateful, I would have done anything she wanted at the time. I think that situation may have clouded my judgment. I had worked for her when she was with Colonel Minh many years before. We had a good relationship then, and she recognized me. That saved me from death that day.

"In any case," he continued, "and for reasons I don't think even I understand, at the same time I was working for Su Ling, I was still up to my old tricks and routines."

He got up and retrieved his briefcase that was left open after Ramadi checked it when he first entered. "I have a disturbing list of disloyal Champas who serve Su Ling and live in Siem Kulea, my lady. I stole it right from her desk when I was delivering a professor's computer I stole for her that had information on it she wanted. I am afraid that is an old habit of mine, randomly picking up papers in people's offices. It has been beneficial to me on occasion in the past. The fact is, I didn't even look at the papers I had stolen until I came upon them in my things when I arrived in Chicago. I put the list away in the event there might be a need for it in the future. It is just another of a long list of things I have done with a sense of protecting you. There are about one hundred people listed who live in the valley, and three work on your personal household staff."

"You are sure of this, Eddie?" she asked, stunned by his revelation.

"Yes, my lady. You will see the documents are in Su Ling's own handwriting, and she includes comments on each of them.

"Su Ling is the one who assigned me to spy on NearNorth Productions while working for her and Hinsu Yameda. They are lovers and co-conspirators. They are ambitious like old Colonel Minh was. Believe me when I tell you she wants what you have, the Siem Kulea valley, everything. I have heard her refer to you several times with a jealous voice. She wants to take you down and is conspiring to do so. I swear it is true. I wouldn't be surprised if you didn't believe me, my lady. But I am telling you the truth."

"Of course I believe you, Eddie," said Mai. "Your thoughts are open to me. You cannot lie to me now even if you wanted to but that does not make this news any less disturbing. Give me your hand," she said.

Eddie reached out to her, and she took his hand in hers. Holding it firmly she said, "You are home now and one of us. You are mine now, Eddie. Whether you want it, or not, you belong to me and you will discover it is impossible to disobey me. You gave yourself to me when you let me walk your mind. I charge you with continuing your mission to ensure the safety of my family and my friends as you have in the past. Keep me informed about anything in that regard having to do with Su Ling and Hinsu Yameda."

Martinez beamed a smile. "I like that I am serving you now officially. I have been doing that previously in my own way with NNP," he said,

Mai nodded and squeezed his hand showing her approval. "Yes, I know that already. But it is a precarious position to be in and you have been lucky thus far not to be discovered, so we will end that now and see where else they might make use of your talents. I am going to report you as an operative of Hinsu Yameda to Catherine and Kelly. You will flee the area after you leave here today. After you get away, call Su Ling, and tell her your ruse has been discovered. I will be very interested to know her reaction. If she seems calm about it, then we can be fairly certain she has others also working inside NearNorth Productions that are loyal to her."

"Yes, and the one who really worries me is the one who came one night and went away again. I gave him access, but he left almost no sign of his presence, a real professional in every way. I left things arranged in a manner such that I would know if he had shown. What he moved, and returned ever so slightly, told me he had been there, and searched the place thoroughly. That greatly concerned me at the time and I have checked their condo again, and again, since. But it has been about three years, and nothing has turned up."

"So we are thinking maybe two operatives still at NearNorth Productions. Even after you are away you might be able to find out more information about them but never say or do anything that would lend suspicion or question your loyalty," she said.

"Yes, I understand completely," he said.

They talked for another hour over their lunch while Eddie related all he knew about Yameda and Su Ling and their operation. Mai suggested a plan for going forward and Martinez refined a few details. Mai gave him her private cell phone number with instructions to call her at any time with anything of consequence to report. He was to be her eyes and ears inside Yameda's organization.

Mai leaned over and kissed him gently on the cheek. "Welcome home, Eddie. Get out of here, make your escape, and call Su Ling. Call me later and let me know what she says."

Eddie smiled at Mai warmly for a moment and then said, "Thank you, my lady."

Then he got up, retrieved his things and left with a final wave as Ramadi rose and stood before Mai.

"Do you wish us to follow him," he asked.

"No, it's not necessary. He is one of us now. We can trust him completely. You may consider him one of our most loyal, and trusted operatives," she said. "He has awakened me, and for the first time, I can see clearly what I must do.

"Ramadi, there are snakes at the door, and we must move quickly to protect ourselves. Let's get back to Siem Kulea. We have lot's of work to do."

Chapter 17

2001 South of Chicago

One hundred miles south of Chicago, Martinez stopped at a truck stop on US 57, and parked in a remote area of the parking lot. He was a new man now with a new purpose. For the first time in a long time he was feeling good about himself. He loved Queen Maisong, always would, and now his life was in line with those feelings.

It was time to call Su Ling, and tell her he had been discovered. Just before making the call he paused, and collected his thoughts as if ready to assume a part he was playing once again that was familiar territory for him.

He waited a moment while the call passed through international exchanges and finally heard her most private line ring. It was the middle of the night in Asia, but he knew she would expect him to call with such dire news, and he was curious to see if her reaction was as Queen Maisong had predicted.

"Yes, what is it?" Su Ling asked, answering her private phone with some irritation.

"This is Eddie. I am sorry to disturb you, but I knew you would want to know right away. I wanted to let you know as soon as I was able that our good luck is over. They discovered my deception quite by accident three hours ago. I am afraid an old acquaintance of mine showed up in a story Catherine was working on and recognized me. I suspect they are busy right now taking measures to protect themselves. I'm sorry," he said, eager to hear her reaction.

There was an extended silence long enough for him to wonder if she had hung up. But then she said, "No, don't be sorry, Eddie. You have performed well, and even beyond our expectations. We have a much better idea of the situation in Chicago because of you, and can act accordingly. I was about to send you on another mission anyway. Which way are you headed now?" she asked.

"I am on the road about an hour south of Chicago," he said.

"Get to the drop in New York at the Chancellery building that we used for the Professor Wenabe operation. I will have some tickets and IDs there. We are setting up shop in Europe, and I want you in charge of security. That is why I had you learning German over the last year. You have been obeying me on that haven't you?" she asked.

"Ja, meine Dame, es ist immer mein Vergnügen, Ihnen zu gehorchen," he replied.

"That sounded pretty good!" she said. "I can always rely on you, and this has come at an opportune time for us. Take care, my pet. You have done well. I am pleased," she said hanging up the phone abruptly.

Martinez almost sneered at the vacant line on his phone.

He thought for a moment, and then smiled to himself. He was surprised at how good he felt. He flipped open his cell phone, and called the secure line Queen Maisong had given him at the hotel to report what Su Ling had told him.

Chapter 18

2001 Egypt Near the Djoser Pyramid

The small group of archeology students from John Hopkins University listened carefully to their professor, Marty Wenabe, as he explained the significance of the hieroglyphics and symbols they were studying on the walls within the Gisr el-Mudir complex from the second dynasty near Cairo, Egypt. This area of the complex was below ground and got light from a few breaks in the stone ceiling. The group of graduate students were cramped uncomfortably within a small corridor, but that did not seem to bother them. They listened with focused curiosity to every word their professor told them. They were dressed in an assortment of loose cotton shirts and work trousers.

Professor Wenabe had a passion for his work, and these summer trips to Egypt with his students was a favorite part of his year. They made tracings of some of the hieroglyphs on the walls of this ancient temple as he explained, "I think some of these are much older than the time they are generally credited. Come with me. I want to show you something very interesting just up the corridor here."

As they got up to follow him around a corner in the complex, a man came up behind them and introduced himself to one of the students. He was dressed in loose khaki pants, and a cotton shirt, and carried a large camera bag hung over his shoulder, which he necessarily guided through the narrow corridor before him so as not to bump the ancient walls.

He called out, "Professor Wenabe?"

The professor turned back upon hearing his name and looked at the man around the heads of his students. "Yes, I am Professor Wenabe."

"I'm Jack Largent. I'm taking photographs at the new archeological site over at the Djoser pyramid area working with a group from the Museum of Egyptian Antiquities in Cairo. I heard you were asking about me. I wondered if you might be wanting a photographer."

"Oh, Jack Largent. Yes, well, I am glad to meet you. You have gained a good reputation among my colleagues. Call me, Marty, and these are young student archeologists from my graduate class at John Hopkins University," Marty said, motioning to his six eager students.

"Since you are here perhaps you would like to do some photography for me right away. I have something of a curiosity I was just about to show my students. Care to follow?" Marty asked.

"Yes, of course! Lead the way," said Jack.

They made their way to the end of the narrow corridor, and a turn to the right led them through a portico into a more open area inside the ruins. Within was a raised structure of stone at the opposite end. Large stone columns went up twelve feet to a mostly closed stone ceiling above the chamber. There were broken areas here and there in the roof that allowed some daylight into the space.

Professor Wenabe led them to the stone edifice that rose about four feet from the floor at the far end of the open area. It was covered with hieroglyphics and showed a broken section near the bottom revealing its hollow interior. There were symbols beside the broken area, and below the open hole in the structure was more writing, but in a different language.

"This is what I wanted to show you. Note if you will the hole in the stone, and the symbols on either side of the hole, and the inscription below the hole. I think they carry some significance," he said, as his students drew closer to study it.

"It looks to have lost some of its luster, and we're missing some of the message I fear," continued Wenabe. "Mr. Largent, could you possibly get a photograph of it for me? I have had little time to examine this particular inscription, and if I could have a photograph to study, that might be just the thing."

One of the female students remarked, "They look like circles, professor."

"Yes, exactly. But what makes these particular circles even more interesting are the rough hieroglyphics just below them, and then there is the writing below that in still another language. They appear to tell a story, but I have not been able to study them at length, and some of them are too worn to be legible anymore," said Marty.

"I might be able to help with that," said Jack. "I have a small remote flash that I can sync with my camera. If we can have one of your students hold it just down there a ways we can use it as an accent light, and I think it will show the edges of these glyphs. We tried it next door at the Netjerykhet pyramid, and got pretty good results."

He handed the small portable flash to one of the students and directed her to hold it about six feet away pointed toward the edifice. Then he stepped back and took a couple of readings with a small flash meter before beginning to take photographs of the circles and the hieroglyphics. For the next few minutes, Jack photographed the edifice covering all sides but focusing on the area of most interest to the professor. After taking a dozen photos from different angles, he nodded to Marty, and asked, "I think I got it. Is there anything else here you need?"

"Did you get this set of letters along the bottom of the column? You will note they do not match the others." Marty asked.

"Yes, I thought they looked like ancient graffiti," said Jack

"Yes, indeed. Fascinating. Timing is everything isn't it, Mr. Largent. How soon can you get me copies of those photos?" the professor asked, eagerly.

"Oh, well, I know a place in Cairo that will process and proof this roll in an hour, and it is about two hours from here by car. I have been using it on the other site," he said.

"Skip the proofs, Mr. Largent. Can you just make me eight-by-ten inch blowups of each photo, and make sure I can see things clearly in them?" he asked. "I would love to see them later today if that's possible."

"Well, I guess…sure. But what's the rush, professor? This ruin has been here for five thousand years at least," queried Jack.

"I should explain, Mr. Largent. Tomorrow is our last day on this trip. After that, we will all be returning to Boston to continue our studies. I would like to discuss the inscriptions in the photographs you just took as a culminating lesson and to review just how much my stellar students have learned this summer."

Professor Wenabe stepped back and gestured around the ancient room they were in. "This is a very interesting chamber. It was a sacred temple built right below the main temple above, Mr. Largent. Only the priests were allowed here in ancient times."

He motioned to the large hole in the in the bottom of the edifice. "I think something was taken from here, and I am hoping that inscription can tell me what. Of course, it could just be an example of ancient vandalism, but I am working on a theory right now, Mr. Largent, and this may be central to it. I will explain tonight when you bring me the photos; say seven p.m.? I am staying at the Luxor, and they have a fabulous chef at the restaurant there. Perhaps you will join us for dinner?"

"Oh please, Mr. Largent. We would all love to see the photos," one of the young girls pleaded.

"Well, I guess I can't say no," said Jack. "Seven p.m. at the Luxor it is."

"Fine, fine...I will make reservations. See you then," said professor Wenabe.

Jack was a little late when he entered the elegant dining room of the old Luxor Hotel. The maître D´ gave Jack the once over, saw his casual dress, and started to send him away from the ultra-formal, elegant restaurant. But then Jack told him he was with the Marty Wenabe party. The maître D´ grumbled a bit, but then relented, and led Jack into the dimly lit interior of the dining room. Jack noticed those dining were dressed formally and felt immediately out of place. When they arrived at the table, Professor Wenabe stood and put out his hand gesturing to the seat next to his around the eight-place table. The maître D´ gave Jack a menu and a final expression of disapproval before he departed.

"I don't think he likes me," said Jack. He looked a little embarrassed as he glanced around at the six students, and the professor. Jack noted the students were dressed like they were going to a school prom.

The professor was quick to mend his feelings. "Rubbish. A little variety will trim his nose nicely. May I offer you some wine? Since you are here as our honored guest, I can finally bring out the good stuff," said the professor, as he signaled the sommelier over.

After telling the sommelier what he wanted, the professor turned back to Jack, and asked, "What do you have for us? I have to say I am as excited as my crew, and beside myself with anticipation. In truth, Mr. Largent, we all arrived here early for cocktails and have been talking eagerly in anticipation of your arrival. I can't wait to see the photos."

"OK, but all of you call me Jack, please. You make me feel as ancient as the pyramids calling me Mr. Largent," he said.

"Of course, Jack. I am Marty, and this is, Sue, Matt, Harley, Bridge… short for Bridget…Meredith, and David," said Marty, as he watched Jack open up the oversize manila envelope.

"I took the initiative to print a couple of them up to twenty by twenty-four inches, and I think you'll see why," said Jack. "Even I was surprised at the detail that showed up using that extra kicker light."

Marty moved away dishes, and glasses, and stood up as he laid out the large print in front of him. It was magnificently detailed showing every groove of the ancient inscription on the stone edifice. Much of the old paint was worn off, but the carved grooves in the stone still revealed the message well. Marty gave a gasp, and the other students got up from their seats and gathered around him. They began to talk rapidly to each other as each seemed to see one significant ancient hieroglyph and then another that held a meaning for them. They were creating quite a commotion and oblivious to their surroundings when the maître D´ once again returned, and asked them to please respect the atmosphere of the restaurant.

They all but ignored his pleas giving him only a sideways glance as they continued to argue about the meanings of the hieroglyphs in competitive earnest. The maître D´ did not like to be ignored and left sharply to consult with the hotel manager.

Jack who had retreated to a chair opposite the group surrounding Marty watched the body language of the maître D´ while he was talking to the manager, and it did not bode well for them. He got up and went over to talk to both of them before things got troublesome for his new friends. He deftly passed them a hundred dollar bill each, and said, "I sincerely apologize for my friends. They have made an amazing discovery out by the Gisr el-Mudir complex today, and that is why they are so excited. This is a large hotel. Do you think that perhaps we can be served in a private dining room? I think we are going to be quite loud with further discussion of what they have found, and we don't want to make any disturbance or cause you any trouble. I really would appreciate it, and I think it will resolve all of our concerns."

The manager smiled in agreement, snapped his fingers, and a bellboy materialized instantly.

Ten minutes later they were ensconced in a private dining room that over-looked the Nile River and were continuing their boisterous conversation, which evolved into more of a debate. Professor Wenabe guided their discourse to areas of further investigation, and the six enthusiastic scholars took notes, and argued their ideas and theories. Marty asked for some presentation materials with more money passing hands, and a bellboy soon arrived with a large marker board, tape, and poster-size paper that quickly filled with hieroglyphs, and interpretations.

Fascinated by the energy level, Jack sat back and watched. Their eager-ness and passion were invigorating. They worked until past midnight and fit their gourmet dinner in as an afterthought blended within the animated conversation. Finally, Marty told all of them to leave with instructions to meet at breakfast in the dining room at seven.

When they were gone the room seemed eerily quiet. Marty poured himself a glass of wine and joined Jack who was sitting alone nursing a glass of his own on the balcony watching the Feluccas make their peaceful way down the Nile under the full moon.

He sat down, and said, "I can't thank you enough, Jack. It was fortuitous that we ran into you today. Honestly, your photographs made this whole trip worthwhile and a rewarding experience for all involved. You saw the reaction tonight of my learned students as they knowledgeably argued their ideas with one another. It was wonderful for me to see, and a fitting close to this exercise. I am very proud of them."

"You all seemed very excited in there, but I only got a little of it," said Jack. "I'm happy I could help. Frankly, I don't think I have seen that level of enthusiasm over any of my archeological photographs before."

"What do you think you heard, Jack?" asked Marty.

"Honestly, I felt like a bit of an intruder so I made myself scarce and opted for a more peaceful night enjoying the view of the river from this balcony. But I think I heard some discussion about the ancient Assyrians which I found inter-esting, what I heard of it, because those photos are from an Egyptian temple. I didn't get much, and what I did hear, kind of ran together for me," he explained.

"Yes, we spent a great deal of time talking about the Assyrian conquest of Egypt. That might just be the key to everything, Jack. You have to understand that the Assyrians at that time were the most powerful nation in the area. Their army developed the horse in warfare. Imagine what it would be like if you were a foot soldier to face an army that was all on horseback. They were the first to use chariots in warfare too. They were ruthless and cruel conquerors of other nations, and that is how they subjugated and held so many diverse tribes together for so long. People of the surrounding nations feared them and most succumbed to their dominance. This lasted for two hundred years and was the beginning of the great empires in the Western world.

"To illustrate my point, there is one story about King Ashurbanipal who had just conquered a rebellious Elamite king. He hung the pickled head of the Elamite king on a wall in his bed chambers while night after night he made love to the conquered Elamite queen. That story presents a vivid picture and mindset of the time. "Around 671 BCE, the Assyrians conquered Egypt. They had tried before and been defeated, but this time with their new battle technologies they were successful, and they sacked Egypt and carried it all back to Nineveh, their new capital. That is why I was excited by the writing below the hole in that edifice, which you photographed in the temple. I couldn't see enough of it before to be sure of what language it was. But I suspected it might be Assyrian, and you helped me prove it."

"So you think there was an object in that structure in the temple that was taken away by the Assyrians. But why would they do that? Was it made of gold or something?" asked Jack.

"I don't know. I don't even know what it looks like. But if it were impressive enough, they would have taken it back to their capital either for its value, or because they believed it was an Egyptian god. The ancients believed that a city could not be rebuilt if they took away their gods, so it was a common practice to carry away a conquered nation's symbols of their gods," explained Marty. "The edifice you photographed got my attention originally because of the circles. The mystery of the hole and the ancient writing around it furthered my interest."

"Ah, yes, the circles. You mentioned them before. Why are they so important to you?" asked Jack.

The professors expression changed and became more serious as he asked, "Jack, have you seen those concentric circles before?"

"Well, I have, professor, but it doesn't mean anything. Nothing to do with here I'm sure," said Jack.

"But it could, Jack. It could be very important. It just might all be connected. Those concentric circles can be found all over the world in almost every culture in some form. I have seen them in China, Central America,

Iraq, India, and now, here. Where did you see them before, if you don't mind me asking?"

"Marty I come from a small valley in Northern Cambodia that dates back thousands of years. I suspect someone with your background would find a lot to work with there. I have to admit I'm hesitant to tell you where I saw those circles," said Jack

"Siem Kulea," said Marty.

"You knew?" asked Jack, surprised.

"I have not been completely honest with you, Jack," confessed Marty. "Word got around quickly in my profession that the photographer who had created the magnificent photographs of the treasure from Thap Cham was branching out, and was available to photograph other archeological sites. By the way, those were excellent photographs, and probably the best ever taken of any treasure collection. I suspect by that effort alone you have received many offers to join archeological sites from my colleagues."

"I am proud to say I received many offers, more than I could possibly accept. That part was entirely unexpected. I have to admit I really like doing this kind of photography after being an advertising photographer for many years. But please, continue. I want to know just how you know about Siem Kulea," said Jack.

"When word went out about your career change, I was already informed, and interested in that find at Thap Cham, and the woman who found the treasure after so many centuries. Indeed, I have read the books written by Catherine Marsh and found out as much as I could about Maisong Sambath Largent, the Champa queen. I admit I am still fascinated on both a professional and personal level with the whole story. I have studied the Champa legend, and I know these circles are significant. What I don't know is why. But you helped clarify a couple of points.

"Our meeting today wasn't entirely coincidental. I knew you were working on the Djoser pyramid site and arranged our outing this summer to be nearby on the off chance I might find an opportunity to get together with you. That is something I have not been able to do since we are usually on opposite sides of the world. As our time here was ending, I arranged for you to get word that I was looking for a photographer."

"I don't understand why you didn't just call us, and ask to come to Siem Kulea, and meet with us," said Jack.

"Sometimes I am too clever for my own good. Many years ago when I was in Southeast Asia, I met a very resourceful man who explained to me that Siem Kulea was much like a fortress for the protection of Queen Maisong and that no outsider could go there. I have spent many years thinking of ways to get you, or Queen Maisong, to invite me to your paradise valley."

"The valley *is* well protected, and frankly Mai would probably have said no to your inquiry. She shuns publicity. Where are you going with all of this?" asked Jack.

"Jack, these circles are connected with an ancient race, and I think they were alien from another world entirely. I know. It sounds crazy, and I admit I thought so myself at first. But there is one person on this planet that refutes that. You know who I am speaking of, don't you?" he argued.

"Mai," said Jack softly. "You think Mai is connected.

But then Jack shook his head firmly in denial. "Look, Marty, Mai is just Mai. She is brilliant in many ways, but a real bumblefuck in others. In any case, I will not talk about her. Sorry. My private life is off limits. I will have to insist."

"I suspected that would be your answer, Jack," Marty said, affably. "I am hoping you will carry my request to her, and let Queen Maisong decide if she will talk to me. I would love to meet her and talk with her. I didn't expect you to say yes, and I am not in any kind of hurry. Get to know me first, and you'll see that I'm not a threat of any sort. This is a professional and entirely personal curiosity, and it isn't my intention to publish anything concerning this topic.

"But, Jack, you should know that there is someone else investigating this, and they are moving faster than I am. If I'm right, Queen Maisong needs to be warned, and protected."

"What did the hieroglyphs say?" asked Jack, quietly getting more anxious.

"I did not tell my students, but in their entirety, they seemed to indicate that the ancients might have been able to control the weather, and the means to do that was somehow contained inside that edifice. It is just a theory so far and a hopeful one at that. I really don't know for sure where this is going," Marty explained.

"So you think this ancient race that might be aliens had some means of controlling the weather. Do you mean here in Egypt or everywhere?" asked Jack.

"I think they were able to control the weather around the world, Jack. I believe the means to do that is still around and we can find it. We just need to look for these circles and find what was taken from that structure in the chamber. I have some ideas about that already based on what we found here. But you didn't answer my question, Jack. Where have you seen these circles?"

"Trust me, Marty, it can't be connected," answered Jack.

"How can I know that unless you tell me," Marty argued, smiling.

Jack got up, poured himself another glass of wine, and handed the bottle to Marty. "I saw them on the door to my wife's chambers in Siem Kulea, Marty, along with a seven-headed snake. I am afraid when I saw it the first time, I overreacted, and embarrassed Mai, and myself. It was not one of my better moments."

Turning toward the view of the Nile River Marty pondered this new revelation. "Seven-headed snake, you say? That's the Naga, Jack. I never made that connection with the circles before. But of course, the Naga is endemic to Southeast Asia. Fascinating."

"Marty, who are these people that you say are investigating this thing? Are you just guessing, or do you have hard evidence there is someone else looking into this theory of yours?" asked Jack.

He turned back to answer Jack's question with some background. "You don't need evidence. They are not trying to hide the fact they are getting involved, at least not from me. Early in the spring several years ago, I returned late from one of my classes and found my home office had been ransacked. I was devastated because they took my computer—took the whole tower. I couldn't figure it out until I realized all of my files and papers on Queen Maisong, the circles, and the Champas, were missing. The only saving grace was that I am meticulous about backing up my files, and they did not find that hard drive, which I kept in another location. But, Jack, I had extensive files and information about Queen Maisong, the Champa heritage, and legend. I feel that I know Queen Maisong as well as anyone, and now I am sure they do too."

"Who are these people, Marty? Who is doing this?" asked Jack.

Marty looked over, and pointed a finger toward him as if to say, "Hold that thought, I'm not done." He continued his narrative. "They left me a card right on my desk. Written on the back was a note that said, 'Don't call the police. We will return all of your files soon, and you will be greatly rewarded for your silence.' One month later, they returned everything. I had even put in a superior alarm system by that time, and it apparently was no deterrent to them. I returned home as before and found everything on my desk. There was an envelope containing twenty thousand dollars cash, and a note saying it was for consultation fees. There was another card with a telephone number on it promising another twenty thousand dollars, if I would meet with them. I called and ended up talking to a woman who said her associate wanted to meet me in person. I had a seminar in New York the next weekend, which she already knew about, and she asked if I would be willing to meet her associate for dinner while I was there. Purely out of curiosity, I agreed. I was determined to give her associate a piece of my mind. Of course, I also wanted to find out what was going on, and to collect another handsome consulting fee. However, I informed her that I would not meet unless she told me right then the name of her mysterious associate. She said his name was Hinsu Yameda, and that he was the CEO of Asian World Investments."

Jack almost dropped his glass. He looked over sharply at Marty and got up. He began pacing as Marty continued to relate his story. "He turned out to be a very cordial, and charming man, and we had a delightful meeting. I daresay we shared an ardent mutual interest in the ancients. We talked all through drinks, and dinner. By the time he left, I was embarrassed to discover I did not know much more about him than when I started. He had masterfully guided our conversation to my own efforts and ideas on the topic. I have to say I fell right into his agenda for the evening. Of that I am certain. I'm afraid I always fall prey to flattery, and compliments about my work. You can readily ascertain I am not the best investigator in situations such as that. But that is the very reason I wanted to meet with you. The more I know about Queen Maisong, the more I want to protect her, and I am confident this Yameda character is up to no good," said Marty.

"You can bet on that, Marty. But he must have told you something or given you some clue about what he knew, or where he was going next with this. Anything come to mind?"

"I am afraid I mentioned to him that China had discovered a very interesting ancient site in the mountains when they were searching for rare minerals. I heard about it through our professional grapevine. They were telling the world it was an ancient Chinese site. When I heard about it I immediately asked to visit the site, and they turned me down. I don't think

Yameda with his connections would have much of a problem going there. Their discovery was about five years ago, and I have no doubt he has already investigated that lead. It might be an important find if my calculations are correct," said Marty.

"And Yameda has all of your calculations?" asked Jack.

"Well, not exactly. I didn't have everything written down in my papers. Come here a minute…let me show you," he said.

They got up and went back to the table in the private dining room, and Marty began drawing a rough map of Europe, and Asia on the whiteboard.

"This is how I see it," he said, as he marked an X in certain spots from Egypt in an Easterly direction. "We are here in Egypt. I suspect there is a site up in Europe, perhaps in France or England. But if we include a site in Iraq that I know about, one in India, and the one in China, and connect them like this," he said as he drew a line between each site forming a zigzag pattern up to China.

"Can you see where the next site might be located, Jack, following the same pattern?" Marty asked.

"Yeah, Siem Kulea," Jack answered. "So you think there are these sites all around the world, and that ancients used them to control the weather "and since you think Mai is descended from these ancients, you think there must be something at Siem Kulea, and she might know about it."

Marty drew a final line from the China site down to Siem Kulea making a nice zigzag line from Egypt. Putting his marker down he said, "I don't think that is a coincidence. But I am pretty impressed, Jack. You're a quick study."

"I get that from hanging around Mai," Jack answered. "But if you are correct they will want to get into Siem Kulea. Do you think Yameda has figured this out?"

"No clue, Jack. But that is precisely what I wanted to talk to you about. What do you think?"

"I have a bad feeling, Marty, a real bad feeling. I think it is time you met my wife. I frankly can't and won't talk about her with you, and I am sure she will want to pick your brain about what you know. When will your work be done here?"

"I will finish up tomorrow. As I said this morning, timing is everything. I will send the kids home on a separate plane, and we can head to Siem Kulea the following day. That is, if you are inviting me to visit?" asked Marty.

Chapter 18

2001   Siem Kulea, Northern Cambodia

Mai arrived late from Chicago insisting that she be flown straight to Siem Kulea without an overnight stay in Hanoi as was the usual routine. As she walked into the back of the White Palace, she encountered the doors to her chambers, the snake doors, which had caused so much ruckus when they first returned nine years ago.

This time, free from the influence of Su Ling, she saw them from a completely different perspective. "Oh, Jack, my darling. I'm so sorry. Oh my God! What was I thinking?" For the first time she understood why Jack had reacted as he did, and she realized why she had been so wrong these many years. It was ironic that she was looking at the physical embodiment of the warning she had expressed to Ramadi not even twenty-four hours ago in Chicago. The doors were a physical representation of Su Ling and everything evil she was conspiring to do to Mai and her people.

When morning came, Mai was still awake sitting at her desk dressed as she was the night before. But her work through the night had produced positive results. She felt born again, clean and fresh. She was ready to set about carrying that feeling to the rest of the valley.

She was without any sleep when her handmaiden Ceva who had stayed up with her all night interrupted her contemplation. "We are preparing your wardrobe. Will Your Majesty be sleeping or working in the fields this morning?"

"Neither, Ceva," she answered. "Please tell Ramadi, Fetu, and Chu that I wish to meet with them in the conference room at eight," she commanded. "Where is Su Ling this morning?"

"I am not sure, my lady," replied Ceva. "I was informed she has been absent from the valley for at least two weeks. I am told she was away the entire time we were in Chicago."

"Who has been in charge in my absence?" asked Mai.

"As always, my lady, Chu has managed the palace very well. She sets a wonderful example for us, and we all depend on her guidance. I hope I am not speaking out of turn when I say we would be lost without her very skilled and organized management abilities."

"Thank you, Ceva. Please, carry my message to my security team and tell my handmaidens I am ready to bathe," she commanded, with a smile. Mai was anxious to initiate her plans and the changes that would truly make her valley a paradise.

She was twenty minutes late when she entered the conference room from her private quarters having dozed off in her bath for a bit. Ramadi, Fetu, and Chu immediately rose and bowed their heads. They all had pads and folders lying on the table in front of them because they were fully aware this was to be a very important meeting. Mai had a particular reason for asking her staff manager, Chu, to attend the meeting, even before the affirmation from Ceva. She sat down and collected her thoughts while arranging her papers in the sequence she wished to present.

After her prolonged and relaxing bath, Queen Maisong had changed into a teal áo dài with the base embroidered in gold Hoa Cuc flowers. She looked fresh, stunning, and regal as usual. Her presence bolstered their sprits, and that was a good thing because she began the meeting with the bad news first.

"I have been up all night working on a plan for dealing with a problem we recently discovered that exists in Siem Kulea. Focus your attention on what I am about to say for my decision on this must be obeyed with utmost dispatch and discretion," said Mai, looking at Chu who was already leaning forward concentrating on the words of her queen. "Su Ling shall no longer hold the awarded title of *Lady* where Champas dwell and obey the Hoa Cuc. In fact, from this day she is in disgrace and a non-citizen within the Champa world. I have indisputable evidence she has betrayed us and is responsible for a traitorous conspiracy planned against our people. She has as her ambition the overthrow of my rule as queen of the Champa people. Further, she along with Hinsu Yameda of Asian World Investments, have been conspiring against my friends, and their financial interests in an ongoing attempt to bring us to ruin.

"I have included Chu in our meeting because I am this moment promoting her to *Lady Chu*, and putting her in command of the valley when I am away. Ramadi, you and Fetu still have the responsibility for security, but Lady Chu must approve any major decisions. I want to make this clear. Lady Chu's word is the final say when I am gone from the valley. I have been too long in making this well-deserved appointment, Lady Chu. I want you to know that your exemplary work has not gone unnoticed by your queen. Ramadi and Fetu, I love and respect you, and even think of you as family, but Lady Chu has a mindset that in every way is more like my own than anyone in the valley. Defer to her. That is my wish in this matter. Am I clear?"

The two security men nodded, and Ramadi said, "Lady Chu, you can be certain of our loyalty, and we are ready to assist you in any way you need. We have been consulting and functioning as Lady Chu suggests for many years already so this will be an easy transition for us."

Lady Chu nodded to them and smiled. "Your Majesty, I am honored by your confidence in me. I always strive to do my best for your safety, comfort, and pleasure. I have the highest regard for my dear friends Ramadi and Fetu. We work very well together, and I look forward to continuing our effort to ensure the safety and security of our valley."

"I know, Lady Chu," said Mai. "I sense a positive, benevolent, and well-organized spirit within you, and that is the sort of leadership I want for my people. Now, you are charged with managing everyone in the valley, not just my household. I will make the announcement this morning. I want you to begin circulating immediately to build a network of loyal followers from which we can have a constant feel for the pulse of Siem Kulea. I am this morning declaring a new birth, a new beginning, and new life for my Champa people. We will be looking forward, and growing with the universe in a positive way."

She gave Ramadi a folder with copies of the list Martinez had given her of disloyal Champas in the valley, and Ramadi passed copies to the others sitting at the table.

"Ramadi, Fetu, and I have already discussed this extensively on the flight back from Chicago. What you see before you is my formal ruling on this matter. I have it on very reliable evidence that there are a number of those living in the valley that are disloyal and conspiring with Su Ling against me. They will be apprehended after this meeting and held for questioning. I want this done quickly with as little notice as possible," Mai began.

Chu nodded in affirmation and showed no surprise at this command, almost as if she expected it.

"What are these lists about, my lady," Lady Chu asked. "Are these the ones you want to join in this effort?"

"Quite the opposite, Lady Chu," Mai said. "Those listed are traitors to me and the Champa people."

"Oh no, my lady, it cannot be!" exclaimed Lady Chu, looking at the three 'traitors' listed from within the palace staff. "An Li has been most loyal since your return to the valley. I depend on her greatly for all that we do. She is one of your most loyal and devoted servants. This is indeed very troubling," she said, as she considered the list.

"Those three staff members listed at the top of this list are loyal to Su Ling, and I want them arrested first, the moment we finish this meeting. Is that clear?" she asked them.

"Yes, Your Majesty," said Lady Chu, looking at the two security men. "It is a sad day for Siem Kulea, I think."

"Lady Chu, I hope I haven't misjudged you," said Mai. "You can have no compassion for those who conspire against us. Your only consideration should be the ultimate safety of my family, my people and me. If that is something you are not willing to do in a most relentless and thorough manner, then I must find someone else. I thought you were of a particular mindset that saw things in black and white especially when it concerns the safety of your queen."

"Indeed, Your Majesty," said Lady Chu. "I have no feelings for those on this list, only the traditions of the valley and our Champa people. I have known for some time that Su Ling was a snake in the flesh, and I did all I could to be certain her ambitions brought you and yours no harm. Those that are loyal to her deserve worse than death in my view."

"Yet you said nothing to me of this knowledge or your concerns?" asked Mai.

"Your feelings toward Su Ling were well known by everyone in the valley, my lady. Her influence over you was obvious. Many nights she even shared your bed. Would you have listened to me if I had done so? I thought it better to watch out for your well being from my position as supervisor of your staff until the situation changed. I confess it was most difficult for me to say nothing, but I always had the eyes of my personal staff watching out for Your Majesty and Princess Devearney," she explained.

Mai nodded, and put out her hand to Lady Chu who took it and kissed it. "You have my ear now, Lady Chu, second to none but my family. Indeed you are commanded to consult with me at any time you think it's necessary. Thank you for protecting my family, and me, even when I was blind to the evil among us.

"Now, back to business. The three presently working within the Palace will be arrested first, and kept separated until they are questioned. I will conduct the interrogation myself so that they can have no secrets from us. Lady Chu, if An Li is indeed loyal as you say, then I will know.

"What of the others—there must be a hundred or so on this list, my lady? Have you decided how and where you wish to examine them?" asked Fetu.

"I am told these people are loyal to Su Ling and are her hand-picked followers. I am not sure they are even Champa. Arrest them, move them up to the work camp, and put them in cells under guard until I can interview them. Do so quietly and with as little notice as possible. Do not mention to anyone what we are doing. If anyone asks, say only they are performing a special task for me. My people will kill them if they find out we suspect they are disloyal. In a few days, they will either be returned to their homes, or ejected from the valley. Only after they have been ejected, will you post their names as traitors. Understood?"

She looked at each of them in turn, and they nodded in affirmation.

"What about Su Ling, Your Majesty? What are we to do with her?" asked Ramadi.

"She does not exist for me anymore. Short of death, do anything you wish. I want nothing further to do with her. Be certain that she is not allowed into my valley. She is not now, and has never been one of us."

Ramadi nodded for he felt this order was long overdue, and it was a command he would gladly obey because like Lady Chu he had noted many of the disloyal actions of Su Ling through the years many of which brought him unrequited anger.

"Lady Chu, you will this day move into the villa formerly occupied by Su Ling. All of her possessions are yours to keep or dispose of as you wish including her jewelry. After we complete the round up of the possible traitors, we will announce that she is a non-person, to be shunned and held in disgrace by all Champa people.

"Her handmaidens, are to be taken with the others up to the work farm until I can examine them. If Hata is there, I want her kept separate from the rest like the three from the palace. I have a very personal session planned for her. Ramadi and Fetu, we still have a long overdue duty to get to the bottom of Cavil's death and this is the perfect time to find out who and why? I suspect Hata will have all the answers we need and if I am right, she will be disposed of first.

"Lady Chu, I want you to increase your staff, and select as many handmaidens, and assistants, as you need. I am aware that everyone looks to you when governing, organizational, or logistical decisions are made. This really is only a formalization of your authority, and well deserved it is," Mai said. "You are free to reorganize the palace as you wish to support your organizational needs."

Mai took a deep breath, resettled herself in her seat, and gave them a big smile. "And now the good news, the news of the glorious rebirth of our Champa nation with a positive vision for our future." Mai passed another paper to each of them. It was a formal declaration of the rebirth of their Champa Faith.

"This Declaration will be reproduced and posted throughout the valley. Every one of my Champa people will this weekend rededicate their lives to me, and to each other in our Champa family as we go forward. This weekend I want my Champa faithful before me as they were the day I arrived in the valley. Together we will reaffirm our faith and the bond we have for each other.

"From this day forward, there will be no further reference, or veneration of the Nagani in snake form as a symbol of our people, and their queen. Only the Hoa Cuc will exist as the sacred symbol of their queen. The Nagani seven-headed snake is a negative symbol, an icon of bad energy and backward thinking. No more. The Hoa Cuc is bright and glorious, and the only proper, and true symbol of our people, our faith, and myself. All representations of the Nagani symbol as snakes are to be removed and destroyed.

Metal will be melted, wood will be burned, and stone will be crushed. Lady Chu, incorporate all Champa faithful in this from within and without the valley. Make it a celebration culminating on Saturday, when we will reaffirm our faith and commitment to one another.

"You will immediately remove the doors to my chambers, and the headboard above my bed, and melt them down. Make it part of the joyous celebration honoring the Hoa Cuc and our Champa faith.

"Set the metal smiths to making new doors for my chambers festooned with Hoa Cuc symbols over concentric circles like the ones that decorate my crown. That is the positive image I want for us as we move forward. In like manner, I will personally pay for new doors for every Champa household that will incorporate the Hoa Cuc image as a sign of their devotion and faith.

Lady Chu interrupted, "My lady, may I respectfully suggest we spend today removing the traitors from our midst and begin the transformation, and rebirth of Siem Kulea on the morrow?"

Mai smiled and nodded. "You may indeed. Thank you. Ramadi and Fetu, go clean up our valley and move the traitors up to the work camp. Do so as discreetly as possible. Start with the three on the Palace staff. Have An Li brought to me immediately. Lady Chu and I will interview her together."

After they left, Mai turned to Lady Chu sitting beside her, and said, "When I returned last night I went to your room while you were asleep, and examined you. I found a most loyal and obedient servant, Lady Chu, with a mindset dedicated to Champa traditions. That is exactly the person I need right now to move forward with my plan for a new Champa nation. Did you have notice of me doing that?"

"Yes, I think I did, my lady. That explains some feelings I've had," said Lady Chu, smiling. "Last night as I slept I felt you were with me asking questions, and spending time talking with me. It was a truly wonderful dream, and yet, it seemed more than a dream."

"I walked around your mind, Lady Chu. Now, with your permission, I am going to take possession of you. I will if I wish, know every thought you have ever had. Your world will center on the welfare of your queen, my family, and my people, as the most devoted follower in my realm," said Mai.

"My lady, I can assure you I have always done my very best to be worthy and the person of whom you speak. At present, you already possess me, heart, mind, and soul."

"Yes, I am aware of this," said Mai. "But I have something new and more expansive that I would like to try and perfect with you as I try to take this ability to the next level. When I am away from here, I would like to be able to see through your eyes that my people are safe, and know how you are acting to protect them as their leader in my absence. This will allow us to be closer, but it will take some time before we can reach such perfection as I desire. Kneel before me, and lay your head in my lap," Mai commanded.

Lady Chu did so quickly, and Mai placed her hands on her head gently. "You should know that I am joined in mind and spirit with the great Queen Dau Te Po and through her I have discovered powers and abilities I am still learning to use. This is one of those abilities. If you are agreeable that I take possession of you, Lady Chu, open your mind to me," she commanded, as Lady Chu closed her eyes.

Mai was surprised when she accessed Lady Chu's inner self because her thoughts from the moment she was born were of serving her queenly goddess. She was fascinated as she explored the subconscious mind of this loyal and devoted Champa woman. Mai found herself admiring Lady Chu in a way she had not expected. If anything, Lady Chu was even more Champa in faith, and beliefs than she was. Mai regretted she had not done this sooner. It was time lost she was going to make up with her over the coming years. She educated Chu's consciousness while she was within to be able to begin conversing in Mindspeak and then she exited, careful to not alter the perfection of Lady Chu's mind.

"OK, come back to me," said Mai, holding Lady Chu's head in her hands. "Please sit with me again.

"How do you feel?" asked Mai.

"I feel happy, Your Majesty, no…euphoric, is a more accurate description," she answered. "You cannot imagine what being in your presence means to me."

"OK, now listen carefully," said Mai.

Then without speaking, Mai said, "This is Mindspeak. Can you hear me? If you can, try answering with your thoughts only."

"Hmmm yes, my lady…Yes!" answered Lady Chu without moving her lips but focusing her eyes quickly on her goddess queen.

"You and I will work on this daily. I am hoping we will eventually be able to converse at great distances. I hope to eventually achieve such perfection. I am also going to try to see with your eyes. I am told by my counterpart, Queen Dau Te Po, this is possible. I have not been able to do that yet, but I am learning. Lady Chu, are you truly OK with allowing me do this with you?"

"Yes, of course, my lady. I am first and foremost your servant to do with as you please. But I confess I am most honored by being chosen by you to be used in this manner. I have always felt that you were with me, and now you truly are. It is an amazing feeling."

"OK, see if An Li is waiting outside," Mai said smiling. "I will examine her right away so that if she is innocent, she can assist you with all of the changes we are making in the next few days."

An Li entered, came before Queen Mai, and knelt at her feet. She looked up with a concerned face as she asked, "You sent for me, my lady?" Lady Chu took a seat at the table and waited, hopeful for a positive examination of her close assistant and friend.

Mai commanded her to rest her head on her lap and was surprised that An Li did so instantly and eagerly. She put her hands on her head and began the examination.

It took longer than usual because Mai found only complete devotion, and loyalty within, and she had to go back many years to discover why Su Ling counted her among her supposed loyal minions. The reason was a simple clerical error. When she petitioned to serve in the valley, she wrote her name as Li An Te. An assistant of Su Ling's assigned to gather those on the list loyal to Su Ling, mistakenly misread her name, sought her out, and added her to the servants in the Palace. She recorded her name as An Li, and that was what everyone called her from that point forward. The real An Li, the one loyal to Su Ling, apparently went away and was never heard from again.

Mai took a deep breath, and removed her hands from the head of An Li and said to Lady Chu, "You are right about her, I am happy to say."

Mai got up, pulled An Li to standing, and gave her a hug. Afterward, she headed for her quarters to get some much-needed rest.

"Chu, what just happened?" asked An Li, after Mai had left.

"You will be the first to know that I am now Lady Chu having been honored by Queen Maisong. You will be my right hand, An Li. My lady found you most worthy. Come now, we have lots to do," she said.

As Lady Chu was walking toward the kitchen, she heard Queen Mai talking to her. *"As we go through our day I will be Mindspeaking with you. If you have something important you wish to tell me, do so through Mindspeak. Even if we are in the same room, use Mindspeak unless what you say is meant to be heard by all."*

Then a moment later, *"Lady Chu, you will tell no one any of this. No one must know that you and I can communicate as we do. Please spread the word that I will have an announcement from the front steps of the palace two hours after sunrise in the morning."*

A moment passed, and then Mai heard, *"Yes, my lady,"* in her thoughts.

Chapter 19

2001   Siem Kulea, Northern Cambodia

There was an election the previous year in Cambodia, and the United People's Party not having gained a majority, secured control of parliament by forming an alliance with the Freedom party. The president was Chunh Ye, but he was mostly a figurehead. Although there was an existing monarchy dating from ancient times, the monarch was also a figurehead like the president and had no power, or influence within the government.

The real head of the government was General Rhee Sonh, the assistant president and head of the United People's Party. He was also the senior General of the Cambodian military. He moved quickly to consolidate his power through a series of arrests and assassinations. General Rhee was the ruler of the country, and he controlled every part of it, except for one particular mountain valley in Northeast Cambodia.

On this day, General Rhee visited the Siem Kulea valley in answer to an open invitation from Mai and Jack. After initial greetings and formalities, they sat down in the palace formal drawing room. The General wore his uniform bedecked with medals, his massive frame straining the buttons over his stomach. He was in his sixties in contrast to his wife who was much younger. She chose for the occasion to wear a turquoise sundress. She was quite beautiful, and Mai made the immediate assumption she was a trophy wife more than a partner. But after a few words, Mai discovered her error in judgment as Chanda acted as a translator for her husband. She was fluent in five languages while her husband spoke only Khmer and a smatter of Thai.

The room was decorated in bright colors accented with many floral arrangements. The servants all wore formal costumes from the time of the old Champa kingdom of a thousand years ago. General Rhee was Khmer by heritage and he was impressed with Queen Mai's preparations for his visit. His normal serious attitude, and stern manner, which made him intimidating and unapproachable, had succumbed soon after arrival to Mai's charms, and the friendliness of the Champa people he met in Siem Kulea. They greeted him like a king, and this was not lost on him, or his adoring young wife.

Mai conversed in Vietnamese because she did not want General Rhee to be aware she could understand and speak Khmer. Chanda translated her words in Khmer to her husband, and Mai noted she did it very well and without bias. When he first greeted Mai, he inquired after her husband. She explained that Jack was in Egypt photographing an archeological site and that he was disappointed he could not be there to meet the legendary General who had finally suppressed the Khmer rebellion. In response, the General reached for her hands and pressed them into his pretending a handshake, but then he ran his hands further up her arms.

Mai was not surprised because she had heard many stories of the philandering General, and his many affairs. He was older now, and considerably overweight, but she could still see why so many women had succumbed to his advances. She gently pulled her hand back, and instead greeted his wife warmly; making it clear to the General she was not interested. She could only imagine how involved their marriage must be, and she found herself desirous of a more personal conversation with Chanda. The General was a bit put off by this gesture because he was used to having his way, particularly with women.

After lunch, they moved to another colorful room in the palace for tea, and when they finally got down to business Mai surprised the General by giving him a gift of a priceless ruby ring. This was matched by a necklace she gave to his wife with similar stones. She explained that these were part of her ancestral heritage and she would be honored if they would accept them as a sign of her friendship and sincerity. They were overwhelmed by these gifts and freely expressed their gratitude.

Mai continued by finally getting down to the reason she had invited the General and his wife to Siem Kulea. She told them that she had strong ties with the Vietnamese and Laotian governments, and they were both desirous of a trade pact with Cambodia. They were hoping she would help them to convince the new government to join them in a formal agreement between the countries.

In short, it promised peace for an area of the world, which had known war for over sixty years. She further explained that Thailand had already expressed interest in signing onto the agreement, and talks were proceeding with the firm backing of China, which had proposed an outline for the idea in the first place. The plan was a part of the growing globalization movement to make Southeast Asia the technical, and manufacturing center of the world.

"It means that you will be a very wealthy man, General, without much more effort than signing your name. More importantly, our Cambodian people will have the ability to join, and even lead the world, in the prosperity of the twenty-first century. There are over one hundred corporations from around the world already looking to open facilities in Southeast Asia. They just need the agreement from the participating governments. You can see that Vietnam has already begun, and is vastly more prosperous than ever in its history. China is undergoing a technological revolution and needs to open factories outside of their country for economic reasons, and they are looking specifically at Cambodia rather than Vietnam. The plans for Cambodia's expansion are many following the Vietnamese example including the enlargement of the port city of Sihanoukville to become the largest port in Southeast Asia." She passed him a sheaf of agreement papers in several languages.

"I have heard many stories about you, Ms. Sambath Largent," General Rhee replied, with Chanda translating as he glanced at the agreements. "I did not expect you would be the negotiator of a trade agreement between our countries. I am quite surprised by this. But on further reflection, I suppose I shouldn't be. You have already charmed and disarmed me, with your valley, and your hospitality. I am sure you leave a similar impression with those less formidable than myself."

"The ruler of the Siem Kulea valley has been a reliable negotiator even between warring nations for thousands of years, General," replied Mai. "I am only the latest version, and I am honored to do so if it will bring prosperity to our people. I find that the surrounding governments truly share in their desire for prosperity for the region, and all of them are eager to discuss such stately matters with me. Because I am not directly involved in any particular state government, they feel free to bounce their ideas off of me, and that has enabled me to become aware of the concerns and particular interests of each. As a consequence, it was easy for me to construct a plan that was advantageous to all of the parties involved. The reception I have received from the other governments has been most positive. Will you consider this agreement?"

"I am intrigued by this, and confess it is something I had not even imagined could happen. If it's as you say, I will do more than consider it. You are a most productive, and charming young lady, Ms. Sambath," he said.

Mai was briefly interrupted as Ramadi entered, and whispered a message into her ear.

As he left, she continued, "General, if I may speak frankly, you have a reputation as being somewhat of a demanding leader. When I first heard this, I was alarmed, but as I always do, I looked into your past, and one item garnered my attention. In the provinces that you personally administer, you spend a great deal of money modernizing production and raising the standard of living for the people residing there. Most importantly, you have invested time and money, into improving the education of the Cambodian people, and that is vital for the new Cambodian twenty-first-century economy. You already have a vision for Cambodia that is centered on the well-being and modernization of its people. I feel very strongly that you and I can work together, and do very well as long as we both respect each other's areas of influence. I want only to live here in my valley with my people in peace. In return, I will do all I can to foster the prosperity of Cambodia and its people along with you. You have evidence of the truth of what I say in the agreement you see before you."

"You would like my government to leave you alone. Is that what you are asking?" General Rhee said, getting to the heart of the matter.

"You speak directly. I find that refreshing. Yes, exactly."

"If I follow your suggestion, you offer to support my government in ruling Cambodia?" he asked.

"Yes, as long as you continue to guarantee the Cambodian people are allowed to grow and prosper, in the new economy we will be building. You must be their champion, General, besides being their ruler," she said.

The General stiffened and became indignant when he sensed he was being skillfully manipulated. His pride spoke next while Chanda continued to translate. "I think you should want to be more respectful when speaking to me, the supreme leader of Cambodia. I am not one to be told what to do, nor will I be toyed with, or manipulated by any of my people."

Mai was disappointed, but she expected this reaction to what she considered positive encouragement to sign the agreement she had outlined for him. She was already aware that he came to Siem Kulea prepared with his own agenda, which planned to present it to her as an ultimatum.

General Rhee perceived he could move forward with his plan and still have this agreement if he wished, including whatever he wanted to do with Maisong Sambath Largent personally. In truth, he saw this visit as an inspection of the valley that would soon be his property and a personal retreat for him and Chanda. Before she could answer, the General continued. "What if I told you, Ms. Sambath Largent, that I have three squadrons of tanks parked just over that mountain with two helicopter squadrons ready to strike this valley?" Chanda looked alarmed and nervous as she translated.

"Then you would be lying, General," Mai replied, bluntly, causing Chanda to sit up straight beside him as she translated in kind. "You have only two squadrons of old Soviet T-54 tanks, and most of them only work part of the time. But I would say that just about now none of them are working because my people have poured our local mash into the engines to ruin them. Even so, you would not be able to get them over my mountains. As for the helicopters, well, come with me, General," she said, motioning them through a doorway outside to the verandah overlooking the valley.

It was a beautiful late afternoon outside as they stood together on the verandah with a number of Champa militia members assembled before them. Mai nodded to Ramadi, and soon four Cambodian soldiers in uniform were brought forward as prisoners and brought to their knees in front of them. When Mai saw what particular militia unit held them as prisoners, she smiled. This was no ordinary militia unit.

"What is the meaning of this?" the General demanded.

"This is my valley, General, and my people protect me and their families who live here with a vengeance. They have their own village council that administers justice and it is without mercy when it comes to the security of this valley and their loved ones.

"These soldiers are members of your advance reconnaissance team, General. I believe they are some of your elite, your best forces. Don't you recognize them? They certainly know who you are," explained Mai. "They were captured trying to come over the west mountains. We followed them after an alert went out of their presence in the area. Soon after that, they were captured, and brought here as you see."

The General only grunted. "I don't know what you are talking about."

"Call off your forces, General. You are being foolish, especially now with knowledge of the agreement I have negotiated for you. The division you have in place ready to attack this valley will all be killed or captured. This is the strongest defended position in Asia, maybe the entire world because the people here act as one to protect us," she explained.

The General looked from the verandah of the palace, and around at the lush green valley replete with exotic flowers of every variety, and could see no sign of any defenses. "Your boast is about to be tested, Ms. Sambath."

"They will all die, General. My people will slaughter them, and then we will come for you. My Champa people are everywhere," she said.

"I am not afraid of you or your people," he said.

"You should be," she said. "Did you happen to notice who it was that captured your men? Take a closer look. They are called the Xua Xamthin. They are a unit made up of very proud women, all grandmothers, and frankly, man for man they are better than your elite. Want a demonstration?"

The General looked at her with disdain, so Mai turned to the prisoners, and spoke to them in Khmer surprising General Rhee and Chanda both, "You men are some of the best of General Rhee's soldiers. You should be proud of that. I will give you your freedom if any of you can defeat any of my militia that holds you captive in hand-to-hand combat. Would any of you like to try?"

The prisoners, still on their knees, looked around unsure of what to do.

Mai continued, as a stunned General Rhee watched, "Please, gentleman, you cannot be afraid. After all, they are only women, and old grandmothers at that. Surely you men can defeat them," she teased.

Ramadi turned around and smiled at her shaking his head.

"Why is your man doing that?" asked General Rhee. "Is this a trick of some kind?"

"No, General," said Mai. "The women living in this valley take its security as seriously as the men. They are all well trained in martial arts. You might say it is a hobby of theirs. Even the men here have trouble defeating them, and they are equally well trained. Your men happen to have been captured by this particular prideful unit, but it does illustrate my point of why attacking this valley would be disastrous for you."

"You can't be serious. They are old women."

"Look closely, General," said Mai. "They are lean and fit. They work hard in the fields every day and train happily after that. These men have threatened the peace of this valley and their families. They want nothing more than to punish them for doing so."

"Get up, you cowards," yelled the General at his soldiers.

All four of the prisoners got up quickly and pointed to different women. Each of the women selected put down their weapons, unhitched their belts and packs, and limbered up a bit before standing before the men.

"Remember, only one of you has to be victorious to gain your freedom. No guns, or knives. The fight will be to the death," Mai said.

The General protested sharply. "You can't do that," he said.

"They are trespassers on my land, General. You condemned them to death when you sent them here without my permission. Even by Cambodian law, I have a right to kill a trespasser," she said. "But in consideration of your protest, I will allow the winner of the contest to decide the fate of the loser."

One of the prisoners charged one of the women before she was ready, but she adroitly sidestepped him and pushed him to the ground. He turned, and got up quickly, like a determined, angry dog, but he was noticeably more cautious the second time. They circled each other, and he attacked again, but the grey-haired woman moved lightly on her feet and deftly parlayed his blows. On his next thrust, she captured his arm, and turned it around behind him sharply, dislocating it and rendering it useless, which brought a painful scream from the man. Deftly bringing him to the ground with a roundhouse kick, she destroyed him bit-by-bit, with kick after kick, until he lay writhing in real pain. Leaving the soldier defeated and broken on the ground, she walked to where she had dropped her equipment. But then the prisoner cursed her from where he lay. She turned, quickly advanced on the suddenly cowering opponent, and without any thought of mercy, stomped her foot into his skull, crushing it, and brutally killing him.

After a pause, her eyes addressed the remaining prisoners. One-by-one the other prisoners knelt back down as before, not wanting to take on the other women. She turned toward Queen Maisong, and calmly stood over the dead prisoner and bowed respectfully.

The women of the Xua Xamthin militia laughed at the prisoners, and talked amongst themselves cheerfully, until their leader brought them to attention with strong words of admonishment.

"I assure you, General," continued Mai, "everyone in this valley is just as capable. Our elite, and prideful senior man unit is called the Hui Hoas. My people are tough and hard, and they take great pride in their military capabilities. But even outside the valley in all directions, thousands of my militia have already organized in the face of your threat. Your division is already surrounded, and targeted, before you even try to move against us. Now as to your helicopters…" she nodded to Ramadi who said something into his lapel microphone. Within a minute they heard the buzz of an engine overhead. It was a small pilotless drone used mainly for target shooting. In a few seconds out of the jungle rose a rocket that swept up and destroyed the aircraft.

Mai walked over to the stunned General and took his hand. "Now we can truly talk about our options," she said, as she led him and Chanda back to the meeting room.

Fresh appetizers and drinks had been served for them. "I heard you prefer gin and tonic, General. I suspect you could use a drink about right now," Mai said, smiling.

General Rhee sat down, took a drink, and then sat staring off in thought. Mai took the time to offer his young wife Chanda a glass of her favorite wine, for which she seemed most grateful, and eagerly sipped.

"We have found two more teams of four on other mountains around the valley, General. I believe we have captured all of your reconnaissance teams. They will all be executed. I leave that determination up to my people, and they will insist on it. I will not interfere with their traditions and eagerness to protect our valley. It will not be pretty. They are a peace-loving people but they can be beastly when someone threatens me, or their homeland. Please understand, General. My people were scattered over Southeast Asia for a thousand years. Now they are one people again, and this valley symbolizes home to them. They will defend it with everything they have."

Still, the General sat, silent in thought.

Mai continued, "General, two months after you were elected, you proposed in secret to your poorly trained and inept military, a policy to annex

Siem Kulea. I heard about that proposal the same day. We have known of your planning, preparations, and even your execution the moment they happened. My people are everywhere mixed amongst the nations of Southeast Asia, and they are at this moment focused on you. If you threaten my people or me, you and those you care about will be killed. I am not your enemy, General, unless you make me one. I assure you, I would rather be your friend and see Cambodia prosper under your rule.

"If you continue to oppose me," she further explained, "I will declare independence and join Vietnam as a province. Since my valley is only five miles from the border, it will be easy to do. I will annex the land between my valley and the border in the process and there is simply nothing you could do about it."

She held out her hand to his wife, and said, "The document is written in Khmer so you can easily read it. Since you won't need Chanda to translate, she and I are going to go on a tour of the grounds while you read the agreement. When we return, I will expect a signed preliminary agreement from you showing your commitment to move forward with these negotiations. Oh, and don't forget to call off your assault. I believe it was to start at dawn tomorrow. I already have your forces targeted, General. They will be destroyed in place if they begin to move. Call them," she suggested, as she took Chanda's hand and left the room.

The General looked defeated as he walked to the verandah doorway, and watched Mai outside introducing Chanda to some of the villagers. He considered all that had just happened. This beautiful young woman who he had heard so much about had out-maneuvered him in every way. He had to admit she had bested him. First with the carrot: the gifts and the trade deal that would indeed make him very rich. And then the stick: the imminent destruction of his forces, and embarrassment for him. Perhaps it would even lead to the overthrow of his government unless she was bluffing. He took a deep breath and got out his satellite phone. He was not accustomed to backing down or losing at anything.

As soon as the commander of his forces answered, he asked him, "Colonel, have you tried to start the engines of your tanks today?"

"General, I am not sure that I understand," the Colonel replied. "We have not started the tanks to preserve the fuel.

"Start your tanks Colonel," he ordered. "Then call me back immediately. Do it, now!"

General Rhee waited patiently admiring the new ruby ring on his finger.

After a few minutes, the Colonel called him back and said, "I am sorry, General. There seems to be some trouble with the tanks. None of them will start. We will try to determine the problem and fix them quickly so we can attack as planned at dawn. I checked, and we seem to be having a problem with many of the helicopters too. But do not worry. We will have everything in place as planned, General."

General Rhee shook his head, and replied, somewhat wearily, "Never mind that. We have reached an agreement. Cancel the operation. Signal everyone that they are to return to base at once. Stand down, Colonel."

He put away his satellite phone, took a deep breath, and reached for his glass. He raised it toward Mai in the distance standing among her people with Chanda. "To you, Ms. Sambath Largent. You have won this round."

The next day they left with pomp and flourish, akin to their arrival. General Rhee hugged Mai and smiled while waving to the many people who cheered them before getting aboard their helicopter.

As they pulled away, Lady Chu said to Mai, "It appears, my lady, you have made a new friend."

"I hope so, Lady Chu," she replied. "But I saw in his eyes the more I gave him, the more he wanted. That one is of the type that wants to control and own everything, and Siem Kulea is on his list. We will have to keep our eyes on him. Always assume the worst so that we can protect our paradise."

Chapter 20

2001 Siem Kulea, Northern Cambodia

Mai was hopeful when she interrogated the two remaining staff members listed as loyal to Su Ling that they would turn out innocent like An Li, but she soon discovered they were what they were reported to be. She sadly turned them over to Ramadi. The very next day and based on that confirmation of her the two house members on her list, she decided to begin interviewing the remaining disloyal Champas as soon as was possible and traveled up to the work farm to meet with them individually. She only had time to meet with half of the ninety-three prisoners before she grew too weary to continue. These intense thought pervasive examinations were taxing to her physical and mental strength but she knew they were necessary and she was driven to see them through. Unfortunately, even though they protested their innocence and she wanted desperately to believe them, every one them proved to be loyal to Su Ling and harboring traitorous thoughts when she examined them. She left their justice to her people who convened a special court nearby and ordered an ancient and traditional form of punishment for them. They would be branded on their cheeks with an ancient sign marking them as traitors to all Champas. They were banished from the valley forever, and not allowed to return to their homes. Marked as traitors they would be released separately in four directions over several days to travel through Champa held lands on foot with only the clothes on their backs. They were not expected to survive the ordeal.

The result was the same the following day when with great determination she examined the remaining people on the list. When the examinations were completed, and she returned to the Palace, Mai was very tired. But before going to bed, she went to her garden to sit and meditate with Queen Po. Upon reflection, she realized that Eddie Martinez had saved her and her people from a disastrous end and she felt an immense debt was owed him. She decided that eventually she wanted him to join her there, and she intended to find a place for him to live out his years with her in Seam Kulea maybe even in the palace.

With the accumulation of bad news and the mind-draining tension of the past week, Mai's spirits found refuge as she shifted her focus on the new birth of the Champa people with the great celebration that was to follow on the weekend.

But then Jack arrived with Marty Wenabe. She was naturally suspicious under the circumstances and not happy to see a stranger brought into the valley. After an initial very brief introduction, Mai insisted that she and Jack get away for a private discussion. Without any explanation, they left Marty on the verandah talking to Jasmine who was assigned to watch him.

Jack sat in a large chair in the parlor, and Mai joined him sitting in a decidedly unqueenly manner across his lap as they talked. "Mai, what happened to the doors of your chambers?" he asked. I was surprised to see plywood replacing them. What's up?"

As an answer, she kissed him gently on the lips, and then quickly again. "That was my apology. We can declare this *'Jack Largent Gets to Gloat'* day, my love. This queen is banning all snakes from this valley. I have decided it is negative energy, backward-looking, and not a symbol that should represent my people in any way including ancient history and tradition. Go ahead. Gloat if you want. I was wrong, and you were right."

Jack responded by claiming a kiss as his prize and pulling her close for a meaningful hug.

Then Mai divulged her newfound intelligence concerning Su Ling, and the reality of disloyal people Su Ling had planted in the valley. She again told him to gloat if he wished for he had earned it by being so patient with her. But he only kissed her on the top of her head, and held her close once more.

Following that revelation, she told Jack of the meeting with General Rhee. From the beginning of their relationship Jack was always a good sounding board for Mai and spoke objectively regarding her choices. He never questioned her decisions concerning Siem Kulea. That was her purview, her right, and responsibility to rule. They both shared a love for her people, and when Jack was around, Mai felt more grounded, and often her decisions during those times reflected it. It was Jack that had reminded her of her unique heritage as the ruler of Siem Kulea in the role of a natural arbiter between surrounding nations, and that it might present an opportunity for a trade agreement benefitting all of the former Indochina area. She was, of course, aware of the history of the rulers of Siem Kulea as arbiters between nations, but she had never put that in the context of the present day. That's what Jack gave her at moments like this: context.

When she was done relating all that had happened Jack said, "So, here I come with this man you have never seen, showing up unannounced. I bet all of your sensors are popping in the red zone right now. But I have no doubt that Marty is the real deal, and we have become good friends. I think when you get to know him, you will like him too."

Mai hugged him closer like she never wanted him to leave again, and then pleaded, "It is just not a good time for me, Jack. I still have some of those people being held up at the work farm in cells. Thank goodness, Ramadi kept all that stuff up there and didn't get rid of it. But I will be nervous until the last of them are put out of the valley. They held a secret court but most of the people still don't know about them. They will go wild around here when they find out they are traitors, Jack. The rumors have already started, and I fear there will be confusion and rioting if this situation is not resolved soon. That is why I chose to give my people something to distract them and celebrate this weekend, the rebirth of the Champa nation."

"Of course, darling, I get it. The timing couldn't have been worse. But Marty is a noted professor in archeology and is very interested in you and the Champa people in particular. He has even been to Thap Cham and conferred with Dr. Bui. He is a genuine expert and I am positive you will like him once you get to know him. How about we do this? I will make an excuse to go off, and take care of a dispute that will take me away for a couple of hours, and you can use that time to talk to Marty. Mai, I sincerely believe we need him, and his expertise. Besides, with your interest in ancient peoples, I am betting that you and he become best of friends. What do you say?"

She let out a breath and gave a sigh of surrender. "OK, but you know what I am going to do to him, don't you?"

"You are going to examine him in your special way, and as only you can. I have no doubt. But I will make you a bet, my beautiful inquisitor. I bet you that you will find he is what you see, and nothing more, deal?"

"OK, deal. But if I find something untoward, he is out of here at least. My first inclination will be to turn him over to my people for their justice. If that happens, no questions. Agreed?"

Mai was suspicious this was just another ruse by Hinsu Yameda to get information about Siem Kulea. She was angry with herself for being so paranoid and wary of Jack's new friend, but she couldn't help it after finding out her most trusted confidant, Su Ling, was a traitor out to destroy her world.

"Agreed," said Jack. They kissed a long bonding kiss, and then reluctantly broke apart to return to Marty who was still waiting for them.

When they returned to the verandah, Jasmine and Marty were engaged in a very animated conversation that appeared to be more of a debate.

Jack was the first to speak and offered an apology. "We're sorry we took so long, Marty. We had a lot of catching up to do. As it turns out I have to leave for a bit and settle a dispute at the north end of the valley."

"I did not miss you at all," confessed Marty, nursing a big friendly smile. "Jasmine, my newest friend here has been most cordial. Within minutes we were lost in conversation. Did you know she is also a big Chicago Bears fan, Jack? She knows all the stats on everyone, and I thought I was the big authority on that."

"Well, I'll have to steal her away from you for a bit. She is going to ride along with me in case I need her. We will return shortly. In the meantime, you and Mai can get better acquainted. I have told her all about you, and she is fascinated to know more," said Jack.

Jasmine nodded, accepting Jack's lead, and followed him out to the stables. After the two left, and with their drinks refreshed, Mai began her conversation with Professor Wenabe in earnest.

"Where are you from, professor? I detect an accent in your English, I think."

"I am half Iranian and half Egyptian," he replied affably. "We traveled and lived in many different countries when I was young, so I learned to speak many languages. My father was a doctor, and my mother was an archeologist, like me. Of course, my father wanted me to be a doctor, but early on I discovered a love for the study of ancient cultures, and civilizations, like my mother. She helped me by insisting that I formally learn the language of the countries we lived in, so I know, among several others, Arabic, Farsi, French, German and of course, English. I also speak some of the more obscure dialects around the area more out of necessity than anything else…"

While having an overtly normal conversation with him, Mai covertly walked around the periphery of his mind. She could not go in depth without making contact with him or having his permission, but even with a cursory examination, she got a good read on him. She was relieved to find he was an honest man with good intentions who was genuinely interested in the background of her people and concerned for her well being. With that secret intelligence, she accepted Marty for the unusual character he was and then opened up to him entirely putting away the cautious but friendly exterior that she adapted with most strangers. She assumed he was a good teacher because she was engaged in the conversation early, and then immersed in it when they got to her favorite topic. She did like him and was soon consumed with friendly delight from his narrative and so much that they had in common. Jack was right about that, and she noted he was three for three that day.

All of this was fascinating for Mai, but with the return of Jack and Jasmine, they broke up for a bit so Marty could freshen up, and Mai could tend to some Palace business. Mai suggested Jasmine give Marty a tour of the grounds and they agreed to get together again for lunch in an hour.

After lunch just as tea was served on the verandah, they finally got down to business. Jack sat next to Mai, and Jasmine was invited to sit with the group making it a foursome.

"Marty, I think it is time we discuss your real reason for coming to Siem Kulea. I suspect you want to explore the valley and its monuments, yes?" asked Mai, smiling at her new friend.

"Yes, Queen Maisong," he said eagerly, "and I want to thank you for providing the services of your assistant, Jasmine, this afternoon. I have thoroughly enjoyed her company as she showed me around your palace and the village. She made me feel right at home, and her admiration for you and Jack is obvious."

He took a sip of tea, and continued, "Several years ago I came upon a legend about an ancient people that came to this planet from another world. You may be interested to know that it is included in the lore of many cultures. What made this particular legend stand out to me was that it also included a symbol for these aliens in the form of a series of complex concentric circles. As I had already seen these circles in different cultures around the globe, I became intrigued. In various cultures they were either plainly portrayed, or had a local icon mixed in with their design. They can be seen from Egypt to China, and even in Central America. The implications are many, but armed with the idea of an ancient alien culture, I pursued the meaning of these circles and developed my own theories concerning them.

"I came to believe ancient aliens did migrate to this planet for a time, and later I concluded that they controlled our world by controlling the weather. It's just a theory, of course, but I believe they built stations around the world that allowed them to do this. Thus, the concentric circles in various cultures. When I plot the known locations of these circles for you on a map, you will see a pattern evolve, and the pattern leads here, to Siem Kulea.

"Jack was a big help in confirming my theory in Egypt when he photographed a stone edifice within a temple there for me. Written in an entirely different language on the bottom of the edifice was an inscription that beseeched the gods to protect them while they moved the sacred artifact to their homeland. I believe that artifact was a device that allowed the ancients to control the weather," explained professor Wenabe.

Mai gave a sigh, and asked, "What was the language on the bottom of the edifice?"

"It was Assyrian, Queen Maisong. And I think they took that artifact back to their capital in Nineveh. This was a time during which Assyrian invaders conquered Egypt. I have seen these same circles in the ruins in Nineveh, but never gave any further thought as to why they might be there," said Marty.

After servants served more tea and departed, Mai asked, "This is all very interesting, but why the sense of urgency I am getting from you and Jack. Why should we be concerned?"

Marty sat up straighter in his seat. "Others are also seeking the answer to these circles, and I suspect by what Jack has told me they have nothing but the worst intentions for you and this valley," he explained.

"Who?" she asked, suddenly focused on the timeliness of this revelation.

Marty looked at Jack, before saying, "Hinsu Yameda of Asian World Investments. I met with him in New York several years ago at his request. His people had burglarized my townhouse and taken my computer, and all of my records concerning you and Siem Kulea. It was a very trying time for me. I had a backup, so I was not distressed about losing the information, but I became concerned for your safety. As I learned more and more about you, I have come to admire you. I confess I feel a need to protect you that I find rather strange.

"This man Yameda," continued Marty, "knows all about you, and he knows about the ancients. I understand that you are the Nagani, the Hoa Cuc, the legendary descendant of the ancients. You are the queen who has been missing for these Champa people to serve and venerate for generations. If that is true, then I believe you hold the secret to everything, to controlling the world as the ancients did. That is why I wished to speak to you in private. Such things are not for public consumption, and I assure you it is not my intent to publish my findings anywhere."

"It is nothing new to anyone that I am the Nagani," replied Mai. It is the core of our beliefs as Champa people. Frankly, professor, I am surprised that no one has come here inquiring about aliens before you. That is also a part of our beliefs. How did you know there are concentric circles in evidence here at Siem Kulea?"

"Uh, well, Jack told me about them with some reluctance, I assure you. I had to pry it out of him, and he insisted he would not discuss you in any way. I had a theory already that they were here based on what I observed at other sites around the globe. It fell into a logical pattern of a sort for me. But Jack only volunteered to bring me here to meet you when I told him about the others who were searching for these artifacts," explained Marty.

"As I said, Queen Maisong, I am a great admirer of yours, and I have been following your story since you discovered the treasure at Thap Cham of the legendary Queen Dau Te Po. I was so fascinated that I traveled to Thap Cham, and talked with Doctor Bui who is the Director of the museum they have erected there to house and study the treasure you discovered.

"Doctor Bui is a fascinating woman, and over several days she showed me parts of the treasure, which were not made available to the public. They were interesting, but I'm afraid I disappointed her when I mentioned that I wished to study the chests they came in. She said she planned to get to them one day, but the contents at that time were her main priority.

"She kindly made the chests available to me, and I spent several days studying them. When I was done, I arrived at a number of conclusions. That ring on your finger is from the second chest, isn't it?" he asserted.

Mai smiled. "Yes, but that is not a mystery, there are many who know that," said Mai. "Why do you ask?"

"Did you ever notice what was on the lid of that chest that held the ring?" he asked.

"Ah—I see. Yes, I did, professor," she said, smiling. She settled back in her chair impressed by his deductive narrative. "But tell us what you saw there, and why it is important."

"On the lid of the second chest were the intertwined complex circles depicted in bronze in an ornate but subtle design as if part of the decoration of the chest. I am positive no one paid any attention to them. But they were the same circles that were on the edifice in Egypt, and that I saw in Nineveh. Grouped with them was the universal infinity sign, the infinity within infinity. This is a symbol that connects with the universe. I believe there was something in that chest that connected you to the ancients, that ring you wear perhaps," he suggested.

"I am not quite ready to take you into my confidence at this time," Mai replied, honestly enjoying the thought process and deductive reasoning of professor Wenabe. "But you're not done yet, are you."

"Not quite," continued Marty, smiling, and feeling every bit as an informed co-conspirator with her. He took another sip of tea and continued. "The third chest, the one next to it, had different symbols imprinted on it. There were the circles again, but this time they were intermingled with the Hoa Cuc flower, the sacred symbol of the queen of the Champas. When I asked to see what was inside of that chest, Doctor Bui showed me a crown, and scepter, which were on display in the museum. In my view, they were common and uninteresting. They did not fit to my way of thinking what I expected to be in that chest. I confess I was confused at the time, but I told no one.

"But this is where it gets interesting. As Jasmine showed me around the Palace today, we came to a room that had a portrait of you wearing another crown and necklace, which Jasmine explained to me that Jack had made of you while you were still living in Chicago. While Jasmine was bowing before it, you can bet I was studying it because it was fascinating indeed. It was not the jewels in the crown, and they were magnificent, but the symbols in evidence on the base of the crown that held the jewels that captured my interest. It was the circles again, mixed with the universal infinity sign, and the Hoa Cuc flower. All of my confusion was resolved because I am positive that was the crown, necklace, and scepter that were really inside of that third chest. I am right, aren't I? I bet the Vietnamese don't even know it," he theorized, proudly.

Jack glanced quickly at Mai who seemed transfixed with an amused smile toward Marty pondering what he had just said. Jasmine, suddenly alert to the situation, got up quietly and stood behind Marty's chair.

"Marty, you are on dangerous ground here," said Jack seriously. "If Jasmine thought you would do anything to harm Queen Mai and that includes revealing closely held secrets, she would protect her queen, and she is ready to do whatever is necessary to do that."

Marty suddenly realizing the implication of what he said, replied, "Oh no! I mean no harm to anyone. I would never reveal such a secret, or even theorize it outside of present company."

He looked up at Jasmine who indeed seemed ready to strike and smiled at her warmly. "I mean your queen no harm, Jasmine. I respect and admire her as you do. I am only interested in recording the history of the Champa people. That is something that is long overdue in my view. With the finding of the treasure at Thap Cham I believe it is time to write it down, even if it's only for consumption here in Siem Kulea."

Mai took a breath, smiled, and waved her hand at them. "Jasmine, darling, relax. Everyone relax. Marty is our friend, I trust him completely, and I am positive he means no harm to me or our people."

Jasmine smiled weakly and leaned over his chair from behind as they talked.

"I have made a decision," said Mai, cordially. "If you will accept my offer, professor, I would like to invite you to record the history of the Champa people. I have been considering such an effort since returning here to Siem Kulea. It is particularly appropriate at this time because we are beginning a new era in our history; a forward-looking, more positive future for my people. But you must accommodate your work according to my wishes? I must insist you work here in the valley where I can protect and secure the results, and none of your research or discoveries will ever leave here. Can you do this?"

"Oh my gosh! Yes, of course, Queen Maisong. I can take a sabbatical from John Hopkins."

"Dr. Bui will be moving here later this year to work on that project with you. She is finishing up on the treasure site in Thap Cham and giving her notice. She, like you, is most eager to begin, and as you will see, there is a lot of history here to research, and record for my people."

He shook his head looking up at the ceiling in honest delight. "I am honored that you chose me to take part in this great effort. In my wildest dreams, I did not suspect such a gift from you. I am very excited, but I confess I am not sure where to start. We must sit down, you and I, and have a preliminary discussion so I can prepare an outline for my research. When did you want me to start?"

"Yes, well, we do have a problem. It is a very big one as it turns out if others are searching for these artifacts as you have informed us. I know precisely what they are because I have one."

Noting the professor's surprise at her revelation, and remembering that she had verified his honesty and good intentions earlier that day, Mai made another decision, got up, and said to the group, "Please, come with me."

She led them inside and down the central corridor, and then down a stairway below the palace. Lady Chu joined them responding to Mai's Mindspeak command. They descended into a large basement area, and to one side among many stored chairs and tables, was a cupboard against a wall that appeared to be left there for storage purposes. Mai located, and pushed a decorative knob on the side of the cupboard. The cupboard popped aside a bit from the wall. She slid the cupboard toward the left revealing another stairway leading down below the palace basement.

"This cupboard and hidden stairs were rediscovered during reconstruction, but it was closed again, and has been left just this way since. I don't think anyone has been down here in a long time although I know personally that Colonel Minh found and explored this chamber," she explained.

As they stepped down into the lower chamber, Marty could see it was very old dating back thousands of years. He observed it was finished, and ornately decorated, even in the dim light. Mai lit a candle sconce on the wall by the door and handed a lit wick to Jasmine to light other candle sconces along the walls. As the room became brighter, it looked to be wondrous and carved out of the stone of the mountain. The ceiling was gold in color and vaulted like the inside of a tomb. The walls were maroon, but eight feet up on the walls began an ornate design of concentric circles in gold that led to the gold ceiling. In various places along the walls were ancient hieroglyphic-type symbols. The left side of the chamber was made up of many rows of shelves that extended further into darkness holding thousands of parchments. These caused Marty's face to light up with delight and literally made his heart race with anticipation.

They were in neat stacks, not rolled, and Marty went immediately to them, pulled out latex gloves from his pocket, and began to examine one carefully. "Oh boy. This is amazing, Queen Maisong. In this dry chamber, these parchments are perfectly preserved like in a prepared environment. I would expect it to be damp down here like a basement and these parchments brittle to the touch. But it is not. In fact, it appears to be an optimum environment for preserving such documents. They look to be in pristine condition. I could spend years studying them. Can I presume you will let me do that?"

Mai was standing proud with her arms folded and smiling broadly like a parent watching her child opening gifts on his birthday. "You are the first person I have brought here, Marty. No one has been here except me. Not even my darling, Jack. I wished to preserve the stored perfection of this vault. This archive is my gift to you that will be returned many times over as you and Dr. Bui, discover and record the story of my people. That said, I insist before you handle these parchments that all precautions be taken to preserve them for posterity. You will consult with Dr. Bui on this, and anything you think is necessary by way of equipment in that regard, I shall gladly fund."

Marty said, "Hmm…this is curious."

"What did you find?" asked Jasmine.

"Queen Maisong just told us she has not shown these parchments to anyone, and yet I saw a photo just recently of this particular parchment. How is that possible?" he asked.

"Who showed you that photo? Oh, let me guess, Hinsu Yameda?" asked Mai.

"Yes, exactly. But how?" he asked.

"Not to worry," said Mai. "We have become aware recently of a few people of questionable loyalty in our midst, and I can easily surmise how he got that photograph. That should not concern you in the least. We will deal with it in due time."

Marty nodded, as he looked around at the many parchments sitting on the shelves going off into the darkness awaiting his perusal.

Mai was amused by his eagerness that verified her decision to show the chamber to him. But then, she took a breath, and declared, "But that is not why I brought you down here. That is not the problem I mentioned. Come, professor, let me show you," she said, taking his arm and guiding him away.

Mai led the group through an arched doorway on the opposite side of the chamber. As Jasmine lit the sconces in that room they saw at one end an intricate stone carving of a dancing woman on top of flowers surrounded by snakes. The sculpture covered most of one wall and almost touched the ceiling. The principal part of the sculpture projected from the wall about three feet, and was painted in brilliant colors perfectly preserved. On raised stands, were vessels of gold holding burnt incense positioned before the carving in a temple-like fashion.

"Oh yes, this is magnificent," said Marty. "It looks to be thousands of years old. It definitely predates the Angkor era, and much, much older I presume. It's interesting that she resembles you, Queen Maisong," His eyes were smiling in wonder as they journeyed the stone canvas.

"This chamber is just full of wonders," he said, smiling back at Mai again, but he also remembered a conversation he had many years earlier in an obscure village on the other side of the mountains with a Latino man who spoke of this same statue. Indeed if the story were true, behind this statue was the magnificent door he told him about.

Even as he recalled that encounter, Mai moved to the right side of the sculpture where it extended out from the back wall and began to pull on a hidden handhold there. "Please help. I'm not strong enough to move it by myself," she said.

Jack and Jasmine moved to assist her and pulled on the sculpture along the same area. It rolled out from the wall grudgingly at first and then easier as they gained some momentum. As they swung the sculpture fully out from one side, behind was revealed a magnificent door of a golden metal. The door seemed to glow and amplify the sconce light from around the room. On the door were sculpted many concentric circles and three-dimensional Hoa Cuc flowers. But there were also snakes ominously intertwined with the circles, and weaving their way around the door. Pushing out further from the surface were six snakeheads warding off anyone who violated their presence.

Marty exclaimed, "Wow. Look at that! Holy Bejeezers!"

Jack smiled, recalling his first reaction to seeing snakes on doors at Siem Kulea. But Lady Chu and Jasmine were not laughing. They had fallen on their knees with their faces to the ground in adoration of this door they instantly and jointly deemed to be sacred.

"Yes," said Mai, looking over at Jack to share the moment with him. "This is what I wanted to show you. Very few people know it is here. I saw it first when I was with Colonel Minh who discovered it. But I have purposely kept this room closed, and the one with the parchments off limits since our return here to Siem Kulea."

Mai said to the kneeling Lady Chu and Jasmine, "I share your reverence for this door, ladies, but just now I need your full attention. Stand, and focus," she commanded them.

Marty stared at the magnificent door for a moment in fascination, and then he ran his hand along the edge of one of the snakes. "This is an interesting metal. It looks like gold, but on second thought I am not so sure that it is. It has an unusual sheen possibly as a result of being so old."

The door was massive, at least nine feet high and four feet wide. "Is this a crypt, or burial tomb of some kind?" he asked. "What do you believe it to be, Queen Maisong? Do you have knowledge of the origins of this door?"

"Not exactly, professor, and therein lies the problem we have. This door was never meant to be found, and certainly never meant to be opened again. Let me show you," she said.

She reached up and pulled on one of the snakeheads releasing it on a pivot, and then she turned it several times to the left, and right. An audible click sounded, and part of the face of the door behind a large Hoa Cuc flower in the middle opened, revealing a compartment. Inside was a strange looking object. Mai reached in and retrieved the object that was about eight inches in length. One side of the object was finished in a snakeskin texture, and a cylinder was formed as if sliced along the vertical from both ends leaving one third missing. On the end, it was flat and notched as if meant to join, and fit, with something else. It looked to be made of solid gold. She handed it to Marty.

"Even Colonel Minh did not know about this artifact. He could never figure out how to open this door. I suddenly had the knowledge to do so when I joined with Queen Dau Te Po, and I think in my excitement I told Su Ling. That was back when she was protecting me from Colonel Minh."

"You joined with Queen Dau Te Po?" asked Marty. "I don't understand."

"We can discuss that later. It is something that I'm sure you will find most interesting. But for now, professor, would you like to guess what this object is?" she asked him.

Marty, Jack, and Jasmine stood mesmerized by the gold and strange appearance of the object. Suddenly, Jasmine became excited, and declared eagerly, "I got it, Marty!"

Mai looked at her sharply with an expression of disapproval, and Jasmine instantly cowered and jumped back a step with her head down humbly, "I am most sorry, my lady. I was taken up by the moment, and forgot my place. Please forgive me for my assuming outburst. With your permission, I believe I will see to my duties upstairs," she said, turning away to leave.

"Jasmine, what do you think it is?" Marty asked, disarming the awkward moment, and not wanting her to leave. "It certainly is a strange looking beast isn't it."

Jasmine turned and stood humbly straight with head bowed respectfully. But when she remained silent, Mai said, "Come on, Jas. You're in it now. What do you think it is?" she asked, smiling and wishing with all her heart she hadn't rebuked her.

"Your Majesty, I think it is part of a mechanism, maybe like a handle, to open this door that curiously has no handle. I bet the other parts are supposed to be in that locked hidden compartment but they are not, and that is what Marty has been chasing all over the ancient world trying to find," she suggested.

Mai walked over and proudly put her arm around Jasmine's shoulder, and gave her a warm hug. "A-plus, Jasmine. I'm impressed. Yes, we are missing the means of opening this door. The door handle is divided into three parts that join together to make it functional. I assure you that the chamber within is sealed tight. This is the only way in, or out...from this world at least."

"Well, I have an idea where one of the pieces might be," said Marty. "Then we will be one step closer to opening this door. This is really exciting, isn't it?"

"But that's just the point I have been trying to make, Marty," explained Mai. "The last thing we want to do is to open this door. That is why the three parts of this ornate door handle were sent away to what were then the far corners of the Earth. The first Nagani closed this door, locked it, and then sent away the three parts of the handle never to be found again. She did not want this door to be opened ever because she wanted to protect her people. I believe inside this door is a chamber of the ancients, and maybe even a portal to another world. Those aliens could come through, and take over the Earth through that same portal. They would make slaves of humans again. The first Nagani thought that if she sealed this door, they could not get out, and their only choice would be to return and leave the Earth alone."

Jack who had been listening in silent fascination asked, "Mai is that fact or legend? There is so much legend blended with the history around here, how can we know what is real, and what is not?"

"You're right, Jack, of course," said Mai. "There is no way to know for sure. And it is impossible for us to determine when the stars will align again, and open the portal."

"Queen Maisong, what are you talking about "when the stars align again?" asked Marty, now very focused on this unique idea. But then he eagerly answered his own question. "Oh! I think I understand. You think the rings are not about weather, but about the stars. If we could interpret the rings, we might be able to define their meaning and maybe determine what stars need to align, or where these ancients came from in the universe."

"That might be, or the circles might be as you have suggested, a means of controlling weather patterns around the Earth. We just don't have enough information at the moment, Marty," said Mai. "I confess I would have known none of this except for knowledge I gained through the ancient Queen Dau Tè Po."

"Obviously the answers to everything might be behind that door, Queen Maisong," said Marty. Surely you can see that might benefit all mankind. Imagine if we could control the weather, and what that would mean for hunger, and poverty on the Earth. We would have enough food for everyone. It would be a worldly paradise."

"Or the end to mankind as we know it," said Mai. "I don't believe it is a risk we should be allowed to take. It would be dangerous, and foolhardy. Remember, I told you the first queen of our people had a direct knowledge of the ancients, and armed with that knowledge she chose to close and seal this door forever. That should be all we need to know concerning any decision on this matter."

I don't understand why someone couldn't just fabricate a handle even of gold, and open this door anytime they want," offered Jasmine. "Those kinds of things are not very difficult to do anymore. I bet we could do it in one of our machine shops in the village."

Mai asked, by way of answering her question, "Marty, of what metal is that handle made?"

"Well, I think it is gold Queen Maisong. It appears to be solid gold."

"We had better put it back," Mai suggested. "I have discovered that whatever it might be, it's a bit radioactive, and it would not do to hold it too long." She took it from him, put it back into the compartment, and closed it once more. She worked the snakehead and locked it back in place.

Afterward, she turned to him, and said, "I believe it is an element not of this Earth. I tried scraping a small crumb for analysis, and it was impervious to my efforts. Whatever it is, the door is made of the same thing, and I am all but positive it is not gold. You did not notice but it is very magnetic, and I suspect an object that fits the shape will not work because I sense it has other properties, perhaps on an atomic level, which will allow it to open the door. It is meant to be only opened by that combined device. We must make sure that never happens. It might even have some sort of concealed trap incorporated into the door for those who try other means of access."

"Oh dear," said Marty. "An atomic door handle. That's a twist. I wonder if the Chinese found such a device at the site they discovered? That Yameda fellow would find a way to get it if they did. He is cunning and devious, that one. I didn't trust him for a minute, but he has a way of convincing you of only the best intentions. Do you know what I mean?"

Mai already knew that Yameda had an object from the Chinese site, but that was not something she wanted to reveal to the group at that time. She glanced at Jack, and his body language showed he was bothered about something. He made a gesture with his head toward the stairs.

Mai thought for a moment and then said, "Lady Chu, would you and Jasmine take Marty upstairs, and set up some refreshments for us on the verandah so we can discuss this further. Jack and I will close up things here."

After they left, Jack turned back to Mai, and said, "Baby, I have lived here in the valley now for over nine years. Why have you never showed me this chamber before? I don't know what to think about all of this. Snake doors are one thing, but I mean, come on, really? A portal to another world beneath our home? Ancient Aliens?" Jack turned slowly around the room observing the painted walls taking on their own lives in the flickering glow of the candlelight. "This is one really amazing chamber, Mai, and from what you have said, what is on the other side of that door is even more so."

"Humans stood in this chamber thousands of years ago, Jack, as slaves. The aliens made them, and used them brutally like trained animals," Mai said. "Look at the drawings on the walls there, and there," she said, as she pointed. "They are worshipping those aliens as gods."

"You are inferring a lot from a few symbols on the wall, Mai? Frankly, I can't make much sense of them. I mean we all worship according to what we believe. They don't have to be slaves. They could be working out of love, and devotion for the aliens. Marty told me the great pyramids were not built by slaves but by a people who truly loved the pharaoh, and believed him to be a god who gave them prosperity and protection. When they stopped believing that, no more great pyramids."

"I just know, Jack. I know. It is in my head like a distant memory. I don't know why but I know. We have to make sure that door is never opened," she said.

Is there more to this that you haven't told me?" he asked.

"Actually there are some things, Jack, but they're not important really. We can discuss them later."

"Queen or no, Mai, I'm not moving, until you tell me everything, and then I will decide when we can discuss the details," he said, standing in front of her.

She nodded and gave a deep sigh in response remembering she had already promised to be candid with him. "OK, I'm sorry. I was kind of delaying telling you to see how things played out. There is a lot going on right now since I returned from this last trip to Chicago. I didn't expect Yameda to know about the door. That bit of information from Marty shocked me.

But it makes sense with Su Ling being so involved in the restoration of the palace, and I am fairly certain I told her all about this door in my excitement when I learned about it."

"OK, so Su Ling and Yameda are now a team working against us," said Jack, "and they want to get inside this door for their own reasons. If she worked for Colonel Minh, it follows that she would have known Hinsu Yameda."

"It is my understanding they have been lovers for many years," explained Mai.

"Where did you hear that?" asked Jack.

"Well, actually from two people. Daniel, of course, told me and then… OK, my love, take a deep breath and get hold of yourself. I found out from Eddie Martinez," she said.

"Eddie Martinez? Who is Eddie Martinez?" he asked, confused.

"You know him. You said you would kill him the next time you see him," she said.

"Holy shit! You mean the Martinez from the trail when I was a prisoner back in the old days of Colonel Minh? That Martinez? How did you meet up with him?" Jack asked, bewildered.

"As it turns out a very different version of him worked his way well within Catherine's security in Chicago. Despite what you think of him, he turned out to be one of the most talented operatives I've ever seen," she explained.

"Come on, Mai. It can't be the same guy. That guy was gruff and unsophisticated. He was an idiot. I can't believe it's the same man," said Jack.

"Positive ID, Jack. I saw him and talked with him. He is a very different person than he was back then, or at least his loyalties are different. He claims to have been devoted to me since his time at Siem Kulea with Colonel Minh. I walked around his mind, Jack. I have no doubt in the truth of his words. He is ready to do anything I tell him to do."

Jack shook his head. "I don't believe this. When did all of this happen?" he asked.

"Last week in Chicago. That's where I examined him."

"You met with him, and you say I'm reckless. Are you nuts? He's a killer, Mai, and a very bad man," said Jack, shaking his head.

"Yes, he's a very bad man, or was. But now he's my very bad man. I control him completely, and I intend to use him. He was a fountain of very useful information about Su Ling and Hinsu Yameda," she explained, calmly. "The truth is, he saved my people and me by shocking me out of my delusions about Su Ling. For that, he will forever hold a special place in my heart and my world. I intend to bring him home to Siem Kulea eventually, where he can find the peace he so richly deserves."

Jack sat down on a large stone in the center of the area and processed all that she had told him. "So he was working for Yameda and Su Ling to spy on Catherine. Does that mean that her security is compromised? Hey, is our security compromised?"

"No, nothing is compromised. In fact, he protected us, and fed them mostly false information particularly where it might have voided our security," Mai said.

"Jack stared at her for a moment considering her words, and then said, "Mai, we have to interrogate Su Ling, and find out what they plan to do. This entire valley is at risk."

"Since my return, we have been taking steps to protect the valley, Jack," said Mai. "It was Martinez who gave us the list of disloyal Champa citizens in the valley. I told you, we have arrested them and interrogated them."

"You didn't say where you got the information before. How many were on the list?" asked Jack.

"About one hundred," replied Mai. "Two were Palace staff loyal to Su Ling. I examined them, and they were found to be traitors. They have already been dispatched along with Su Ling's personal maid, Hata."

"Dispatched, you mean killed? You executed them for being disloyal to you? Do you even have the power to do that?" he asked.

"If those three were allowed to leave, or escape, their knowledge would put the entire valley and specifically our family in this palace, at grave risk. They were traitors, and I had them executed," she said. "Please don't question my decisions regarding this matter. We agreed long ago, this is my area of responsibility alone and what I decide is final. I am saddened that two of my own palace staff, close to my family, harbored a wish to bring harm to us, Jack. My people would rip them apart if they knew and got hold of them. In our Champa world traitors are dealt their fates without compassion. Once guilt is proven without a doubt, justice is swift. I walked their minds and I have no doubt of their guilt. Ramadi has already taken care of it quietly."

"What about the other one hundred or so? Are you going to execute them too?" he asked, still questioning his own feelings on the matter.

"Many of them are still being detained up at the work farm at present as they are being processed. As I said, I have interrogated each of them individually. The procedure drained me mentally. It took a few days, but I had to be sure before condemning them. While they lied, hid their feelings, and protested their innocence, when I walked their minds, I found out the secret, traitorous thoughts they harbored. They will be marked as traitors, and sent from the valley."

Jack nodded. "So you let them live."

"Honestly, they will be lucky to live out the year once my people find out about them, " Mai replied.

Jack took her in his arms and hugged her very close. Then he kissed the top of her head, and said, "Baby, you have been through a lot while I was gone. It appears we are at war with Yameda. Have you imprisoned Su Ling?"

"No, she has been away since I discovered her intentions. I talked to Daniel about it. He told me they have been separated for three years, and he suspected her relationship with Yameda for a long time before that. Su Ling was Yameda's mentor when he was still a teenager. They have a long, and perverted relationship. Daniel promised to help, but he said he would not deliver Su Ling to us. He still loves her."

"What do you think they will do next?" asked Jack.

"I have been deliberating on that a great deal. This whole thing just keeps adding on levels of complexity. But at least we are aware of their intentions now, and we can move to protect ourselves. Yameda is super intelligent and cunning. I told you after our meeting in Paris that I thought he was coming after us. I am sure of it now because he wants what is behind this door.

He nodded in agreement and she said, "Let's get this sculpture back in place, and then you can help me blow out the candles."

Chapter 21

2002 Siem Kulea, Northern Cambodia

B rad Martin was the CFO of the financial division of Catherine's corporate empire in Chicago. But Mai was the data and analytical genius behind the remarkable success of that division. Though they were thousands of miles away from Chicago she insisted on working primarily from the Siem Kulea valley. Thus it was necessary to have the best communication systems available between the valley, and the rest of the world. She made good use of the ancient renovated temple that was attached to one end of her palace, turning it into her communications and computer center. Inside housed one of the best cybertech facilities in the world. It was manned by a staff of more than thirty well-educated, ultra-intelligent Champa followers she had personally tested and trained. They were intensely loyal and ensured that her financial ideas and strategies progressed with the proper attention paid to the most minute detail. They were always watching out for anomalies that might prove a detriment to their queen, and her friends.

Mai was distressed when she discovered that Su Ling had betrayed them and with evidence of traitors within her own palace staff, she told her financial team she was going to conduct a security review of them as well the following day. When one of the team failed to show, she became suspicious. Further investigation revealed he had been another Su Ling loyalist embedded by her among the team. She was further surprised to find out that Su Ling had been getting copies of all the financial reports they sent to her as a regular routine. Her staff felt they let her down and they were all on extra alert now looking for any attacks that Hinsu Yameda might be directing toward their network.

That very morning there were a few events that turned up at the same time, which represented a possible danger for Queen Mai, and those she cared about.

The first was an apparent covert attempt to take control of Catherine's company, NearNorth Productions. Someone was buying up stock in the company in small amounts, and from several different sources primarily using shell companies as a front. They appeared as innocent, and disconnected public stock market investments. This activity was not new to Mai because she had been watching it for several years. She thought there was only fifteen percent of stock being held by outside investors but her team of financial experts had recently shown her data that indicated the number might be as much as twice that amount. Since Brad Martin and Mai, did not allow any amount of stock to be on the market that would put the ownership of NearNorth Productions in jeopardy, there had to be someone on the inside who was dumping protected stock on foreign markets and then concealing their transactions. It was on the Hong Kong exchange where the most recent, and damaging trades, had occurred.

Mai responded by buying up all remaining outstanding stock, and ensuring any further sell orders would be purchased first and automatically by an anonymous shell corporation of her own. She could do this because with her team making use of algorithms of her unique design she had a jump on other buyers in the trade markets around the world. As fast as the automatic computer-driven stock exchanges were, she was faster by fractions of a second, or more specifically her algorithms were, and she controlled all of it. She parked her intercepts on specific choke points where electronic data commonly traveled that allowed her to examine these automatic transactions as they went out to world markets. Even Catherine was not aware of this, and only a very few members of her piously loyal team knew what she was doing.

She did not meddle and did not interfere with everyday stock market activity. She only monitored NearNorth Production stock to protect herself and her friends from attacks, and hostile takeovers such as the one that had now surfaced. The formulas and algorithms she created to determine stock market trends were far in advance of anything used by those in the industry. Her only challenge was to be careful not to introduce something so profound that the more antiquated systems would take exception, and make her presence known.

There were very few computer systems in the world she could not access if she really wanted. With her in the lead, her team of cyber experts could penetrate almost any firewall, but they were careful not to use this expertise unless needed, so as not to expose themselves, or their superior technology. Mai saw what others could not even begin to see in numbers and data, and she was smart enough to leave it alone until she had a use for it.

The next event had been waiting to happen for many months when Lady Chu called out to her for help through Mindspeak, and a moment later the alarms sounded signaling an unauthorized helicopter launch.

She jumped from the desk in her office with the Mindspeak message from Lady Chu, and hurried out to the pad in the rear of the palace. The daily delivery helicopter was there with blades spinning ready to take off. Lady Chu was lying on the ground dazed, and two of her staff were attending her. There was a large jewelry case turned over next to her with precious jewels falling out of it. Mai could immediately tell among them were jewels from her collection.

She saw Ramadi speaking through a megaphone ordering the helicopter to stand down. Fetu, and two other members of her security team held MP5 automatic weapons pointed at the helicopter. Ramadi gave Mai the megaphone and picked up a sniper rifle with a high-powered scope and laser sight. He could not miss at that range as he honed in for a body shot, and the laser scope danced a red dot on the center of Su Ling's chest. She was in the open doorway of the helicopter looking desperate and holding a gun on the pilot.

Mai put her hands on her hips, and just watched as Su Ling pleaded in unheard words for her life. Finally, Su Ling stopped, put down the gun, and went on her knees in the doorway of the helicopter with her hands folded, pleading toward Mai.

Mai calmly walked to the first two security men in the row and lowered their rifles with her hands. She looked up purposefully at Su Ling in the helicopter. Then she went to Fetu and lowered his rifle as well. She took a position beside Ramadi holding the most powerful and accurate of the four rifles and waited a full ten seconds as he aimed his weapon at Su Ling. The tension built as she looked long and hard at the traitor she had trusted, and loved for so many years. The red dot of the laser sight bounced around her white blouse menacingly. Then Mai calmly reached up and lowered that rifle too.

Mai held up the megaphone, and said, "Now we are even, Su Ling. I have saved your life three times this day just as you saved mine. I owe you nothing, and I tell you now that you no longer exist for me, or my people. You are banished from this valley forever. All Champa people will shun you. You are a non-person to us." She waved to the pilot giving him permission to leave. After the helicopter lifted off, Mai handed the megaphone back to Ramadi and turned away with tears streaming down her face to see about Lady Chu.

She did not know it then, but she would regret the decision she made that day.

Chapter 22

2003 Ubon, Thailand

Hinsu Yameda rose from behind his desk to greet General Rhee with a warm, welcoming handshake. They exchanged pleasantries, and spoke in Khmer; a newly acquired language for Yameda and Su Ling. This was a necessary part of Yameda's dark plan because what he was to discuss must remain a closely held secret for it to succeed. After his meeting with Mai in Paris five years earlier, he adapted and moved to another strategy. General Rhee was always a big part of that plan even if he didn't know it yet. Since his embarrassing failure at conquering, and bullying Queen Maisong, General Rhee had settled down to become a good citizen and leader of the Cambodian government.

One entire side of Yameda's office consisted of windows looking out over the Mun River. It was a beautiful visage, and once again General Rhee found himself admiring the view and considering such a location for himself. This was not his first trip to Ubon to meet with Yameda. But the prior meeting was cut short when Yameda would not support, or give him the expertise he needed to make his ambitious plan successful.

"I think I love the view from your villa more than any other I have seen, Hinsu. You have chosen a site for your estate well. I hope that one day I can have such a view from my villa. How have you been, my friend? I was surprised to receive your call since you turned down my offer concerning Siem Kulea," said General Rhee.

"Yes, well, plans have a way of changing, and we must adapt, mustn't we? May I offer you a drink, General? I believe you like gin and tonic as I recall," offered Yameda.

Yameda pushed a button before guiding the General to a couch overlooking the view of the river outside. "Let's sit over here a bit more informally as we talk, shall we?" he proposed.

Only a moment after sitting, a young woman appeared with a tray of drinks and appetizers. She sat them down in front of the two men.

They toasted to "our mutual prosperity" offered by Yameda, and then he got down to business. "If I may speak frankly, General, your plan as presented to me had no chance of success against the defenses of Siem Kulea. I wish you had listened to my words of caution in that area as I have heard you were stopped even before you started."

The General played with the rim of his drink as he considered his answer. "Ms. Sambath Largent is a formidable opponent, Hinsu, and I am not embarrassed to say she seduced me with an offer that promises great wealth and a comfortable life for me."

"And she also showed you explicitly how she would defeat you if you tried to attack Siem Kulea, is that not true?" Yameda asked.

"Yes, and in the face of that, I had no choice but to accept her offer. As it turns out, it was a wise choice because foreign investments are already streaming into my country. Since we are speaking frankly, I must tell you I have no further interest in attacking Siem Kulea."

"Indeed," answered Yameda, "and I would always advise caution when planning any scheme against Ms. Sambath. I myself have been defeated by her financially several times. I learned to follow her lead and have gained considerable profits from doing so.

"But what if I told you," continued Yameda, "That there are untold riches at Siem Kulea that boggle the mind. Within Siem Kulea may be the power to rule the world, General."

"I think Hinsu," answered General Rhee, "that your ambition may be getting the best of you. First your father, and now you with worldly ambitions. Nonsense. I will have no part of any such scheme. All of that talk is pure folly and a waste of my time. If you have nothing else, then I should be leaving," he said, putting down his glass and getting up.

Yameda stood up quickly before him. "Wait, General! I did not build my financial empire and considerable wealth with ambitious schemes of foolishness. Be patient with me for five more minutes, and then I think you will have a better understanding of what I have in mind. I want to show you something," he said, moving toward the bookcase behind them.

He pressed a button that caused a panel to slide aside revealing a hidden safe. He quickly worked the combination to open it, and removed an object wrapped in a dark blue velvet cloth. It was about eight inches in length. He placed it on the table in front of General Rhee.

He untied the cord that was pulled tightly around one end and removed a golden bar-like object. It had a snakeskin texture on one side and was triangular along the length.

General Rhee was fascinated as he looked at the strange object. "Is it made of gold?"

"No, but I think it is something even more precious because that element does not exist on this Earth," said Yameda. "What do you think it is, General?"

"I can't imagine," he said. "I wish my wife, Chanda, were here. She is much smarter about such things than I am. I am afraid this is all very curious to me."

"Imagine there are three objects similar to this one that fit together to make something," said Yameda. "Does that give you a clue?"

"May I," asked the General as he picked it up in his hands. "It is heavy enough to be gold. I suppose the end where the indentations are would be the front. I don't know, Hinsu. What is it?"

Yameda sat down beside General Rhee and took the object from him. "It is one-third of a door handle for the most magnificent door you have ever seen, General, and where do you suppose this door is located?"

General Rhee considered the question, and then answered, "Siem Kulea?"

"Yes, the door is under the palace at Siem Kulea. I have seen it, General, with my own eyes. This is part of a door handle that is the only means to open that door, and behind it, I believe are riches beyond imagination. But more importantly, I believe behind that door is the means to control the world."

"This still sounds like a bit of fantasy, Hinsu. But you have my attention. Tell me what you know of this," he said as he offered his empty glass. "Please, I am suddenly most thirsty."

Yameda got up and ordered more refreshments on the intercom at his desk. When he returned, he stood before General Rhee and told him what he knew of the ancients and Siem Kulea.

Just as he finished, the door to his office opened, and Su Ling entered wearing a short tight cocktail dress with a plunging neckline. It had been over two weeks since the incident at Siem Kulea, and she was well on her way with a plan for her revenge, and to secure access to the ancient door for her and Yameda.

She walked up to Hinsu, and gave him a big kiss saying in Thai, "Sorry I'm late, darling. I wanted to shower after my swim."

"General, this is Su Ling. She is my partner in every way and has as much knowledge as I do concerning what I have told you," Yameda explained.

Su Ling walked over, leaned down toward the General, and gave him a big kiss on the cheek while she made sure to entice him with her cleavage. "I am pleased to meet you, General Rhee," she said. "I have heard a lot about you. Is it true that you have three wives?" she asked in Khmer.

Yameda interrupted in Thai, "Darling we were just getting to the reason I asked General Rhee to meet with us. Save your questions for later. I am sure you and General Rhee will have time together to discuss such things if you wish."

"Oh, too bad. I am curious as to how he keeps them all satisfied," she teased. She picked up her wine from a newly arrived tray of drinks and offered the General his drink, as she sat down next to him.

General Rhee had not taken his eyes off of Su Ling since she joined them, but after taking a sip of his fresh drink he collected himself, and asked Yameda, "You were saying this door is at Siem Kulea?"

"I have seen it, General. I swear, and so has Su Ling. I only had a one-time chance to see it, and that was only because Su Ling was partly in charge during the reconstruction of the Siem Kulea palace. Unfortunately, I could not get a photograph of it then as Queen Maisong's security team sealed off the area from anyone shortly after that. But it is there. All we have to do is get control of Siem Kulea.

Yameda sat back down opposite General Rhee, and said, "This object is one-third of the door handle. Su Ling says another third is contained within the door itself. Queen Maisong showed it to her when she was under Su Ling's control while still working for Colonel Minh, and she even taught her how to access it from the secret panel where it is hidden. We are working on finding the last part now, and we have a good lead."

"But you can't get to the door unless you can get control of Siem Kulea, and that is where you need me, I assume," said General Rhee.

"Yes, exactly. If we went into the Siem Kulea valley, it would be a criminal invasion. If you go in, it is simply putting down a rebellion of a group of terrorists bent on overthrowing your government."

General Rhee thought for a moment. While he considered his options he rested his hand freely on Su Ling's bare leg beside him. She did not resist and instead smiled back at him.

"You want me to set up an operation once more to annex Siem Kulea, and take possession of it," he concluded.

"No!" replied Yameda. "That way you have already tried, and we can be certain it will not work. That is not the way to conquer Siem Kulea. We have another more subtle plan, which we are positive will be successful. All we will need you to do is come in afterward, and take over. For that, we offer you half of everything we find."

"How much do you think that might be?" asked General Rhee.

Yameda, hearing his response, knew General Rhee was convinced. "Su Ling estimates the jewels in Ms. Sambath's vault alone to be a treasure worth a billion dollars. Beyond that, there is the palace, land, and the most important part, what is behind that door. But you must agree up front, General, that Su Ling gets the valley. She wants to own the valley after all is done. Agreed?"

General Rhee got quite serious, pursed his lips and thought a moment as he pretended to consider his decision. But then he nodded, and said, "Yes, I think we are in agreement. What is the plan? I will need to prepare my forces."

"No General, in great secrecy prepare only a small elite force and even then disguise the operation as normal training. Tell no one of your plans. It is important that you never mention Siem Kulea to anyone at any time. In fact, gather and practice with this elite force well away from that valley.

When we are close, and can give you an exact time, and date, we will be in touch. Su Ling will act as my emissary with messages between us. Please tell no one, not even your wife, of what we have agreed here today. I must insist on that. Queen Maisong has her informants everywhere. Trust no one but Su Ling and I. We will take care of all the details. Is this agreeable to you?" Yameda asked.

"Yes, I will look forward to hearing from you," General Rhee answered, running his hand along Su Ling's leg possessively.

But then General Rhee had a thought. "Who gets Queen Maisong when she is captured?"

"If she disappears completely, I do not think you will get any argument from me or Su Ling," said Yameda.

"Indeed," answered General Rhee looking out the window in thought.

Chapter 23

2005   Siem Kulea, Northern Cambodia

With the dawn of another day, Mai put most of her concerns behind her while practicing her favorite form of therapy. She was up to her calves in muddy water working in rice fields not far from her palace. She wore purple rubber boots in the mud at the begged request of her handmaidens who were charged with bathing her afterward. Many of her people worked with her that morning as part of a concerted effort to get all the fields planted before the rainy season. The morning sowing of crops was an organized effort of everyone living in the valley dating back centuries as part of their tradition. They enjoyed working at that most fundamental task in their natural environment, and they even sang together as they planted. It was a special time when they bonded with each other, their ancestors, and their queen.

But then as Mai reached back for another seedling from a hanging shouldered basket carried by one of her people nearby, she lost her balance and fell over, landing full-front into the muddy paddy. She turned over quickly and sat there stunned and embarrassed for a moment. The sludge firmly held her hands, torso, and feet.

It was not the first time, and it would not be the last that Mai fell down in the mud, but that did not make it any less worrisome for the devoted Champas working beside her. They dropped what they were doing, and rushed to help their queen. When she was finally freed and helped to her feet, she was in a most undignified manner covered in mud from head to foot.

One little boy seeing her muddied appearance, pointed and laughed with unrestrained glee at her. Under most circumstances it would have been the penultimate moment in a slapstick comedy if Queen Maisong wasn't the object of the joke. Once again, everyone was paralyzed in shock at this insult toward their queen.

Because of their very quiet and stunned concern, the boy's laughter was amplified across the field. It became an awkward moment as Mai with muddied hands on her hips turned and looked at the boy with a raised eyebrow and a stern expression on her face. No one moved as the boy at last realized the error of his unfettered reaction to her mishap. He looked around at everyone with angry faces toward him and humbly lowered his head ready to cry in self-conscious remorse. But then Mai, breaking into a huge grin, galloped through the muddy field awkwardly until she stood right in front of the boy. Looking like a malevolent, sodden, Asian scarecrow, she stood over the tearful boy in pretended anger with her hands on her hips. After a moment, she raised the boy's chin and he was surprised to see her grinning from ear to ear. She leaned in toward him and gave him a tongue-accented raspberries. The boy giggled, and answered her raspberries with a version of his own, even putting his hands on his hips matching her pose. She laughed, delighted, and everyone laughed with her.

After a moment of fun, Mai quickly washed off some of the mud in the dirty water where she stood brushing away any help. One of her handmaidens assigned by Ceva, who simply refused to let her go into the fields without her assistance, handed her a clean cloth to wipe her face. As she cleaned around her eyes, Mai saw the mother of the little boy drag him away by his ear toward the other side of the field. Mai called out for him to return to her. The mother let go of him, and he made his way eagerly through the muddy paddies until he was beside her again.

She bent down, straightened the collar of his dirty shirt, and asked him, "What is your name?"

"I am Beni, my lady,"

"Well, Beni, today I want you working right beside me as my personal and favorite assistant. I think you are perfect to retrieve each new seedling for me from the basket, and hand it to me so I won't slip again. Can you do that?" she challenged him.

"I think I can. I will try, my lady," he replied, smiling eagerly.

She nodded to him, and he reached up and retrieved a seedling, and handed it to her. She took it and began singing again as she bent down, and planted it. He quickly got the next one and waited with a big smile for her to reach out for it.

An hour later Mai walked into her chambers from the garden verandah still sprinkled with dried mud from head to toe. Mai in her late thirties was in the best physical shape of her life. She pulled off the latex gloves her handmaidens insisted she wear when she did her fieldwork. She stood with her hands out, and they removed her muddied clothing as she watched her still sleeping husband lying in their bed that he once said looked like a boat.

With an evil grin, she got an idea, and suddenly ran naked to the bed, and jumped under the covers snuggling up close to Jack. At first, he was startled, and then realizing it was Mai, and without ever opening his eyes, he put his arms around her and pulled her to him warmly. "Good morning, my love," she whispered as she snuggled in closer, kissed, and chewed on his ear intimately. Her handmaidens, never surprised at the antics of their queen, silently backed out of the room, and waited nearby.

Still with sleepy eyes, Jack hugged and kissed her. He turned her over onto her back and began exploring her body with kisses. He loved Mai in every way imaginable, and it was moments like this that never got old for him. They had almost died for each other, and their union was proven and blessed on many levels, and in many ways. But that boundless love was challenged as Jack's kisses landed on a spot of dried mud on her neck. He pulled back stretching out his arms and opened his eyes to look.

"Wha...! Oh my god, Mai! You'll get the bed all muddy!"

"Who cares!?" she replied.

"You'll get me all muddy!" he said.

"My intention exactly. If you won't come out to the fields with me, I will bring the fields to you. Now shut up, and make love to your queen, slaveboy. I am so hot. I can't stand it!"

Muddy or not, that was an order Jack was pleased to obey. This part of their relationship never got old, and later as they lay arm-in-arm Jack smiled to himself contemplating Mai's morning mischief.

Mai had a thought, kissed his shoulder and said, "Jack, darling, I am having second thoughts about you going on this mission with Marty. Iraq is still too crazy dangerous, and this whole thing seems foolhardy. I know I supported Marty's idea of going there to get the artifact, and it is very important that we get it, and control it. But I am worried, baby. Something is wrong. I can feel it."

Jack knew enough to respect when Mai got one of her feelings. She, unlike most people, had a sixth sense for danger, or more accurately, when her universe was out of line. She was always right, and no doubt that second persona, Queen Dau Te Po, had a lot to do with that. It was hard enough arguing with one woman, but two was impossible, and they were both queens.

They had been going over this quest for the lost artifact for several years as she and Marty narrowed down all of the possible locations where, if it still existed, it might be located. Marty was now convinced it was at Nineveh, the ancient Assyrian empire capital, and he was all but certain he knew exactly where it might be if it was still there. They were ready to go once before but then the Iraq war started, and it was impossible to get permission to enter the country. Then when things seemed to be settling down in Mosul, their destination city and the site of the ancient Nineveh ruins, insurgents formed an uprising, and the 101st Airborne responded making it one of the hotspots of the war.

They instead examined in person the other possible site locations for the missing artifact while they waited for the conflict to settle down in Mosul, and eliminated them one-by-one on site. Soon that part of the conflict ended, followed by a lull in the war as the Americans solidified their hold on the country. They again applied for visas, and permission to enter the country, to no avail. To their chagrin, the peaceful lull in Mosul ended once again, and the war looked to be heating up in that area as Americans withdrew from the North leaving it for the Kurds to administer. Mosul became a stronghold for the Sunni factions of Iraqis, most of them former soldiers in the Iraqi army who under Saddam Hussein controlled the vast numbers of Shiite ethnicities that outnumbered them in Iraq. Marty convinced Mai and Jack that they had to go now or risk that the artifact would be destroyed, or lost, as the looming battle threatened the ancient ruins area. He had a plan for getting into the country through the back door using CIA resources supplied by a friend.

Marty was expecting to meet him in Ankara, Turkey that same night. They were to go into Iraq the following day on a private charter contracted by the CIA.

"Don't worry, Mai," he said. "I'm not a fool. If things really look bad, we'll take a rain check and head back home. At worst, I will beg off, I promise."

"I know I can't talk you out of it, and I'm not sure I want to, but you better come back to in one piece, Jack Largent! What time is your flight?"

"A helicopter is picking me up at eleven," he said.

"Is Daniel flying you to Bangkok?"

"No, I am flying out of Ubon to Ankara. Daniel is taking Devi to Bangkok for her flight to Chicago. What time is it?"

"Mmm...not sure. I came in around nine."

"Nine! Holy crap. I better get going!"

Minutes later, Mai was lying in bed as Jack called out fully dressed from the adjoining suite after his shower, "Mai where is my photo vest? I can never find it after your handmaidens clean up."

She laughed to herself. That old photo vest had seen more wear than it deserved. Why he liked it so much she couldn't imagine. But it was one of her favorite things too because it personified Jack and everything she loved about him. She jumped out of bed, and ignored her handmaidens trying to wrap her in a housecoat.

"You want your photo vest?" she asked, smiling while arriving naked inside his dressing area.

"I believe that was what I was asking about," he said, teasing a smile back at her.

"Kiss first," she demanded.

He gave her a long meaningful good morning kiss, and she said, "It's right behind me hooked on the door where *you* hung it, Jack, you goof" she said, laughing.

But that morning's last minute kiss-fest was abruptly interrupted by their sixteen-year-old daughter Devi who entered their bedroom without warning. Seeing them wrapped together, and her mother naked, she declared, "Oh come on, you two. Don't you ever get enough?"

"Never!" said Mai, laughing and kissing Jack's ear.

"I will have to leave soon," said Devi, "and if you want to share any breakfast with me before I go, you'll have to put your passion on pause, and come right now. Everyone is waiting to serve breakfast, and I, as their begged emissary, am asking if you are going to join me, or not, or do you want it served in bed? Really mom, they're all waiting, and Lady Chu not wanting to interrupt you, sent me to ask you what you wish to do."

"Well, there have to be some benefits for being a queen although with you two I feel most of the time like an Evanston housewife. Come here, and give us a kiss.

"Tell me again why you are so dressed up today, Devi? What's going on with my little angel?" Mai asked, as Devi leaned in and kissed her and Jack.

"Daniel Vega is warming up his helicopter right now, and flying out in ten minutes to take me over to Bangkok, mom. I am off to Chicago to meet up with Charlie, and bring him back for the summer. I have to go to UCHI while I am there, and get my classes for fall too. And what's with all the dirt, mom? Gawd, you're a mess! What the heck, and you're so forgetful!" Devi declared.

"Oh, no. I was just in another world for a minute with your father," Mai said, giving Jack a look, and feeling the aftermath of their lovemaking.

"He's leaving to Iraq on another mission with Marty, and admittedly it is pretty important this time. I just wish it was somewhere else. All of my loved ones are deserting me; another typical day at Siem Kulea for this queen. I will have to muddle through somehow," she pouted. "When are you and Charlie coming back for the summer? I can't wait to see him. I bet he's as big as an ox!"

"Three weeks, mom. We're in Chicago for a week or so, then to Andhra Pradesh, India, for Kelly's charity on the way back. I don't look forward to that. It's going to be well over one hundred there, and sweltering with no decent place to stay. We will be back by June," she said.

"OK, I think I have it. Jack, when did you say you would be back? Oh! I am getting lonely already."

"Hard to say, really. Marty seems to know exactly where he needs to go and what he needs to do. We will get in and out real fast, and I will call in daily to keep you informed."

Mai gave a mock pout and looked at him sideways. "You better," she said.

"Devi, tell them we are on our way right now," she said, clapping her hands. Three handmaids entered bowing. Ceva held her robe for her. "I am going right to breakfast. No…I am going for a quick shower, and then I will go right to breakfast. I guess I had better get this mud off me. Although I think I look good in mud. Darling, do you think I look good dressed in mud?" She joked as she struck a naked pose for Jack.

He looked at the silly persona of his beautiful wife posed as a mud sprinkled statue, and laughed at her playfulness. He glanced at her handmaiden Ceva who, in spite of her reverence, and devotion had a twisted smile on her face. Mai could be a very serious queen at times, especially when it came to protecting her people. But most of the time she was like this. "Mai, I have to leave. Get into the shower and wash off!"

"Yes, sir!" she said. With a smile, she gave him a mock salute.

Almost as they arrived for breakfast, Devi was called out to board the helicopter to Bangkok leaving Jack and Mai alone on the verandah opposite the garden.

"Have you told her about Charlie yet?" he asked before putting a fork of eggs and sausage into his mouth. Charlie is Catherine and Kelly's son, fathered by Jack.

"Relax, even if your deal with Catherine and Kelly precluded you making your parenting known to Charlie, and acting as his father, I told Devi long ago that you were married to Catherine for a bit and that Charlie was your son by her. I have no doubt she has told Charlie. They tell each other everything. Frankly, I have always felt your supposed one-year marriage to Catherine nullified that part of the agreement but you both have honored it nevertheless. So stop your silly speculating and let's have a nice relaxed breakfast before you go off to play GI Joe."

The two teenagers, though world's apart, were best friends, loved being with each other since the time they were children, and spent their summers together usually in Siem Kulea. Devi once told them she liked being with Charlie because "we are of the same mind." Jack could not resist, and whenever Charlie was around, he made a point to spend time with him as much as possible, and give him some male influence in his upbringing.

In the fall, they would both be attending the University of Chicago together. Devi was a year younger, but possessing a genius IQ, had qualified and entered college two years early, a year ahead of Charlie. Devi had several majors. This year it was Computer Science. Charlie was majoring in Accounting, and had plans to go to law school after that.

"I have to get going, Mai. The helicopter will be here any minute, and I have to get my gear and bags out to the pad," he said, as he started to get up.

"Jasmine is going with you, right?" she asked.

"I haven't asked her. I want her to be putting the studio back together, and cleaning up while I was gone," he said. "This is supposed to be a quick in-and-out. Just us boys. Besides, it might be..."

He left the sentence hanging, and Mai took it up tossing her napkin down on the table as she did. "You are such a phony. You're not taking her because you think it *is* going to be dangerous."

Mai picked up her cell phone, and punched in a number. When the call was answered by Jasmine, she commanded, "Get your things together. You are leaving with Jack in a few minutes. Pack three days to a week. Get the equipment you packed for Jack yesterday in the studio, and bring it out to the helicopter pad. Don't be late."

"With respect, my lady, I am already packed, and was just heading out to the pad. I did not intend to let Jack go without me. I know he needs me, even if he does not," she said, as Mai hung up the phone without replying; surprised, and then, not surprised by Jasmine's comment.

Jack smiled at her as she put her cell phone down on the table. "OK, I guess she is going." He jumped up from the table.

"Not so fast, handsome, before you desert me, give me a good-bye kiss I can remember you by."

Jack was thinking the same thing. "I am going to miss you, darling. I will get back as soon as I can."

"Be safe, and don't do anything stupid," she said. "Marty can get carried away and not pay attention to what is going on around him...please, Jack, for me. Don't take any undue risks. Promise?"

As he left, Mai called to Jasmine using Mindspeak this time. "Jasmine, be sure the two of you are well armed, and bring the emergency cash packet, and anything else you think you might need to protect yourselves. You and Jack will be flying on a jet charter out of Ubon so there won't be any problem with customs."

"Yes, my lady. I have already done that. Do you know of a further danger of which I am not aware other than the ongoing war over there?" she asked. "I have been keeping up with the news, and it looks like our final destination city in Iraq is starting to get dangerous again as Americans withdraw from the city."

"I am not sure, but you might be heading into the middle of a real war. It is only a feeling. Jasmine, I want you to know that I love you dearly and am grateful every day that you are here with us and go with Jack on his many archeological excursions. You are more like a daughter to me than a loyal servant. You and I have a bond. I have prepared you for just this circumstance. Protect Jack. I know you won't let me down," she commanded.

"I am ready, my lady. You needn't worry."

Jasmine was among the best of the elite two hundred of her combat trained Champas, the best in the valley, but even so, worrying was exactly what Mai was doing.

Chapter 24

2005 Chicago

Detective Lieutenant Frank Haleran sat at his desk in the small office he occupied in the Police Headquarters building on Michigan Avenue. After twenty years in the Robbery-Homicide Investigative Division, and five in the Counterterrorism and Intelligence Division, he was now off on his own in a quasi-independent unit called Special Operations. Now in his early fifties, he did not have the energy he once had as a rookie, and his waist was expanding a bit over his belt. His grey hair, and somewhat wrinkled face spoke to his many late nights on the job. He started his career as a lawyer, but a few years out of law school a local gang member killed his brother, a Chicago street cop, when he intervened in a robbery attempt. For several reasons, Haleran did a left turn and joined the police force as a rookie street cop like his brother had been. He worked up through the ranks always demonstrating a discerning mind, and his record of solved cases was proof of that. He had an eye for finding the truth at a crime scene, but it was his gut that often set him off on the correct path for a solution.

His wife, Virginia, who he met in law school, was now a superior court judge. Together, they tried to keep up with their daughter Amanda who was a junior in high school, a stellar and very active student contemplating college. With their two careers successful and on power drive, that was always a challenge, but one where they shared a mutual dedication.

He tapped his fingers on the thick brown file folder on his desk marked "Most Secret" in one place and "Confidential" in another. He had just finished his second examination of the folder, and was pondering how to proceed. In this super-charged post nine-eleven atmosphere even the most absurd accusations of terrorism were given undue merit. He was handed the file the night before over drinks at a north side bar by his Chief of Police and immediate boss who asked him to look into it as a favor. Most cops would think this file was a career maker for an ambitious detective, but he knew it was given to him because it was a pile of crap that the chief didn't want to have anything to do with. Haleran already had a career and had risen as high as he wished to be. He had no desire to stop being a detective, and his current position gave him the autonomy to choose the cases he wanted to personally investigate.

This file was political through and through. A second-term Senator by the name of Earl Beacham Grimes who was on the Senate Judiciary Committee had passed it to the Chief because some of the alleged malfeasances were based in Chicago, and the Chief owed the Senator a favor. The Senator wanted the Chief to do his dirty work for him in preparation for Senate committee hearings he proposed on the alleged terrorism activities. Put another way his assignment was to find the proof of the criminal activity the Senator was alleging to be used as ammunition during those politically charged hearings.

Haleran already knew about Senator Grimes. Five years earlier he had been in all the headlines when his high-society wife of three years died in a boating accident on Lake Michigan. Grimes inherited her old-world family wealth, and some suspected him of murder at the time. But nothing was ever proven, and the autopsy apparently backed his story that she fell overboard during a storm and drowned when he could not find her. With a lack of evidence, and because of his political clout a lid was put on the story, and it was wrapped up forthwith with a cursory investigation and autopsy.

Haleran didn't buy that story then, and now he was supposed to help the same man crucify someone else. He hated politicians because they were always making good cops waste their time on their flighty political schemes while the real work that needed to get done sat unattended and added to a growing list of unsolved crimes.

This time, for several reasons, Haleran decided he would extend his investigation by checking out the Senator too. What was his motive for wanting to bring down this individual? What did he gain from it? There was always a motive, and most of the time it was about money.

He pulled out a yellow legal pad and began scribbling in pencil what he knew. He had a big state-of-the-art computer right in front of him, but he didn't like computers. He didn't trust them and liked to keep his considerations private. Writing in pencil helped him to collect his thoughts, and organize his thinking.

At the top of the pad, he wrote "Queen Maisong Sambath Largent", and underlined it several times.

Unbeknownst to the Chief, he knew Mai Largent personally and had met her several times when she and her husband still lived in Chicago. He liked her then, and there is no way in hell she was a terrorist. There just wasn't enough room between his ears for that idea.

He has known Jack Largent for over 25 years. Back in the old days, they used to play volleyball at an old gym on Lincoln Avenue every Wednesday and Friday night. It was the kind of place where the same people showed up on volleyball nights, and over the years they all grew to be good friends. Volleyball was from nine to eleven, and then they would shower, and retire to the bar area that was in the basement of the old gym. The bar was one-hundred years old, and they shared old stories over drinks and cards into the late hours. Some of the men even stood up at Jack's wedding on that crisp early morning when they married at sunrise on the shore of Lake Michigan.

He knew Jack had been a very successful advertising photographer, judging by the size of his studio and townhouse above in downtown Chicago. He remembered how he talked about Mai when he first met her. He fell both feet in love with Mai, and he seemed to have an extra bounce in his step after that.

The folder alleged that Mai was a terrorist and a murderer, guilty of trading and bank fraud, and with circumstantial evidence, attempted to make a case for that. Haleran opened the folder and looked at the news photo of Mai Largent taken during a visit to Navy Pier in Chicago. He knew Mai spent several weeks each year in Chicago while working as a corporate vice president for NearNorth Productions in their financial division. The company has risen over the last fifteen years to be one of the largest production companies in broadcasting specializing in investigative reporting much like the popular Sixty Minutes program. Its financial division has subsidiaries that include stock trading, and data mining companies that are among the top handful in the world. They are worth billions.

Haleran again considered the evidence suspiciously with his friendly bias. What was the endgame here? What was Grimes after? These were powerful people in that tree house he was going to be shaking. Why take the risk unless perhaps Grimes was on the offense to deflect attention off of some wrongdoing of his own. It would be easier to discount some investigation that Catherine Marsh was working on if he could bring criminal charges against her, and her organization. He made a few notes and pointed arrows toward that idea.

Haleran had a hard time sleeping most nights and used the crutch of a good book before going to sleep to help him relax before dosing off. He had some of his favorite books on the shelves of his small office. Two of them, which he thoroughly enjoyed, were non-fiction and factual accounts of two of Catherine Marsh's investigations. One was entitled, "Queen Dau Te Po and the Champa Treasure", and the other was "The Notorious Colonel Minh".

But the subject of both books, at least peripherally, was Mai Sambath-Largent, and they painted an entirely different picture opposed to the circumstantial evidence of the criminality that Grimes alleged in his brief.

The folder said she had been a terrorist working with Colonel Minh to overthrow governments and conquer Southeast Asia. But from what he had read, her ambition was not to empower Colonel Minh, but to kill him. She was, in fact, responsible for thwarting his plans, and defeating him before he could start his revolution. So that part of the folder was as phony as a paid television pundit.

The folder further claimed she was guilty of stock manipulation. The circumstantial evidence presented in the folder only showed dates that NNP invested and divested stock, which mirrored the same fluctuations in the market that followed. There were a dozen examples of this, and it made a good circumstantial case. But there was no proof of insider trading, nor had anyone brought any direct evidence forward showing Mai to be doing anything illegal. Nevertheless, Haleran decided he would have to look into that aspect further. But he already suspected there was nothing to it because he knew that Mai was a very smart professional when it came to the financial markets.

The last thing that they accused Mai of was libel, a civil case at best. They claimed she was using her position as head of the Data Mining Division of

NearNorth Productions to make false claims of improper procedures concerning subprime mortgages being followed by other banks in an obscure area called derivatives. Such claims caused many wealthy clients to flee those banks and put their money in banks recommended and supported by NearNorth Productions, which did not deal in such specious policies.

He sat for a moment thinking of the good times playing volleyball on a team with Jack at Lincoln Turners back in the old days. He sure did miss those games and the guys on and off the court. He did not have Mai's telephone number in Cambodia, but he did have Jack's, and he thought it would be a good time to catch up with him. He thumbed through his Rolodex and found the number. Picking up the phone, he punched in the overseas number with a big smile on his face.

He listened to a series of clicks and silence for about ten seconds, and then a woman came on the line speaking in a language he assumed was some form of a regional dialect. She switched to English when he explained why he was calling, but the lady informed him that Jack was away on a photographic assignment. Expecting to hear a no, he asked if he could speak to Mai, and the woman replied she would see if she was available.

In just a moment, Mai came on the telephone asking, "Is this Chuggy Haleran, the volleyball player friend of Jack's?"

"Mai, how are you? It's been a long time. How are you doing, young lady?" he asked, thinking no one had called him *Chuggy* in years.

"I was just getting ready for bed when my handmaiden told me there was a call from the United States. When she told me who it was, I dropped everything. I have to tell you, sometimes I wish we were back there in Chicago, Chuggy. Those were some of the best years of my life when Jack and I lived above the studio. I miss you guys," she said.

"Yeah, I know what you mean," he replied. "But come on, Mai. I hear you are a famous queen living in a remote paradise. I think you got the brass ring."

She laughed. "Well, it has its moments. I'm sorry Jack is away. I know he would love to catch up with you."

"Actually, Mai. I called because I wanted to talk to you about something. I hope I didn't call too late. It really was a spur of the moment thing, and I forgot to make a note of the time," he said.

"No, you're fine. It's about ten p.m. here. It's planting season so we get up early before it gets too hot. Frank, are you still a police detective?" she asked.

"Yes, I am, Mai. I'm a Lieutenant now with sort of my own area of responsibility. I have thirty years in so I can leave anytime I want. The fact is I don't know what I would do if I didn't come into work each day," he explained.

"We are the same in that, Frank. My favorite thing to do here is working in the fields with my people. I can't imagine a day without finding something to do. I just cannot sit around doing nothing. I think I flunked queen school," she quipped. "You're not going to believe this, but I was just thinking about you today," she told him.

"For god-sakes, Mai. Why would you be thinking of a fat old Chicago police detective? Is everything all right with you?"

"Yeah, sure. Things are really great for the most part, Frank. But we have a daughter. Do you remember Devi?"

"I think so, she was two the last time I saw her. She would be, what, fifteen or sixteen now, right?"

"Yes, exactly. She is flying to Chicago right now to register for school and visit for a bit. The thing is I am getting all kinds of bad vibes, Frank. It isn't based on anything in particular…maybe I am just being a mother, but I have to admit I am more worried than usual. I take this call from you as a sign, and so I am going to ask you something I have been thinking about for a while now."

"Sure, Mai. What is it?"

"How would you like to work for me, Frank? I need a smart investigator with lots of experience like you. The fact is, our corporate interests are getting very complicated, and we have issues all the time that require someone with your skills. Does that sound like something you might be interested in? I figure you are making about seventy, or eighty thousand a year. I could double that if you work for me."

Haleran was silent for a moment until Mai asked again, "Frank?"

"Mai, do you know a man by the name of Senator Earl Beachem Grimes?"

"Yes," she answered. "Isn't he the man that Catherine thinks killed his wife, that wealthy society friend of hers?"

"Yeah, that's him, and he is for some reason trying to give you a lot of trouble. I have a file here that the Chief gave me to follow up on where he accuses you of being a terrorist and involved in stock manipulation among other things."

"That's ridiculous, Frank. You don't believe any of that do you?"

"No, Mai, I don't. But you are damn lucky this file landed in my hands, and not someone else. He has just enough circumstantial evidence here to make it seem legitimate, and that could cause some other detective trying to make his gold shield push a case like this forward in the present atmosphere after nine-eleven. Things like this tend to end up on the nightly news, and before anyone knows any better, you are judged guilty without there ever having been a trial," he explained.

"Why would he do it?" asked Mai. "Why come after me? I don't have any connection to him that I know of."

"I have been asking myself that same question since this file landed on my desk," said Haleran. "He connects Catherine into his allegations like it is some sort of conspiracy to manipulate the stock market. The fact is you've been so successful in guiding Ms. Marsh's corporate investments, it appears to be improper. But as I said there is no direct evidence proving it. I think there is more to the story, and I am going to keep digging."

"Frank, I swear to you we have never done anything improper in any of our transactions or dealings in the stock market," Mai declared. "I have been buying stock in Catherine's company quietly because it appears someone behind the scenes is scheming to try a hostile takeover, but again we are doing nothing illegal."

"You or Catherine have apparently caused some trouble over something called derivatives whatever that is. Back in my law school days, I was somewhat of an expert in corporate law and even worked with a major bank here in Chicago regularly. But a lot of what is going on now is beyond me. Things move a lot faster now than they did thirty years ago. From what I can make of it he is accusing you of libel by claiming some competitors are selling bad stocks," said Haleran.

"Oh god! I don't believe the audacity of that man," said Mai. "We've pulled all of our money out of banks that are selling derivatives, which are in fact, bad stocks. We've recommended to our customers that they do the same. That's just good business on our part, nothing more."

"OK, I thought that was the case. Not to worry. I'm on it and will hold this file close. But you see why it would be very bad timing for me to go to work for you right now, Mai. It would look bad for you, and as I said you don't want another detective heading up this case," he explained.

"Yeah, thanks, Frank. I see what you mean. I am going to call Catherine, and let her know what is happening with Grimes. She is going to go ballistic.

"But Frank, could you do me a big favor?" Mai continued. "Could you take some time to check on Devi, and be sure she is OK, and not doing anything stupid while she is there in Chicago? My daughter is very much like me, and that worries me to death. I would consider it a personal favor if you would."

"I'll do you one better," he said. "My vacation time is stacked up beyond what I will ever be able to use. I will take a couple of days, and check on her, and on her security too. Who you got working this?"

"In Chicago, it will be Catherine's crew," said Mai. "Probably someone Big Ben Washington assigns. I'm not sure."

"OK, I will look into it just for old times sake. Can you send me her schedule? You can fax it to this same number, and it will go right through. Say, how's the weather over there?" he asked.

"It's really gorgeous this time of year, Frank. Why don't you come over, and get your feet muddy? I bet you would love it. We plant rice every morning."

"Oh, I don't think my back is up to all that stooped labor, Mai. I will pass on that, but it would be nice to visit. I have never been to Asia although I have thought about it. I just never got around to it.

"We will make it an open invitation then. You can write it off as a job interview. Give me a heads up when you're ready, detective," she said. "And Frank, if anything else develops or you just feel the need to consult me, you will call me, right? Don't hesitate, or think twice about it. Here is my direct private number."

After she dictated her direct telephone number, he replied, "Thank you, Mai. I just may do that, and I will let you know how things are with Devi," he affirmed.

"Thank you, Frank. I feel better knowing that. Be careful and watch your back," she said, hanging up the telephone.

"Always," he said to the dead line. He remembered Mai as being a very sharp, and together young lady. Yet she disguised it behind an affable, and approachable personality. She was the kind of person he knew you could learn a lot from by listening, rather than talking. He trusted her instincts, and if she was getting bad vibes over this trip, he was going to find out if there was anything to it.

Chapter 25

2005 Chicago

When Catherine first heard they were being investigated by the FBI, and audited by the IRS, she wasn't surprised, nor was she concerned. Confounded, and irritated would have more correctly described her state of mind.

This was always happening in her investigative journalism end of the industry, and to some extent even expected. Her publications in print, cable and online, were among the few who had spoken out against getting involved in the war in Iraq. More than most she knew the facts, and they just didn't match with the story the administration was telling the American people.

But this time it was different, and her old friend from high school, and sometimes informant from inside the FBI had called, and asked for a private meeting to talk with her about "some serious matters."

When he arrived she led him into the lounging area of her condo, and he greeted her partner, Kelly, with a hug. She provided a coffee service for them while they heard what he had to say. Catherine could tell he was concerned, and so she began the conversation with some trepidation.

"Come on, Warren, I would think you would be used to this by now. You know we experience this kind of thing several times a year because of trumped-up political ploys that go nowhere. Why should this be any different?"

"I know, Catherine, but you are aware I'm sure that even perfectly innocent people can spend years being tied up in court with some of these inquiries and investigations."

He flipped the latches on his briefcase sitting on the white couch beside him as he answered. "They're not after you this time, Catherine. That's the thing. They are going after your friend, Maisong Sambath Largent. She's an officer and major shareholder in your company, and they appear to be trying to get to you and paint a black mark on your company through her. She is being accused of international terrorism, stock market manipulation, embezzlement, fraud, drug smuggling, and murder. They are attempting to build a case with Interpol to put a warrant out for her arrest."

Catherine gave him a look for a moment, not sure she heard what she had just heard. She glanced at Kelly who had her hand over her face stifling an incredulous laugh. She too realized what she just heard was beyond ridiculous.

"Mai? That's just nuts," Catherine said. "They couldn't arrest her even if they were successful. Do you have any idea how farfetched this whole thing sounds? Who's behind this, Warren, and where are they getting their information?"

She was dressed elegantly wearing a sweater over her silk shirt and wool pants, but she still felt a chill. She got up to check her thermostat. It was raining and cold outside, a little unusual for Chicago at this time of year. She pushed the temperature up higher than normal, and laughed to herself as Warren removed his suit coat at the same time. When she was done, she sat down again this time right up against Kelly who was observing Warren with a look of amusement over the top of her coffee cup.

"I really am not allowed to tell you any of that, Catherine, and I probably shouldn't have told you what I did, but they are obviously trying to get at you by association. I just heard the Senate Judiciary Committee is holding a special hearing to investigate the charges."

"The Senate Judiciary Committee? Oh, wait! Warren, its Grimes again isn't it? Come on, tell me, Warren. It's Grimes, right?" she demanded. She looked at Kelly who nodded and shook her head showing her contempt for the Senator.

He reluctantly nodded. "But I have seen the charges and the evidence, Catherine. They make somewhat of a good case this time, especially with the stock manipulation charges. I read it over, and it though it's entirely circumstantial it might be enough to get to a grand jury.

"Who else is involved?" she asked. "Grimes, even as a Senator, alone doesn't carry enough weight to get the Justice Department involved. Who else is behind this? I know you well enough that you have already looked beyond the judiciary committee to see who instigated this. Who was it?" she persisted.

Warren hesitated and fidgeted in his chair. "I'm not supposed to know this, and if it gets back to me, it could mean my job, Catherine."

"I don't want you to tell me anything that you don't want to, and you wouldn't be here if you didn't think something was hinky about the whole thing anyway. Come on, Warren. Who else is behind this?" demanded Catherine.

"Beaulieu," he replied softly.

"Beaulieu! They're not even an American company. They're French for god's sake. What the hell! What are we talking about, foreign lobbyists bringing pressure in Congress? Oh wait." she said as she paused a moment in thought. Then she turned to him and said, "I get it. I really get it."

They were interrupted as Ward her butler served pastries. Warren absolutely dove into the pastries, and when Kelly poured him another cup of coffee from the silver service, he downed that too.

"Warren, we can make a full breakfast for you if you wish," offered Kelly. "Have you been missing your meals? I don't think I have ever seen you so quick on the draw when it comes to eating sweets."

Warren laughed as he reached for another pastry. "I missed breakfast this morning, and I'm going to miss lunch because I have to catch a plane at O'Hare in two hours. I'll have to grab something quick at the airport. They have me running all over, Kelly. It's the Homeland Security people. We are all over the country checking every rumor. We don't want to get caught with our pants down again. Everyone is walking around looking over their shoulders. But you must know that. How many orange alerts have they put out already? Everyone is acting like Al Qaeda is some big organized group when in reality they're a bunch of dumb radicals that took advantage of our freedom and lax security.

"Kelly, this coffee is the best," he opined. "You should open up your own shop on Michigan Avenue."

He reached for still another pastry as Kelly pushed the tray toward him on the table between them. Catherine had been thinking meanwhile, and she spoke as she made her decision, "Warren listen to me. This is an end-around to shut us down. That's all it is. There is no substance to any of these charges."

"What do you mean? Shut down...what...who?" he asked, getting out his notepad from his briefcase.

"Warren, you know Mai. You've met her. She is a genius, especially when it comes to computers and financial data. That simple fact has given our company an advantage for the last decade as she used her percipient judgments to ensure that we made investments in the right areas, and moved away from those that were suspect according to her methods. In our company when she says to buy, or sell, or invest here, and not there, we don't even ask why anymore.

"Do you remember back in 1999 when Congress passed a bill that deregulated the banks?" she asked.

Warren nodded with his mouth full of pastry, and his hand jotting down notes.

"It canceled the Glass-Steagall legislation that was passed way back in 1932 after the great depression with the express purpose of never having another Stock Market crash like we did in 1929. That original bill protected us by separating commercial banks from securities and investment banks for almost seventy years. When the banks were no longer regulated, that meant they could take chances, and speculate more. They could combine an investment bank, with a commercial bank without regard to the consequences. Previously the consequences were the stock market crash of 1929,"

"OK, I follow you so far," said Warren. "So, what does this have to do with you, and Beaulieu?"

"Over the last few years with the volatile housing markets, there has been a trend for making a lot of bad loans to those people who would not have qualified for them in previous years at the same banks. These loans were then bundled together, and sold to other banks, and then repackaged, and sold again. This kind of speculative buying and selling would not have been possible when the banks were regulated. This has been going on for several years as the market was deregulated, and one of the largest companies dealing in derivatives, that's what we call these kinds of bundled loans, is Beaulieu. If this story ever breaks it could cause a major recession. It is a huge financial bubble ready to burst," explained Catherine.

"We are about to do a big story on it," she continued. "That's why they are trying to shut us down. Mai has been the primary individual in our company steering everyone we know away from banks doing these kinds of deals. She says what the banks were doing after deregulation is a disaster waiting to happen. Mai is our in-house expert who understands the implications of this better than anyone, and she is heading up this story. That is unusual for her since she never steps across the aisle to participate in our investigative reporting division.

"Mai, and Brad Martin, who is the head of our financial division, have very carefully steered our company away from these investments, and into much more solid holdings that can withstand the crash that is coming."

"Are you saying the stock market is going to crash?" asked Warren.

"One hundred miles an hour right into a brick wall," she affirmed.

Kelly snuggled a little closer to Catherine against the cold. "Does it seem colder in here to you, Cat?" she asked.

"I just turned up the thermostat. I think a cold front is coming in off the lake again. I haven't checked the weather, but I bet we get hit," Catherine said.

Kelly nodded, and said to Warren, "We have also moved all of our charitable trusts away from these banks. I handle most of that side of our affairs, and we don't want to take any chances. It's going to be a real mess, Warren. I have spent many hours discussing it with Mai."

"Why isn't anyone doing anything about this?" he asked.

"It is like the elephant in the room, Warren, because another thing that has happened with deregulation is that banks have purchased other banks, and some of them have gotten too big to let fail. If one of them fails, it will bring the rest down. Everyone knows it's there, but if anyone says anything, we all lose. Our company is somewhat protected, but we have friends that will lose everything. Some of the big brokerages on Wall Street will cease to exist," she explained.

"But you're preparing a story on it, and they want to stop you from releasing that story. That's your assertion?" he asked.

"We have a story, have had a story for several months. All done. All ready to go. But we cannot bring ourselves to release it. The crash would be worldwide, and devastating for almost everyone. So, we wait, not wanting to precipitate the inevitable."

"OK, but why go after Mai? You are the ones going to do the story," he said.

"Well, there are still more parts to this story," said Catherine. "We are the third largest data mining company in the world because of Mai, and her people in our financial division. Data mining has become huge, and allows companies to invest to the greatest advantage, and save millions of dollars yearly. Beaulieu is the number one data mining company in the world. But at the same time, they are also a major principal involved with the marketing of derivatives. They know, Warren. They can see where all of this is going, and they know that they are defrauding their investors. Yet they continue to do it. But if you check, I bet you will find out they or their subsidiaries are also into hedge funds, shorting stocks, and are betting against the market at the same time. It is the worst kind of insider trading, and stock manipulation there ever was, and they are the ones accusing Mai of stock manipulation. How hypocritical is that?"

"Your company will look bad if they bring this Senate investigation, Catherine, even if none if it is true," he said. "The cable news pundits will have it out there as if it were all true just because somebody says they are investigating your company."

"When are you meeting with Senator Grimes?" Catherine asked.

"My boss is meeting tomorrow morning at the request of Senator Grimes," Warren answered. "I suspect he wants to monitor our investigation, and put his slant on things."

Catherine got up and left down the hallway. In a few minutes, she returned and handed the FBI agent a folder. "Have your boss look over this before meeting with Grimes. You will note that we have found he has a number of accounts at Nassau banks in the Bahamas totaling several million dollars, which were funded just this year. With those account numbers, I just bet you that you can trace an account back to Beaulieu. What do you think?"

"Where did you get this information?" he said. "Those banks are very private about their clients, and frankly impossible when it comes to getting any information out of them."

"We have our resources," explained Catherine. "After all, we are one of the major investigative reporting networks in the world."

Warren shook his head, and said "Wow!" He checked his watch and got up abruptly. "I'm sorry, but I have to run, or I'll miss my flight. Kelly, thanks for the pastry and coffee. I guess I didn't know how hungry I was. Mind if I take a couple more for the flight?" he asked, as he put two pastries into a napkin, and placed them into his briefcase before closing it.

He collected everything, put on his suit coat, overcoat, and turned to give Catherine a kiss on the cheek. "Well I came to give you a heads-up, and you've given me a bombshell. I don't know whether to thank you or be worried. Either way, this is going to be an interesting few weeks."

"Call us after the meeting with Grimes. I want to know what happens. Be safe," said Catherine, as he was leaving.

As he opened the front door, he turned and said, "Oh, I forgot to mention something, and it might be important. There is an Asian organization that has mercenaries working in the Chicago area. We have lost track of them, and know only that they arrived in Chicago a few months ago, and then disappeared."

"Asian? That's unusual, isn't it? Are we talking the Middle East, or Orientals, and do you have any idea why they're here?" she asked. "You are not saying they are planning an attack here in Chicago, are you?"

"We know little about their intentions, only that they have come to this area, and disappeared. They have been very adept at covering their tracks, and we are a bit concerned about it. I thought with your connections you might be able to find something. These are reported to be Hmong mercenaries from Southeast Asia. Let me know if you hear anything," he said, going out the door.

Catherine watched him leave even as her intercom informed her that Mai was on line three. She put on the speakerphone, after telling Kelly it was Mai on the line.

"How you doin', girl?" she asked, settling back, and putting her feet on her coffee table. "Kelly is here too."

"I'm getting lonely, Cat. All my loved ones have abandoned me. Devi is on her way over to you, and Jack is going to...get this...Iraq!"

"Iraq! Is he nuts? Did anyone bother to tell him there is a war going on over there? Why in hell would he do that? Hey, Mai, you have to put a leash on our boy. This is a bad time, and that's a bad place for one of his crazy archeological photo-safaris. You have to stop him. This is a bad idea," Catherine said.

"Too late," Mai said, "and I'm afraid it's my fault. In consulting with our friend professor Marty Wenabe, the archeologist, we think we know where there is something we need to find and protect. They've already left. I'm worried, Cat. I even sent Jasmine with him to watch over him for me."

"The super-girl martial arts expert?" Kelly asked.

Mai laughed. "Yep, she's all that, but they won't be using martial arts in Iraq, Cat. Damn, I feel so helpless. But that's not why I called."

"And why was that? Oh, by the way, we're set to fly over the fifteenth of July; Kelly and I. Charlie will already be there. Can't wait!"

"Well, I called to remind you Devi is flying there, coming in tomorrow morning. Be sure she has good security. My danger sensors are running maxed out, Cat," explained Mai. "Something is not right, but I can't see it yet."

"Not to worry, I will put Ben on it personally. But there is something else too. I had my friend Warren Stamp from the FBI in here today, and he told me that they are going to open an investigation of you in connection with the Senate Judiciary Committee. You are being charged with stock manipulation, fraud, terrorism and even murder. He says the charges on paper look substantial, and I told him it was an end-run to try to shut down our investigation on derivatives. What do you think?" she asked.

"Well, that is a coincidence," Mai said. "I just had a similar conversation with an old friend of ours that works high up in the Chicago Police Department. He has been handed a file that originated from Senator Grimes accusing me of the same crimes you just mentioned."

"Yes, exactly," said Catherine. "He seems to think attacking me is the best way to get me to back down on my investigation to prove he killed his wife five years ago. I know he did it, but I just can't prove it, and so far he has gotten away with it. But there is more this time. It is not just he doing this. Le Beaulieu Financière Mondiale out of France is also behind it."

"Beaulieu? Cat, that is something we have been monitoring very closely here," said Mai. "Remember I told you that Asian World Investments was secretly buying stock in European corporations? If our estimates are correct, they now have a controlling share in Beaulieu. There are a couple others we have put on that same list, but you have to admit that makes sense. We knew they were coming after us but who would have expected something like this? It's crazy and insane. Cat, we should share our information with the Committee, and bring charges against them. We have enough real evidence to make the charges stick. They are really criminal. But can they bring charges against foreign companies?"

"I gave Warren a copy of our file on Grime's Nassau accounts. That should shut the whole thing down for now. He won't want that coming out," Catherine explained.

They were silent for a moment as both sides pondered what might happen next.

Mai spoke first. "Cat we have to think about this. Something isn't right. This isn't the end game. They're playing us."

"Well, we think it is either to get us to drop the story about derivatives, or to stop investigating Senator Grimes," said Catherine.

"No," said Mai. "That's too obvious. There is something else going on. I can feel it. They are trying to distract us from something. Let's put our heads together and think about it," suggested Mai.

"OK, Mai. We're on it," said Kelly.

"With all of that I have completely forgotten about Jack going to Iraq," said Mai. "Sometimes I think, Cat, we should just forget the whole thing, and retire. We both have enough money to never be able to spend it all. Why do we do this?"

"I can't help myself, and neither can you. It's not about the money, never was. We love this stuff. You love computers and data, and I love telling stories. It's what we do," said Catherine.

"Oh my gosh! I almost forgot, and as an asterisk to all of that, I can tell you that you have a mole in your financial department that is making NearNorth Stock available," said Mai. "I didn't authorize any sale of stock, and I know Brad Martin didn't either. Not to worry though, I am blocking all sales on my end, and even buying the stock that becomes available before the rest of the market sees it," said Mai. "My team here is working their way back to the source, but he covers himself really well."

"Who could it be, Mai? It would have to be someone higher up, right?" asked Catherine.

"No, just someone who is good with computers, and has access to our network command level. It could be anyone who can get access to the network. Remember, Eddie warned us he thought Su Ling had another operative in NNP. Give me a couple of days, and my guys will track it down. We have a better lead this time," said Mai.

"There is something else I need to tell you about," Mai said, and she proceeded to tell them the entire story about Su Ling, Yameda and the ancient door beneath the palace. She explained that the stakes were very high, and just how dangerous their adversaries had become.

"So be alert, and watch your backs. I will stay in contact. Remember Devi comes tomorrow. Please protect her. "

There was a pause in Mai's words while she instructed one of her aides. Momentarily, she came back on the line.

"I have to go, more meetings," she said finally.

"OK, Mai," said Catherine. "We love you, and you watch *your* back."

As Catherine slowly hung up the phone, she looked at Kelly's worried face, and said, "Let's be sure Ben is at the top of his game."

"Mai has never been one prone to exaggeration," said Kelly. Where do we start?"

"Let's put our heads together, and make a list," suggested Catherine.

Chapter 26

2005 Mosul, Iraq

Jack, Marty, and Jasmine made it to Iraq. But for all their effort they found themselves sitting on a cement floor leaning up against a metal wall in a crowded, noisy, airport hangar with hundreds of other detainees. American soldiers of the 101st Airborne stood guard in tan fatigues, and IBA vests, while people yelled to each other in conversation against the constant prop and jet noise just beyond the large hangar doorway open to the busy flight line. The rest of the airport and the city of Mosul were closed off to them, and in spite of their pleas to the Army Master sergeant who was running the show, they were told in no uncertain terms they were to stay put until further notice.

They were dressed in light tan khakis, and they only had their carry on luggage. The unauthorized charter airplane they arrived in left on orders from the military with most of their belongings minutes after dropping them off. Upon landing they were told not to get off of that airplane, but they did anyway because their mission was so important. Marty's pleas that the CIA sanctioned their mission were ignored due on the lack of any paperwork supporting his claim.

Marty sat with his head leaning back against the hangar wall with his eyes closed. Jack looked at him momentarily, gave a sigh, and deadpanned, "Well, here's another fine mess you've gotten us into."

Marty smiled at that, opened his eyes and looked over at him, "Hey, that was pretty good. I like Laurel and Hardy. I bet none of this generation even knows who they were. Jasmine, do you know who Laurel and Hardy were?" he asked, encouraged by Jack's attitude.

Jasmine thought a moment. "Was one of them that hobo with a cane, and mustache?"

"Nope, that was Charlie Chaplin," explained Marty. "These two were comedians that came along a bit later, one big and fat, the other small and thin."

"No clue, Marty. Sorry," she said.

He looked at Jack in triumph. "My point exactly."

"You seemed deep in thought a minute ago, Marty. Where did you go?" asked Jack.

"I was thinking about where we are going, or more correctly, where we would like to go: Nineveh, the ancient Assyrian capital. I have always meant to come back here, and spend some more time studying that site, and the ancient Assyrian culture in detail. Wait till you see it, Jack. You can still see some of the walls remaining from that great city that was here over twenty-six hundred years ago. I find it fascinating…but I don't want to bore you with my ramblings about ancient history."

"Pardon the pun, professor, but you have a captive audience. It looks like we have a boatload of time at the present, now that we're stuck in this hangar until tomorrow morning. Since I've been photographing archeological sites all over the world, I've become a huge fan of the ancient cultures. I am constantly amazed at what I see. But I admit I know next to nothing about the Assyrians. They must have been one of the lesser cultures back then, right?" asked Jack.

"Oh, heavens no! The Assyrians have not been covered in the history books because they were ruthless, demanding, and not as glamorous as the more well known empires that succeeded them. They ruled this area of the Middle East for over two hundred years. Theirs was the first great empire and they were ruthless and cruel conquerors. This area of the world had been a loose group of city-states, and warring tribes before that time. They are given credit by historians for taming the many disenfranchised city-states, and unifying them under one rule. They set the stage for the more familiar empires that followed, the Babylonians, the Persians and even Alexander the Great.

"Nineveh, the magnificent capitol of the Assyrian empire, covered sixteen square miles and its walls were fifty feet high and fifty feet thick. I'm not exaggerating, Jack. Long after the empire fell the walls and city were still here and standing almost intact. In fact, the Persians called it a 'ghost city' when they came here two hundred years later. It was completely empty, and they thought the gods built it. It was even larger and grander than Babylon, the city of ancient legend whose descriptions fill the history books. That's how magnificent it was. But as impressive as the Assyrian empire was, it was crushed and disappeared over a relatively small period of time–fourteen years," Marty explained.

"How did that happen if they were so powerful?" asked Jack, surprised.

"They grew soft, decadent and none of their subject neighbors cared for the harsh manner of their rule. A population growth and a severe drought proved to be the final straws that felled the world's first great empire. They were attacked first by the Medes, and then the Babylonians joined them. Soon the Scythians joined in, and the Egyptians too. Everyone attacked them at once until there was nothing left. That was around 615 BCE. But the Assyrians changed cultures and warfare in ways that were revolutionary for their time. They were the first to have entire divisions on horseback, and chariots that moved at great speed. They were the first to have their army armed with swords of iron, and they built this magnificent city Nineveh as their capitol that was unrivaled at the time in its magnificence and grandeur."

"I can't wait to see it," said Jack.

"I'm afraid there is not much left of it now by comparison. But perhaps when we are there you can imagine how it must have been."

"What happened to that contact you said would take care of us once we got here? I believe your exact words were, 'Don't worry, it's all arranged,'" asked Jack.

"I don't know. I'm as surprised by all of this as you are. I really thought he would be here to greet us when we flew in," replied Marty, "Especially since I had no paperwork to prove this was a CIA sanctioned mission."

Jack was lost in thought for moment, and then said, "OK, Marty, Jasmine and I are going to get out of here as soon as we can. The army guys told me that the Sunni factions here in Mosul are forming a separate guerilla army targeting all Westerners in general, and Americans in particular. There is a civil war between the Sunnis and Shiite factions about to break out. This whole thing is ready to pop, and this place is crazy unsafe for us. Even the soldiers don't want to go into Mosul proper. They say there are snipers everywhere, and something called IEDs, whatever that is. Nothing is worth getting killed over. Let's get out of here on the next cargo plane. What do you say?"

"IED stands for Improvised Explosive Device, boss," said Jasmine "They are like homemade bombs the insurgents have made from unguarded Iraqi artillery shells. Apparently, it was not the policy of the administration bureaucrats running the American occupation to secure Iraqi weapons, and arms when they disbanded their army. There are a lot of those home-made kinds of explosives all over Iraq now as a result."

Marty did not answer for a minute, and just sat with his eyes closed again. After a moment he opened his eyes and turned to Jack with a serious expression, "Look here, I can't leave. I have to stay. I know that if I leave I will never find the object Mai and I are hoping to find. It really is important. This is the most important thing I have ever done in my life. I strongly feel that, and especially after what Queen Maisong has done for me, I can't let her down. But you take Jasmine and get out of here. I understand completely. I hoped the conflict in Mosul was over, but now with this new uprising as Americans leave, it is getting dangerous again. I'm sorry I got you into this. But we're so close now. I have to stay, and I have to find some way of getting out of here, and to the ruins."

"I'm not going anywhere. I'm good, boss," insisted Jasmine who was wearing a dull green scarf over her head following the custom of Iraqi women. "We can handle this. I think we should stay with Marty. He's right. This is important to Queen Mai."

Jack noticed that Marty squeezed her hand, and continued to hold her hand beside him. *When did that happen* he wondered? Jasmine had been with him on three of their four field trips to various possible sites looking for the missing artifact around Asia and the Middle East, and these trips usually lasted about a week. He had entirely missed that. Jasmine gave a glance toward him looking for a reaction to her statement. She saw him looking at their hands, and quickly pulled hers away.

Jack studied their faces and saw them in an entirely different light. After a moment they both let out a breath and settled back. Jasmine wrinkled her nose and looked back at him with an awkward smile.

"Come on, you guys. When did that happen? How long have you two been lovers?" asked Jack.

"Almost since the first day," replied Marty. "Remember when I was joking about her at Abydos? We had already hooked up by then. The truth be known, I fell in love with her the first day when I met her at Siem Kulea, and she gave me the tour around the Palace."

"Jas, why didn't you tell me? I would think I would be the first person you would tell," exclaimed Jack.

"It's complicated, boss. I was afraid if Queen Mai knew Marty and I are involved she wouldn't let me go with you, and send somebody else on these trips. She might think I would not watch out for you," Jasmine explained. "Frankly, I have been a bit distracted. Please don't tell her."

Jack noted she had started calling him 'boss' like Kelly used to do and, no doubt she picked that up from Kelly. He didn't for a minute believe she had really been distracted. She took her responsibilities seriously, and she had sworn a vow to her queen. At the most, she probably geared back to a superior bodyguard-assistant level, he mused.

He looked around the very crowded hangar as another group of soldiers came in from the open door leading to the flight line. There were people in all types of dress standing or sitting in place around the large hangar. Jack suspected a good portion of them were reporters with news services not directly affiliated with the United States. They all looked upset, and he could relate.

"I'm happy for both of you. I think it's a great match. I just wish you had told me. I'm surprised I didn't catch on sooner. Now I understand why you were already packed when Mai called you. You planned to go anyway, didn't you, Jas?"

"Yep. I was getting ready to call Queen Mai when she called me, and I will be diligent, boss. I promise. I managed to bring three Sigs, and three extra clips for each of us in my backpack. They never even checked it. Some security!"

Jack saw a Lieutenant walk in, and pass around salutes. He decided it was worth a try, and got up to go ask him some questions.

It took a few minutes to get near the busy Lieutenant, but after a moment he was able to get his attention and managed to pull him aside for a conversation. "Lieutenant," he began, "I am Jack Largent, an American citizen. My friends who are also American citizens and I are archeologists on a mission sanctioned by the CIA. We only need to spend a short time at the ancient Nineveh ruins site north of here; two hours at the most, and then we can clear the area. My friend is Professor Marty Wenabe from John Hopkins University. He is a world-renowned authority on Middle Eastern Culture and History. It would be a great favor if you would release us to go and take a quick look."

"I have no paperwork or brief on that. Do you have paperwork on your mission?" the lieutenant asked.

"No, I'm afraid not. There was supposed to be someone meeting us here that would have handled that," explained Jack.

"Well, I'm sorry, sir," the Lieutenant replied. "I have strict orders to hold all Western civilians here for safety reasons. This is Mosul, Iraq, and in case you haven't noticed the war is still here in spite of our efforts to clean out the insurgents. Besides, this airport is located South of the city, and on the opposite side of the river from the Nineveh ruins site. To get there, you have to travel through heavily populated Sunni areas along very narrow streets that are all but impossible to get through safely in a vehicle. You may have heard that the other day two American mercenaries were hung and burned, on a bridge in Baghdad. The Sunnis do not like Americans right now, sir. They consider us allies of the Kurds and the Shiites who they hate with a passion. You will not be permitted to leave this hangar. That remains in effect through tonight. Tomorrow morning early a flight is coming in to transport you all out of the country."

"But, what if we don't want to leave in the morning?" asked Jack.

"Sir, you have placed yourself in the middle of a military operation without anyone or any government's permission as far as anyone can tell. I am not sure how you even found a way to get here under the circumstances. This is a very serious, and dangerous situation, and we don't have the time or resources to protect you. Please return to your friends. We will remove you from here as soon as we are able. Sergeant!" he said, calling over an MP who was standing nearby. He gave him instructions to take Jack back to where he was sitting.

Jack sat down again, and after a moment said, "Well, that was a waste of time. The worst part was that he was right! Damn, I hate this place."

"Well it wasn't all for naught," said Marty. "While you were talking to the lieutenant, Jas was approached by that man over there sitting by the door. He said his name is Hakim, and he works for the friend of mine who was supposed to meet us when we arrived. He found a way to get us out of here, but he told us we have to be ready."

"Ready for what, exactly?" asked Jack, thinking that Marty was holding back on him.

"I am as clueless as you are. I swear. But really, are you game? Jasmine is willing, but she won't go unless you do." said Marty.

Jack looked at Jasmine and realized the predicament she was in. She loved Marty and wanted to stay with him, but she swore to Mai, her queen she would protect *him*. As silly as that sounds, it was just the opposite. So, he thought, *in for a penny, in for a pound. He would stay with his friends.*

"Yeah, let's do it," he said.

As the afternoon passed, more Western refugees assembled in the hot and muggy hangar area. Most passed the time in quiet worried conversation while others took the time to find something to lean against and take a nap. Then as the sun got lower in the sky, the situation changed abruptly. Rockets began hitting the airport, and there were lots of explosions outside on the flight line; one or two at first, and then many more, some in bunches, some several minutes apart. Detainees in the hangar began screaming and trying to find places to protect themselves, even though no rockets were hitting anywhere near the hangar area. The managed order quickly turned to chaos as some of the troops retreated behind sandbagged areas, while others formed a protective barrier around the more eminent civilian detainees gathered in one corner of the hangar.

Then one of the rockets landed very near outside of the hangar creating more chaos within. Suddenly, the man Hakim showed himself and signaled for them to follow him through a side door. In all the confusion they were able to escape unseen into a carpool area outside and adjacent to the hangar. They kept low, and made their way hurriedly through rows of Humvees and military vehicles. They worked their way to one of the Humvees on the outside of the parked group. They crouched by one, while Hakim, carrying a duffle bag, took a look inside.

He signaled to them, and they all quickly got in. Hakim changed his shirt to an American military uniform shirt, and he handed Marty who sat in the front seat with him a military jacket, which he quickly put on over his civilian clothes. They both put on helmets that were inside the Humvee. Rockets were still exploding along the flight line as they raced away. Hakim drove with focused determination, and as they neared the perimeter guard, they did not slow down. Their luck held, and they rushed past the guards who gave them little more than a glance. Once beyond the airport perimeter, Hakim was able to avoid the conflict areas, and navigate the narrow streets. There were scattered groups of people here and there carrying their belongings fleeing the city toward the north.

They crossed a bridge, and after ten minutes, they came to a large massive ancient gate and wall structure. There were many crumbled remains of buildings fading into the distance. This was the ancient Assyrian city of Nineveh ruins site. Marty sat up in his seat looking out of the window and became visibly excited. It was late in the afternoon, and they did not have much time before dark. They would have to work quickly.

"Take us around to the other side, to the remains of the temple area. Please, hurry, Hakim," he said. "Is Amir going to meet us?"

"I do not know, professor. He said only for me to bring you to the ruins, as you requested. I am afraid Mosul is about to be turned into broken ruins like these. I love my city, and it is sad.

"Here we are," he said, as they pulled up before the half walls of an ancient temple. One end was restored to about half of its full height, but Marty went to the opposite end toward a wall that backed up against the wall of another building and extended out three feet making the entire structure about six foot thick.

Marty was leading them with a hurried pace, almost running, as he said, "Come on. As I recall it's over here. Hurry! Anything could happen. I have to say, I have never felt so anxious before."

Hakim retrieved the duffle bag he had brought with him from the truck. When they reached the wall, Marty quickly went through the tools inside the bag until he found a small hand pick, and hammer. In the late afternoon light, he moved his hands along the structure and stopped finally in the center where he saw eight concentric circles inscribed about twenty-four inches from the stone floor. He put on latex gloves and ran his hands over the circles as if trying to make a connection with them. Then without warning, he hammered the pick into the center of the circle design and began working a hole into the stone.

Jack was intrigued by Marty's enthusiasm, but as much as he wanted to share that with him, he was very nervous about their situation. They heard a great deal of gunfire in the distance marking the opening forays in the latest battle for Mosul. He fidgeted with his hand on his camera as he looked around at the deserted ruins about them. This was not a circumstance he foresaw when he decided to join his good friend as part of their plan to protect access to the secret door in the chamber beneath the White Palace.

Marty was down on his knees picking away at a small hole that he was now widening. He was off to a good start because the section of the wall he had chosen to attack with his pick proved hollow, and the hole that he had made grew slowly larger. But it was taking too long, and that only added to Jack's anxiety. Storm clouds formed overhead as the sun fell lower on the horizon, and they enjoyed a welcome cool breeze that now swept over the ruins.

Jack noticed Hakim looked nervous as he cowered down by the back wheel of the Humvee parked thirty yards away. It had gotten them out of the airport because it was an American military vehicle. In this area, it stood out like the golden arches of a McDonald's restaurant. Hakim kept looking down the road, and appeared ready to jump up, and leave with the first sign of any trouble.

Jasmine was vigilant and kept lookout while pacing silently behind Jack and Marty. She scanned the many ruined walls surrounding them. Now and then she stopped to focus on an area when she thought she saw movement.

"Jasmine, please go over, and stand by the Humvee, so Hakim doesn't leave us stranded here in no man's land," Jack said. He spoke louder than needed to remind Marty they were not in Egypt working in the Valley of the Kings.

"OK, boss. I'm on it," Jasmine replied. She was wearing one of the Sigs she had retrieved in a holster at her waist. "Whatever Marty is doing we'd better hurry. I'm not sure, but I thought I saw some movement in those ruins over on the other side."

Jasmine walked away with something else on her mind. She remembered there were four M-16s behind the back seat in the Humvee and they looked to be loaded. They would be way more useful if they got into a firefight than the Sigs any day.

"Jas is right. This is crazy. Come on, Marty. We have to go. I've got a bad feeling about this too. Even the sky looks like a storm is coming," said Jack, watching the dark storm clouds pushing down on them forcefully from the East. The sounds of gunfire seemed to be getting closer.

Marty turned around from where he was picking away at a hole in the platform just under the flat top portion, "Jack, as volatile as this area is, we may not be able to return here for some time, and I think I have found what we came for. I just need to dig a little more to get it out." He glanced over and saw Jasmine standing on the road by Hakim checking their newly acquired M16 rifles. "OK, I am tired of being coy with this. Hand me that large pick over there."

More out of frustration than anything else, he finally hit the wall four times viciously with the pick like a treasure hunter and not a respected Doctor of Archeological Studies from John Hopkins University. As the stones gave way, falling onto the old temple floor a small dark wooden box not more than one-foot square and deep, and held together by aged greenish metal, was revealed within the large hole Marty had formed with the pick.

"Jack, look! I think we found it!" he exclaimed.

As he examined the heavily inscribed box in its hiding place, an elated Marty declared, "I believe these inscriptions are from the time of King Ashurbanipal, the last great king of the Neo Assyrian Empire. It was probably hidden here before Nineveh was sacked by the Medes and Babylonians about 612 BCE."

"Wow, sometimes you amaze me!" said Jack honestly surprised. "Wait. Let me get some photos as you pull it out. I want to record this," he said raising his camera and stepping back a bit to photograph the whole scene.

Jack started moving about Marty taking photographs with his new digital camera from several angles. Marty laid out a velvet cloth on the ground near the wall. He removed the gloves he was wearing and acquired new latex gloves from his jacket pocket. After putting them on, he carefully removed the box from the hole he had made in the wall and set it down on the clean cloth.

"It was that inscription below the hole in the edifice in Egypt that you photographed, Jack, that led us to here. Let's quickly see what we have, and get out of here."

"The box is a bit heavy," he said as he turned it around in his hand looking at the carved and ornate surfaces of the box. "OK, I am going to try to open it. Get your camera ready, Jack."

With a fancy pocketknife from his pocket, Marty carefully pried back two clasps on one side of the box and raised the lid. What he saw startled him, and thrilled him at the same time. Inside was an intricately detailed object, which looked to be made of the same golden elusive element they had seen on the door in the basement chamber at Siem Kulea. It was curious because it did not look like the artifact in Siem Kulea as he suspected it would. It was a disk, round in shape about five inches across. The top was exquisitely engraved with a concentric circle design, but eight points were defined by hoa cuc flowers and snake designs like the ones on the door in Siem Kulea. Directly in the middle was a larger engraving of the Hoa Cuc flower."

"Jack…Jack, do you see this?" Marty asked.

"Yes, I see it, move your head in closer to the box, Marty…a little closer. There. Hold that!" Jack said as he continued to take photos.

"Jack this was not expected. I wonder how it fits in with our theory. I can't wait to study it."

"Marty," said Jack as Marty continued to extol on the importance of what they had found without looking up at him.

"Marty," he said again as Marty ignored him while he studied the object carefully.

"Marty!" Jack said louder as he put a hand on his shoulder.

"What, Jack?" Marty asked as he turned around. Forming a half circle around them on the ruins floor of the ancient stone temple were six Iraqi soldiers all carrying AK-47s pointed at them, and bearing unfriendly expressions.

Marty closed the box and put it down quickly. Following their commands, he put his hands behind his head and assumed a kneeling posture as Jack had done. Marty spoke Arabic, and he told them he was part of an archeological group studying the ancient ruins. They did not respond as Marty continued to explain.

Then everything happened at once. Hakim and Jasmine were running toward them from the Humvee carrying M16s, and one of the soldiers turned his AK-47 toward them and aimed. Jack responded from his kneeling position by pushing the barrel of the soldier's gun upwards as he fired at the sudden movement sending a burst of bullets up in the air. The other men turned on Jack with their weapons, but then a loud voice yelled at them in Arabic. The Iraqi soldiers quickly collected themselves and lowered their weapons slightly as Hakim and Jasmine joined the group breathing heavily and pointing their M16s back at the soldiers. The man who had yelled was wearing the Iraqi army uniform of a Colonel, and he quickly took charge of the situation. Marty first, and then Jack, stood while the Colonel was busy dressing down his men, and sending them to guard the perimeter. He turned to Marty with a serious expression, and Jack was surprised when he spoke perfect English.

"You see the trouble you cause me, my friend?" he said slowly, breaking into a huge smile. Then he grabbed Marty by the shoulders, and hugged him as if they were brothers. Jack and Jasmine looked at each other in surprise. This must be the friend Marty had told them about thought Jack.

The Iraqi Colonel told Marty how worried he was when he heard he had decided to return during all the current chaos. He informed them they had been prohibited just recently from entering the airport as Iraqi nationals, "Hakim has always in his own way been very resourceful, so I left it up to him to make contact with you at the airport." They held each other at arm's length talking like true comrades who genuinely cared for each other.

After a moment, the Colonel turned to Jack and Jasmine. "Please forgive my rudeness but Marty and I have a long, wonderful history together. We have been in many tight spots have we not, my friend? But I suspect this might be one of the most dangerous. You are as foolhardy as ever," he said to Marty, before turning once more to Jack and introducing himself.

"My name is Colonel Hamad Amir. Most of my friends just call me Amir." I hope you will be among them," he said, as he kissed Jasmine's hand and shook Jack's.

"I am Jack Largent, Marty's friend, and photographer. This is my assistant, Jasmine."

"I don't think I have ever seen you actually dressed in your uniform of rank," remarked Marty. "I must say you look like a bit of a despot."

"Ah, yes. I think I agree, but my soldiers give the proper response upon seeing me in this manner of dress. So during these difficult times, it is very useful. We are not an army anymore, only security forces, and the insurgents attack us as much as the Americans. We must get to a safer location," said the Colonel.

"Ah," he continued, seeing the box on the ground, "you did indeed find something! May I have a look?"

"Of course, you of all people will appreciate this, Amir. We have talked about this many times," said Marty, reaching down, and lifting up the ornate wooden box he held in the velvet cloth.

The Colonel took it in his hands for a moment and handed it back to him. "It's a little heavy for such a small box, no? Have you opened it?"

"Yes, go ahead, and lift the lid. I am afraid I must hold it with both hands to be safe."

Colonel Amir held up his hands with a question on his face, and Jasmine on cue reached into Marty's coat pocket and pulled out a set of latex gloves. "Thank you, Miss…Jasmine, is it? Marty, why have you not brought this young lady…" he said, stopping mid-sentence as he opened the box and saw the object for the first time.

"Oh, by Allah, this is extraordinary!" he exclaimed. "The quality of this artifact is amazing, and in this setting it is unbelievable. But I am not sure what it is. Do you know what it is, Marty? It certainly is unlike anything I have seen before."

Jack leaned in to have a close look himself before taking more photographs, but upon seeing the artifact clearly for the first time he was surprised like Marty that it did not look like the other part for the door to the chamber in the palace basement. He presented a curious expression and remarked, "It certainly is interesting."

Amir realized there was more to this story. "Well, I see you have made a great find, Marty. Come let's get to a safe place, and talk about this. Hakim, please rid yourself of that vehicle you brought from the base, and meet us back at my father's place. Get your things ready. We are leaving tonight."

Chapter 27

2005 Mosul, Iraq

They drove back across the river using the Colonel's van taking a roundabout route that avoided any apparent danger and exposed them to mostly empty and deserted streets. After ten minutes, they parked in the rear of a storefront that looked like an old antique shop. Its windows were boarded up.

"This belongs to my father," explained Colonel Amir as they got out of the car and he led them inside. "He and most of my relatives departed Mosul to the north a week ago. We could not go to my place because that is the area unfortunately where the gunfire you are hearing is coming from. The conflict has already restarted there."

In the distance, they heard a great deal of gunfire as Marty mentioned. "That sounds like the war has again returned to Mosul," said Jack.

"That is nothing, my friend," replied Amir. "Wait until morning. Then you will hear the cruel cacophony and chaos of war that has no boundaries for friend, or foe, and preys on innocents mercilessly. I fear this war that has come to our country will spread like a disease across the Middle East."

Through a stone garage structure, they made their way to a back patio that was partly covered on one side, and open on the other to a beautifully kept garden. They all sat around a large table where Marty placed the artifact gently.

Servants appeared anxiously, and Colonel Amir looked surprised. He thanked them for their loyalty, but instructed them in Arabic that after they prepared dinner, they should leave, see to their families, and depart the city. He wished them well, and bid them stay safe in the upcoming conflict.

He joined his new friends at the table and switched back to English. He explained to Jack and Jasmine that he and Marty were fellow students at John Hopkins University several decades ago. While attending the university, they became best friends and explored many of the historic sites around Iraq together. Amir named his first son, Martin, after his best friend. It was Marty who stood beside him when his wife died giving birth to his daughter, Sadie.

It was over many late night conversations that they proposed the theory of ancient aliens visiting Earth, and causing the spark that allowed humans to evolve into cognitive beings. The circles became the symbol of their theory when they were found all over the world yet according to any historical record had no cultural nexus.

Once drinks arrived, Colonel Amir held up a glass, and proposed a toast, "To old friends and new in times of peril." They all touched glasses, and as they again settled back, Colonel Amir noted, "You seem fascinated with the artifact in the box, Jack."

Jack was not sure how to answer. He was not sure if they could trust Colonel Amir with their secret. "It is more beautiful and I guess different than I expected."

"You expected to find this object? I sense there is a story here that you three share, and I do not. Please, will you include me in your confidence?" he asked smiling.

"What confidence?" asked Marty with his hands out in a question.

"Come on, my friend. There is obviously something going on here that you three share and I do not and perhaps at the very moment of what appears to be our greatest victory together. We have both talked about this many times over the years. We have both sought proof for what others thought was an outlandish theory. But now when it seems we might have that proof, you leave me out in the cold. You must tell me what is going on here." he protested.

"Amir, my friend, I'm afraid it has gotten a bit complicated. I have been told a secret connected with this object at a solemn moment of great trust, and that I have vowed to not tell anyone. Jack, what do you think?" Marty asked.

But before he could answer Colonel Amir continued, "Marty, this object that appears unique in many ways, which you found in a wall constructed before 600 BCE appears to lend credence to our theory. You would not even have come to this theory of ours if I hadn't walked you around the sites in Iraq, introduced you to the knowledgeable people in my country, and interceded with authorities. I daresay the very artifact you found today, you would not have found if I had not shown you that site with the concentric circle carvings. Of all the people in the world I would bet my life that you would be one I could count on to share everything with me," said the Colonel with growing frustration.

Marty lowered his head embarrassed. Finally, he said, "Jack we need this man if we are to get out of here with this artifact safely. I trust him as a friend, brother, and with my life. Can we tell him why this artifact is so important? I believe he has a right to know."

Jack reached over and opened the box again showing the round artifact with the snakes and the circles, and the Hoa Cuc flower settled in the middle. Colonel Amir was surprised to see Jasmine bow her head reverently toward the artifact.

"Yes, I would love to join in your knowledge of this," said Colonel Amir. "Why is your assistant bowing toward the artifact, Jack? I saw her do that at the ruins too. Tell me, please."

"Colonel, you noticed the concentric circles and the snakes printed on the artifact within," began Jack. "But I bet you made little note of the symbol right in the middle. Both Jasmine and I saw that instantly. It is the Hoa Cuc flower, the sacred symbol of her people, the Champa people, dating back thousands of years. It is the symbol of their queen who they must obey without question.

"My wife, Queen Maisong, the current Champa queen, is in fact descended from the ancient rulers of the Champa kingdom. They last ruled as a kingdom around 1000 AD before the Dai Viet army from the North, and the Khmers from the West overwhelmed them. They are a very intelligent people, and were culturally advanced and very sophisticated for their time. They were at the center of the trade routes through Southeast Asia, and are largely responsible for civilization maturing in Asia."

"So this Hoa Cuc flower has a meaning as a symbol? Your wife is this Champa queen for real?" asked Amir.

"That symbol you see in the center of those circles is imprinted in the form of a birthmark on my wife's hip," said Jack. "Her people believe that the person, and I think it has always been a female, who possesses that birthmark is the legitimate heir to the ancient rulers of their people. My wife, Queen Maisong, now rules, and lives in peace with her people in the Siem

Kulea valley in Northern Cambodia, over six thousand miles from here." He paused to look at him, and let that thought sink in at the same time hoping Marty noted he had neglected to mention the door they hoped would connect with the part of the handle device they had already seen in Siem Kulea.

Jack shook his head as he continued. "All of this is fascinating to me, and I tell you I have been enchanted for many surprising years around my wife, Mai. It seems when I just get things figured out, something new surfaces to confound me."

"Well, let's consider the possibilities," said Amir. "We have an extraordinary disk inside of a box that had to be placed there before 600 BCE, which contains the concentric circle design and this time, with the snakes, and the Hoa Cuc flower in the center. The disk and even the box for that matter could be much older. By tradition, the concentric circles symbolize life in the universe or universal life. It is also a language, a mathematical language, and a connection to all things physical, and spiritual in the universe. That alone would seem to connect your wife with other beings in the universe. That's one possibility."

"Wait," interrupted Jack. "I want to make one thing clear. Mai, my wife, is very intelligent…super intelligent. She's a wiz like no one else with data, and numbers. But she is not an alien, and not a god in spite of what her people believe." Jack put his arm around Jasmine as he finished.

"But, Jack," said Marty, "She is connected. She is connected to the ancients by the evidence we see before us."

"She is connected to the gods," said Jasmine. "The gods speak through her. That is what we believe. I worship and obey her as do all Champa people. That is our duty."

"I admit it is baffling, and fascinating at the same time," said Colonel Amir. "I wonder, Marty. Would you see if the disk could be removed from the wooden box?"

Marty looked at him abruptly, and then wondered why he had not proposed the same idea. He nodded, put down his glass, and pulled some latex gloves from his jacket pocket like before. Jasmine smiled at this. She had already grown accustomed to the idea that he always had a pocket full of latex gloves.

Marty passed around latex gloves to Jack and Amir, and said, "Jack I want you to lift up the box, and while I hold the disk gently turn the box over. Be very careful. Do not make any quick movements. Amir, you have your hands ready to catch anything that might unexpectedly fall out. OK, here we go, gently now. Very gently."

Jack raised up the box about a foot from the velvet cloth on the table. Slowly he turned it over. At first, it looked like the disk was a part of the box itself but then it began to move out from the box exposing an unexpected thickness of a polished solid gold-like metal. As Jack turned the box on more of an angle, the disk showed a bottom beveled edge after about two inches, but it did not drop out. It continued to extend out from the box on an unusually shaped bar. As the shaft grew in length to two inches, Jack raised the box a bit higher. Finally, with a triangular shaft of about eight inches, the entire artifact fell out into Marty's hands. Jack turned the box over and set it back down on the cloth.

Marty turned the unusually shaped object around for everyone to see all sides with a broad smile on his face.

"Marty, it is what we were looking for after all!" said Jasmine. "It is a part of the door handle."

"Door handle? What door are you speaking of?" Amir asked, looking at her and then to Marty. "

Marty took a deep breath and looked at Jack who had his face buried in his hands.

Jasmine realized her mistake. "I'm sorry, Jack. But you already mentioned the door, didn't you? Oh, crap! But it doesn't make any sense to hide what is so obvious anyway. I mean if you have a door handle you must have a door somewhere."

Marty nodded, and said, "And I respect my friend too much to play this game any further.

"Amir, there is a door in Siem Kulea beneath a white palace, which is unlike any door you have ever seen."

Marty proceeded to tell Amir about the door and all he knew about it including the part where Queen Mai insisted that it should never be opened.

"All of this is fascinating indeed," said Amir. "I can now see why you have risked everything to try to recover this artifact. But it does seem to me that the more we know, my friend, the more questions we have."

Marty nodded. "Exactly. Jack, you know even with what has been found and revealed to you and me in the last few months, all of this was an unproven theory, still just a mystery. But I think we can agree now that there actually were ancients living here on Earth long ago and that there is something of great importance behind that door.

"Only we at this table and a few in Siem Kulea know of this, and no one at this table would ever reveal the secret, even Amir. I know him. He is like me, an ardent explorer of our ancient history. We are brothers in this, and I know of no other man I would trust like Amir. This secret is safe with us Jack."

Jack nodded. "I don't know how you feel about this, but I must insist that any decisions made about this artifact, or anything else related, must come from my wife."

"I think we agree with you, Jack," affirmed Marty. "We must seek answers and permission to proceed forward from the one person on Earth who has a direct connection with the ancient past. As extraordinary as that sounds, we all see the connection and are enthralled by it for separate reasons. We will follow Jack and Jasmine's lead, and beg permission, and counsel from Queen Maisong."

"My friends," Amir declared, "This looks to be the adventure of a lifetime. To Queen Maisong," he said as he raised his glass.

They all smiled and raised their glasses in a toast.

Jack's thoughts were reflective. Fifteen years ago Mai found the ancient Champa treasure near the temple in Thap Cham Vietnam. Fifteen years ago she helped to defeat, and destroy the agenda of Colonel Minh to conquer, and rule Southeast Asia. And fifteen years ago when Vietnam declared her a national hero of the People's Republic, she fled the publicity and the obligatory appearances that overnight made her a Vietnamese celebrity. Her friend Catherine even wrote a book about it making her an international star. She did not want publicity, only to live peacefully among her Champa people protecting any secrets the valley might hold. She had gradually accomplished her goal of living peacefully in Siem Kulea. This could mean the end to all of that.

Marty asked, "Amir do you have a case large enough to hold the object so that it won't be damaged as we transport it?"

"Yes, as a matter of fact, I have just the thing," replied Amir. He left and in a moment returned with a large square Halliburton aluminum case and sat it on the table next to the artifact.

"Perfect," said Marty. "That will do nicely."

Chapter 28

2005   Mosul, Iraq

A moment later a young man and woman dressed in jeans and polo shirts came out onto the patio with food from the kitchen. The young woman declared, "Poppa, we are back." She went around to where Colonel Amir sat and gave him a hug and kiss on the cheek.

"Is everything prepared?" he inquired of them.

"Yes, poppa," the young man replied, Hakim helped us. Two vans are all gassed up and packed in the garage ready to go. The servants have all left. We have only to get in and be on our way."

Amir switched to speak in English. "Please let me introduce my daughter, Sadie, and my son, Martin," said Colonel Amir. "You know your Uncle Marty, and these are my new friends Jack and Jasmine who will be going with us tonight. Go ahead, and bring in the rest of the food and then sit down, you two, and let's eat a good meal before we head off into the unknown."

As the meal progressed, Marty commented to Amir, "He is huge, I think he has grown three inches since I last saw him. Are you still trying for the Olympics, Martin?"

"I think those dreams are permanently on hold, Uncle Marty," Martin replied.

"Most unfortunate," said Marty. "I have no doubt that when it comes to accuracy with a firearm of most any variety, there is none finer."

"He will do much better in America I think," said Amir. "Maybe he can compete as a member of the team from the United States."

As they finished the meal, Amir explained his plan. "We are leaving Iraq tonight at midnight. American helicopters are meeting us about fifty miles north of here at a small airfield. They will fly us out to Turkey where we will be responsible for our own transportation from there. I have made arrangements for that already."

Jack was surprised. "I thought you were a Colonel in the Iraqi army."

"Yes, correct, but I am a Colonel of rank by my title in the province as Director of Antiquities. I have no military experience like my son Martin who has military training and is as you have already heard an expert marksman. In any case, since our agreement with the American forces in Mosul we are but a small security force, and not really part of any army at all. In fact, with the insurgents rising up again you might say we are right in the middle of it. That is one of the reasons we are getting out of here tonight. It is no longer certain who our friends are, and Sunnis, Kurds and Shiites alike are drawing lines in the sand.

"But I might as well tell you, I have worked since my time as a student in the United States for your CIA and predicted in reports that I filed with them, everything that happened after the Americans invaded. They knew all of this chaos was going to happen, and they let it happen anyway.

"Do not misunderstand," Amir continued. "I was never a fan of Saddam Hussein. But the devil you know is better than the devil you don't. This is a huge mess your country, and your president have created. As strange as it may seem, you needed Sadam Hussein in power in Iraq to keep the Middle East extremists in check. He was an extremist, but a balance to other extremists and particularly here in Iraq. In the Muslim world, it is always Shiite against Sunni. By ousting him, you are going to have radical revolutions all over the Middle East, and they will all point their swords toward the west. Mark my words!"

Amir took a sip of wine, but everyone could tell he was not done. "I am convinced the people who brought this war to Iraq had as part of their agenda to have my country in chaos so they could profit from the confusion. Why else would they invade without a plan for governing the aftermath of the war? Why would they disband the army that kept order in our country instead of converting it for keeping the peace afterward? Why would they allow huge stockpiles of weapons, and small arms all over the country to go unguarded inviting further revolutions and uprisings as we see happening here in Mosul? The local rebel militias will make thousands of homemade bombs from all of that. They are bringing in pallets on airplanes of American dollars that disappear overnight. Someone is profiting from all of that, and I can assure you, it's not the Iraqis. I warned my contacts in your CIA this would happen. But nothing was done. That was either gross incompetence or a well-conceived plan with a hidden agenda. I vote for the latter.

"I feel that my family and I will not be safe here now, so I am getting them out right away before it is too late. I am sad for my country, and I tried to prevent it. But moneyed interests have prevailed, and my country and people were sacrificed simply for greed," said Colonel Amir.

"Poppa, I saw a boy today named Yusuf who used to be in my classes at school," said Sadie. "He was carrying an AK-47 and very proud of himself. When the war began all the young men picked sides, and I don't understand them anymore. They are all crazy, Poppa, and they all have guns. He told me I belonged to him, Poppa, and actually ordered me to leave my work as a nurse volunteer at the clinic and join them. He talks like he owns me."

"Do you love him, Sadie?" asked Amir.

"I hardly know him, Poppa. He was just one of the boys in my class that I never talked to, and now he talks like he is important and he can just tell me what to do," she replied. "I was shocked when he told me that."

"That's why we are getting out of here tonight. You see?" Amir suggested, looking around the table. "Everyone is going crazy. The city is being turned over to gangs, and radical extremists."

He gave Sadie a hug. "Remember, you can tell no one we are leaving. No one! Do you understand me? Do not tell your friends, no matter how much you trust them. You too, Martin, do you understand? There are spies everywhere, and you will put our lives in jeopardy."

They both answered wearily, "Yes, poppa."

Chapter 29

2005 Mosul, Iraq

They took two vans. Six of them rode in the first with Amir driving, and Hakim followed in the second. The plan was to have a backup, just in case there was a problem. Amir did not anticipate any trouble because all the conflict was happening south of Mosul. Only refugees were moving north. But there were bandits, stray former Iraqi army units, and insurgents everywhere. So, they made sure their group was heavily armed. Jack and Jasmine were proficient with many weapons, and they both now carried the M16s that Hakim had saved from the Humvee. There were no lights on anywhere, but Amir and Hakim had night vision goggles that Amir had acquired from his American contacts. They had an extra pair, and Jack suggested they give them to Jasmine because she had the better eyes and the tactical training. They also had radio contact with each other through wireless collaboration ear buds, another toy supplied by the CIA.

Jasmine devised a tactical plan for trouble. They were to divide into three teams, Amir and Sadie, Marty and Jasmine, Jack and Martin. Hakim who was also military trained would work independently. With this plan in mind, they set out for the airfield. Hopefully, they would not have to implement it.

They exited the city through mostly dark narrow streets without incident, although they saw many armed men barricaded at intersections along the way. Outside the city, it cooled down a bit. The sky was very clear, the stars were out, and they were moving along at a fast clip. At one point Hakim reported there was a vehicle following behind them, but later he could not see it anymore. About ten miles north of Mosul they left Highway Two and headed toward Tel Kayf on a smaller, and bumpier road. After a few miles, they came to a roadblock.

It was very dark, and to Jack, it appeared there were two armored personnel carriers on either side of the road with machine gun mounts on each. Jasmine, sitting in the front right seat had a more precise and enhanced view. She told Amir the vehicles were non-functioning and destroyed. They could, however, make a formidable defensive position. Three soldiers saw them and moved to the middle of the road to block their way and they all carried AK-47s. Amir stopped down the road momentarily while they discussed the situation. Jasmine pointed out they were dressed haphazardly, but mostly in some form of Iraqi soldiers' uniforms. Amir suspected they were bandits. He told Hakim to keep back a distance, and pick the safest way to proceed. After taking a quick vote, it was decided to speed up and not stop for the roadblock.

Amir told everyone to buckle their seat belts. They were not more than a quarter-mile away from the roadblock. Amir started up with his foot all-the-way down on the gas pedal raising his speed quickly to over sixty miles per hour. As he got closer, the soldiers raised their weapons as if to fire, but then moved to the side of the road suddenly to avoid the speeding van. For a brief moment, it looked like they had made it through, but too late Amir saw the road had a large ditch dug across it. The van hit the ditch violently and rolled over twice landing about fifty yards ahead beside another wrecked vehicle.

Fortunately, the van landed upright, but the engine was smoking, and it was too damaged to continue. In the immediate aftermath, they were all stunned, confused, and taking personal inventories when Jasmine yelled, "Everyone out, let's go. Stay down!"

They all acted as one and immediately responded to her command.

"Sadie is hurt!" yelled Jack, from the back. "I think she has a broken arm."

"Get her outside, and bring her gun," ordered Jasmine.

Jack and Martin helped get Sadie out, and the rest quickly exited hunkering down behind the van. The Iraqi soldiers began firing at the van from behind the armored vehicles on either side of the road. Bullets were pinging on the metal, and dusting the ground nearby. Jasmine hurriedly peeked around the front wearing the night vision goggles to assess the situation, and to form a plan. They had AK47s supplied by Amir, but thus far they had not returned fire. After a moment, the gunfire from the soldiers stopped.

Hakim was still watching all of this while waiting down the highway. Without lights, they did not know he was there on that moonless night. He drove off the road. Slowly, and carefully, he made a big circle around everyone. He came to a stop beyond the other side of the van about fifty yards away and on their left side.

After a while, the Iraqi soldiers came out from their positions behind the armored vehicles and stood mostly in the open. They carried on a party-like banter between them confident those in the van were unarmed.

Hakim worked his way closer from his van, found a good shooting position, and suddenly began firing on the Iraqi soldiers. The surprised bandits immediately took cover and began returning fire toward Hakim. They did not seem to want to get into a firefight that night as after an initial response their return fire became minimal and sporadic. Jasmine assumed they planned to wait until morning when they could better assess the situation and press their advantage, or maybe their ammunition was low and they wished to conserve it. She observed what appeared to be a squad-sized unit of about eight Iraqi soldiers opposite them. They appeared to be stragglers and not well organized. She could not decide if they were actual soldiers or bandits as Amir had suggested.

She gathered everyone together behind the van and took charge without asking. She sent Jack and Martin to flank the armored vehicle on the left while she and Marty would go around to the right. Amir, Sadie, and Hakim, who had joined them, would return fire from behind the damaged van, and keep the Iraqi soldiers occupied, and concentrating on them.

Hearing her plan, Hakim, and Martin at first looked at her quizzically, but Jack advised them, "You would be making a huge mistake not to follow her lead. She has trained extensively for this and even in the United States. She is usually in charge of our militia maneuvers in the valley where I live. Believe me, she is by far the best trained among us. We have many like her in the valley where we are from. Martin nodded satisfied with the explanation and because she had a good plan. When they were ready to go, he and Jack quickly headed out around the left side to flank the armored car and the Iraqi soldiers on the left.

Jasmine grabbed Marty's arm, and said, "Come on, we can't let them get organized. Do what I tell you, and you'll be fine. You know how to use that weapon right?"

"Well, I think so," he said, sheepishly. "Honestly, I have never had to use one of these. You just pull the trigger, right?"

Jasmine took the weapon, pulled back the slide and set the selector on single. "Now you just pull the trigger. It will kick, so be ready for that. The most important thing is don't hesitate once you identify your target. They will kill you if you do. Shoot, and worry about it later."

"Okay, I think I have it," he said.

She leaned over and kissed him quickly. "Stay close, and follow my lead."

Amir and Hakim stayed by the van and began firing at the soldiers. Amir told Sadie to stay down as he and Hakim fired a few shots here and there to keep distracting the Iraqi soldiers. Sadie didn't like it but kept down just the same. She took the time to care for her arm making a sling out of her hijab. It was her left arm and she was grateful for that as she could still function well with her right.

The desert was empty, but filled with small holes and rocks that made the going a bit tricky. There were a few small hills, and uneven ground that allowed them to circle around unseen from the road. Martin and Jack came around the left side of the armored vehicle from behind, and had the drop on four Iraqi soldiers on their side of the road within ten minutes. They stayed low and hidden while they waited for Jasmine and Martin to signal that they were in position.

Jasmine and Marty had a similar situation circling around on the other side of the road, but ran into a problem. On their side of the road one lone Iraqi soldier had positioned himself back thirty yards from the rest, keeping an eye down the road in the opposite direction for any more oncoming cars. Not having seen the arrival of Hakim, had made the Iraqis more cautious. Jasmine decided he had to be taken out before they could ambush the other Iraqis hiding behind the armored vehicle on their side of the road.

She told Marty to stay back while she worked her way up toward the Iraqi soldier in silence. It was very dark in the desert that night as the moon had not yet come up. Slowly, and methodically, she came upon the Iraqi soldier from behind. She pulled out her MK3 navy knife, and grabbing hold of the soldier from behind, sliced his throat quickly from side to side in one motion being sure to hold his mouth silent with her hand. With his life gone, she slowly lowered the dead soldier to the ground. Then she turned and made her way back to Marty.

Marty, keeping an eye on the Iraqi soldiers behind the armored vehicles, did not see what Jasmine did, and gave a quick nod when she returned.

They moved off toward the trucks from behind, and took up positions facing the Iraqis on the opposite side of the road from Jack and Martin. Jasmine tapped her earbud to let Martin know she was ready. Martin yelled in Arabic and ordered the Iraqis to drop their weapons and to get down on the ground with their hands behind their heads. On each side of the road, there was one Iraqi who felt braver than the rest and attempted to fire toward Martin. Jasmine on the right, and Martin on the left dropped each of them with a single shot. With that, the rest put down their weapons immediately, and put their hands above their heads.

Jasmine, Jack, and Martin efficiently herded them together into a group on the right side of the road. While Martin and Jasmine kept them covered, the other two searched them, and then lined them up together sitting on the ground against one of the armored vehicles.

After getting the all clear from Martin, Colonel Amir joined them and began questioning the Iraqi soldiers while Martin and Jack watched. The soldiers told him they were ordered to guard this road and not let anyone pass. Since they were so few, they decided to dig up the road so any vehicles would have to go between the damaged armored personnel carriers and around awkwardly or crash. Amir understood considering the small size of their force that it was actually a good tactic.

Marty was relieved the gunfire was over. He took a breath, and said to Jasmine, "You were pretty impressive out there. I think I like this macho side of you especially since I have already gotten to know your feminine side so well."

But Jasmine was only half listening as she was still in combat mode and watching the scene around them intently. She observed Amir talking to the soldiers, and noticed that one of them kept glancing off toward the desert behind them. She turned, and again scanned the horizon; this time more carefully with her night vision goggles, looking for anyone who might be sneaking up behind them. Amir standing next to Jasmine and Marty was trying to take a friendlier approach with the soldiers. He commended them for their strategy with the hole in the road, and he was passing out cigarettes. But then Jasmine spotted three more soldiers coming up behind them stealthily.

She turned, and warned the others, yelling, "Look out, there's more coming!"

She pushed Amir away as bullets began landing around them and pinging into and off of the Humvees. She fired back in a spray of focused bullets that killed one of the attacking soldiers. But as she turned on a second of them she was herself shot with one of a series of bullets meant for Colonel Amir. It sent her flying back brutally and down to the ground in pain. Marty and Jack fired back and missed, but it had the effect of making the two remaining soldiers seek cover. Before they could do so safely, Martin already had them lined up in his sights and dropped both of the retreating soldiers with accurate shots in quick succession. The whole encounter was over in less than a minute. After that, the silence screamed at them as they looked around on all sides for other soldiers. They waited a tense and breathless moment, but there was no one else.

Marty dropped his rifle and ran immediately to Jasmine's side to check her wound. Sadie rushed over, and pushed him out of the way with a command, "Get out of the way and assist me, Uncle Marty. Lately, this kind of work is all I do as a volunteer at the hospital." She tore open Jasmine's blouse with one hand and began administering to the wound. Amir was at her side and said, "What can I do?"

Sadie said, "Poppa, get the first aid kit. Martin, guard those men. They are filthy bandits and should all die. If they move, shoot them!" Sadie winced as her broken left arm was still painful and hanging untended in the makeshift sling.

The wound was in Jasmine's left shoulder. Sadie pulled out a pack from the military first aid kit her father brought, and Marty opened it for her. She started to clean the wound but gave up and decided to instruct Marty how to do it instead as her left arm became very painful. He quickly and efficiently cleaned the wound with disinfectant and put a compress on it following her instructions. He taped it all up and said, "Come on, let's get her out of here. Help me get her over to the other van."

Martin said, let's get all the vitals out of the damaged van just in case we are not done tonight. Can she walk?" he asked.

Jasmine said, "I'm OK," but she struggled to get up, and Marty and Jack helped her walk slowly to the other van. After settling Jasmine in the middle seat, Jack returned and retrieved the large Halliburton aluminum case in which they had packed the artifact. He put it on one side of him, and held Jasmine on the other.

Amir was irate and resentful as he dressed down the remaining soldiers. Martin came over with his gun always pointing at the soldiers and his finger on the trigger. He said in English, "Poppa, we have to shoot them. They may have friends nearby they can contact. Go to the van. I will do it."

Amir had always been a peaceful man, and though he knew his son was probably right, it was hard for him to reason with more killing. "They are Iraqi's, son," he said, "We can tie them up."

"Poppa, they are bandits, gangsters, shit dogs of no value. They disgrace Iraqis like us. Sparing them might cost one of us our lives. Besides we have no time. Go, I will do it!"

Amir shook his head, and walked toward the remaining van as behind him he heard several bursts from Martin's AK-47. He was sad for everyone that night.

As they continued toward their rendezvous, Amir checked his watch. It was 0230 hours. They had thirty minutes to go five miles by his reckoning. He gave everyone an update on their situation.

"I think the small private airstrip is about five miles up this way, but we have to be careful not to miss the turn-off. As I said, it is seldom used. There should be a small wooden sign with a dirt road leading off to the right. It will say 'Kazar airstrip' in Arabic and English," Amir told them.

They started off again into the dark night. Hakim drove and Martin rode shotgun. Both were wearing night vision goggles.

After twenty minutes they became convinced they had missed the turn-off and began debating whether to turn back. Sadie who was in the second seat with Amir overheard their discussion, and told them, "Keep going, poppa. I know it is just a bit further. I have been there too and more recently several times on ambulance duty. Go further. I'm sure, I am right."

They went another five minutes, and were relieved to find the turn-off. They arrived very soon after at a small airstrip and noted it was deserted. They waited until 0300 hours when Martin lit a single flare and put it out on the dirt strip. In the night sky, it illuminated the area and could no doubt be seen for many miles especially if the pilot was wearing night vision goggles. They waited anxiously, and in a few minutes, they heard the lovely whup-whup sound of a helicopter.

There were actually three helicopters, a Chinook and two Apache gunships as escorts. The Chinook landed, and a crew chief exited. He came over to the group and explained they were looking for Colonel Amir. Colonel Amir introduced himself and informed the crew chief that they had one person wounded with a gunshot in the shoulder, and another with a broken arm. The crew chief nodded, spoke into his helmet, and two more men descended from the helicopter with a stretcher. The crew chief told Amir they had a trauma team on board during these missions because almost always there were wounded.

The two medics took charge of Jasmine, checked her vitals, placed her on a stretcher, and loaded her onto the Chinook. They quickly, and efficiently hooked her up to an IV pack and gave her morphine. The others climbed aboard the big Chinook assisted by the crew and buckled in. Sadie was finally getting her arm properly tended, and the medic who was applying a bandage around the military splint was having a friendly conversation with her at the same time.

Marty sat as close to Jasmine as they would let him and watched them tend to her wound.

Jack sat on the other side of him with the large aluminum case that contained the artifact. He asked Marty, "How's Jas doing?"

"Better than me, Jack," Marty replied. "I'm getting too old for this kind of thing. I was so selfish in my personal agenda I disregarded the danger to the rest of you."

"That's not true," insisted Jack. "We could have opted out at any time. As it was. you accomplished the mission. You should be proud of that, Marty. You kept us going with your focus and determination."

I have to tell you," he replied. "I don't know what I would have done if she had been killed back there. She saved our lives, Jack."

"Yeah, Mai will be proud of her for that. Can she talk?" he asked.

"I think she is high on morphine right now and resting. Let's let her rest," said Marty. He went forward to beg some water from the crew chief.

Amir came over, ran his hand along Jasmine's arm, and sat down beside Jack. "She's quite a woman. She was in her element out there. I would not have believed it if I hadn't seen it. I hope I can find the words to express my appreciation someday."

"If you want to thank her, to really thank her, tell Mai what she did. Tell Queen Maisong, and Jasmine will be very grateful to you for that, I promise," said Jack.

"Oh yeah, the Champa thing. OK, I will do that. Queen Maisong must be quite a woman herself. I can't wait to meet her," Amir said.

Jack nodded, and asked, "Where are we headed now?"

"Incirlik Airbase, Turkey. We will check in there, see to her wound, and then get her up to Ramstein Air Force base near Frankfurt to a really good hospital. They are the best in the world for these kinds of wounds. I have talked to the crew, and they called forward and made all the arrangements for her already," Amir said. "She is going to get VIP treatment all the way."

"Thanks for that," Jack replied.

Chapter 30

May 2005   Chicago

It was nine in the morning and overcast with dark rain clouds in Chicago when Devi Largent arrived at Midway airport aboard their family Bombardier Learjet from Bangkok, Thailand. As the cabin attendant opened and pulled back the door, she unbuckled, got up, stretched, grabbed her phone, backpack, and purse, and headed for the exit door of the full-size jet she had all to herself.

Standing in the doorway of the aircraft and looking out at Chicago's Midway Airport, she spoke her thought, "Finally!" But she immediately broke into a big smile when she saw Big Ben and Michael, the two body-guards who worked for her Aunt Catherine, waiting for her at the bottom of the airstairs.

She loved Big Ben like family. He towered over her but bent down so she could give him a hug. "I hoped you would be here." She turned to Michael, the other guard who was a former Seal and looked fit and handsome. She smiled. "Hi, Mike. Good to see you too! Looks like Aunt Catherine sent the first team on this one."

Catherine was not in reality Devi's Aunt, but she was considered family ever since Devi had known her, and was always referred to as 'Aunt' like her life-partner, Kelly. Devi got into the waiting limousine and made herself comfortable in the back seat. She grabbed a cold bottle of water embedded in the ice tray beside her while they put her luggage in the trunk.

As they were pulling out of the private gate, Devi saw a young lady standing beside a suitcase on the sidewalk looking neglected, and a bit worried. The young lady gazed toward the city apparently waiting for her ride.

On a whim, as a few raindrops fell onto her window, Devi called up front, "Michael, please stop. I want to see if we can help that young lady."

Michael stopped, but Ben protested as Devi began to power down her window, "Miss Devi we were ordered specifically not to stop, or let anyone into this vehicle. I think we should just continue on to your breakfast with Miss Catherine and Miss Kelly if you don't mind."

"Really? You want to leave that young lady standing out there in the rain when we have a whole limo empty? Ben, please, let's see if she needs a ride," Devi said.

"Now you sound like your mama, Miss Devi. Would you mind terribly if I take precautions before you go welcoming all the robbers and kidnappers into your vehicle?"

Devi rolled her eyes at him and said, "Well, Ben I looked, and she seems to have left her Mac-10 at home with her suicide vest."

Devi lowered her window, and called out to the young lady, "Could you use a lift into the city?"

The young woman looked to be in her early twenties, blond, with shoulder-length hair. She wore a tan coat, and straw hat over a print dress. She seemed surprised the limousine had stopped, and even more so that the person inside was a young Asian girl. She processed Devi's inquiry, and replied, "Well, yes, if you don't mind. I think they forgot about me, and it looks like it's starting to rain."

Ben got out of the limousine and approached the young woman. "May I see some ID Miss?"

The young woman looked unsure but opened her purse, and found her wallet. She was fumbling with it, when Ben took her purse from her and looked through it.

"Hey," she protested, "You can't do that."

"I'm sorry, miss. I need to check to see if you are carrying any weapons. Just doing my job," he said.

"Ben, you're being rude, and embarrassing me. Miss, are you carrying any weapons?" Devi asked a bit sarcastically.

"Huh? No! Why would I be? Look, I think I will just wait here, OK?"

Devi opened her door, and said, "Get in, before Ben decides he needs to pat you down." The girl looked confused for a moment and then decided to climb into the limousine.

"Ben, put her suitcase in the back please," Devi ordered.

Ben gave Devi a look of exasperation. He was obviously frustrated and took a deep breath. He held the door as the young lady got into the limousine, and sat beside Devi.

"Miss Devi, your Aunt Catherine is on the phone," said Michael from the front seat, as the girl settled in.

Devi picked up the car phone from the console at her side, and said, "Hi, Aunt Catherine! How are you? I just got in."

"So I've heard. What is going on, Devi? I hear you're giving your guards a difficult time. Let me be clear, young lady. When it comes to security, you obey Ben, not the other way around. Understand?"

"Aunt Cat, this has gone way over the top." She smiled at the young lady as she talked on the phone. "It's starting to rain outside, and I asked Michael to stop so we could give a young lady a ride into town. That's all. She looks like the girl next door, not a terrorist, or anyone who would want to harm me. Why doesn't anyone trust my judgment on this? I mean she's from...where are you from?" she asked the young woman who was listening intently to her conversation as they sat parked by the side gate of Midway Airport.

"Madison, Wisconsin...Audrey Goodnight," she said, holding out her hand, affably.

"Madison, Wisconsin...her name is Audrey Goodnight. Come on, Aunt Cat, trust me on this, OK? Now we have to give her a ride, or I will really be embarrassed. Besides, this is not who we are, running around afraid of everyone," Devi said.

"OK, tell Ben and Michael I said it was OK," replied Catherine. "Be good, and I will see you for breakfast at Saint Marie in thirty minutes. Be smart, Devi. Don't give your security a hard time. They only want to protect you. Tell Ben to get on the line, and I'll say goodbye to you for now."

Devi pushed the hold button, and called up front, "Ben, she wants to talk to you," Devi said.

"Thank you so much," Audrey said honestly. "You surprised me by stopping. I hope I'm not causing a lot of trouble."

"No problem at all. Sometimes we just get overly cautious, that's all. Where are you going?" asked Devi.

"Well, I don't have a place yet, so my new job put me up at the Drake Hotel for a week until I find a place. I am not sure where that is, have you heard of it?" she asked.

Devi called up front. "Michael, we need to drop her off at the Drake on the way in, OK?"

"Yes, Miss Devi," answered Michael, from the front.

"Let's start over," Devi said to Audrey. "I am Devearney Largent," she said, reaching out her hand, and smiling. "Everyone calls me Devi."

"This is really nice of you. I am Audrey Goodnight," the young woman said repeating her name.

Devi laughed, and involuntarily scrunched her face prompting Audrey to say, "Yeah, I know. My name sounds made up like a stripper. Actually, I am a reporter; well, soon now anyway. The Chicago Herald just hired me. I start tomorrow," she said putting her hand out to shake with Devi. "This is my big adventure, just in from Madison, Wisconsin."

"What's your middle name?" Devi asked.

"Huh? Oh, Jane, why do you ask?" she said.

"Well, I was thinking since you are just starting, you could make your pen name A.J. Goodnight, or Audrey J. Goodnight, or A. Jane Goodnight, just a suggestion, and I apologize for laughing. It wasn't about that. I was thinking about us and how difficult we make everything. I never would have thought what you said anyway. But now that you mention it, you are beautiful enough to be a stripper, and you have the body for one too," she commented, smiling back at her.

"I like you," Audrey said, nodding. "You speak your mind, don't you, and thanks for the compliments. But I think all of that will get in the way of people taking me seriously. I really am a good reporter."

Devi suddenly brightened up. "Audrey, coincidentally you are in good hands! My Aunt is Catherine Marsh, the television reporter. You might be interested to know she had the same problem as you when she started."

"How did she get around it?" Audrey asked.

"She tried everything, and it took time. Put your hair back away from your shoulders, wear glasses and dull down your looks a bit until they can see your real talent. Men can be so shallow sometimes, but most of the time it's not personal. Oh, and stay away from any affairs in the office. That's professional suicide," Devi said.

"Hmm. That's pretty good advice. Where do you work?" she asked.

"I'm only sixteen, so I don't work anywhere real, or professionally yet," said Devi. "Mom says I'm like her only I get to be a teenager. She tells me to enjoy it while it lasts, and mom is always right."

"Only sixteen? Really? You sound and act much older. Do you live in Chicago?" Audrey asked, noting she was leaving the airport when they first met. She was a bit surprised Devi was so young; dressed in designer jeans with an expensive sequined sleeveless top, and traveling in a chauffeured limousine with a bodyguard. *Who was she really talking to*, she wondered?

"No, I live in Siem Kulea, Cambodia. I just flew in this morning too. We have lots of close friends here, and I am meeting my half-brother Charlie so I can take him back to Cambodia with me for the summer. In fact, he is Catherine Marsh and her partner Kelly's son."

"OK, hold on. Let me think about what you just said. So, your father is also Charlie's father, right? Oh, wait! I think I know who you are. Cambodia! Your mother wouldn't be that queen who discovered that ancient treasure a few years ago, would she?" Audrey asked, with a bright face that mirrored her enthusiasm.

"Yes, exactly! My mom is Maisong Sambath Largent, the queen you were talking about. We live in a valley in Cambodia that is so beautiful, and remote, I sometimes find it hard to believe we are on the same planet," she explained smiling.

"But I don't quite remember everything. Weren't there some bad guys who wanted to take over Asia or something?" Audrey asked. "I was still young myself when it happened, but I remember being fascinated that your mom found that legendary treasure, and then found out she was really a queen. That's every young girl's fantasy like Snow White or something."

"My mom was pretty brave then, and my dad too," said Devi. Then she told her the story about her mom, and Colonel Minh, and how she almost ended up in very different circumstances.

"What happened to Colonel Minh?" asked Audrey.

"The Vietnamese Special Forces showed up at the last minute. They killed him, his followers, and ended the rebellion. A few years later, my mom bought the property that makes up the Siem Kulea valley and rebuilt it. When the word got around that she was back, all the Champa people began migrating there, and that's how it is today."

"Hmmm, good story, maybe a book in fact," said Audrey.

"Well, you are too late on that one. Aunt Catherine already wrote it, two in fact. You'll have to do one on me instead," Devi said in jest.

"OK, when do we start?" Audrey said, joking back.

Devi smiled. She really did like this young lady. She knew she had to be a great writer, or they never would have hired her at the Herald, especially now when reporter jobs were so hard to find. She wanted to know more about her. Who knows maybe Aunt Catherine would be interested in hiring her. She was always retaining the best young talent for her NearNorth Productions.

As they pulled up at the Drake Hotel and the doorman opened their door, Devi said, "Hey, it's early. How about you drop off your bag with the concierge, and then you can join me, Aunt Catherine and Aunt Kelly for breakfast. I want to hear your story too."

"Sure! I mean, you don't think they would mind do you?" Audrey paused a moment in thought, and then said, "Oh, I can't just show up, and invite myself to breakfast. It isn't proper." She continued arguing that she wasn't dressed for an expensive restaurant, but Devi pointedly leaned back, and displayed her own choice of clothes for the day.

"Trust me, it doesn't matter. You're my guest, and I insist. At least you're wearing a dress," said Devi. "In fact by this time tomorrow, some designer will probably be redoing their fall collections to reflect your taste. Not to worry. When you're with Aunt Cat, nobody will say anything. They'll all be so envious they can't help themselves. Come on. I invited you, and I bet Aunt Catherine will want to meet you too, especially since I made Ben stop to pick you up, and you're a reporter. Who knew!"

"Well, OK," said Audrey. "I have nothing planned today anyway other than walking down Michigan Avenue and getting a feel for the city. Hey, do you know anyone looking to rent an apartment for cheap to a young reporter just starting out in Chicago?"

Audrey felt privileged at all the attention she and Devi received as they exited the limousine and took the elevator up to the top floor of a tall building where the restaurant was located. The staff apparently knew or were alerted to Devi's arrival because they treated her with deference and respect. It was almost too much to take in all at once, she thought. What's next? She couldn't believe her luck, and couldn't wait to see.

She did everything she could to not show the pure excitement, and awe, she felt as she followed Devi making their way toward the back area of the restaurant. There were flowers everywhere, and the ceiling was a glass atrium that gave the bright room the look of a patio. The view on two sides was of the Chicago Lakefront, and there were sections behind flora and plants, which seemed to offer the privacy desired by a few. People were talking with every kind of body language, serious, happy and animated. Audrey thought she recognized well-known celebrities sitting at some of the tables. She could not tell if people were really looking at her, or Devi, but they definitely were being noticed as they made there way toward the back. But then she realized that having two large bodyguards walking with them probably had something to do with it.

Audrey was stunned as they approached their destination, a booth off to one side, and itself allowing for some privacy. Devi's Aunt Catherine and Aunt Kelly were indeed there but on the other side of Catherine sat Johnny Jericho, the Hip-Hop star, and her current heartthrob. *"OMG,"* she thought. *"No way!"*

The handsome young man dressed in street styled jeans, hair and grunge t-shirt popped up from his perch in the booth, and said politely, "Good morning, ladies, I am Johnny J. I was just leaving which is unfortunate since you two attractive ladies are just sitting down at our table."

But Devi ignored him, and said to Kelly who had joined them, "Aunt Kelly! I have missed you so much!" She greeted her other 'Aunt' with a warm hug, and a kiss on the cheek.

Kelly said, "May I introduce you to Johnny Jericho. Johnny, this is my niece, Devi Largent, and her friend Audrey Goodnight. They're just in from the airport."

Audrey smiled at Kelly very impressed that she knew her name and then turned to the rock star, and said, "Pleased to meet you, Mr. Jericho." He held her hand, and would not let it go.

"Hey listen, I am just heading out for a rehearsal at Navy Pier for our big show this weekend. Perhaps you would like to join me," he offered, directly to Audrey.

Surprised, Audrey at first considered his offer, but then said, "Oh I would love to, but I can't just now. I have appointments all morning, and I'm afraid they are very important ones. Can I possibly get a rain check or a pass for later?"

The rock star pulled out a card, scribbled something on the back of it, and handed it to her. "Call this number, and it will get you backstage Saturday night," he said. "That's my producer. I will tell him to expect your call."

With that, he said goodbye to everyone, and to Audrey in particular. As he departed, Devi and Audrey replaced him in the booth; Devi sitting beside Kelly, and Audrey sitting beside Catherine.

Devi was amused as the conversation ensued much as she thought it might. Catherine was honestly fascinated with Audrey, especially when she found out she was a new reporter hired by the Herald. In a way, she looked like a young Catherine; same hair, skin tone, basic body style. Devi surmised Catherine saw herself twenty years earlier and had thoughts about taking Audrey under her wing.

"Well, you are full of surprises, young lady," Catherine commented. "You just turned down an invitation from one of the hottest rock stars in show business today. I don't know if you're very smart, or very dumb. Whichever it was, you reacted quickly and to the point. What, Audrey, may I ask, were you thinking?

"Really?" she asked Catherine.

"Yes, I'm quite curious to know how your mind works," Catherine explained.

"Ms. Marsh, it was a weak contest at best. I had a chance to go spend the morning playing gaga over a dreamboat rock star, or have breakfast, and talk to one of the most successful female journalists ever. He can move my libido, but you can move my life. See what I mean? No contest. Game over!"

Catherine looked at her silently for a few seconds as she processed what she had just heard and knew about the eager young lady sitting next to her.

She pulled out a pad and pencil, and handing it to Audrey, said, "Interview me."

Devi gave Kelly's arm a friendly bump, "Uh-oh, here we go again. Anyone having a Déjà-Vu?"

Audrey was caught short, but in the next moment she pulled out her purse, put on some glasses, retrieved the pad and pencil, and wrote something. Then she said, "I will get to the general questions later, but I would like to start with something I am personally curious about that Devi mentioned to me earlier. I understand you had a difficult start breaking into the news business as a female. How has the television news industry changed for women since you started twenty years ago?"

Catherine was impressed with her response and her first question. She nodded and said, "Actually it is quite a bit different in some ways, and not at all different in others."

"Yes, I can imagine that would be true, but perhaps you would care to elaborate, or give some specific examples of what you mean? I suspect your own career may have opened doors for many young ladies like myself wanting to pursue a career in journalism."

"Well, you had to be careful back then, especially if you were attractive," said Catherine. "Men didn't regard you as anything but a fixture like a pretty lamp, which I might add they liked to turn on and off at the drop of a hat and a chilled martini. You had to dress down your looks, or men, who ran everything, wouldn't take you seriously, not that they ever did anyway. The good and provocative stories always went to men. Women were all categorized with a first impression by men who had mostly one thing on their minds. A sexual harassment suit was unheard of in those days. If you protested you were fired, usually for a made up reason. I worked at three different stations before I settled in at WNYJ with a real professional boss. There were some bad rumors spread around town about me, none of which were true. It was unsettling, to say the least. Men judged women by their looks and in that good-old-boy network that was hard to overcome."

"Like you just did me," said Audrey.

There was a short pause while Catherine considered Audrey's response.

"Perhaps a little. But not entirely, I assure you. That was mainly my surprise that you seemed so insightful for one so young," Catherine said.

"Well, then you haven't been paying attention, because that niece of yours sitting over there is a lot more insightful than I am, and I'm seven years older than her," she said, toasting her water glass to Devi and mouthing a *thank you* with her lips.

"That said," she continued, "in your opinion where is the greatest opportunity for a young woman starting a career in journalism in Chicago today?"

Catherine smiled, and said, "You know that already, or you wouldn't be sitting next to me. Don't ask unnecessary questions you already know the answer to unless you're looking for a quote because your subject may flee your interview with the next breath."

"OK, then," said Audrey, "Of all the stories you have done which was the hardest to get or most frustrating for you?"

"That one's easy. It's on-going, and is sitting right over there across the room," said Catherine.

Audrey turned quickly, but initially, didn't understand what Catherine was talking about. She saw some people she didn't recognize, a couple of celebrities, and then she saw Senator Earl Beacham Grimes sitting at one of the tables. He was balding with white hair and a plump face. He wore an off-white suit and his skin held a reddish tint. He was very famous, but she didn't really know why. Only that he was someone talked about as a possible vice-presidential nominee. She didn't pay much attention to politics, having not even voted in the last election.

"The man in the light suit sipping his coffee and staring at you?" she asked.

"Yes, that's the story, only I haven't gotten it yet. That's Senator Grimes," Catherine said. "He's sitting there to provoke me. He knows he got away with murder, and he thinks that neither I nor anyone else can touch him. I have been trying to get the story for five years."

"What did he do, Ms. Marsh?"

"He killed his wife, Audrey, as sure as I am sitting here now," Catherine said. "She was an old friend of mine from the time we were little girls together. He killed her and inherited her vast family fortune. He did that five years ago in what he claimed was a boating accident on Lake Michigan. There was a storm, and she supposedly fell overboard and drowned. Her body showed up several days later. It was ruled as a death by accidental drowning. They found lake water in her lungs, so it seemed airtight. But I'm convinced he did it, and now he taunts me with it. Over my friend's grave, I swore never to give up until I got him."

She returned the Senator's stare from across the crowded room, until he finally raised his glass, and toasted her.

Catherine turned abruptly toward Audrey and said, "You want to work for me? The job is yours. Your first assignment is to find evidence proving that Senator Grimes killed his wife. You will be on probation for six months while you prove to me you are up to the job. Or you can go work for the Herald tomorrow morning. What's it going to be? Your choice."

"Aunt Catherine..." said Devi.

"I'll do it, I want to do it," said Audrey excitedly. "I'm not sure where to start though. I don't even know where my office is, but I don't care. Thank you, Ms. Marsh. I won't disappoint you."

"Catherine..." again said Devi, trying to get her attention.

"What won't you disappoint Ms. Marsh about?" asked Senator Grimes now standing right in front of their table, and addressing Audrey. "Good morning, young lady. I am Senator Grimes. I assure you the horrible stories that Ms. Marsh continues to spread about me are entirely untrue," he said offering his hand.

Audrey sat back ignoring his hand, as Catherine said, "You have a lot of nerve, Senator. Leave us alone. Don't make me have you removed." Catherine motioned to Ben who was watching everything in an obscure area off to the side, and with her nod began to move forward.

"You see," he said. "She really doesn't like me. Don't bother yourself, Catherine. I was just leaving. Is this your latest bloodhound seeking to find something to bury me with? I wonder, my dear, did she tell you that the first assignment she gives all her new charges is to find evidence proving that fantasy that I killed my wife. This has been going on for years, and no one has found a thing because I'm completely innocent. I would sue her for harassment, but it's not worth my time or money."

"Please leave, Senator," said Kelly, sitting beside Catherine who was now trembling in anger.

"Well, good day, ladies. I wish you well, Miss. What is that old Sherlock Holmes quote? Ah yes, 'The game is afoot!'" he said, laughing as he left.

"God, I hate him," said Catherine while Kelly rubbed her hand quietly.

"He's a fool," said Devi. "He thinks no one can touch him. But you will, Aunt Cat. You'll get him."

Audrey looked at the three of them and saw their honest enmity and determination. She wondered what she was getting into, but on the other hand, she could not deny the incredible opportunity that had just dropped into her lap. "Looks like I have some work to do," she said. "When can I get started?"

Catherine took a deep breath, collected herself, and said, "Not today. Today you and Devi play, but tomorrow you report downstairs at NearNorth Productions on the third floor to Jamie Wilton, our Personnel Director. What are your plans today, Devi?"

"We're going to take a walk down Michigan Avenue, and after that Audrey will get my first class tour of Chicago. I think we need to find her a place to stay that is convenient and safe. The Herald was paying for her to stay at the Drake, but since you just hired her, I bet that's over. I bet there might be a small apartment in your building, Aunt Cat, that could be part of her incentive pay," suggested Devi.

"Oh, no you don't, princess. What are you, her agent now? Let's see how she does first before adding pay incentives. However, that said, since you are taking her around, I think we can put her up for a few days in one of our spare bedrooms until she finds a place. It might be a good idea for you to take her by the Herald so she can give them notice, and let them know what is going on. Tell them they blew it by not picking her up this morning. Then come by the office and show her where she will be working starting tomorrow. Be sure to talk to Finn who will have a key for her and show her to her room in our condo. By then, I assume he will have a desk for her too. That way she will lose some of the first day anxieties we all get."

"I don't know how to thank you, Ms. Marsh. This is all like a wonderful dream."

"Last thing. Devi, while you are out and about today, you stay close to your bodyguards. I promised your mother we would take good care of you, and I mean to do it. Are we clear on that, young lady?" she cautioned her.

"Yes, Aunt Catherine. I'll be good. I promise," she replied.

Catherine smiled, "Audrey, it looks like you've been kidnapped. It's your fault you have made such a good impression on us. Fair warning. I am going to work you hard the first few weeks to see if you are up to my standards, and deserving of this opportunity. But for now, let's order. I'm really hungry and we have lots to do today."

Chapter 31

May 2005   Chicago

Victor Daniels by all appearances was simply a bored middle-aged man flipping through channels on his big-screen projection TV. It was another night of reruns, and while he waited, and trained over the last year, he had endured more than he wanted on the oversized television. Playing a middle-aged bachelor during this waiting game wasn't the life he imagined when he set up this operation, and now continuing to play the part was wearing on him making him ever more restless. Usually he fought his overactive, detailed intellect by vigorously planning and preparing his operations. But this particular affair had drawn out so long, there wasn't any planning left to do. If anything, it was overplanned with every contingency accounted for.

He lived on the North side of Chicago in an invisible brownstone, which blended in with the other identical brownstones on his block. He was as invisible as the brownstone he lived in with average height, build, and features. He was a very uncommon man hiding within a common disguise.

He was, in fact, one of Interpol's most wanted men known ignominiously as 'The Crow' because of his high pitched voice inadvertently recorded on the wiretap of another suspect. It was a name that amused him, and that he now embraced. He was a thief, a criminal taskmaster who looked nothing like the rare, and blurry images, that accounted for what police were using to identify him. He had already proved the fallacy of those images by coming through customs at O'Hare Airport without so much as a blink from security officials. Once settled in Chicago, he tested this further by brazenly going to a well-known neighborhood cop bar just down the street on the corner from where he lived. Some of his acquaintances that first night are now counted among his best friends, and join him every Thursday night playing poker into the late night hours. He considered this research for his current assignment.

His temporary persona flipping houses and renting brownstones was only a front, but it helped to keep him physically, and mentally fit. He was there to carry out a plan that required precise execution, and special-forces level skills. He was the best at what he did, and though he had never taken an assignment with the challenges involved in this particular one, he was very well compensated for his time and trouble.

The security around their victims was comparable to that of a political candidate, and their adversaries were unusually talented in their protection efforts. They had almost started once before only to find that at the last minute one of the victims had changed plans. Based on the last information from his client the latest variation of the plan was imminent. That was fortuitous because the contract, which had already been extended once, and for which he was paid half up front, was up in three weeks. One way, or the other, he was packing it in and leaving. In his mind, he had already overstayed his welcome, and he was bucking the odds of not getting caught. He had made that very clear to those who hired him. Unlike his usual modus operandi this was a joint mission by which he incorporated foreign mercenaries hired and trained by the client. He needed them involved as a necessary prelude for his plan to work. Thus, he had been patient to that point, but as far as he was concerned, this operation was drawing to a close one way or another.

He heard a soft ping coming from his computer. *Another message from Asia* he thought as he began typing in a long password. He hoped they were being careful. Every message sent back and forth from his computer was bounced all around the world, and even then scrambled, so that only the end units could make sense of it. But his adversaries were skilled, maybe even better than he was with this ever-evolving technology. In his profession, one couldn't be too careful.

The message read in an obscure Burmese dialect; "otwwap 3220032p".

He answered with a coded acknowledgement. It was on. His curious expression turned into a firm nod, and a smile. He was ready. They had been training, and waiting for this moment for months. Just the fact they had hired him showed how determined these people were. He had no doubt that by this time next week both young victims would be taken, and their fates would be in the hands of those who hired him. Ironically, the impending success of his plan was the part that kept gnawing at him.

He made a few cryptic calls, and then sat back, and went over the plan once more in his mind. They had members of their team embedded as workers where Charlie Marsh was doing an internship, and even within NearNorth Productions. They knew everything NearNorth Productions did to secure the safety of their people. His plan was perfect, but it needed someone with his cleverness, and audacity to pull it off. He smiled to himself. That's why he got paid the big bucks. It was just this kind of attention to detail, which ensured the success of his plans. He was feeling the ramped-up excitement he always experienced at the start of one of his pursuits.

Then he had a thought. He went over the plan one more time.

Chapter 32

2005 Chicago

On that crisp Chicago morning, Catherine was working in her office on the 30th floor of the NearNorth Productions building in downtown Chicago. With several dozen stories in production at various stages as was their routine, the investigative division at times seemed more like a newspaper than a cable news program. She was busier than ever with a host of diligent young reporters who were eager to prove themselves while working for her and Howard Landell, the overall Head of Production. The new young girl, Audrey, who she just hired was indeed competent and talented, but thus far had not shown the out-of-the-box thinking that Catherine had hoped to find in her after the short interview a week ago. She was considering that perhaps it was time to reevaluate her potential at NNP and assign her accordingly when Finn, her secretary, buzzed her that Mai was on line three. She picked up the phone ready to assure her that Devi had arrived safely. But Mai spoke first without the usual greeting.

"Cat there is a lot of activity on the internet right now between groups we normally monitor for security reasons. We have some intercepts that might be something. We really don't know for sure. But they are talking, and that usually means that something is up. Can you corral Devi for me, and be sure she is protected? I will feel a lot better. You know how she gets. She totally does not understand how dangerous some people can be."

"Of course, Mai. Ben and Michael are with her right now. She said something about coming here this morning and taking Audrey with her to register for her classes. Then, they plan to go to lunch, meet up with Charlie, and spend the afternoon together. She has made a new friend, a young girl who is working for me now and just starting out in journalism from Madison, Wisconsin. She is really sharp. You will like her. I'm afraid I have had her burning the midnight oil just to feel her commitment, and determination, so she and Devi have not been together since the first day. I promised Devi she could whisk her away today," said Catherine.

"I would rather they were not out, and about, OK? This is serious. Something big is going down soon. I'm sure of it," warned Mai. "Let her take care of what she has to do for school, do lunch, but then keep her close. Please do that for me. I have to go. We are just finishing up a meeting over here. Talk to you later."

"OK, not to worry. We have it covered. Bye," said Catherine.

Catherine hung up the phone with Mai and pushed the intercom to tell Finn to have Audrey report to her office.

Five minutes later, Audrey knocked on the glass door of her office and was beckoned to enter. Even after a week she still felt a little nervous talking with Catherine who she greatly admired and who kept her at arms distance as her boss at work. On the other hand, since she was staying in a spare bedroom in their condo, she and Kelly had become like family and enjoyed spending time together.

Catherine looked up and saw her, but continued reading for a moment. When she was finished, she put down the folder, and said, "So, a day off today. Kelly told me you are going to lunch with Devi. Apparently, you're also going with her to get registered first."

"Yes, thank you, Catherine. I appreciate the time off. I admit I am a little tired from the long hours, but I'm getting a real feel for the routine around here, and fair enough, you warned me that you would be working me hard the first few weeks. I know it's like boot camp, so I don't mind. We both know it's necessary and why."

Catherine sat back in her seat. She had her hair up in a bun and was wearing little makeup. She had on a light beige skirt and a white blouse. "OK, I'll bite. Why am I working you so hard?" she asked, somewhat amused at the bluntness of her new reporter.

"Well, based on what you've told me, I think you're trying to see if I have the attitude, determination, and grit to stand up to your measure of what a good reporter should be. I'm taking that as a compliment. If anything it drives me to work even harder."

"You are quite presumptuous too, aren't you?" commented Catherine with a straight face. She did indeed like Audrey very much, but was not about to let her know that yet.

Audrey only smiled, and nodded, so Catherine continued. "You've been here a week, and I haven't seen any progress on the assignment I gave you concerning Senator Grimes. So, I am assigning you to Doug Corval's group. Frankly, that assignment was just one of my hopeful whims with new hires. I am always hoping fresh eyes will turn up something. This is the story they are currently working on, and this will help you get caught up on their progress," she said, handing her the folder she was perusing.

"Uh…but oh, I think I have actually made some progress, Catherine. I think I have found something, which seems to prove something untoward happened. It's pretty amazing, if you ask me."

Catherine put down her pen and looked at her. Audrey had her full attention. "What are you talking about? What did you find?"

Audrey opened a manila folder she held in her left hand and presented Catherine with an aerial image of an estate that bordered Lake Michigan.

Catherine looked at the image quickly. "Yes, I have seen this already. It is a Google overhead image of Senator Grime's house. You are not the first to see this image. You will have to do better than that if you want to keep working around here." Very disappointed, she handed the image back to Audrey.

"Yes, Google," said Audrey nervously. "The first thing I did was Google his address, and then I got the map, and called up the Earth view. I printed it out and left it on my desk totally ignoring it for a few days. But then I realized that the image I had was probably different from a Google image five years ago of the same house when the Senator's wife died. I contacted a technician at Google and asked him if they could send me an image closer to the date and time I gave him of the coordinates that included the Senator's house. He told me they had thousands of images of those coordinates from about that date. He said they usually pick the best ones for their earth views and recycle them accordingly. Some areas are redone daily and some are never changed according to what resources they have. I begged him to send me the best he could find from that date and he obliged by sending me seven images. I was very disappointed when I saw them because like the one you just saw, there didn't appear to be anything in them. Then, just yesterday morning, I was thinking about something else while staring at this image that was the top one laying on the stack of seven, and I saw something I had not seen before. I don't think you notice it unless you are staring at it like I did because it was fall and the Senator is wearing a yellow jacket."

"Fall? Senator...what are you talking about? What do you see?" Catherine asked grabbing the photo she handed her. "I don't see anyone or even any humans in this photo. It's just like the other one."

"Yes, but we got lucky. I think this one is a little better," she said, handing her still another photo. "Look and see if you notice what I did. It may be nothing, but it looks like something. At least I think it does," Audrey said, handing her the printout. Catherine looked at the print that showed the Senator's estate that bordered Lake Michigan on the East. It was a bit fuzzy, but you could make out tables and chairs on his patio, and a path leading down to his boathouse. His boat was parked next to a pier that ran along one side of the boathouse.

Catherine looked at her, shrugged her shoulders, and shook her head as if to say "What?"

"Look between the trees on the other side of the boathouse. It is mostly covered with trees but look carefully, and see what you see," said Audrey.

At first, Catherine saw nothing, but then she stood straight up, and sat back down again and said, "Oh my God! Do you think? Is it possible it was right there all the time?" She laughed out loud, shaking her head. "This proves there is a God!"

In the printed Earth view from Google on the other side of the boathouse, there was displayed mostly trees that were a celebration of yellows and oranges, in fall colors. But between the trees right by the shore was a man in a yellow jacket who appeared to be holding the head of a person underwater.

Audrey said, "I followed up to see if I could get it any clearer. You will note there is specific time and coordinates embedded in the image in the lower right corner. I made some calls and talked to another technician braced by that more specific information. I told him I loved the image of this house enhanced by the fall colors. It was a selling point, I told him, with the lake and the colorful surroundings. It would be perfect if I could get a clearer image of the same scene during that time. The very nice gentleman I spoke with informed me that the technology on their end could only go so far but he would send me the best they could get with those specs. I told them to send it Fedex ASAP. They charged me fifty dollars plus shipping for this image. I hope I didn't overstep my bounds. I forgot to okay it before I gave them our Fedex number." She handed another image to Catherine that seemed to have worse color but had slightly better resolution, and one could definitely tell a man was pushing or drowning a female in white pants and a pink blouse by the shore of Lake Michigan.

"I checked the time this was taken, and it was that morning before the storm came on the seventeenth. Remember it hit that afternoon on October seventeenth? So this was before Senator Grimes said he took a boat ride with his wife out on the lake, and then they got caught in the storm. And he didn't find her body anyway, so that is not what he is doing. She was found two days later by another search boat out on the lake itself, not by the shore.

"I'm not sure if this is the clearest image they can get but I took the liberty of having two of your staff follow up on it. You know, Jill and Freddy, uh, Ms. Banks and Mr. Warner. Well, actually they volunteered because in their words, 'This was the most important story in the building.' Well, we checked, and when his wife was found drowned in the lake, she was wearing a pink top with white pants."

Catherine was looking away nodding to herself in thought, but turned back suddenly and asked, "Whom did you tell? Never mind. Get them in here right now. Go. Hurry! I want a meeting right now!"

A few minutes later, Audrey returned with the two staffers she worked with as a reporting team. One was a reporter like her, and only a little older, and one was a production assistant about the same age. They looked like college friends. They were all young, smiling, and excited as they took seats opposite Catherine's desk.

"Calm down, all of you," ordered Catherine, seriously. "I want to know who you three have told about this Google photo. Does anyone else know? This is very important. Tell me."

They were silent for a moment so Catherine further explained, "Look, I can understand that you are very excited about this, but I do not want this story to get out before we're ready to spring it on the public. So if you have mentioned it to anyone, loved ones, friends, tell me…no recriminations here. We just want to try, and keep a lid on it until we're ready. You didn't know my wishes, and even I would have been tempted to spread the word. So, please, tell me if you have told anyone, so we can button this up right away."

They looked at each other for a moment with inquiring eyes. "Well, Catherine," said the young red-headed reporter, Jill Banks, "We all work in the same department, and even our cubicles are adjoining, and self-contained, so we pretty much shared the information with each other, and speculatively. But we recognized the importance of this story and knew it was top secret especially since we had not verified it, and we only did that an hour ago to our mutual satisfaction. I don't think it got out of our area. "

"Of course, I talked with the technician at Google like I mentioned before, but I did not mention anything about Senator Grimes or explain what I was really after. I am positive he didn't have a clue about that," added Audrey.

The others agreed and swore they had not told anyone else. Catherine looked at them thoughtfully in silence for a moment giving them time to say more.

When they didn't, she nodded her head and smiled. "Good, keep it that way. This is going to be our secret. If you can keep your mouths shut for the next two weeks before we air this on our Sunday night show, I promise you all will have bright futures with me. Am I clear on this? You have my back. I'll have your back. This is top secret, and you will tell no one. If this gets out, I can promise you, your careers in this industry are over."

One of the three actually gulped, but they all nodded as Audrey said, "We understand fully, Catherine."

"OK, let's all agree on what we see here in this photograph taken by the overhead satellite, and is reproduced on Google. I still can't believe this. Audrey, how often do they change their satellite images?" she asked. "Do you think there are more we can look at?"

"It varies apparently. But in this area they change them a lot because it is a major metropolitan area in the United States. It might be worth following up and perhaps we should consider putting in a major request for a full 24 hours of imaging of whatever they have. But that might take a while. Their turn-around time on such requests is about four weeks and they have a backlog of requests. It was fortunate I made a quick connection with that technician during my initial inquiry and I think we got lucky on the seven images he chose to send me.

"Catherine, I know it is your first inclination to follow up on it, and to see if there are any other images like this one. But you might want to reconsider going any further down that road. I am positive we can keep this a secret here, but if we go requesting a lot of images around a certain date and time, someone is bound to catch on."

"Yes, I see what you mean and I agree with you," replied Catherine. Right now I am thinking we shouldn't risk that. We have an excellent image right here that we can go with. Do you happen to know the name of the technician you talked to that sent you these images?" she asked.

Audrey checked her notes. "Yes, I have it here. Why? What do you have in mind?"

"Perhaps we can talk to him outside of work and arrange a deal to get more images of what we need. We would have to be very careful about it as you suggest—meet him in person and discuss it over dinner or something. Where is he located?" Catherine asked.

"Probably San Jose, California. I think an older man; someone who looks rather official should approach him outside of the office and present an abstract offer over a cup of coffee. If we get him onboard, then we give him the rest of the story with the offer of a bonus attached," Audrey said.

Catherine considered what Audrey said for a moment. "Yes, we need to discuss this further, you and I," Catherine said. "Amazing." She took a breath, smiled at them and said, "OK, I believe we have a photo here of Senator Grimes drowning his wife in the lake before he took her out on a boat, and dumped her overboard. Does everyone agree?"

They all shook their heads affirmatively.

"Does anyone have anything to add to that assertion, or have a counter-argument of any kind?" she asked.

Audrey raised her hand. "I have something to consider. Wouldn't the chemical composition of the water along the lakeshore be different than the water out on lake? Wouldn't that show up in an autopsy?"

"Yes, it should have," answered Catherine. "But remember there was only a cursory examination given afterward and a quick autopsy. They weren't looking for anything like that. I bet if we get the body exhumed, they might be able to examine that idea more closely."

Catherine was positive they wanted to run outside, and tell the world what they knew as she stared at them, all still smiling, and so bright and eager. She was young like that once, and not so long ago either. What a story!

She called to her secretary on the intercom, "Finn, get Miles, and Howard Landell, on the phone right now. Interrupt them if you have to," she said, while the others looked on. "Oh, and see if Gerald Doyle is still in the building."

"We are going to feature this in two weeks…no, wait…it will have to be three because we will want to play it up the last few days before we air it. The ratings are going to go through the roof!

"OK, sit down and let's get organized," she said, as Miles Bowen knocked on her door while entering. Miles was the senior producer on her successful cable show, "Newsworthy".

"Miles, our new reporter here has broken the story on Senator Grimes. I want to air this as soon as we can with a proper presentation, and to my way of thinking that is in three weeks and it will encompass the whole hour. Do you see any problem with that?" she asked, really hoping for a no answer from him.

"Three weeks, Sunday, the twenty-first," he said to himself, thinking about the Newsworthy schedule. He pulled out his Blackberry, and worked through it quickly. "That's the one-on-one with you, and the First Lady, for a personal tour of the White House. We set that up months ago, but it kept getting moved from their side for one reason or another. It's all set now, due to shoot next week on a very tight schedule," he said.

"Move it again," said Catherine.

"Uh, but Catherine…" he started to protest, but then caught himself.

"Miles, we have a ratings monster on our hands, and it only works if we break it first. I'm not happy about waiting even three weeks to do it. I don't want to hear any argument about this, nor do I want you telling anyone what we're doing. You handle the whole production personally. You call the White House and cancel. Do your best to reschedule, but my heart was never in that story anyway.

"Next, talk this over with Howard, and make sure this story that Audrey, Jill, and Freddy are working on is your priority. Give them anything they need to get it done. I will be the on-air reporter and personally head the group on this one. One thing we will for sure need is graphics and film. Since they are relatively new, we also need someone to work with them on the script. Scratch that. I will do the rewrite, and work closely with them on the script. We will want teasers a few days before it breaks and on all of the primary networks, and cable channels. I want the word out there that something big, Earth-shaking, and historic is going to happen.

"Next, get these three into the reserved thirty-fourth-floor production facility, and close it up tight. No one goes there without clearance. Guard it like Fort Knox. Fortunately, I think we have most of the graphics, photos, and footage we need in-house so we will not have to go outside for that. Get a good editor…."

"Catherine?" interrupted Miles. "I have this," he said. "I'm on it. I know what to do, keep it in house, and lock it tight."

Catherine took a breath, and smiled, "Of course you do. Miles, I am so crazy excited over this. OK, get going! Start with getting these three off of this floor. Get them each an assistant. Make sure they are people who know how to keep their mouths shut," she ordered, as Miles began to leave the room hurriedly.

"Miles!" she said, stopping him momentarily. "Where are you going? You don't even know the whole story yet."

"Doesn't matter just now, Catherine," he said. I need to take care of a few things right away if we're going to keep this quiet, and in-house, so, got to run. They can brief me on the story, and what they need, in say…one hour in my office," he said, looking at them for any objections. Receiving confirming nods from each, he closed the door and was gone.

Catherine looked after him pleased once more with his professional initiative. She turned to the three young staffers who she noticed for the first time all had pads out and were taking notes. She actually chuckled to herself. "OK, so get your lists ready, and meet with Miles in his office in one hour. After that I want you all working exclusively in the thirty-fourth-facility until this is over. I am going to make an outline this afternoon of the show, and I will divide the responsibilities for each of you to gather material, and prepare a script for me to work on. Start by moving your offices upstairs. If anyone asks, tell them you are working on a special project for me, but say nothing else by way of explanation.

Catherine paused, took a breath and looked at them seriously. "This is a very special moment in our profession. You are experiencing the fabulous feeling and great fulfillment of finding a blockbuster story. This kind of event in our professional lives is very rare. This is journalistic treasure, and you should take a step back and savor the moment. It is worth remembering for the rest of your lives. We must not waste its value, and we must be sure to present it to the world in all its shining glory. I am very proud of you," she said, just as the door opened and Devi walked in.

"What are you doing here?" asked Catherine, a bit put off by her assuming interruption of the planning of her triumphal television presentation.

"I came to get my girlfriend, remember? They told me downstairs she was here, meeting with you. She is going with me while I get my classes, and then we are meeting Charlie when he gets out of his intern job," she explained.

"Oh no! Not now. You can't do that now. I need her here. Sorry, Devi. She has just broken a big story, and I need her working on it," explained Catherine.

"You have put me off all week, Aunt Catherine, and I am leaving tomorrow. This is the last chance I will have to really spend some time with her, and I found her! Come on, can't she just take this afternoon off? Please?" pleaded Devi. "Consider it a favor to mom," she added.

Catherine shook her head and smiled to herself. If it were Mai asking, she wouldn't think of saying no. She owed Mai a hundred favors. Still, the timing couldn't have been worse. She sat back and thought for a moment before answering.

"OK, we're mostly getting organized this afternoon anyway. Audrey, you go take a break but be prepared tomorrow, and for the next two weeks to not get much sleep. You will be heading up this team and I expect you two, Jill and Freddy, to support her with everything you have, and doing the best work you've ever done. While you are gone, Audrey, we will get you set up upstairs with the others," said Catherine. She dismissed them and watched them go out the door talking, and laughing with each other.

Right away, she picked up the phone to remind Big Ben to be particularly alert for their safety that day and to bring them back to the NNP building after picking up Charlie.

After making that call, she returned to the surprising new project that Audrey had just gifted them. "You two," she said to Jill and Freddy, "Make sure that her things are properly moved and cared for. This is as big as it gets. Do not talk to anyone about it. You're all bright and young, and what you don't have in experience you can make up for with energy and eager-ness. If there is anything you need come to Miles, Finn, or me and we will make it happen. We don't want this to get around so come to us and only us when you need something."

Catherine paused in thought. "You make a pretty-good team I have to admit. Now is the time to show me what you can do, you…Musketeers," she said, smiling, and remembering her own beginnings as a reporter. "Let's all meet with Miles in one hour and get this show on the road!"

Chapter 33

May 2005   University of Chicago

The two young ladies spent two hours together getting Devi registered in long lines at the school administration building. "I'm glad that's over," said Devi. "I hate lines. Registration seems to get more fucking complicated each year. Thanks for doing this with me."

Audrey smiled and then had a thought. "It shouldn't, I mean about the complicated part. I remember for me it was like automatic, especially my junior and senior years. But that was at the University of Missouri School of Journalism. Are you switching majors or something?"

"Yeah, that's it," explained Devi. "I'm working on my second major in two years. I have kind of an accelerated program my mom worked out with them. She changed my curriculum four weeks into my first year when I said college was stupid and mundane. I can speed read and I have an eidetic memory. I just look at stuff and I get it. At the time I was ten weeks into the semester and I had already read through all of my textbooks mostly out of boredom. One of my teachers even tested me when my mom pressured the administration to put me into a special program. I sat down and took his two semester finals for that year right then and I missed one question on one of them and was perfect on the other. When it got to the essay section of his test, he said he had never seen answers as complete as mine and if he hadn't watched me the entire time he would have thought I cheated somehow. Then he surprised me with ten more difficult written questions just to be sure. He never told me how I did but after that, the administration was willing to work with my mom on changing my program. Instead of cutting my curriculum back as most do, she doubled it because she is one of the few people who understands me. I take about thirty units a semester this year, half in undergrad and half in post-grad. It is the only way for me not to be totally fucking bored by the classes. I don't think my mom will let me continue here much longer anyway. She is always worrying about my safety."

"And you change character on campus too I've noticed," said Audrey.

"Huh? I don't think so. What do you mean?" asked Devi.

"You use a lot of cuss words when you didn't before. Since I know you otherwise, it doesn't fit your character. They stand out like a sore thumb on you," Audrey explained a bit judgmentally.

"That's funny, Audrey. I do use cuss words around here. It is automatic for me like it comes with the territory. I change into my campus-mode character without a second thought."

They stopped to buy drinks and sat on a bench under a large oak tree. The campus was between semesters and only a few students were around. But a few paces away Michael and Ben were sitting, and enjoying sodas as they watched over their young charge.

"My mother says cursing is a sign of weakness brought on by insecurity, and a response to peer pressure with the idea that it will make you fit in, be one of the crowd, and more acceptable," said Audrey, playfully challenging her.

"Wow! When did your mom talk to my mom?" asked Devi. "She says the same thing only she adds it is a sign of ignorance and disrespect. I have done it so much around here I never notice I'm doing it. Everyone I know around here cusses commonly. I guess I thought it would help me fit in."

"Did it work?" asked Audrey.

After a moment Devi's eyes watered, and she shook her head sadly. "I don't fit in anywhere, Audrey. Sometimes I get really lonely. The truth is I don't know how to act with anyone anymore. It's impossible to be like everyone else when you have bodyguards always following you around. Boys are afraid to talk to me, and the few girls who pretend to be my friends only do so because they want to be friends with a princess, not me, not the real me."

"So you cuss trying to say to them, 'Hey! I'm just like you!'" observed Audrey.

"Yeah, I guess I do," said Devi smiling through tears. "That's really lame, isn't it? Most of my friends are adults, like Aunt Kelly. She's my best friend. We talk on the phone all the time. Oh, and Charlie, of course. I tell them things

I would never tell my mom, especially Aunt Kelly. She used to be my dad's assistant in his photography studio before she married Aunt Catherine. She's really cool. Sometimes I think she knows me better than I know myself."

"You seem to have no problem talking to me," said Audrey, handing her a handkerchief. "I think a lot of that is in your head."

"No, you're different. You're approachable, open. You don't put up a façade. You don't play to me like others do trying to win my favor," said Devi. "Besides, we've had a thing going from the start and that is very rare for me. I wish everyone treated me like you do."

"I'm a farm girl from Wisconsin, that's all," said Audrey.

"I'm a farm girl too," said Devi.

"Come on, what do princesses do on farms besides ride horses," teased Audrey.

"I milk cows and feed the animals, slop the pigs, plant crops. I work right beside my mom and everyone else in the valley. I have to say I like that almost as much as being on my computer doing code. It's great therapy," said Devi.

"Your mom works in the fields?"

"Every day!"

"Sows and harvests?"

"Yep!" said Devi. "We all do. It is part of our tradition."

"That's really cool! I imagined you lived in a big palace with servants falling all over themselves to attend you."

"I do, and I work in the fields too," said Devi.

They got up, tossed away their cups in a trash can nearby and started walking back toward their car. Audrey was laughing. "You get the best of both worlds. I wish I could experience that. I got half of it at least. Maybe someday I will get the other half."

"If I can pry you away from Aunt Catherine, I want to take you back with me to Siem Kulea this summer. Then you'll get the other half. Trust me, you'll find it very awkward at first. People bathing and dressing you is something that takes time to get used to if you're not born to it. You should see my dad. He still winces when he's sleeping in my mom's chambers, and all the servants arrive in the morning. He doesn't like it, but it's part of the tradition. Personally, I like that part," said Devi.

"Wait, so your dad and mom have separate bedrooms?"

"Huh? No...not exactly. It's not like it sounds. The palace in Siem Kulea is huge, and my mom has her own private wing, the queen's chambers, which is a separate suite of rooms. Her bath and bedroom are sumptuous and fitting for a queen. It opens up to a private garden where I love to spend my time. Then there is her private office, the amazing library, and there is even an observatory where we study the stars," explained Devi. "My dad is often away on photography trips, but when he is there he always sleeps with mom. He doesn't like to sleep in her big bed. He thinks my mom's bed looks like a boat and I already mentioned the servant's morning routine. There used to be a seven-headed snake on the headboard too. That's gone now. In fact, my mom got rid of all of the snake representations in the valley," said Devi. "I am personally happy about that."

"Why did you have representations of snakes in your valley in the first place?" asked Audrey.

"That was the Nagani," explained Devi. "It was a symbol for the first queen, the mother of all Champas, and to our ancestors. But mom felt it was a dark, negative symbol of her ancestors. She replaced it with the Hoa Cuc, the flower that represents her. I like that a lot more, and it seems to have lifted the spirits of everyone in Siem Kulea. Like I said, my mom is always right.

"Our valley is all about the old traditions, heritage, and beliefs, of the Champas. My mom and dad are doing their best to protect that although it can get awkward at times, especially for my dad. When we first came to Siem Kulea, my dad was not allowed in her wing of the palace without her express permission. I found out when I was a little girl and ran into my mom's quarters, and he stayed by the door. It had nothing to do with my mom, and everything to do with her being the Champa Queen. It is out of respect for our people that he makes an effort to respect all of their traditions," said Devi.

"Anyway, mom changed all that when she found out about it. After that, my dad had complete access everywhere. But he dresses and bathes himself. He insists on it and he doesn't like everyone fondling over him, although he insists they take care of mom and me. Personally, I like it.

"My mom changed a lot of how they used to do things. Let's face it, times have changed. A thousand years ago my dad would have been kept in quarters with the rest of her consorts all day. Can you imagine that?" They both laughed. "But as it is, my dad is the real boss in our house. I mean, mom does what she wants. She is the queen, after all. Dad never tells her what to do in public, or around the servants. I have never seen him order her to do anything. But somehow, in the end, she always does what *he* wants. I picked up on that many years ago. What about you, who has the last word in your family?"

"I think like most families around here, it goes back and forth. But I don't know if I told you, I'm adopted. They're not my real parents," said Audrey.

"Oh, I'm sorry," said Devi.

"No, there is nothing to be sorry about. I was adopted as a baby, and my adopted parents have been wonderful. I love them very much. They told me when I reached eighteen that I was adopted. They gave me this photograph of my real father," she said.

She unfolded a four by five black and white photograph she took from the folds of her wallet. In the photo was a young man holding a baby standing on a shoveled walk in front of a house with lots of snow around. The man was smiling.

"He is handsome. This photo could be taken anywhere around here. Did you ever try to find him?" asked Devi.

"You know me. Of course, I did. He set up a trust fund for me, which never left me wanting for anything. But I could not break it, or find out who he was, or who my mother was either. Strangely though, with all this, I love him, Devi. I really love the man in this picture, and would love to see him and be with him. Does that seem weird?"

"No, not at all. I think the biological connection is binding although I firmly believe there is something more beyond that, especially in my case. We girls love our fathers usually more than our mothers. I love my dad more than my mom, but don't you ever tell her that. I feel very comfortable with him, and he is the only male besides Charlie that I feel that way about. He's a very talented, and special man. Well, he would have to be to put up with my crazy mom, and me," joked Devi.

"That must be hard for him living in the valley," said Audrey.

"No! Not at all. In fact, sometimes I think he is more popular than we are. All the people love my dad. When he's there, he's always at someone's house helping them to fix a roof, build a porch or just to visit and talk.

"Do you travel much?" asked Audrey.

"I have been all over the world…twenty-five countries so far," said Devi. Earlier this year Jasmine and I did the world on the cheap. It was my most favorite trip ever."

"Where did you go?" asked Audrey.

"It wasn't where we went, London, Paris, Rome, Egypt, Japan. It was how we went. We went as young, middle-class college students. It took us a month. It was my mom's idea to give me a different, fuller perspective on the world. The idea was just to mingle without deference and 'mix with the masses' as she called it. But it was also kind of an experiment. I had a chip implanted in my shoulder that they can use to track me if I am ever kidnapped. It is supposed to be very advanced technology. The whole time we were gone, they were seeing when, and if, they could track me…kind of perfecting the technology. I'm pretty good at spotting such things, but I never saw my bodyguards although I knew they were always watching us and monitoring the chip."

"Did it work?" asked Audrey.

"Not as well as they hoped. In the end, you had to be in the same city or area to pick up the signal from the chip. So it isn't like they can find you from a great distance. They were disappointed in the results, I think. But I still have the chip in my shoulder."

"I can't believe your mother let you do that. That sounds very danger-ous, two ladies traveling alone. Did you have any problems?" asked Audrey.

"No, I was safe the entire time, but let me explain," said Devi. "Our valley is set up so that all men and women living there must serve in the security or militia for two years. They must be weapons, and martial arts trained. Also, they spend two weeks every year retraining. It is something we are very proud of. I'm skilled at martial arts too, and I'm a pretty good shot. Out of these trained Champas, there are two hundred elite warriors.

"Jasmine, who was with me on that trip, is the best of our best," she continued. "Of all the men and women who have qualified mentally and physically, through very rigorous testing to be called warriors in our valley, Jasmine is the best. On that trip I mentioned, we had some guys, now and then, coming on to us, but all I had to do was kiss Jasmine, and they backed off. Good for them too because Jasmine would have cleaned their clocks! You should see her. She even has a six-pack!" said Devi laughing.

"Hmm, it seems the women in your valley traditionally are more dominant than men," said Audrey.

"Huh? No. But I can see where you might think that because of what I said. But only my mom is dominant. Her word in the valley is absolute, except maybe for my dad, but that is only because she loves him so much. Otherwise, our social relationships are pretty much like the rest of the world. Our females have the same responsibilities as men when it comes to work, and security. That's all. But each family decides how they go just like everywhere else.

As the limousine sped away from the curb, Devi said, "Ben, we are going to Edith's right across from where Charlie is interning. Do you know where that is?"

"Yes, Miss Devi," Big Ben replied. "I sure know where Edith's Barbecue is. Mmm-mmm, I can't wait. Her barbecue is even better than mine, and I'm over ready for lunch."

Devi laughed. "Me too, Ben, me too."

Chapter 34

2005 Incirlik Air Base, Turkey

Jack rushed over to the main counter in base operations at Incirlik Airbase, Turkey. He flagged down an NCO and begged permission to use the telephone. They had been at the United States Air Force Base six hours, and now he was watching them wheel Jasmine out to a C-9 medevac aircraft along with fifty other Americans wounded in Iraq.

It took him a while, but he finally got Mai on the telephone and told her that Jasmine had been shot, and they were flying her up to Ramstein airbase in Germany.

"What were you thinking, Jack?" asked Mai. "Why didn't you put her on our plane and get her back here? We can take good care of her."

"I know, and I thought about that, darling. But listen for a moment, and consider that our plane was not anywhere near here and first I would have had to find a charter that could properly take care of her while we were transporting there. Also, these doctors deal with bullet wounds all the time, and the best in the world are at Ramstein airbase in Germany where they are flying her now. She is not being treated like the rest of the soldiers, Mai. She has been given every priority like she was a general or something. Marty's friend, Amir, had something to do with that. He is in the CIA, I think. I will be with her all the way, not to worry."

"Mai, you should be proud of her. She saved Amir's life for sure, and the rest of us probably along with it. She was amazing," said Jack.

"What are you talking about? What happened, Jack? How did she get wounded? I don't like this at all. You're scaring me," said Mai.

"We got involved in a fire-fight at a roadblock on our way to the small airbase that was our pick up point to get out of there. We dealt with that handily following Jasmine's lead. We were mopping up, and getting ready to continue with our escape. But then some more mercenaries ambushed us, and Jasmine really came through at the risk of her own life. She spotted the bad guys first, and killed one of them while pushing Amir out of the way before she got shot herself," explained Jack.

There was only silence on the telephone and Jack thought he lost the connection. "Mai? Are you still there?"

She was crying when she answered at last. "Yes, I am still here. I am so afraid of you risking your life like that, and I'm proud of Jasmine. I have grown to love her very much, Jack. She has become very special to me almost like family. Why didn't you call me right away? Come home, Jack. Come back to me as soon as you can."

"I broke my cell phone during the ambush. In fact, there were three cell phones between us, and all of them were lost or broken. This is the first chance I had to call. But, Mai, the most important part I almost forgot to tell you. We found what we were looking for. We found a part of the handle at the Nineveh ruins site. It is magnificent, Mai. You can easily see why ancient humans treated it like a sacred object of worship,"

"I hope you are being careful with it," she said.

"Yes. Not to worry. We have taken extra precautions to protect it," Jack said. "It is in one of those big aluminum Halliburton cases that Amir owned, Mai."

Jack looked up to see Marty waving at him. "Mai, I have to go. Marty is waving at me to board. I love you, darling. I will see you soon," he said. "I will call you from Ramstein, and fill in the details," Jack said.

"You better," Mai said. "I love you, Jack Largent."

Chapter 35

2005 Chicago, North Clybourne Avenue

Thirty minutes later the two young women found themselves on North Clybourne going to meet up with Charlie when he finished his day at the law firm where he was interning.

As the limousine pulled up to the curb in front of a line of red brick storefronts dating from the 1920's, the two ladies did not wait for the bodyguards to open the door. They burst out of the limousine, with Devi announcing, gleefully, "Just you wait and see. You won't believe it. This is the best. It's perfect in fact: the atmosphere, the smells, and the food. Come on!"

Devi smiled broadly as she opened the door of the old barbecue restaurant that showed its character proudly as if the atmosphere where you ate was just as important as the taste. She looked back at Audrey who was smiling too and caught up in her enthusiasm. The smells and surroundings were as Devi remembered, and she couldn't wait to put that first bite into her mouth. She had been anticipating this moment while she traveled all the way from Cambodia. This wasn't the reason for her coming to Chicago, but it was at the top of her list of the most treasured fringe benefits, and this memory had been sitting comfortably in the back of her mind for a week. She waited to come here because she wanted to bring Audrey with her.

They entered and found a booth by the window up front in the nearly empty restaurant. It was two in the afternoon, and the lunch crowd had long since departed. The two guards, Ben and Mike, who entered just behind them, took up a booth on the side farther from the front where they could see the whole serving area and keep a good eye on Devi. They too had big eager smiles on their faces.

Almost immediately, a young black waitress came to their table and gave them a menu before she struck a pose with her order book. "Hello ladies, welcome to Edith's. Can I get you something to drink to start you off?" she asked.

"Coke is fine for me please, and I already know what I want," said Devi. "I want a pulled pork sandwich with slaw, and some of Edith's home-made baked beans. Oh! Can I have some sauce on the side too…the more spicy kind? I have been anticipating this moment for nine thousand miles."

"Nine thousand miles? Where you from, girl?" the waitress asked, with a curious smile.

"My home is in Cambodia, but we have a lot of friends who live in Chicago. I came here last year and never forgot it. It's all I have been thinking about since I left Cambodia. Really! I'm not kidding. You got the hook in me!" Devi said, smiling eagerly.

"Yeah, I hear that a lot. Momma's cookin' does that to everybody. I'm glad you like it," said the waitress, proudly.

She looked at Audrey who smiled, and said, "I'll have the same."

"OK, two pulled pork sandwiches, two cokes, coming up," she said, as she walked away to take the order from the two bodyguards sitting three tables away.

Devi smiled at her back, and then turned, and looked out the window at the modern office building across the street. It was in sharp contrast to the seasoned character of the red brick storefronts, and warehouses, of North Clybourne.

Audrey said, "You're right. If the food is as good as the atmosphere, this is going to be a real treat. Is that where Charlie works?"

"Yep," replied Devi. "He should be coming out the door any minute now. So, what was going on when I interrupted your meeting with Aunt Catherine this morning? It looked like something big was happening."

Audrey's face turned into a huge ear-to-ear grin. But then she caught herself. "Sorry, I made a promise not to tell anyone until we broadcast. But you're right, it's a really big story, and I found it. I am so psyched, Devi, you can't imagine. I admire Catherine so much, and I want to prove to her that she made the right choice in hiring me. I'm walking on a cloud right now, but I am truly sorry. I mean that. I can't talk about it. She made us all promise to tell no one. Top secret," she said crossing her lips. "But you'll know very soon, and it will blow your mind!"

Devi looked at her eye-to-eye in silence mimicking her smile as a fellow conspirator for a long moment. "You got the evidence on Grimes, didn't you? You did it. I know you did!"

Audrey continued her huge grin now wanting desperately to share.

"Come on! I won't mention it to anyone. I promise," begged Devi.

Audrey took a big breath and then said, "Oh god! I am dying to tell someone what has happened. You have to promise…you have to swear that you won't tell anyone. Honestly, I am going to break at the seams if I don't share what I've done with someone. I am so proud and so thrilled. I can't keep it in any longer. Yes! I found the evidence that will convict Grimes. I got him, Devi."

The two young women squealed in delight and then looked quickly around at the almost empty restaurant but no one was paying any attention other than Devi's bodyguards who couldn't hear their conversation.

"That's amazing, Audrey. Do you know how long Aunt Catherine has been after him? I am so proud of you. In a way it is my victory too. I found you afterall."

"Yep, without you, I wouldn't have even had this job. I can never thank you enough for that," affirmed Audrey. "Okay, but now that I have gotten that out of my system, let's forget about it, okay? Please, please, please, don't let anyone know. Promise."

"Sure, I am good at keeping secrets and I will enjoy keeping this one in the next few weeks as it plays out. Wow! Okay…moving on. I promise."

To change the subject, Audrey offered, "So tell me about Charlie."

"I already told you Charlie is my best male friend in the world. He is a freshman at the University of Chicago in the fall where we just registered me," she explained. "But I will be a sophomore."

"Wait, about being a sophomore; you said you were sixteen and then you told me you are taking a special advanced curriculum. Are you some kind of genius, or something?" Audrey asked, already aware that Devi was very smart.

But Devi decided to play with the comment. "Yes, something like that, I guess. I don't know. I have been told I am off the charts intelligent." She fluffed her hair and struck a prideful pose with her nose in the air as Audrey laughed.

Devi continued with the pose for a moment pretending to put on airs but then broke into a big grin, "But I don't think of myself as any different than anyone else. I just look at stuff and get it and that makes school boring for me. My mom asked me to stick it out because I need it for the social aspect of it. But I already told you I am a failure in that department."

She broke it off and turned to Audrey smiling. "But wait till you see Charlie! He is a hunk! The funny thing is, I love looking at him, being with him, and talking about things with him, but I feel not one iota of sexual attraction. Of course, in our situation, that's a good thing. But you would think there would be something. I know I'm not gay like Aunt Catherine and Kelly because girls don't attract me either."

"OK, but something must turn you on," said Audrey.

"Computers. If I could have sex with them, I would," she said, chuckling. "Seriously, I love data and programming. I created a new logic board at Siem Kulea based on a chip I designed. We were getting some interesting, but weird, intercepts on it when mom made me shut it down. She said that Queen Dau Te Po told her to."

"Who is that, a friend of your mom's?"

"No," Devi said, thinking a moment. "She is an ancient legendary Champa Queen who mom talks to in her thoughts sometimes. That's all.

"Hey, you're a reporter. Look at those men with the laundry truck making a delivery across the street. What looks funny about them?"

"Hmmm, well let's see," said Audrey, looking to where she pointed.

She observed a large white truck that was parked across the street to the right of the entrance of the law firm where Charlie was doing his summer internship. The entrance was elevated with a dozen steps coming down to the street. On the side of the truck it read, *Bodine's Towel and Linen Service.* She watched two men on the opposite side of the truck, working with a two-wheeler and a stack of packaged towels.

"Well, there's a couple of things," Audrey said. "The one man's uniform doesn't fit well. Looks like a bad day at the laundry. His sleeves are too short like they shrunk. They look like they are in the middle of a comedy routine. I bet they don't even know there is probably a delivery area in the back of the building. Oh, and they keep changing the bundles they are delivering." Audrey said laughing.

Devi noted that and nodded smiling with a scrunched nose in affirmation to her, but then she turned quickly away from the window as the front door of the restaurant opened again, and a burly middle-aged man dressed in a raincoat and rumpled suit entered.

"Uh-oh, cop," she whispered to Audrey.

The white-haired lady who she thought must be the actual Edith, and who was busy wiping down the counter across the aisle from them, shook her head smiling. "Detective Haleran, where have you been? I think I aged ten years since you was last in here."

"Mama, it has only been a couple of months. You know I can't stay away from you for long," he joked. "You're just too good looking for any man to resist."

"Oh, you the biggest liar I know," she said. "But I also know you have to get your fix on my barbecue ribs too. I got your number, detective. So what brings you up this way today?" She was all smiles, and unconsciously licked, and crunched her lips as she spoke.

Haleran sat down at the counter while mama Edith poured him a cup of coffee without asking. "I was interviewing some wits up the street and thought I would drop by, and say hi. How you doin', momma?" he asked, honestly caring.

"OK, I guess: a little older, a little slower gettin' around. You know. We ain't youngin's like we used to be, detective."

"Yeah, I get that. I am at the age now where my joints remind me all the time I'm not a kid anymore, especially on long trips."

"You want the usual?"

"Same as always, mama. You know what I like," he said, while looking around at the others in the restaurant. Mama Edith's Barbecue used to be on his beat when he started as a rookie many years ago. Since then, he had been transferred to other divisions, and did not get up to this area of town as often as he used to.

"Yeah, I know what you like, detective, and you know your money's no good 'round here after what you did for my son. You changed his life, detective. I can never thank you enough for that," she said.

"That was nothing anyone else wouldn't have done, mama. He's a good kid. I heard the other day he got his detective's shield. He only needed someone to point him in the right direction," Haleran insisted.

She gave him a look and rolled her eyes. "You know, and I know what you did, detective, and since then, you have always been like a father to him. Mmmm, mmmm, we were lucky you were there at the right time."

Haleran continued to gaze around the restaurant while she talked, and saw the real reason he was at Edith's that day: princess Devi sitting with another young lady in the booth near the door. "What's their story? They waiting for someone? They both look like they should be in school."

"No idea, Frank. They just wandered in here, and sat down about ten minutes ago. They been here before though. They knew what they wanted without lookin' at my menu. We're 'bout ready to serve them both pulled pork sandwiches. If you so damned curious 'bout everbody, why don't you go introduce yourself, and do your own detectin' work?"

Haleran had been tailing Devi around town for two days. Her bodyguards were good, excellent in fact. Haleran was adept enough to stay far enough away so as not to attract attention. This afternoon he was on the trail again and was personally happy when she stopped at Edith's.

The first thing he noted that first day when he caught up with Princess Devi was that she looked like Mai only younger. He even imagined it was Mai for a bit. Closer up the young princess was quite attractive, but her eyes are what got his attention the most. She had what he liked to call 'listening eyes'. He remembered Mai's were like that. They were like recorders always on, always thinking.

She was dressed in designer jeans, and a sweater, and her bag had to cost a big chunk more than his paycheck. She looked out of place in that old booth that had as much character as she had style. He wanted to meet her, but he hesitated another minute trying to decide on an approach. Finally, thinking of nothing else, he decided to be direct.

He walked over to the table where the young ladies sat, and introduced himself flashing his detective ID and badge briefly in his wallet.

"Hello, I am Detective Frank Haleran, Chicago police. Mind if I sit down?" he asked.

"I bet if I said 'yes' you would sit down anyway, wouldn't you, Lieutenant?" Devi replied smiling as Audrey scooted over making a place for him.

"How'd you know I was a Lieutenant? Hey, you're pretty quick, aren't you," he commented, trying to get the young women to feel more relaxed with him. "You picked that up from my ID?"

She looked at the fiftyish, grey-haired lieutenant with the amiable face, and said, confirming his assessment, "You are Lieutenant Frank Haleran, Chicago Police Department Headquarters badge 3189."

"That's pretty good," he commented, honestly surprised. "Damn good, in fact. What is your name?"

"I am Devearney Ann Largent, sixteen years old, and I live in Siem Kulea, Cambodia. I am here visiting my friend, Charlie Marsh, who works as an intern at the law firm across the street. He should be meeting us here after he gets off work. I will be starting my sophomore year in the fall at the University of Chicago with Charlie. This is my friend, Audrey Goodnight, from Madison."

Haleran ignored the pretty young blond on his right for the moment, and smiled, "Starting Sophomore year next year, huh? Mind if I see some identification.?" he asked, fully aware everything she said was the truth. He wanted to see how she represented herself to strangers in general, and authorities in particular.

Devi reached into her purse and handed him her passport. It was a diplomatic passport. As he studied it, Big Ben suddenly appeared with Michael at the end of the table and said, "Can I be of assistance here, Miss Devi?"

Devi looked up, and said, "Thanks, Ben, but we're fine. Everything is OK. This is Lieutenant Haleran of the Chicago Police Department. He's just checking us out. I guess he thinks I should be in school or something."

When Haleran looked at her curiously, she explained, "I overheard you talking to that lady. Is that Mama Edith?"

As the two bodyguards relaxed and went back to their seats, Haleran replied, "Yeah, that's her. A nicer woman, and a better cook you'll never meet."

"You carrying?" she asked, as he handed back her passport.

"Huh, oh, yes I'm armed," he answered.

"May I see it?" she asked. "What kind is it?"

"I don't think so. Mama Edith doesn't approve of firearms," he said, as their sandwiches arrived. Mama Edith put a plate full of baby-back ribs in front of Haleran with a side of beans at the same time. She put down his half-filled coffee cup and topped it off.

Haleran picked up a rib and took a big bite. He involuntarily closed his eyes for just a second but when he opened them again he looked over at Devi who only sat, and stared at her sandwich with big eyes matching her smile.

"It tastes a lot better if you actually put it into your mouth," he said, glancing over at Audrey who was already working on a mouth full of sandwich and smiling at his comment. She dabbed her cheek with a napkin.

Devi looked over at him and gave him a face. "Lieutenant, if you knew how long, and how much I have anticipated this moment, you would understand why I want to cherish it for just a bit longer. This barbecue is like a fine wine. You should smell it first and enjoy that before your taste buds take over. But that said, I was just now thinking I need to get them cooking barbecue like this in Siem Kulea."

"So you're a fan of Edith's. I think you and I have found something in common. It's a thirty-eight, Smith and Wesson."

Devi looked at him confused. "Oh! For a moment I thought you were talking about my sandwich. Wow, that's really old-fashioned!"

"The sandwich, or the gun?" he asked, enjoying the back and forth with her.

Devi made a face. "The gun, of course! But it fits with the whole image. You could be in a movie, Lieutenant. You look like a Hollywood version of a police detective. I mean, who wears trench coats these days?"

"They issued them with the badge back in my day," he joked.

Devi glanced outside as something caught her eye. "Oh I think that's Charlie now," she said, seeing a tall blond young man starting down the steps wearing a canvas fedora. He stopped a moment, and removed his raincoat as he realized the drizzly morning had turned into an exceptional afternoon. She stared at him much the same as her sandwich, for being with him was something else she had been anticipating for nine thousand miles, and thus far they had only had one rather brief meeting as he had been out of town.

But something wasn't right. To her horror, one of the towel service workers bent down, and retrieved a machine pistol from between a stack of packed linens. She gave a surprised start as the two workers from the towel truck began approaching Charlie from behind.

Charlie, seeing her in the window from across the street, started to wave, but she only got a very brief look as a large green Peterbilt semi truck-and-trailer prevented their view when it passed between them, moving slowly down Clybourne Avenue.

After it had passed, she saw just a glimpse of Charlie being led behind the linen truck by the two men. It was hard to tell, but she was almost positive he glanced across the street again, and he looked worried.

"He's being kidnapped," she uttered to herself as she realized what was happening. "BEN, CHARLIE'S BEING KIDNAPPED!" Devi yelled frantically. "They're putting him at gunpoint in that white linen truck across the street!"

The two guards looked up, and then, dropping ribs and napkins at once, moved with surprising speed out the door before Sergeant Haleran even reacted. He threw his napkin on the table and rushed after them.

Outside, the three men pulled their guns, and rushed past parked cars hurriedly toward the white truck. But as they started across, one of the kidnappers who were both Asian came around the front of the truck, and began spraying them with bullets from a Mac-10 he held at his waist. His method wasn't accurate, but it was effective. Shots were hitting all around them puncturing cars, windows, and pavement alike. As determined as the guards and detective were, the three were forced to seek cover immediately, and they withdrew back behind parked cars from the overwhelming firepower. It was lucky that none of them got hit in the opening barrage. Bullets were landing all around them, breaking car windows, and puncturing metal ominously. The noise in the narrow street was deafening.

They hunkered down behind cars trying to protect themselves in front of Edith's with bullets zinging everywhere nearby. They grabbed a few inaccurate shots back at the assailants when they could. Storefronts became pockmarked with bullet holes, and some glass windows in the buildings broke as they were hit. Sensing an opening, Michael rose and walked with determined focus toward the truck as he carefully aimed, and fired again, and again, at the armed kidnapper. Michael was an excellent marksman, and he seemed to hit the gunman several times. That staggered and knocked him back momentarily. But the gunman kept on coming and fired relentlessly. Then Michael was himself hit in the shoulder. It spun him around and knocked him down on the pavement on his back. His gun landed several feet away. Big Ben tried to get to him, but was driven back immediately by another fusillade of bullets from the automatic weapon the kidnapper held.

"Michael, talk to me. Are you OK? Can you get to us?" Ben called out, from behind the wheel of a car.

"I'm shot in the shoulder...can't move very well. But I'm OK. Stay where you are, Ben. I think this guy is wearing a vest." Michael called back. "I will try to reach my gun."

Haleran, still crouched down behind a parked Chevy Impala, waited for the man with the automatic weapon to have to change his clip. In spite of being hit at least once by Michael, he seemed unfazed and didn't stop shooting. Haleran had only seen that once before, and that time the assailant was high on drugs.

It seemed to take longer than expected but finally, the assailant's clip ran out of bullets. As soon as that happened, Haleran hurried out into the street, grabbed Michael's feet, and pulled him back behind another parked car. The other gunman fired at him several times from the driver's seat, but his aim was inaccurate, and all the shots missed Haleran and the big guard.

Just as they arrived safely behind the cars once more, the linen truck started its engine, and began to pull away from the curb hurriedly. When the kidnapper with the Mac-10 stopped firing to get into the truck, Big Ben and Lieutenant Haleran stood, and began firing in earnest at the truck popping the tires and causing the engine to smoke. The effect was to leave the truck pulled awkwardly out from the curb about four feet, and facing them head-on with two flat tires in the front.

It became quiet for a moment, and a standoff ensued, as the kidnappers seemed to be considering what to do next. The kidnapper with the Mac-10 again got out of the truck, but stayed protectively just behind the front bumper. A police car arrived with its siren blaring, and parked facing the truck on the street from the back right, blocking any escape in that direction. Soon after the police emerged from their vehicle, they were fired upon, and they returned the fire from behind the open doors of their police car at the kidnappers. Haleran immediately identified who he was to them, and explained the situation in a few yelled words.

Big Ben yelled, "How's Michael?"

"He will be OK," answered Haleran. But even he was surprised as mama Edith suddenly appeared with some towels, which she used to prop up Michael's head behind the safety of the parked car. She began setting about putting a compress on his wound.

"Hey, you look like you know what you're doing, mama, but, you shouldn't be out here. This is getting crazy real fast." Haleran commented.

"Detective, you don't know everything about me, do you? I've seen plenty of shootings in this neighborhood, and was even a nurse assistant at a clinic for years before my fam'ly moved from the Southside. That was a long time ago, but you never forget some things," she explained.

Haleran didn't have time to convince her otherwise. He settled for telling her to keep down behind the car. He didn't like it, but he had other things to worry about.

Another police car arrived behind the rear of the truck, and parked further away down the street. The officer quickly got out, and moved stealthily along the sidewalk from car to car until he was almost at the truck itself. The kidnappers did not see him moving in closer from behind.

Just then, the second kidnapper began recklessly coming at them again around the front of the truck with his Mac-10 firing on full. Bullets hit the cars in front of Haleran and Big Ben, mercilessly pinging off in menacing ricochets, some making holes with a loud thunk-thunk as they did. Big Ben crouched down even lower as his right forehead was streaked by a wild remnant from a bullet that hit the surface of the car in front of him. But then one of the other policemen on their right side from behind the open door of his cruiser, shot the assailant twice in the chest, and this time the man went down. Things got tense as the assailant lay flat, and still for a moment. Nobody moved, not wanting to expose themselves. Then unbelievably, the assailant struggled up again, and began firing once more with marked determination, this time in a duel with the cop who had shot him. The same cop shot him again, and emptied his clip into him with all the bullets hitting his chest, except one that landed in his neck. The assailant went down for good this time on his back with his arms spread out above his head as he lay on the ground. He was pooling blood on the pavement from his open neck wound.

Just then, there were shots from inside the truck as the cop who had approached stealthily from behind along the sidewalk leaned into the open side door facing the sidewalk, and shot the driver. The same police officer quickly climbed in, and examined the body of Charlie Marsh that was laid out on the floor of the van with his hands cuffed behind him.

"You OK?" he asked the young man.

Charlie couldn't answer, but nodded eagerly as he had a gag stuffed in his mouth preventing him from talking. The officer quickly removed it, and freed his hands before he yelled "Clear!" from inside the truck.

From the right-back side, the two police officers slowly got up, and began moving cautiously toward the kidnap van.

Haleran and Big Ben ran around the front side of the truck anxiously, and with some relief watched as the uniformed officer checked to see if Charlie was OK. The officer was a bit older, a police Sergeant judging by the stripes on his sleeve, maybe in his forties. He examined Charlie like he had some experience. An ambulance arrived, and within seconds an EMT took over and was asking Charlie questions while another was attending to Michael.

Seeing the 15 pinned to the uniformed officer's collar, Haleran said, "You're a long way from home, Sergeant. I'm Detective Lieutenant Haleran, Headquarters Special Operations. That was good work."

"Thank you, wrong place right time, I guess," he replied. "I'm Sergeant Daniels. I was comparing notes on a case with officers at District eighteen earlier. When the call came in I was a few blocks away, and on my way back, so I came over here, and just happened to pull up at the right spot to intercept them from behind."

Charlie saw Big Ben peeking in the back of the truck, nodded to him and said, "I'm OK, Ben. Look's like we escaped another one. Hey, did you get hit?" he asked seeing the blood on Ben's forehead.

"Just a flesh wound, Charlie. Nothing to worry about," answered Big Ben.

"What does he mean, another one?" asked Haleran of Big Ben.

But just at that moment, they heard three more gunshots from back inside Edith's Barbecue. Haleran and Big Ben with two other uniformed cops turned quickly toward the sound of the shots, and ran across the street back to the front door of the restaurant.

Just outside the door, Haleran stopped and told Big Ben to wait outside.

"Not with Miss Devi in there I won't," Ben said. "You going to have to shoot me too if you going to keep me out of there right now."

Haleran nodded, but then told the two uniforms to go around the back of the restaurant. Then he and Ben went into the restaurant quickly, but cautiously, with Haleran in the lead. Just inside the door, they assessed the situation as they looked around with guns drawn.

The waitress was behind the counter frozen holding her face in shocked surprise. On the floor near them was an Asian man who appeared to have been shot once in the head. His gun lay on the floor nearby. Closer to Haleran was another Asian man lying on his back across a stool by the counter holding his bleeding right shoulder where he had two wounds. On the ground at his feet was a 9mm Mauser. Both men were dressed entirely in black.

The girl, Devi, had a gun drawn, and pointed at the second man in a shooting position, with her elbows resting on the table in front of her, and her hands making a cradle for her gun. The other girl, Audrey, was drawn back in the booth with fists clenched. Her eyes were huge, and her mouth was open in surprise.

After taking just a glance to see that it was he who had entered the restaurant door, Devi spoke to Lieutenant Haleran, keeping her eyes on the two assailants, "I put two bullets in that one, Lieutenant, but I only tried to wound him," she said, speaking calmly. "We will need him for questioning."

Haleran looked at her in surprise. She had a passive look on her face more robotic than human.

"We will need…" he repeated, stunned by her statement. " Put the gun down, young lady! Gently. Put it down on the table!"

Devi ejected the clip, cleared the chamber, checked the barrel, and set the gun down on the table. She searched around collecting her spent brass from the bench still acting somewhat methodical in her actions. When she was done, she sat straight with her hands folded on the table, and looked at him as if following a well-practiced exercise.

"Are there anymore suspects around?" Haleran asked her.

She shook her head. "I don't know, Lieutenant. They came in from the back so there might be an accomplice out there," she said, pointing toward the right end of the counter.

Suddenly remembering, she looked at Haleran, and asked, "Charlie! What about Charlie? Where is he? Is he OK, Lieutenant?"

Haleran told Big Ben to keep an eye on the wounded suspect who didn't look like he was capable of moving anyway, and walked toward the back door. "Charlie is OK. They're checking him over, but he's fine. Just stay put until we clear the area," he directed her.

Haleran met the two uniforms just outside the back door. "All clear here, detective," the first one said. "We saw a blue Toyota van pulling away pretty fast in the alley as we came around the back. We did not get a good look at the driver. He looked to be Latino, or Asian, but I couldn't say for certain."

"I'm Detective Lieutenant Haleran from Headquarters Special Ops. Did you get a license?" asked Haleran.

"No sir," said the first cop.

"The license plate had mud all over it," added the second cop.

"Should I call it in, anyway?" asked the first cop, as they heard sirens arriving on the street in front.

"Yeah call it in, and make sure more EMTs, and the crime scene techs, are on their way," said Haleran. "You guys get it taped off back here, and get someone to guard this part of the crime scene. Tell whoever is in charge out front we have an additional crime scene with one dead, and one wounded inside the restaurant. Tell them to be sure to block off the street on both ends all the way back to the corner. This place is going to get overrun pretty fast."

As Haleran came back into Edith's, he saw Ben looking very concerned, and sitting in the booth talking with Devi who had moved to the other side, and was holding hands with Audrey. They were turned looking out the window. "Ben, go see to Michael. Please, I'm OK," said Devi.

"Tell him we are very proud of him," Devi called after him as Big Ben hurried back outside.

Haleran returned to the front area, checked the wounded assailant who hadn't moved, and faced the waitress. "Are you alright?" he asked.

"I'm OK, Lieutenant," said the young black woman. "Just a bit shook up. It's been a long time since we had a robbery in here."

"What happened?" he asked her.

"Those men came in from the back. Surprised us all," said the waitress. "We didn't see them until they were right on us. We were all watching you outside, and keeping low because a couple of bullets came through the front window, and shattered the little window on the right.

"They had guns pointed right at us, and they ordered me to get on the floor," she continued, still acting nervous from the recent events. "That's when the girl shot them. They looked mean. I think they were going to kill us. That one had death in his eyes," she said, pointing to the dead man on the floor.

Just then, Mama Edith came through the door, and interrupted them as she went to the waitress and gave her a long hug. "Are you OK? They wouldn't let me back in here until just now," she said. "I was worried sick about what I would find in here."

"Yes, Mama, I'm OK," she said, but then she started crying anyway.

The waitress collected herself in a few short sobs with Mama Edith still holding her. Finally, she took a deep breath, and said, "That girl saved our lives. I'm sure of it."

Haleran grabbed a couple of napkins, and picked up the two Mausers the suspects had been holding. He ejected the clip in each one, cleared them, and put them safely on the counter. He patted down the one suspect that was still alive and lying across the stool. He found no identification and a lone switchblade. He checked the man on the floor and found no pulse. He patted him down, and found no ID on him either.

Big Ben was back after seeing Michael off in the ambulance, and talking low in the booth with Devi as Haleran walked over to them. "That was some pretty quick thinking, Miss Devi. You're sure you are OK?" Ben was asking her.

"I'm OK, Ben, really. I'm just kind of dazed. It was just like our drills only it was real. How's Charlie?" she asked in return.

Big Ben observed that in spite of her protests, her fingers played nervously on the table as she talked. "He's OK, Miss Devi. He's being looked over by the EMT guys. They took Michael off in one ambulance and the other that just arrived is taking over care of Charlie. They're keeping him flat on his back while they're observing him. He was hit hard on the head by one of the kidnappers when he tried to resist as they put handcuffs on him. I think they want to be sure he doesn't go into shock or anything like that. But I don't think he's hurt bad. It's kind of confusing out there. There's lots of Indians, and no chiefs," he explained.

She nodded in answer to Ben's summary as Haleran reached over, and picked up her gun still sitting on the table where she had placed it. "An HK P2000 9mm," he said. "Good weapon. Can I assume you have a permit for it, Miss?"

"Of course, Lieutenant," she said. "It's in my purse."

"We will need to call your parents. I think you said they're in Cambodia. Is there someone close we can call here in town to take responsibility for you since you are still a minor?" he asked hiding his favor to her mother.

"Yes, but Ben already called my Aunt Catherine," said Devi.

Haleran nodded knowing she meant Catherine Marsh. He stood up, and looked outside seeing lots of policemen standing about with no direction. He wondered what happened to the instructions he gave the two officers in the back. He turned to the big guard, and said, "I think I got your name, Ben is it?" he asked.

Big Ben looked over at him and nodded.

"Ben, would you do me a favor. Go out there, and tell them we need an officer in here ASAP. I want someone taking charge of this wounded prisoner. Also, be sure the EMT guys know there is a wounded man in here. I think they forgot about this guy."

Ben nodded, and went back outside as Haleran continued talking with Audrey about her age, and where she was from. Ben returned a minute later with two uniformed officers following. The first one introduced himself. "Lieutenant Haleran, I am Boyd from the one-eight," the officer said.

"Are you ranking?" asked Haleran.

"I was first on the scene after it was over, Lieutenant. But my sergeant just arrived, and he is busy securing the crime scene outside. We've got four cars from District eighteen alone."

"What's your name, again?" asked Haleran.

"Boyd, Lieutenant."

"OK, Boyd good job. But understand, there are two crime scenes: the kidnap shooting out there, and another almost simultaneous shooting in here. Go make sure your sergeant is aware of that, and get an EMT in here to look over this suspect," Haleran ordered.

He looked at the remaining police officer, and ordered him, "Stand over there, and keep an eye on that suspect. He's unarmed and hasn't moved, but I don't want him to try anything cute."

Haleran turned back toward the booth where Ben, Audrey, and Devi still sat. "I want you three to move out of the booth. Stay to the side away from the bodies, and move back to the rear of the restaurant. Sit around that big table in the rear until the detectives get here to take your statements."

Another Emergency vehicle arrived near the front of the restaurant with sirens on until they slowed, and maneuvered to a stop outside. Within seconds, two EMTs came into the restaurant. "There are two suspects here," Haleran said to them pointing to the two men by the counter. "This one is dead I think. The one back there is wounded in the shoulder."

The first EMT followed Haleran's direction to the second suspect just as he slid from the stool unconscious to the floor leaving a trail of blood on the stool over him. The EMT went to work quickly on him, but it was obvious after a few moments that he was dead now too, and not going to respond to the EMTs efforts to resuscitate him.

"He dead?" asked Haleran as the EMT moved over to the rear table to look at Big Ben.

"Yeah, the bullet nicked an artery, and it mostly bled out before we got here. There wasn't much hope without someone catching this one right away," the EMT explained while he worked on the flesh wound on Big Ben's forehead.

Haleran nodded. A medical examiner arrived followed by two crime scene techs. The medical examiner gave Haleran a nod in recognition, and took a moment to observe the scene before going to work on the first dead suspect.

A few minutes later two plain clothes detectives, one short and one tall, but dressed in almost identical brown suits, arrived and looked around as they entered. Seeing Haleran they walked over. "Hey, Frank, what the hell are you doing here? I thought you were assigned to Headquarters Special Ops," the shorter one said.

"Petri and Donavitch. Good to see you guys," he said smiling. "I really walked into something this afternoon. I'm actually on vacation."

"What have we got, Frank?" the tall one named Donavitch asked.

Haleran rubbed his forehead. "I was just sorting it out myself. Here's what I know," he said, as he proceeded to outline the events of the previous thirty minutes to them.

As the story unfolded, the detectives' eyes got bigger, and at the end, Donavitch exclaimed, "Jesus, Haleran! It sounds like the Wild West. You OK?

"Yeah, we didn't have any casualties, except for the guard who got hit. It's a shoulder wound and I don't think it's life threatening. We were lucky. But these guys were serious, and listen, you two, I still have a bad feeling about this. Something isn't right, but I can't put my finger on it right now. Look, why don't we move over to the back end of the restaurant, and sort this all out while the Medical Examiner and the CSI team do their thing," suggested Haleran.

"We'll need your weapon, Frank," said Petri inspecting the firearms that Haleran put on the counter. "We have the guard's from outside but we still need to get the weapon from the other guard."

"You want the rest of these ribs, detective Haleran?" said Edith, with a rag in hand ready to clean the table where they had been seated before.

"No, don't touch that table, Ma'am," said Donavitch. "That's part of the crime scene. Please stay back away from that area." He motioned to the uniformed cop who was supposed to be protecting the crime scene to do his job.

"I guess not, Edith," said Haleran while in the process of turning over his gun to Petri. "I will have to take a rain check under the circumstances."

"Well, I want mine. I'm famished!" said Devi, from the back of the restaurant. "Is it OK if she brings it over here?"

"Let me make you a fresh sandwich," said mama Edith. "I will bring it over to you with a fresh coke. Does the young lady with you want one too?"

"Well, yes, I guess so," Audrey said, following Devi's lead, but still not recovered from all the excitement.

The two detectives joined Big Ben and the two young ladies sitting around the round, red-Formica table in the back of the restaurant. Big Ben sat next to Devi on one side, and Audrey on the other.

The detectives introduced themselves as Haleran collected Big Ben's weapon. Then they sat down at the table and got out their notebooks.

Petri began. "Let's start with the younger girl. The shooter. What is your name, Miss?" he asked, taking notes on his pad.

Devi gave her name, background, and why she was there exactly as she had for Lieutenant Haleran earlier. Exactly.

In a few minutes, Mama Edith delivered fresh sandwiches and cokes to the two young ladies, and they eagerly began eating them. She also placed a fresh plate of ribs in front of Big Ben who was surprised and thanked her with a big smile for thinking of him.

Petri watched Devi eat her late lunch as if nothing had happened, and he couldn't reconcile it with the two dead bodies on the floor, or the attempted kidnapping. "You don't seem very concerned about all that has happened, young lady. I would expect most people in your situation to be pretty upset by now. Care to explain?"

Devi was finally enjoying her barbecue sandwich and looked irritated when he interrupted her. At first, she ignored his question, but then she put down her much-desired sandwich with a frown, wiped her mouth, and faced him directly. "Hmmm, let's try to figure this big mystery out shall we, detective? Oh wait, I know! The answer is simple. I'm hungry! I haven't eaten since breakfast. Case solved. You can go now." She looked at him like he was an idiot for bothering her, and then asking what to her was a stupid question. He was about to challenge her again when she continued. "Look, detective, I am not the weak, and emotional little girl you have already type-cast, and expect me to be. If I acted like that when those animals attacked us, I would be a prisoner, or dead right now. My mother and father taught me to be strong, analyze the situation, and act decisively. That's what I did. I assessed the situation, saw what needed to be done, and defended myself. Now I am eating my lunch, or at least trying to. I keep getting interrupted. Maybe you can leave me alone, so I can finally enjoy some of this delicious sandwich in peace. Big Ben can answer your questions."

The two detectives were surprised by the directness of her statement. After a moment Petri asked, "Who's Big Ben?"

Ben raised one hand while holding a rib in the other. "That would be me, officer." He put down the barbecue rib, wiped his mouth, and said, "Maybe I can help clear things up for you, if you don't mind me explaining. I am Ben Washington. I work for NearNorth Productions and am assigned with Michael, the wounded man they took away in the ambulance, to guard Miss Devi and Charlie Marsh today. Miss Devi is distracted because that sandwich in her hand was something she was eagerly anticipating and why we came here to this restaurant today to wait for Charlie to get off work across the street. Everything that has happened, including your questions, are working to ruin that experience for her. You might want to take a nicer, less belligerent approach to your questioning especially with the two young victims here. I called Ms. Kelly, Ms. Marsh's partner, and she called Mai Sambath Largent, Miss Devi's mother in Cambodia, immediately. We have trained extensively for situations like this since these young people are in constant danger because of who they are," he explained.

"Just who *are* they?" demanded Petri. He glanced at Donavitch as he felt the situation starting to slip away from him.

Devi was focused on her sandwich as Big Ben answered. "Charlie Marsh, the young man out there resting his head, is the son of Catherine Marsh and Kelly Ryan," Ben said. "You know Ms. Marsh, I'm sure. She is the billionaire television reporter, writer and philanthropist. Charlie is the heir to all of that."

"Oh shit," said Petri, involuntarily.

"And Devi here who is trying against all odds to finish her lunch is an Asian princess," said Audrey, a bit more excited than she really intended, but loving the looks on the detective's faces that resulted from her declaration. "A real Asian princess. Her mother is Mai Sambath Largent, the Champa Queen. You may remember the big deal about fifteen years ago with the finding of that ancient Champa treasure in Vietnam. She was the one who found it. She now lives in Northern Cambodia very much like a queen, and as a very respected, and powerful citizen of Cambodia."

"And who would you be?" Petri asked her.

She looked at him surprised. "Me? Oh, I'm Audrey Goodnight, and this is my first week in Chicago, detective. This has been more exciting than anything in my entire life. I'm a new reporter at NearNorth Productions starting just this week."

"Oh great!" commented Petri. "A princess, a reporter, two bloody shootings, and an attempted kidnapping. What could be more complicated? Would you excuse us a minute?" he said motioning his partner to a corner leading to the restrooms.

"You left out Charley, Ms. Marsh's son," added Audrey flippantly. "How about, 'a billionaire TV personality's son'? I think that will fit the alliteration nicely. I think I will add it at the beginning when I write about it," she said with some sarcasm, taking sides with Devi because she too didn't like their hostile attitude.

The detectives just stared at her for a moment not sure if she was making an attempt at humor or what. After a bit they turned back to their intense discussion and didn't see Audrey share a high-five with Devi.

Haleran watched the whole encounter from a stool nearby. He, of course, knew who the parents and relations were of the two young women and the young man outside. He decided to leave his favor to Mai out of the investigation, and stick to the facts of the incident. It was a bit amusing for him to see Petri and Donavitch get flustered with each new revelation. He walked over, sat down at the table, and said, "I don't think the detectives like the can of worms you just opened, Ben. Watch them." They all looked over at the two detectives talking intensely to each other. "In a moment Petri will reach for his mobile phone, and call in to his Captain who will be here very shortly."

The group sitting at the table watched with smiles as indeed Petri did make a call on his mobile phone before both detectives returned to the table, and sat down. By then, Devi had finished her lunch, and sat forward with her hands folded on the table signaling she was ready to answer questions. She gave a conspirational smile to Haleran and then turned back toward the detectives and waited.

Donavitch shook his head and took a deep breath. "If you're ready now, Miss Largent, I would appreciate it if you could tell us about the shooting. Take us through it bit-by-bit if you please." His approach changed with the realization that this was no ordinary case, and they were going to have a lot of supervision from downtown very shortly on everything they did.

Petri gave him an approving nod, as Devi began. "When they came in, the two Asian men I am talking about now, they looked at me first, and then went for Chantelle, the waitress. I suspect they were told to do so just in case there were any weapons behind the counter. They told her to get on the floor. That's when I saw the mark on the back of the first man's hand. It was the mark of the Black Hand, a Hmong gang of mercenaries from South Asia. It is like an oval with three lines through it. They usually work for Asian warlords but can be hired out by anybody for the right price. They are heavily involved in the drug trade mostly out of Malaysia. This is the third time they tried to take me."

"You? You think this was about you?" Petri was incredulous. His attitude toward Devi continued to be less friendly, and Big Ben gave him a disapproving look. Donavitch nudged Petri's hand slightly signaling for him to back off with his attitude.

"Yes, detective, me, and Charlie, of course. They would not come here to rob mama Edith's. This was planned. They knew I was coming to meet Charlie, and someone set up the whole thing."

"Other than you are both children of wealthy parents do you know of any reason anyone would want to kidnap or harm you? They seemed pretty determined," asked Haleran, who also felt there was more to this story than everyone was saying including Mai.

"There *is* something else besides the usual reasons," said Devi. "My mother knows, but she hasn't confided in me. It might have something to do with her, and Aunt Catherine, thwarting those people's plans to take over Southeast Asia fifteen years ago. But I think it is something else entirely. I don't even know if it is the same people we are talking about." She shook her head, and said, "I honestly don't know, but this won't be the last time. Is Charlie OK? How come they haven't released him yet? Is he hurt?"

"Charlie is OK. You don't need to worry about him. You seem pretty good with that gun. Where'd you keep it? In your purse?" asked Haleran.

Devi nodded a thank you at his reassurance that Charlie was OK, and explained, "Yes, Lieutenant, it's a custom-made designer purse with a gun holster incorporated into the design and hidden on the side."

She showed them a hidden compartment that blended into the beaded design. "As soon as they came in, I had my hand on my weapon. I could have shot them through the purse, but then they both looked at Chantelle for a moment, and that gave me the chance to draw and fire properly. It was just as I had trained for. I learned to shoot when I was ten after they tried to take me the first time. I can put a tight group in at fifty yards with it. I have a permit to carry a concealed weapon, and you saw my diplomatic passport."

The uniformed Police Sergeant Daniels came from the front of the restaurant, and said, "Lieutenant Haleran, the young man, Charlie Marsh is still pretty shaken. He has been released by the EMTs. I have him outside, and he asked if he could be taken home. He mentioned something about the Asian girl, Devi, going with him. I volunteered to drive them since I have already given my statement to these detectives. Is it OK?" he asked.

"Detectives?" Haleran asked for approval.

"Yeah, sure on the boy, but tell him we might have more questions later," said Donavitch. "I am not sure we can release the girls yet."

"Oh! Can we go too?" asked Devi getting up from the table. "I'm afraid all of this is finally getting to me. Please, can he take us home with Charlie? We're all going to the same place," she pleaded. "Besides Ben knows everything about us, and can give you all of the information you need right now. Ben, did you call Aunt Cat?"

Big Ben was nodding while listening on his cell phone, and then held it out to the detectives. "Detective, this is Miss Devi's Aunt Catherine on the telephone. She wants to speak with you," he said.

Donavitch took it, introduced himself, and listened for a moment answering with a "Yes, ma'am" every few seconds. Finally, he said, "Yes, sir, I will see to it right away." and gave the phone back to Big Ben.

"Looks like we are done with you, for now, Miss Largent," he said.

"That was Catherine Marsh on the phone?" asked Petri.

"And the Chief," said Donavitch. "He is with her. Sergeant, you would be doing us a favor if you take them back to Ms. Marsh. Walk them right to the door, and drive carefully."

"I'll go along just to be safe," said Big Ben.

"Oh no you don't," said Donavitch. "We still have lots of questions. You sit tight, and finish your barbecue."

The two young women got up and headed for the door with Sergeant Daniels following behind. He nodded to Haleran who nodded back a thanks for stepping in when they needed it.

Devi went to the counter where mama Edith stood, and said, "I think that was the most delicious meal I have ever had, mama, in spite of all the interruptions. Thank you. I will be back." She gave her a hug, and followed up with, " You can bet on it."

"Oh, sugar, you make me so proud," mama Edith said. "I made a bag full of goodies for you to take with you. Thank you for all you did for us today," she said, as she handed her the large bag. "You a very brave girl."

After they left, the three detectives sat down with Ben at the back table. Haleran said, "You know, fellas, this is going to take a while. You have to eat, and this place has the best barbecue around. What do you say?"

They nodded, and Haleran called over the waitress for menus. Big Ben said, "I think I could use a few more ribs too, Lieutenant, if you don't mind."

Chapter 36

2005   Chicago

Devi, Charlie, and Audrey relaxed for the first time since the shooting started. They headed south on Clybourne toward Catherine's condo on Oak Street, riding in the back of a blue and white police cruiser driven by Sergeant Daniels. Devi and Charlie were sitting next to each other, and held hands while they eagerly told each other their perspective of the attempted kidnapping at Edith's.

Devi looked up front through the bulletproof, glass partition at the police sergeant escort, and asked, "Do you know where Charlie lives?"

"Well not exactly," answered Sergeant Daniels, in the front seat. "But I have been to NearNorth Productions, and it is my understanding that Ms. Marsh is in the same building. Right?"

"Yes, that's right! We're all going there. Thank you for driving us," said Devi from the back seat. "Can you turn on the air conditioning? It's kind of warm back here."

"Uh, yes, miss," answered Daniels. "But I have to apologize because it doesn't work very well. But not to worry, we'll be there in a few minutes anyway."

Daniels turned the switch, and he heard the hiss as the gas began filling the back seat of the police cruiser. The rear seat compartment was completely sealed off from the rest of the vehicle. This was something that took him several months of work in his shop to perfect along with the gas input.

He shook his head. *Amazing. It had worked.* He looked up and watched in his mirror as they all began falling asleep behind him. He heard a faint,

"Oh no," from the girl, Devi, before she too collapsed over the young boy's legs.

He had spent almost two years learning everything he could about being a cop in Chicago, and to the point, he was more like them than the real ones. He could talk, dress and act like a cop. His uniform was perfect, not new, slightly worn, and even the shoes were 'cop' shoes. He spent so much time with the cops on the west side, they welcomed him as one of their own, and now all of that time at the bar, and playing cards into the very late hours had paid off.

He turned west and headed for his shop where he would switch cars. He took a moment to push a preset on his cell phone, which sent a signal to those who had hired him indicating he had the two kidnap victims, and everything should continue according to plan. Four more digits gave them the exact time of the rendezvous. No doubt, they had already heard their version of the kidnapping had failed and would be surprised to get his message. But that had been his plan all along.

The two victims would be helplessly unconscious for several hours, and he would have plenty of time to get them into the prepared shipping containers, and to the airport. He had only to make the exchange, and it was done.

Every time he finished one of his assignments he disappeared completely with a new identity. Even if someone considered him a loose end and wanted to kill him, they could never find him. When he was ready, he would let it be known through a select few circles that he was in the market once more.

This was his life. He loved this moment in every operation, when he had completed an operation successfully and was on the other side. The rush he felt was what he lived for, and he had to have it. He wasn't crazy, or a psychopath. He wasn't a serial killer, or a killer of any kind for that matter. He was a businessman, a craftsman, with a peculiar set of superior talents, which enabled him to accomplish the goals of those who hired him even under the most unlikely, and difficult circumstances. He had no wife, or family. He only had his work, and he took great pride in being the best.

He smiled to himself again. This time, on this job, everything looked to have gone wrong. But that was all part of his perfect plan. From the beginning, when his client submitted the proposal to him, he knew it would fail. That was what he wanted to happen so he could implement his unique twist on it, which would make it perfect. Thus, even though he saw the flaws in their scheme immediately, he didn't bother telling them because it fit into his perfect plan. All along they assumed he would be a back up just in case something went wrong. They never thought he would be a cop actually ensuring their plan to kidnap the two victims did not work.

Yes, this was better. This allowed him another hour before anyone realized what had happened, and by that time the two victims would be well on their way to god-knows-where.

He pulled into an alley between an industrial building and a supermarket. He got out and looked around carefully. It was deserted. He checked one in a line of nearby dumpsters and found it filled mostly with broken cardboard boxes. He opened the back door of the cruiser and pulled out the young blond woman. He threw her over his shoulder and walked over to the dumpster and gently tossed her inside. He closed the lid over her afterward. She was not part of the deal, and if he took her to the airport, they would most likely kill her, or worse. She didn't deserve that. She was all apple pie, innocent, and just in the wrong place at the wrong time.

He checked the area again. Nothing. No one anywhere. He got back in the cruiser and pulled away.

Another mile further west, he pulled into another deserted alley and stopped in back of an old car repair garage. He waited while the overhead door opened, and then he pulled into a mechanic's bay. This was his shop where he kept more of his equipment and prepared the vehicles like this police cruiser. Twenty-four hours from now the entire garage would go up in flames, as would his two-flat on Dixon leaving nothing behind to trace to him.

He opened the back door and pulled the young man out first. He was heavy, over two hundred pounds. He used a fireman's carry to lug him over to the specially converted casket, reengineered as a wooden crate on the outside. He dropped him in with his head resting on a pillow. He spread him out to be sure his limbs were resting comfortably, and then he locked his arms and legs in the soft cuffs that held him firmly within. If the boy awoke early, he could not escape. He removed his belt, and glasses, so they would not harm him during the flight. He placed an oxygen mask over his face and turned on the temporary supply. Then he closed the casket.

Then he took up the girl and lifted her over by the casket. Her outfit was a bit bizarre. It had a metallic lining, and accents here and there, which could be uncomfortable during the long flight. Without hesitation, he removed her clothes and jewelry. He left her in only her underwear resting in the comfortable folds of the casket with her head resting on a pillow. She looked like a sleeping angel. He noted this and took an extra moment to secure her comfort, and safety by adding a blanket over her. But then he put on the mask as he had done with the young man, and secured her arms and legs in the cuff bindings. She was now a prisoner, and her fate was sealed as far as he was concerned. He collected her purse, and jewelry, and put them with her in a closed-off holding area in the corner of the casket.

He was still uncomfortable with the whole operation, and the sooner it was done, the better. He agreed to the job because he owed a former client a professional favor for getting a friend of his out of a very difficult situation and that client had asked him to take this job in return for that favor, adding that his fees would be tripled. What the client had done for his friend had seemed an impossible task, and the client left no doubt that one day he would ask and expect him to return that favor. This was not the kind of thing he had ever done before or liked to do, and though his feelings kept barking at him, he did his best to ignore them and get the job done so he could put it all behind him as a debt paid. He had no doubt that there wasn't anyone in the world who could have pulled this off as he did. He even rehearsed alternative scenarios that would get the two young victims into his police car to supposedly transport them back to Catherine Marsh's condo.

He dollied both of the crates over, and loaded them into the back of an oversized panel truck parked on the right of the workshop, and closed it up. He checked his watch. He still had plenty of time before anyone would be snooping around or looking for them. Even so, he didn't take a break. He had practiced this routine many times, and he was less than an hour from his payday and his next new life.

He went into the bathroom of the garage where the first of his two new looks that night awaited him. He took off his clothes, and then peeled back his fake hair, and pulled the inserts out of his cheeks. Then he began putting on his new face, and disguise. After a few minutes of careful work, he made final adjustments to his cap, and did an inspection. He was a completely different person in the mirror.

He went to the wall and set the timer for twenty-five hours. That was when this garage would burst into flames leaving no sign he had ever been there. Quickly, he took one last look around, got into the van, opened the garage door, and pulled away. That part was over.

Thirty minutes later, Hagen, his real name, arrived at the cargo side of O'Hare airport, and showed his fake credentials to the guard who barely glanced at them. How ironic he thought that in this age of terrorists, and nine-eleven, no one checked the cargo carriers while they practically undressed travelers on the other side of the airport.

Hagen drove for a mile down one side of the long tarmac arriving at a very large hangar. As he pulled up to the hangar, he flashed his lights three times, and the big door on the side opened up slowly. When he had room, he drove right inside next to a large Boeing cargo jet. He backed up to the lift, which would take the crates up to the belly of the aircraft, and got out. Two Asian men and a woman approached him and started to introduce themselves.

"No names, if you please," Hagen told them. "Let's get this done."

"We thought our operation had failed and were in the process of packing up and getting away," said the Asian woman. "You surprised us with your text message, but we were elated nonetheless. It appears your reputation was not unwarranted. My congratulations to you."

They unloaded the van and placed the crates on the lift. Hagen punched in a button combination that freed the locks on one, and the container opened automatically revealing the sleeping Devi Largent. The Asian woman nodded, and one of the men reached in and took her pulse. The man looked back and nodded an affirmation to his boss. Hagen noted her smirk that signaled her feelings leaving one thing apparent judging by the look on her face. This young lady would not survive this operation unharmed. That bothered him, unlike any other operation he had ever worked on. Once again, he struggled to put the thought behind him as he pressed a button, and the crate-casket sealed again. Though he was most wanted by Interpol, he had never harmed an innocent person in his life, until now. Why was he doing this? He was forced to ponder that question while those thoughts distracted him.

"And the other?" asked the woman after a moment interrupting his thoughts.

Hagen again punched a key combination, and the other crate opened revealing a sleeping Charlie Marsh. The same routine was repeated, and once again Hagen closed and sealed the crate.

"I have delivered the package as I was hired to do. Now I want to see the payment put into my account."

"Of course," said the woman. "It is already done. You can check now if you wish. You have performed most brilliantly as we expected. I want you to know I am personally a fan. Your reputation will grow with the news of this assignment."

Hagen opened his laptop, quickly typed in his password, and found his account. His considerable balance had grown by an enormous amount; more than three times what he was usually paid. He was glad to be done with this operation. The one thing he had learned from this was that he didn't like kidnapping people, particularly innocent ones. He had considered walking away many times, but in the end he was obliged to get this done, and he had. Now that it was over he swore he would never do it again. He handed the control to the woman.

"You have not told me the code," the woman said.

"There is no code anymore. It was removed automatically when my payment arrived."

The woman pressed the button on the remote, and the lid to Princess Devi's crate opened. "Ah, very good," she said.

"Good day," said Hagen, as he turned and left. He got into the van, started up, and pulled away from the hangar. He looked back to be sure he was not followed, and then was careful to watch for signs of snipers. But they had what they wanted, and were done with him. They were concentrating on getting the crates aboard the aircraft. He drove a few hundred yards down the tarmac and pulled between two hangars to watch the aircraft take off. In just a few minutes the aircraft pulled out of the hangar and taxied out to the runway. In a few more minutes it was gone.

A moment later, Hagen was gone too.

Chapter 37

2005 Chicago

Catherine took the glass of wine Kelly offered her and sat down across from Police Chief Wilcot. They sat in the living room of her thirtieth-floor condominium waiting for Devi and Charlie to be returned to them with an air of anxious anticipation. Catherine took one sip, and then cradled the glass of wine and stared out the window at a view of Chicago's north side.

"Chief, it's after five. Are you sure we can't pour you a glass," Kelly asked. "One of our friends owns a vineyard in France, and he sent us a case. It is absolutely the best."

"Uh, no, Kelly, thank you anyway," he answered. "I'm afraid I won't feel at ease until young Charlie walks through the door. I feel like the boy is my own grandson. I have known him since he was a toddler bouncing on my knee like I did his mother a long time ago. I cannot believe that they would try to pull off something like this in my town. We were lucky. We will have to learn from this. These people mean business."

"Indeed, we know that only too well already," said Catherine. "This makes the third attempt. They are certainly persistent, and I am prepared this time to be as ruthless as they. I am going to use all of our resources to hunt them down and expose them."

Ward, the family butler, entered, and inquired, "Ms. Kelly would you like me to serve some hors-d'oeuvres, and are you planning on eating dinner here tonight, and if so, would you suggest a time?"

"No Ward," she answered. "Just put things on hold for now. We've made no plans yet. Tell the staff to stand by, and we will let them know when we know. I think we will be staying in with just family, and possibly Chief Wilcot, but we're not sure."

"Yes, ma'am," he said, before turning and departing the room.

It was starting to get dark outside as storm clouds filled the skies. They sat silent in thought for a few minutes. The police chief got up and paced about. Catherine commented, "I wonder what is taking them so long."

The police Chief looked at her sharply and then retreated to the hallway where an aide awaited him. "Any word yet?' he asked.

"No sir," replied the assistant.

"When did they leave? They should have been here by now."

"Yes, sir. I will check again. It has been almost an hour, sir," the aide confirmed.

The aide called on his cell phone, and after a minute looked sharply up at the Chief. "I see. I'll get back to you. Stand by. I think the Chief will want to talk to you, Captain," he could be heard saying.

The aide turned to the Chief and confirmed that Devi, Charlie, and Audrey had left an hour before being driven in a police cruiser by Sergeant Daniels from District 15.

The Chief took his cell phone, and asked, "Anyone with Daniels escorting the three young people here?"

"No sir," replied the Captain. "I wasn't there, but the two detectives on the scene reported that considering the status of the three individuals, they were happy to get them away from the scene, and back to Ms. Marsh. It is only a twenty-minute trip, sir. I don't understand it."

"Did you try getting them on the radio?"

"Uh, yes, sir, about fifteen minutes ago, and again just now. I'm afraid there has been no response," replied the Captain.

"Put out an APB on the cruiser and Sergeant Daniels immediately, Captain. I mean now! Who are the detectives on the scene?" he demanded.

Sergeants Donavitch and Petri, sir," replied the Captain. "And there is a Lieutenant Haleran here also."

"Frank Haleran? Put him on. Get that APB out immediately, Captain," he repeated.

After a moment, Lieutenant Haleran came on the line, and said, "Chief Wilcot this is Lieutenant Haleran. Did I hear right? Have the three individuals not arrived at Ms. Marsh's yet?"

"That's right, Frank. I don't have a good feeling about this," replied the Chief.

"Jesus H. Christ, Chief. It's been an hour. They could be anywhere. But I would bet on the two main airports. I would blanket there first."

"So you think this is real, Frank?"

"Yeah. I do. Something has been hinky about this whole thing from the beginning. I haven't felt right about it since I got here earlier this afternoon."

"How'd you get involved in this anyway, Frank? Did this have something to do with that folder I handed you last weekend?

"In a way, sir, it did," he said. "That file you left with me looked phony, and by pure coincidence, I knew the accused from a long time ago. I think you knew it was bogus too, or you would have given it to one of your young detectives to run with. I called Jack, the husband and got Mai, the accused. We caught up with old times, and then I laid it out for her. As I said, it was phony and she had no trouble convincing me of that. She asked me if I would check on her daughter Devi who was visiting Chicago. I was doing just that when this all came down. My bad luck."

"Well, it's my good luck. I need someone I can trust to consult with on this thing. I'm at Catherine Marsh's. Get over here ASAP," ordered the chief.

"Sure, Chief. But first I'll call District 15, check on Sergeant Daniels, and get back to you. I strongly suggest that you stop all flights out of Chicago, corporate, commercial, and cargo, and quick, sir. We may already be too late. If this is what we think it is, then these guys are sharper than anything we have ever come up against. I'll start heading over there," said Haleran.

"Get here as soon as you can, Frank," said Chief Wilcot. He gave the cell phone back to his assistant, and facing the living room entryway, felt heartbroken. The Marshes were like family to him. He considered Catherine like his own daughter, and he had no doubt she felt the same toward him. He had even proposed at one time to Catherine's mother. He had to be strong because all hell was about to break loose, and his had to be the most discerning mind in the room. They were all depending on him. This was not his first involvement in a kidnapping, but none of the others were so personal. He took a deep breath and stepped back into the luxurious living room where he was greeted by the anxious faces of Catherine and Kelly.

He sat down close to the two partners, and after a short pause began. "Catherine there is no other way to say this, and there is still some hope that I am wrong. I want you to know that. I believe Devi and Charlie have been taken."

There followed the sound of breath catches, and exclamations of denial. Kelly and Catherine stared at him in hopeful disbelief, followed by tears that welled in their eyes. Catherine shook her head slowly, then fell into Kelly's arms, and cried in earnest. Kelly held her close, and rubbed her back as she looked over at Chief Wilcot sadly.

"I have an APB out right now, and we are blanketing the airports. This operation was very well planned, and executed. They were one step ahead of us all the way."

"I don't understand?" said Kelly anxiously. "What happened to the police escort they had coming back here from the crime scene?"

"We are checking on that right now," said the Chief, as his assistant interrupted him and handed him his cell phone once more.

"Yes, Frank," he answered.

"Chief, I checked with District 15," said Haleran. "There is no sergeant Daniels on their staff. The guy was a phony. He took us all in. I'm sorry, Chief."

" I see. OK. Tell Captain Forney to set up an emergency task force on this. Come right over here. Oh, and tell the techs at the crime scene this is a priority job now. It takes precedence over everything else they are doing. I want everything processed yesterday. Got it?"

He gave the cell phone back to his assistant, turned, and faced the ladies again, this time with a worried face.

"It seems the police sergeant who was supposedly escorting the three young people back here was not a real policeman at all. I am afraid he took us all in. We have had reports of a man wanted by Interpol operating in our area for some time, but we were never able to find him and assumed he was passing through. I think he just showed up," said the chief.

"You said there were three. Who? What three? I thought they were escorting Devi and Charlie back here," said Kelly.

"There was a young reporter with them by the name of Audrey something. I didn't get her last name," said the Chief.

"Goodnight, John. Her name is Audrey Goodnight. She is a young reporter I am most impressed with, Devi met a few days ago leaving the airport," explained Catherine, wiping her eyes. "Oh my God. I can't believe this."

"You say she met her just this week. That is a bit of a coincidence, don't you think?" asked the Chief.

"You don't think she was involved, do you?" asked Catherine.

"We can't rule out any possibilities," said the Chief. "I know this is not the best time for this, but I need you to sit with me and answer some questions. I have my best man, Lieutenant Haleran on his way over here, and I will want him to sit in with us. He should be here in a few minutes. While we are waiting, you may want to call the young girl's mother. She is in Cambodia, right?"

"Uh, excuse me, sir," said Big Ben coming into the room his right forehead covered by a large bandage. "I just heard that Miss Devi and Charlie have not arrived. Is that true?"

"Yes, I am afraid so," said Chief Wilcot. "We are acting on the assumption that they have been taken. Is there anything you remember about the man who called himself Sergeant Daniels that might be helpful?"

"He looked real, Chief. I mean there was nothing that looked wrong about him. He knew what he was doing. He acted like a cop, looked like a cop and talked like a cop. Heck, he even shot one of the assailants to save Charlie. We all thought he was a brave hero. I can't believe he was a fake. I don't know what to think," he said holding his arms out apologetically.

Ben, why weren't you with them?" asked Catherine.

"Ms. Marsh that was the deal Ms. Devi made with the detectives on the scene. She could only leave with Charlie to return here if I stayed there to answer their questions. Michael was wounded, and at the hospital by then. Since they had a police escort, I thought it was OK. I'm sorry, Ms. Marsh. I let everyone down. I feel terrible about this." He stood there shaking slightly, and his lips quivered holding back his own tears.

"Ben, no, no. You didn't let anyone down," she said standing up, and moving next to the big guard she had known for sixteen years. "Oh my God, what are we doing? You faced up against a machine gun this afternoon to save Charlie. I've heard all about it," Catherine said. "They fooled everyone, Ben. We all got fooled. Now we have to find them, and bring our babies ho..." and she began to cry all over again. They had never actually been taken before, and the realization of that was too much for her. She was compliant as Kelly took her shoulder, and led her back to sit on the couch.

The police chief asked, "Is there a place where we can set up? They will most likely be calling you before long. We will need to move quickly, no matter what they say," he explained.

Chapter 38

2005   Iowa truck stop

Just over the Iowa border, Hagen stopped at a travel center to get a cup of coffee, and have a bite. He had no doubt he was safe now from everyone. No one could trace him, or find him. He smiled to himself. It was just as it always had been. Patience, planning, and getting your priorities straight. The three P's that were so important to him. Waiting for the right time was just as important as being prepared when it happened.

It was the thrill and nothing else that drove him to accept each assignment. But this one had been to repay a debt, and he was glad it was over. This job had taken two years, at five million per year, and a final payoff for a total of twenty million. It was over in a few minutes. But if he were teaching a class, he would say it was a textbook example of his philosophy. It was perfect in its planning, and perfect in its execution, even to the first part of it not working, turning the crime scene into chaos, and allowing him to work his magic. If it were not for the actual victims he had delivered he would have been over-the-top elated.

He had already discarded the face, and the van they had seen when he transferred the crates to the clients. Finally, he was himself again, Mr. average, Mr. invisible. He looked so bland he seemed like a prop in the faded orange booth of the mostly empty diner. He fit in and became part of the environment no matter where he went.

He took off his jacket, and as he did, he felt in his pocket the pink billfold he discovered in the police cruiser that belonged to the young woman he put in the dumpster earlier. He had meant to throw it away when he found it, but instead unconsciously transferred it into the pocket of his new identity much like he did his own wallet. Most who practiced his particular profession would have done away with the girl as a loose end. But that was never his way. Besides, she was all Midwest, milk, and honey; what life was all about. She didn't need killing. He smiled thinking about her.

Nursing a hot cup of coffee, he began going through her billfold. He would dispose of it later. She had only twenty dollars and a single credit card. He perused her driver's license, and after a while, he put it back in the clear plastic pocket where he found it. He reached inside under the license and found a photograph. It was folded into fours, and he carefully unfolded the very creased image.

What he saw when he opened it was something that would change his life forever. He felt an eerie tingling all through his body. He took a second to be sure of what he was looking at because what he saw was impossible.

It was what he thought, and it was instantly at the center of his universe like a lightning bolt from the almighty. The world seemed to spin around him in a dizzying array as all his memories swirled into one incredible moment he never expected. He did not believe in coincidences…ever. That had helped him survive many difficult circumstances throughout his shadowy career. Now he was experiencing one, and he had no doubt it was just that: a coincidence. It was impossible, but there it was just the same.

He stared at a black and white picture of a man holding a baby wrapped in a blanket standing on a freshly shoveled sidewalk in front of a house covered in snow. The house was a four-room post World War Two housing development type like many seen in small towns in the Midwest of the era. The photograph was about twenty-two years old. He knew that because he was the man in the photograph, which had been taken by the agency handling the adoption of his daughter. His wife had died during childbirth, and soon after he gave the baby up for adoption. He knew his hidden, and dangerous life was not one that included taking care of a daughter. Though he never knew what happened to her, he had provided nicely for her in a blind trust that was attached to the adoption. Now she had returned to him in a most unexpected, and bizarre manner.

But then he had another thought. Of course! He must have made a mistake, and put his photograph in her billfold by accident. Hah! He wasn't even supposed to still have it. He just got them mixed up, that's all.

He retrieved and opened his wallet and was surprised to find his copy of the same photo. He laid them out side by side on the table. They were identical.

He shook his head in disbelief. Her billfold instantly became a thing of deep and honest reverence for him. He lifted it, kissed it, and held it to his cheek for a moment. He could still smell her scent on it.

His decision was made instantly, and it was irrevocable. He got up suddenly, put a twenty-dollar bill down on the table, and hurried out to his blue Toyota Camry. A minute later, he was on the expressway heading back to Chicago. He was 200 miles away, and he would be there in less than three hours.

He was moving contrary to every principle he believed in that had safeguarded his success for these many years. It didn't matter. Finding that wallet had sent his life into a tailspin. What had he thought? "All honey, and apple pie," and he threw her into a dumpster! His motive then had been to be sure she was concealed until the victims were out of town. He threw his daughter into a dumpster like she was the trash, and the symbolism pummeled him mercilessly.

He knew he shouldn't have done this job. He knew it. He had second-guessed himself over, and over, the last two years. He never kidnapped anyone before, or even hurt an innocent person. He kept asking himself why did he do it? Why? He hit the steering wheel again, and again in frustration. There were no coincidences. He believed in that as his own mantra for survival. He was meant to get this message, and it went right to his soul. He was in a pit, and he was falling deeper and deeper into that abyss. He felt an uncontrollable urge to climb out of there, to right that wrong, save his daughter, and those two victims. That one act he performed so commonly as with all the other misdeeds of his life had become his nexus, and his life turning point.

He realized at that moment that all the money and wealth he had accumulated meant nothing compared to the daughter he still loved after all these years. He had given up hope of ever finding her because the trust was double-sided, and he was blocked from knowing who her adopted parents were as part of the original contract. He had tried once, and even with all of his resources, he couldn't track her identity or whereabouts. He had paid well for that security. It was the best, and in the end, it had prevented even him from breaking it in reverse. It became an empty void in his life that at the worst times nagged at him.

But now in a most bizarre way, he had found her, and he realized nothing else mattered. He was going to make it right, and he would start anew. But first, he had to get his daughter out of that dumpster and to safety. He began to imagine a hundred things that could happen to her there. He drove faster.

Chapter 39

May 2005 Chicago

Haleran was settling down in the makeshift command center set up by the Chicago Police in a spare room at the Marsh condominium just as his cell phone buzzed him.

"Frank, this is Mai. I'm falling apart here. What can you tell me?" she said.

"I'm sorry, Mai. These guys were as slick as anything I have ever seen. They used a fake cop to kidnap them successfully after we had won a shootout stopping what we all thought was the attempted kidnapping. We even killed four of them. The cop was supposedly taking them back to Ms. Marsh's, and we think he kidnapped them for real, and they disappeared after that. They have been missing for about three hours now."

"How could you be fooled by a fake cop, Frank? I remember you being sharper than that."

"His plan was ingenious, Mai. He came off as a hero, even to risking his life and killing one of the kidnappers himself. He had us all fooled, I'm sad to say. I've never seen anything like it."

"OK, what are you doing about it?" she asked, pragmatically. Mai had spent the last three hours crying and with help from her inner self was now recovered as much as was possible. She replaced her grief with a determination to save her daughter from any circumstances. Nothing was going to stop her from getting Devi back. She hoped they brought her to Asia because her vast network of Champa faithful would quickly work to save her. But that was just a hopeful wish and she honestly believed they meant to take Devi to Europe instead where she had no such help.

"I advised the chief ninety minutes ago. My thinking is they got them out in freight maybe on a private cargo plane of some sort. I doubt they are still in the city. I advised the chief to check the flight plans of all cargo aircraft leaving O'Hare for the last two and one-half hours. There is a task force working on that and other leads."

"Frank, the kidnappers are most likely working for the Asian World Investments Corporation headed up by a man named Hinsu Yameda. It might pay to see if they, or any businesses connected with them, had any aircraft chartered that left O'Hare, or even Midway. I cannot give you too many details on their motives, but they have been after a means to control me for many years now. This is the third attempt on our kids," Mai said.

"Asian World Investments, where have I heard that name before?" Haleran asked.

"It's a part of my past, Frank. That was the company headed by Colonel Minh back in the old days."

"Oh yeah...now I got the picture," he said. "So, a revenge thing then."

"No, something much more complicated. I have no doubt they are the ones that took our kids," Mai said. "Something else you should know. Devi has a chip embedded in her shoulder, which will give a return signal in the form of a beeping sound if you access it in the same area from not more than fifty miles away. Farther than that and the device does not read. I can give you the unique frequency. It will work with most police portable equipment, and act as a homing beacon."

"Well, we have to first figure out what city they were taken to," he said. "They could be halfway to China by now. But just in case, I will have a search done around the two airports. Go ahead, and give me the frequency, Mai."

"One thing, Frank. It would not do for the kidnappers to get this information so you will want to reveal this to only those who can keep their mouths shut. Are we agreed on that?"

Haleran assured her he had the unit in mind he would relay the information, and they were good at keeping things in-house.

After she gave him the frequency, and he handed it off to an assistant, Mai continued. "My bet is they will take them to Europe. They will want us to think they took them west, and toward Asia. But I think they took them east instead."

"Based on what? Do you have proof, or are you just guessing?" asked Haleran.

"Right now, I really have no evidence to support that is where they took them. But AWI has new facilities in Europe they have built, and organized, over the last few years. I am getting my security team here ready to move quickly when we have better information."

"Mai, this is not something you want to run off half-cocked about. Let the trained experts handle this. It is the best bet to get your kids back alive."

"Frank, I want you to be my eyes and ears there. I want you to keep me informed. Will you do that for me…as an old and trusted friend?"

"I work for the City of Chicago, Mai. I'm a cop. I am not sure how that will work. We don't usually give out information on an ongoing investigation to private individuals for good reasons."

"That's wise under most circumstances, Frank, but not in this case. The fact is I have information you need, but I cannot tell you, and you will have information I need. I am your best bet to pin down the whereabouts of the kidnappers, and our kids. Tell me you'll keep me informed on everything you find out. Promise me, Frank. It's very important to me," Mai pleaded.

"Mai, are you OK? I can't imagine what you must be going through."

"Yes, I am now, Frank. I have a close friend who is consoling me and helping me to focus."

He thought about what she asked of him and said, "Yeah, OK then. I guess bringing you in on this can't hurt. I will get right back to you as soon as I know something. I promise. In the meantime, you find a way to stay calm because I need that wonderful mind of yours to help us think this thing through."

"OK, call me when you hear anything," said Mai, hanging up.

Chapter 40

May 2005   Chicago

A loud sound from somewhere nearby brought Audrey awake as if from a fog, or a confusing dream, and to the smell of something very foul nearby. Her head hurt, and then her body as she realized she was lying strangely with her leg tucked back up under her. "Am I dreaming?"

She adjusted her position slightly and realized she was on something unstable that moved with her, and was poking into her back. She strained her eyes to see but it was unusually dark, and she could see nothing. "Where am I?"

Her head ached as if from a hangover, and she tried desperately to remember why she would be in this situation. With no answer, her fear grew, and panic was not far away. She heard a squeaking sound and jerked her head suddenly toward it. It was dark, very dark. But she sensed something, and then was able to perceive a reflection in a pair of small eyes very close, and sniffing her face. She jumped and felt it crawling away on her chest. She screamed and sat up abruptly hitting her head on unforgiving metal. Whatever it was ran off her and scurried away.

She pushed on the metal less than a foot above her head, but she was in an awkward position, and it resisted. She sobbed, and screamed again, and getting no answer, lay back trying to collect her thoughts. It didn't work. She had no idea where she was, or why she was there. Just then, she heard the sound of a loud motor nearby, and a metal-on-metal grinding sound right underneath her. Everything began shaking, and moving, carrying her with it.

Audrey became terrified and screamed as loud as she could. It was the worst bad dream she ever had, but she was certain it wasn't a dream. Other creatures began scurrying over, and around her, and she nearly gagged at the smell of one that rested on her lips for a moment.

Audrey kept screaming, and the loud motor stopped abruptly. She paused for a moment feeling herself continue to rock from side to side. She screamed as loud as she could again, and cried for help in desperation. She felt herself being lowered and then landing on the ground with a loud 'thunk'.

She continued to cry for help when suddenly the metal lid over her head lifted away bringing a torrent of fresh cool air, a street lamp, and a jovial black man with fat jowls. He was wearing a smile and a city sanitation cap as he peered in at her. She went from sobbing, and fearful to relieved and happy in an instant. It was all crazy. He was a trash man. She was in a trash bin. There was a great relief for her in just understanding that simple fact.

"Oh my God! Thank you," Audrey exclaimed, "you cannot imagine how happy I am to see your smiling face. Please, can you help me get out of here?"

"Well, sure, but first I have to ask what're you doin' sleeping in a trash container on the south side, young lady?" he asked. "This is a bad part of town. You should only sleep in trash containers on the north side of town," he joked. "You're covered with garbage too!"

"Really? You think this is something to joke about? Well, I'm not laughing," she protested.

He was taken aback by her response but smiled affably. "Oh, missy, you have to forgive me. That's just my way. It's how I deal with the bad things of this world like this situation here. My name is Leo Jefferson, and I'll be your rescuer this evening," he told her, still smiling.

She smiled back finally, finding his method disarming. "Thank you, Leo. I'm Audrey Goodnight, and I'm certainly glad you came along."

He continued to wear a big smile, as he said, "OK, come on, missy. Let me help you out of there. Whoeee, this dumpster stinks."

He stood on a raised two-foot cement structure that marked the perimeter of the trash area in his grey soiled coveralls and pulled her by her arms up and out of the dumpster. Audrey struggled with one knee on the side of the dumpster and then dropped down onto the asphalt alley between it and the truck. But as she jumped down, she scraped her leg across some glass at the top of the container and opened up a small gash in her leg, which began to bleed. She did not notice at first, as she was just happy to get on solid ground again.

"If I was going to go sleeping in a dumpster, missy," he said, "I certainly wouldn't choose one in back of a supermarket. They's full of rats. You could've been eaten alive," he informed her.

She gave him another look but blended it with a scrunched smile this time. She was still in a daze, and could not make sense of where, or why she was in that alley. But then she felt the gash on her leg and grabbed at it with one hand as she tried to stand up.

"Oh, missy, you're bleeding," he said, with genuine concern seeing the blood rolling down her leg. "That's quite a wound. Hold on, I got a first aid kit in my cab."

He rushed off, and in a moment returned with the first aid kit. He brought with him a pint bottle of vodka. "I ain't got no antiseptic, missy, but this will work. Put that leg out here now, and let me work on it."

He sat down on the cement stoop, and she laid her leg across his leg. He poured the vodka over the wound and used some gauze to clean it up.

"Do you have a clean rag?" she asked.

He reached into his inside jacket pocket and handed her a handkerchief. "I haven't used this at all. Will this do?"

"Thanks," she said. "You're nice." She took the handkerchief, poured some vodka over it, and brushed over her lips and face. "I had a rat sit on my face in there. Ugh! I hope I never do that again!" Then she took a swig, swirled it around in her mouth, and spat it out nearby.

He wrapped up her leg with gauze as he asked, "So, how did you end up in that container, missy?"

"I don't know. The last thing I remember is being taken in a police car to my employer's condo," she said. "I'm not sure how I ended up here. I was with some friends, and they're gone too. Wait! Can you look in the other trash bins?"

Leo finished wrapping her leg and then checked the other five large metal dumpsters one-by-one, finding nothing. "Nope, they's empty Missy. Just you sleeping in dumpsters tonight," he said, smiling. "Oh! They might have been kidnapped. We need to call the police. Call 911. Please," she begged.

"What's going on here?" asked a man walking up dressed in a dark blue jacket, and tan slacks and shining a flashlight on them.

"I found this young lady in the trash bin here. She says she, and her friends might have been kidnapped, and we're just getting ready to call the police," the trash man answered, suddenly aware that his situation did not look good.

The man held out a badge toward them, and said, "I am a police detective, off duty now, but I can take over from here. Are you alright, young lady?" he asked.

"Yes, I think so. I'm just confused, and my head aches. But listen, I think I was kidnapped, and I don't know where my friends are. They were kidnapped too," she said, earnestly.

"OK, slow down, miss. You say you were kidnapped, and your friends are missing? You had better start from the beginning. When did this happen?" the plain-clothes detective asked.

Audrey, as best as she could, related the events leading up to her abduction finishing with the fact that she had no idea of how she ended up in the dumpster behind the market.

The detective looked at the trash man, and said, "What is your name, sir?"

The trash man explained his name was Leonard Jefferson and recounted finding Audrey in the trash bin as he was doing his rounds.

"Could I see some identification?" asked the detective who had a pad out, and was taking notes.

After the detective examined his driver's license and wrote down his name, he handed it back, and said, "OK, Mr. Jefferson, I have your statement and identification. Is there a number I can reach you at for any further questions?"

The trash man gave him his telephone number, and the number of the company where he worked, along with the name of his supervisor. The detective told him he could be on his way, but to leave the six trash dumpsters untouched He eagerly jumped back into the cab of his truck and pulled away into the next block leaving Audrey, and the detective alone.

"It looks like you're hurt. I think we had better get you to a hospital, and get that checked. Do you live in the area, Miss?" he asked. "My car is right over here in the lot," said the detective.

Audrey followed, still confused, and got into the blue Toyota Camry. After they were both inside, the detective said, "I want you to look at something."

Her head still clearing, Audrey settled in her seat, and then looked at the old photograph the detective handed her.

"That's my picture!" she said, jumping away from him. "How did you get that?" Fear blended with her confusion.

"That's not your photograph, Audrey," Hagen said, with more calm than he felt. "That is mine. This is yours," he said, as he handed her an identical old photograph, but this one bared creases from having been folded.

Audrey looked at the two identical photographs and held them in her hands side-by-side illuminated by the streetlights through the car window.

Audrey looked at him shaking her head slowly. "What is this? I don't understand," she said, confused. "How did you get my picture? You're not the policeman who—Oh my God! I think you are! You are the same man. Oh my God, Get away from me," she said, as she pushed against the passenger-side door, and then turned desperately to find the door handle to get out.

"Audrey, please. Wait! I'm your father, the man in the photograph," he said softly. His eyes began to water with the meaning of the moment.

She stopped struggling with the door and turned back to look at him. "If you compare the photograph to me you will see that is true," he said. "The picture is twenty-two years old, but the resemblance is still there. Please calm down, and let's talk for a moment, and then you can go. I promise I will not harm you, or hold you captive against your will. You are free to go anytime you wish. I only want to be sure you're OK before you do."

"You're my father? Really? I...you don't know how long I have yearned for this moment," she spoke very quietly, but then shook her head. "But no, not like this. This is impossible. What did you do to us? How did I end up here? What happened to my friends?"

He shook his head. "They're gone. They've been taken away, and I do not feel good about it. Audrey, you have to believe finding you like this is a real shock for me too. I can't tell you how sorry I am. All I ask is for you to give me a chance. I will do everything I can to make it right."

"Make it right...what are you going to make right?" she asked, as her thoughts sailed in several directions at once.

"The kidnapping. I am going to turn myself in, and help the authorities to get the two young people back," he said.

Audrey paused in silence for a moment and even relaxed a bit. "And me...are you going to make that right too?"

"Audrey, I am the man in the photograph. I'm your father. I swear it's true. When I opened your wallet and saw that photo, I was thrown into a tailspin because suddenly nothing mattered to me, but saving you and making sure you were all right.

"When I first saw that image from your wallet, I was sitting in a truck stop in Iowa. I had gotten completely away, again. Another successful operation. But when I saw that photograph, I realized I had been caught by the only person in this world who was capable of stopping me cold," he confessed, sincerely.

"I am an internationally known criminal, and a man wanted by Interpol. I think their latest name for me is "The Crow." I have been doing what I do for thirty years. I have money in banks all over the world, and investments worth millions. I have had no reason to ever worry about money, or anything until now.

"Why didn't you come, and get me? If you loved me, why didn't you come for me? I tried to find you once I knew I was adopted," she said.

"I love you, Audrey. I have always loved you, and I have never forgotten you. I did try to find you, but my access was blocked, and very well hidden just like yours. I paid for that security when I put you up for adoption to protect you. I was afraid that evil life I led would somehow get entangled with yours, and my enemies would find out about you and bring you harm. This photograph is the proof of what I am telling you now. This is the image I look at every night before I go to sleep."

She studied the images for a bit and even compared one to him in the dim light of the front seat. Then she looked at him, and said, "I don't know what to say. Why did you do it? Why did you kidnap my friends? My father would not do that. My father is a wonderful man who loves me," she pleaded.

"Yes, and the proof is sitting in front of you right now. When I thought you were in danger, I gave up everything I had worked for my entire life. Nothing else mattered to me but your safety. This is the most reckless thing I have ever done. I did it for you, and I am willing to do a lot more so that I will never lose you again.

"I have never been afraid in my life, Audrey. But I am trembling with fear right now. All I can say is, please give me a chance. I love you so very much." He bowed his head unable finally to hold back his tears.

She heard him sobbing as he said quietly, "I want to spend the rest of my life with you now that I have found you. But I really messed up this time. You know we have to save those kids first, and then after that, I may be sent away for a very long time. I am ready to accept that, but I am not ready to lose you now that I have found you. Please forgive me. Please give me a chance," he pleaded once more.

She believed him because she had always had faith in her father, wherever he was.

"What are we going to do now?" she asked, softly, not sure what was happening with them. She wanted to burst across the front seat and hold him in spite of everything. But she didn't know how yet. She wasn't afraid of him anymore. But she wasn't sure what he intended to do with her.

"*We* are going to take you back, and I'm going to turn myself in," he said, sincerely.

He wiped the tears from his eyes and smiled through the remains of them. "Can I at least get a hug? I want you to know that although I have not seen you these many years I have never forgotten you. I could never know who adopted you just as they could not know my name. It was to protect you. It looks like they did a good job. You are a beautiful, intelligent, young lady, and though I have no right, I am very proud of you. You look just like your mother."

She gave up any resistance, and burst across the seat suddenly, "Oh, father," she said, and kissed him on the cheek and hugged him as if her life depended on it. She held him tight and felt the moment she had imagined for many years.

Still holding him, she asked, "Father, isn't there some way you can help them without turning yourself in, or at least find someone to discuss the situation with?"

"I have been friends with several street cops for over a year, but I would not put my future in any of their hands," he told her.

She hugged him close again but then suddenly she pushed back, and said, "Oh, daddy, I stink! I'm filthy. You'll get dirty."

"I don't care. I've never been happier in my life," he said, honestly. "They named you perfectly. You are an Audrey."

She ignored him because her mind was still looking for solutions to their unusual circumstances. "Daddy, there was a police Lieutenant at Edith's that seemed pretty together, and he was nice. Maybe you could talk to him," she suggested, hopefully.

"Yes, I remember, Lieutenant Haleran. He did seem to have his act together." He thought about it for a minute and then said, "OK, we have to do something. We can't just sit here. Those kids are getting farther, and farther away. But I have a few cards up my sleeve I can still play. Let's see if I can get hold of him. I think he said he worked at headquarters."

Audrey sat back and watched her father fondly while Hagen called. He got some information, and then made another call. He waited, and then Haleran answered.

"Lieutenant, my name is Hagen. Please do not try to record, or trace, this call for both our sakes. I will explain why this is important. I am the one who kidnapped the three young people this afternoon. You knew me as Sergeant Daniels. I have the young lady named Audrey with me now. I am ready to turn myself in and help you recover the other two, but I would like to discuss an unusual situation with you first. I hope you believe me when I say I have done a complete one-eighty on this, and I will do everything I can to help get them back. I have some information that will be a huge step toward doing that. Will you meet with me?"

"Let me speak to Audrey," said Haleran.

Hagen handed her the cell phone. "Hello? Lieutenant?" she asked.

"Audrey, are you OK?" he asked.

"Yes, Lieutenant, I'm fine. Please believe what this man has to say. We both had a bit of an epiphany, but we can explain that to you after we meet. This is all for real. He wants to help," she said, handing the cell phone back to Hagen.

"OK," said Haleran. "Talk to me."

"Lieutenant, do not tell anyone of this call. There is a mole close to Ms. Marsh. I am not sure who it is, but they, the people who hired me to kidnap the two young people, knew everything Ms. Marsh, and her family did. They are probably monitoring what the police are doing right now. We will meet you in room 205, at the Starlite motel, at Barry and Ashland. If you do this officially, and bring a bunch of police, I am certain the kids will be killed, no matter what I do. If you work with me, we might just be able to save them. Will you do it?"

"Yes, the Starlite Motel, Barry and Ashland, room 205. It will take me about thirty minutes to get there," said Haleran.

"In a way that's good because Audrey needs to take a shower. I will explain when you get there. Lieutenant, Audrey is in no danger. She is the one who encouraged me to contact you about this. By pure coincidence, she is my long lost daughter. I know...it sounds crazy...but we will explain when we meet. See you soon," he said, hanging up.

Haleran privately told the chief he had a hot lead he wanted to follow up, and that he would be away for a bit. The Chief only half heard him because he was distracted by a hoard of Federal agents, some FBI, some from Homeland Security, who just arrived, and were in the process of making a new command center out of Catherine's large main conference room. Chief Wilcot was surprised at the quick response until he found out that these particular perpetrators from Asia had been known to be in the country, and both entities had shared some angst over that information. He nodded an OK with the proviso that Haleran check in often for updates.

Thirty-five minutes later, Haleran pulled up at the motel. It was well lit, and he could see no one suspicious hanging around. Still, he unholstered his thirty-eight and held it down cautiously as he climbed the stairs to room 205. The room was all the way in the back, but just at the top of the stairs. Haleran knocked on the door, not sure what to expect.

Audrey answered, and opened the door wide as Hagen advised her to do. He told her Haleran would want to see the entire room before entering. Hagen was sitting on a king size bed with his hands up in the air. Haleran entered and went right to Hagen. He turned him over on the bed and handcuffed him.

"This is only for safety reasons, Hagen," he told him. "I am not sure what to make of any of this, but when in doubt procedure is always wise."

"It's OK, Lieutenant," Hagen replied. "I told Audrey you would do this. Until you can trust me, I expect to be treated like this or worse."

Haleran nodded and turned to look at Audrey who was dressed in a white bathrobe that was too large for her. She turned around demonstrating she was unarmed. "I can take this off if you insist, but I assure you, I'm unarmed, and I have nothing on underneath."

Haleran patted her down just the same, "What was your part in this kidnapping? Did you help plan the setup?"

"What? Huh? No! Oh no, Lieutenant. I was kidnapped too. In fact, I spent most of the night in a dumpster behind a supermarket on the south side of town. When he took us, he didn't know who I was," she said. "That's why I'm wet. I just took a shower to try to get the smell, and gook off of me. The hot water here is not working well, and there was only one of those motel soaps. So, I may still smell a bit like dumpster trash."

"How did you figure out she was your daughter?" Haleran asked Hagen.

Audrey showed Haleran the two photos she still had with her. "With these. We both kept them in our wallets. He found mine, and his life changed, forever I hope."

"Are you this master criminal Interpol has been harping about for a couple of years?" asked Haleran.

Hagen looked at Audrey and raised his eyebrows. "Yes, I am."

"And you let yourself get caught because you unexpectedly found your daughter?" asked Haleran, still not sure he was buying his story.

"Actually, Lieutenant, I threw my daughter into a garbage dumpster like she was trash. Try for one moment to understand that I have loved her all my life, although I did not know where she was. After I had gotten away and was sitting at a truck stop in Iowa, I found her copy in her billfold of the same photo I carried all these years. The sudden realization of what I had done hit me hard like a hammer. I almost fainted. Really. I set speed records from the Iowa border getting back here, and I got to her just as she was being lifted into the back of a garbage truck. Nothing else matters but getting my life, and my soul back on the right side of things," he explained.

Audrey sat down on the bed beside him, put her hand on his shoulder, and looked up at the detective.

Haleran as a father himself believed him. As crazy as it sounded, he knew it was true. He shook his head and smiled at the whole thing. This was one of life's crazy ironies.

"I'll be damned," he said, after a moment having considered this unlikely turn of events. "You look very different from the cop you portrayed before. I have to say if you didn't swear you were the same person, I wouldn't know you."

Hagen gave a shrug, then rolled over on the bed, and sat up with some effort. "Unfortunately for us all, I am really good at what I do. But I'm ready to answer all of your questions, and help get the two young people back." Audrey was snuggled up against his shoulder.

"Who hired you to kidnap Devi and Charlie?" asked Haleran.

Without hesitation, Hagen said, "Asian World Investments, a man named Hinsu Yameda. But I worked with a female assistant of his by the name of Su Ling. They never told me their names, but I am cautious, Lieutenant. I always determine the name of whom I am working for before I agree to the deal. They never knew my name."

Haleran nodded. He thought of what Mai had told him. His information checked with that.

"What information do you have that will help us find them?" asked Haleran.

"I always protect myself when I am dealing with people who I believe would have no scruples about double-crossing me. Devearney and Charlie were packed into coffin-like containers within shipping crates. I know it sounds ominous, but as long as they don't wake up, and panic they are being transported quite comfortably. These crates were specially fitted with a tracking device I hid within the larger coffin giving the aircraft the designation VR4598. You can follow this GPS data that will read like a transponder if you have the right software to interpret it. He held out his hand, with a small thumbnail USB drive. Attach this to a computer, download the program, access the FAA flight controller data archive, and you can find it quite readily I suspect. You have only to check the flight paths for that number, and you can see where the aircraft went. Understand, it is not a transponder, and won't show up on normal FAA screens. But with this software, the GPS location of the aircraft can be pinpointed. That would be a start. I am ready to do anything it takes to get them back, and I assure you I am the best at what I do."

"Why wouldn't they detect such a device when you turned over the two victims? I would be willing to bet they can detect any electronic devices," Haleran said.

"The device is on a timer and doesn't activate until one hour after I dropped them off. That leaves ample time for them to check for such a device before it switches on, and the device itself is probably undetectable anyway. I will bet you it is working now. I haven't checked yet. I can't access the FAA from here, without being detected. They are very particular about who has an access to their data. Ordinarily, I would go to another one of my locations that would disguise my identity."

Haleran looked at Hagen stunned for a minute as he processed what he had just been told. He pondered what to do with this information, and then flipped open his cell phone, and punched a number.

In a few moments, he heard a friendly voice. "Frank, do you have some information for me?" Mai asked.

"I think we might have a lead, but we need your help. As it turns out I have the kidnapper here with me. He is ready to turn himself over to the police and help all he can to get Devi and Charlie back. But I wanted to tell you what he said, and see what you think," said Haleran.

"And the young girl, Audrey, Frank. Don't forget about her. She is just as much a victim as our kids," said Mai.

"No, she is OK, and safe with me here, Mai." Haleran quickly explained the circumstances, and what Hagen had just told him about the embedded fake transponder number.

"Do you have a computer laptop in the room there?" she asked.

"Yes," answered Haleran, "but Hagen tells me he cannot break into the FAA system from here," said Haleran. "He has the chip with the program but does not have a way of accessing the FAA. I am ready to run with it downtown."

"No, Frank, please don't do that. I am positive that will get our kids killed if we let the FBI handle this. Our effort must remain top secret, especially if there is a mole on Catherine's staff. Our security is better than any police, or paramilitary organization in my opinion. Let us handle it. Put this man, Hagen on the line," she told him.

"OK, Mai, I am going to put my cell phone on speaker, and lay it on the bed so we can all hear," said Haleran. When he was done, he introduced Hagen to Mai.

"Mr. Hagen, can you access the internet from there?" she asked.

"Yes, ma'am, I am a bit of a computer expert myself," he said. "I can access the internet from almost anywhere. I set up this emergency location hideaway because I have access to three different wifi signals in the area."

"Turn on your computer, plug in the USB chip that you spoke of, and then give me the IP address," directed Mai. "Turn off any firewalls you may have installed to block others from accessing your data. I am coming there to get the information from that chip."

Hagen showed his cuffed hands from behind his back, and Haleran unlocked the cuffs releasing his hands. Hagen turned on his laptop, the latest and best PC version available. He worked the keys quickly, plugged the computer chip into a slot on the back of the computer, and worked the keys some more. After telling Mai his IP address, he said, "I am all yours. Go for it."

For a moment nothing happened, but then data began streaming across his screen at a maddening pace. The three watched as the data flowed for four minutes, and then stopped, leaving a blank screen. Then his system returned, apparently as it was before.

Mai said, over the cell phone," Give me a moment. I will be right back to you. Please leave the line open."

Hagen looked perplexed, so Haleran asked, "What's the problem?"

"She just downloaded my entire computer memory, not just the chip. She didn't have to do that. What's she up to?" he asked, feeling very vulnerable, something rare for him. He knew there was information on there that a smart computer analyst could use to locate him. But then he reminded himself; he was not playing that game anymore. He had nothing to hide.

"She is checking you out, no doubt," Mr. Hagen. "Remember we have only your word so far of your good intentions. Don't worry. You're with the good guys now," Haleran told him, smiling.

Hagen put out his hands for Haleran to put the cuffs back on, but Haleran brushed him off. "I think we can forego that for now, but don't expect any special treatment, if we go back to headquarters. I still don't know where this is all going."

Mai came back in ten minutes, and said, "OK, we have found something, Frank. We have accessed a remote FAA screen, and I can see that identifier at 17:45 hours leaving Newfoundland, and heading for Iceland.

"It does put them on course for the destination you mentioned previously, Mai," said Haleran.

"Yes, Europe. My bet is that it is heading for Salzburg, Austria, Frank. Asian World Investments has built a large complex there including airport facilities. But they also built a good-sized clinic at that location, and it would be a perfect place to hold two captives as prisoners until they get what they want from me," she said.

"Mr. Hagen, did those who hired you ever mention where they were taking Devi and Charlie once they had them?" Haleran asked.

"No, I was only to deliver them, and that ended my part in this," Hagen said.

"How do you want to proceed, Mai?" Haleran asked.

"I was hoping you would ask me that question, Frank. Does that mean you are willing to let us handle this our way?"

"Mai, when I left Ms. Marsh's condo an hour ago, the circus was already started. It was pure chaos with the Feds all vying with one another for jurisdiction. They were busy blaming each other for letting this happen while the Chicago police just looked on helplessly. That show is going nowhere. My instincts, which are usually right, tell me the only hope those kids have is your team. So yes, you can handle this your way."

"I have a few more questions for Mr. Hagen, Frank," said Mai.

"OK, he is listening. Shoot," said Haleran.

"What airport, and hangar, did you deliver our kids to?" she asked.

"It was O'Hare, on the north end, 2013L Aviation Road in the commercial cargo area. It was one of the very large hangars," said Hagen.

"Look, you two," he protested, "Audrey is still suffering from her ordeal during the kidnapping. She needs to go back to Catherine's where she tells me she is staying temporarily. She needs to get cleaned up and get some proper rest. I hate to think what will happen when she walks in though."

"I can always say she was found in the dumpster, and I was called to come and get her," said Haleran.

"What about me?" asked Hagen. "Are you going to have me arrested?"

"You are the one who found her standing confused by the side of the market. She told you my name, and you called me. Simple. It's not a great story, but enough to get us through until we come up with a better one. What do you think, Mai?" he asked."

"Yes, we want to keep Mr. Hagen around, so we can find out what else he knows about our friends. I have a feeling he can still be very useful. However, I would not reveal yet that you have Audrey. That is just inviting trouble, Frank, and I bet she is not up to enduring any close examination at the moment." said Mai.

"I'm having second thoughts about that, Mai. I'm a cop, and that would be withholding evidence," he said. "Honestly, I am having trouble justifying that and Audrey's presence too. I know the Feds would intercept the airplane as soon as it lands but then there is the inevitable hostage situation and shootout that would follow.

"And then there's this to consider. Mr. Hagen tells me there is a mole embedded at NearNorth Productions close to Catherine and they have known our every move thus far. It might do well until we can determine who that is to keep both Hagen and Audrey's situation secret," Haleran said.

"OK, do what you think best. But I have a few more questions for Mr. Hagen before we close the conversation for now.

"Go ahead, Mai. We are still on speakerphone," Haleran said.

"Mr. Hagen, what kind of aircraft did they load the crates into?"

"It was one of the biggest ones, a Boeing cargo plane. Really big. I was surprised. But when you see the hangar you will see that it could easily fit in there. The hangar was very large too," said Hagen.

"Did you get the tail number by any chance," Mai asked.

"No, I'm afraid not. I was concerned with getting out of there in one piece, so I did not think of that," he replied.

"OK, that's all for now. I may be contacting you at Ms. Marsh's later tonight so stay close Mr. Hagen," said Mai.

"Now please take us off speakerphone. I wish to talk to Frank in private," she said.

After the speaker was punched off and as Frank listened, Mai said, "Frank my computer team tells me Mr. Hagen is as he said very skilled on computers, and quite the hacker himself. However, they also tell me that as far as they can determine from police, and Interpol reports, his nefarious activities have been aimed at and limited to suspect corporations and organizations controlled by cartels, and criminals. That seems to be his modus operandi. It also means that most of his victims are not going to be candid with the police about their losses. My gut is you can trust him, but be alert. I know it is your instinct to arrest him, but I think we would be wasting a valuable asset in our effort to get Devi and Charlie back if you do. If you believe his story, then you have to agree he has a much more positive reason for wanting to help us.

"Let's stay in close touch throughout this. You can call me at this number anytime day, or night, even when I am in the air. We are leaving here within the hour, and heading for Munich, Germany," she continued. "I have a secret I would rather not reveal yet, which may help us greatly in our effort to get our kids back. Thank you, Frank. Your decision to come to me with this means a lot," Mai said.

"Can I tell Catherine about all of this?" he asked.

"Yes, but if Hagen is right about a mole, then I suggest you do it without anyone but her partner Kelly present. No one else should know. We will set up a trap soon for the mole. But right now let's let the Feds think they are running this show. Where do they think the kids are anyway?"

I am not sure, Mai. When I left, they said something about tracking the transponder. I guess I will find out when I return," he said.

Chapter 41

May 2005   Chicago

Haleran called ahead and talked with Catherine and Kelly. Catherine said the FBI and Homeland security had taken over her conference room with a dozen or more agents, and the effort had turned into frenzied chaos in her opinion with lots of loud disagreements between them. They were pulling out all the stops and had marshaled all of their people in response to this kidnapping by foreign terrorists.

Considering the possibility of a mole lurking within Catherine's organization, the decision was made to keep the presence of Audrey and Hagen a secret for now. Haleran warned them not to let anyone, even their staff, know what they were doing. Kelly told Haleran how to bring Audrey and Hagen in the back, away from the crowd of reporters out front, and the Feds who had taken over the investigation. Kelly met them in the basement of the building. She took them by a private elevator to a suite on the thirty-eighth floor used mainly by visiting guests of NearNorth Productions.

Once settled in, Audrey was allowed to take another shower while Kelly retrieved a change of clothes, collected her make-up and bath items. Kelly cooked and served her a meal after that. Finally, they gathered in the small living room area to discuss all that had happened. Kelly's original distaste for Hagen mellowed a great deal in that first hour.

Catherine suddenly came into the room and seeing Audrey went directly to her and gave her a warm hug. "I am happy you're OK," she said. "At least we have you back safely."

She turned to the man sitting in one of the chairs and walked over to him. Hagen was uncharacteristically nervous and stood as she approached. "You're Hagen?" she asked.

"Yes, Ms. Marsh, I am. I am very sor…" he began. But he was interrupted by a harsh slap across his face from Catherine, and then another, and another. Hagen just stood there while she pounded him with her fists on his chest like hitting a wall.

Kelly hurried to her, and stopped her from hitting him by catching one of her hands in her own, and slowly drawing it down. "Cat, stop. This isn't helping," she said.

"It's helping me!" she cried out, over tears. "How could you? How could you do this horrible thing?" she asked, not caring at all about his answer.

"No, I deserve it," said Hagen. "Let her do what she wishes. I have no answer for her because at this moment I cannot understand myself how I could have done this."

Audrey placed herself between Hagen and Catherine. "Catherine, he's my father," she said. "Please, for me, stop," she said.

"What?" asked Catherine. "What are you talking about? Is this some pretense you've cooked up to try to get out of this?" she asked Hagen.

"I am afraid it is true, Ms. Marsh," said Haleran. "In one of life's more screwier situations these two found each other after twenty-two years, and that is why Mr. Hagen has done a one-eighty and doing all he can to help us find Devi and Charlie. Please, if you'll sit down for a moment, we can explain."

"Please, Catherine, for me. Please listen," said Audrey.

Catherine sat down with Kelly on a small sofa opposite the others. Kelly had her laptop out and was following the events downstairs in the newly formed command center with an ear bud from the computer. Audrey sat next to her dad on another sofa opposite while Haleran occupied a chair facing them. Haleran told Catherine what he knew from beginning to end.

"Thanks to Mr. Hagen we think we have a breakthrough and know where they are headed with Devi and Charlie. Mai is on her way to the vicinity with her security people now. On my own, I decided that was probably the best chance to save the kids. I have seen too many operations like the one downstairs go badly."

"For real? You think you can save them?" asked Catherine, with a hope she had not felt in several hours.

"Yes," said Haleran. "Mr. Hagen gave us that opportunity, and Mai is running with it. I should be arresting Mr. Hagen right now, but I am convinced that is the wrong course of action in this instance. The thing is we need to keep this under our hat. We must continue like we know nothing because there is definitely a mole close to you in your organization. Mr. Hagen says he is positive because they have known all of your movements for the last year. That is how they were able to pull this off, and that is why we are meeting privately right now to discuss this."

"Who is it?" asked Catherine looking at Hagen directly.

"Mr. Hagen does not know only that he or she exists," said Haleran.

"However, I have an idea," said Hagen. "Kelly, can I borrow your laptop a moment?"

"I am not sure that is a good idea," said Haleran. "Mai tells me you're an expert with computers."

"If that computer is connected to the local network, I think I can use that computer to search for any illicit transmissions from the thirtieth floor. That might help narrow down our options for a mole," he said.

"But my offices and my people are on that floor," said Catherine.

"That might not matter because what I am looking for would be unauthorized, and piggybacked onto something routine you do every day. They will be disguised as something else, and at the command level. If I am on the network, I can look for it if you will allow me to try. Please, I am on the good side now. I have great skills. Let me help, please," he asked.

Catherine nodded, and Kelly handed over her laptop across the glass coffee table to Hagen.

While he began pounding on the keys, they discussed how they were going to handle Audrey's return. They decided not to mention Hagen at all for now. When Haleran cautioned them that they could be accused of participating in a criminal conspiracy, Catherine picked up the phone and called Chief Wilcot.

Fifteen minutes later he was sitting with them in a chair near Haleran. Catherine recounted the whole story and then informed him she needed the biggest favor from him she had ever asked. She told him what it was.

"You think you can get back Charlie and Devi?" he asked her. "Because I have no doubt those bozos downstairs can't do it, and the Chicago police's jurisdiction stops at the county line. Mother of Christ, what a mess. Both of those institutions downstairs in their own world are very capable, but they are equally incapable of working outside the box, or with each other. Of course, I will go along with this, Catherine. What choice do we have? But I want Frank here to be informed at every stage of your planning, just so I know how much trouble I am getting into," he quipped. "But let's be clear. You are working with the Chicago Chief of Police now in a separate investigation if anyone asks. I have authorized it as necessary based on the firm evidence of at least one mole within Catherine's organization. Yes, that ought to handle that issue for the interim."

"Chief, did they say downstairs which way they think the kidnappers went with Devi and Charlie, when they flew out of here," Kelly asked.

"Yes, they think they are in Wichita, Kansas. They have followed a corporate aircraft there that headed west."

Suddenly, Hagen spoke up, "I've got him! Someone is communicating by piggybacking a message through the condominium network router to… it looks like an Asian server. Is there a room near the kitchen in the condominium, maybe your home office or something?" he asked.

"No, that would have to be Ward Nedson, our butler, in our servant's quarters. He lives in the condominium. You don't mean he's the one? Why would he be involved?" asked Kelly.

"I can't believe Ward is a mole working for AWI. That's just crazy," said Catherine. "I refuse to believe it. He's proven entirely trustworthy and heard countless privileged conversations while working here. You're wrong, Mr. Hagen. Maybe we should look into your motives for saying such a thing."

Hagen nodded as if he understood her bias. "Look, there is one way to find out. He's online and communicating right now. Go see," he suggested.

Haleran looked at Kelly. They both jumped up and left the room quickly.

They made small conversation for a few minutes and after a while Chief Wilcot commented, "It is commin' on 3 a.m., Catherine. I think I will have to make my leave. But you know I am always ready to take your call if you need anything. It has been a long night."

He gave Catherine a hug, a kiss on the cheek, and left the room.

Catherine, Hagen, and Audrey realized they were alone together. At first, it seemed awkward, but then Catherine offered, "You should be very proud of Audrey, Mr. Hagen. She is rare in our industry. She is very talented, and just today, or yesterday now, she broke a major st…"

Kelly came suddenly through the door and sat down with her arms folded in silence. After a pause she looked up at Catherine who had a question on her face. "We caught him red-handed, Cat. He looked like a kid with his hand in the cookie jar," Kelly said.

"Did he say why he did it?" asked Cat.

"No. But Catherine I saw his personality change right in front of me. He said to tell you he was sorry he didn't get to see you ruined. Perhaps someday we will find out what that was all about. Lieutenant Haleran whisked him away before anyone noticed, and gave him to two cops outside who put him in a squad car. He told them to take him to headquarters and keep him in a private secure cell by order of the Chief. He told me he would keep him under wraps until they could get answers and were sure there were no other moles within the organization," said Kelly.

"Mr. Hagen, I guess I owe you an apology," said Catherine.

"Don't be ridiculous. I will be repaying you for the rest of my life, Ms. Marsh. Right now, I am pledged to do all I can to undo that wrong," he said sadly.

Not long after that exchange, Hagen looked over at Audrey sitting with her head resting on his shoulder, and said, "I think we all need to get some sleep. Please, can I stay here close to Audrey? I promise I won't impose on your hospitality, and I will stay out of the way. I am not going to try to run away. I made a promise to Lieutenant Haleran to put myself in his hands. If he decides to arrest me, then so be it. I have found my daughter, and I am not going anywhere.

Kelly jumped up, and said, "Come on, I will get you fixed up. We can talk some more in the morning."

In spite of all the events of the evening, Kelly went to bed hoping to get some rest. She woke up in a fitful sleep an hour later finding that Catherine had not joined her, and was probably still at the command center worrying over things.

With sleep no longer possible Kelly got up and got dressed. She pulled her hair back in a ponytail, and without makeup went out to the kitchen for a cup of coffee. It was 4:30 a.m. As she poured a cup, Audrey joined her coming through the private back door of the condo from upstairs. "I couldn't sleep. I'm still worried about them, Kelly. Have you been up all this time?" she asked

"No, I got an hour, and then couldn't sleep myself. How is it finding your father after all of these years?" she asked.

"I shouldn't be under the circumstances, Kelly, but I am very happy in that regard. I really like him, and he has sacrificed everything for me. It is one thing to find your daughter, and step back into her life, but it is another thing entirely when it means that doing so you have to give up all you have, and maybe even go to prison just to do that. I can't explain what I feel very well. I should be better at it as a reporter."

"No, I get it. He's your father, and he does appear to be a nice man, but for his criminal record. As to that, there is something to be said about being the best at what you do. Mai says she has checked his record at Interpol, and he had a particularly focused modus operandi. He robbed corporations and organizations that had criminal affiliations. His favorite targets were money-laundering operations for the cartels. Much of informed law enforcement liked what he was doing, and that is why they haven't really made a concerted effort to catch him," explained Kelly.

"Then why is he on their list, most wanted even?" asked Audrey.

"I think the cartels have many of their own people within law enforcement and may be influencing that. But even so, if the good guys like what he is doing, they can't seem to condone it overtly. In fact, they will want it to look like they are after him to throw the cartels off. That's my thinking on the subject," said Kelly.

"I haven't properly thanked you or Catherine for letting me move in with you when I showed up here last week," said Audrey. "That was really nice, but the best part was that the two of you made me feel like family. I have to laugh though. Catherine is like a big sister here, but at work, she's a pretty tough boss."

"That was all Catherine's idea. She likes you, and frankly, it's nice to have another young person staying with us," said Kelly. "Grab your coffee. Let's go see how they are doing at the command center."

"Wait, do they know I'm back?" asked Audrey.

"We are going to a room that overlooks the conference room and has a one-way glass window. No one will see you," explained Kelly.

When they got there, they saw the conference room was packed with every seat filled with strangers they had never seen before.

"This is the communications room we are in," explained Kelly. They were elevated looking down on the conference room through a long thin window. She pushed a button, and they could hear the conversation from the conference room. There was a heated debate going, and Catherine was at one end of the large conference table tapping her fingers while staring through a well-dressed man sitting among other men dressed in suits on one side.

"Uh-oh," whispered Kelly. "When Catherine taps her fingers like that, she is really upset. Something is wrong. We can talk because they cannot hear us in there so if you have any questions, just ask."

Everyone was concentrating apparently on Mai's voice coming out of a laptop sitting on the conference table, and projecting into the speakers of the conference room.

"I think you're wrong, Director Morris. Please believe me. They are not there. I would even bet that the kidnappers went in the opposite direction, and we do have some information that supports that theory. You must proceed with great caution. These people have already shown us they are very elusive. How did you arrive at your conclusion that this was the right aircraft, if I may ask?"

Director Morris rolled his eyes and looked with disapproval at his team of agents on one side of the table. "Will somebody please tell me why we are wasting our time dealing with the parents of the kidnap victims at this time? While we all sympathize with the situation we cannot let ourselves be distracted with emotional theatrics. Please someone spare me so I can concentrate on my team and the upcoming operation."

Kelly turned to the technician concentrating on the control panel console to her right. "Lloyd, what's going on in there? Do you know?"

"Yes, Miss Ryan. Apparently, there is a bit of a territorial dispute going on between Homeland Security, and the FBI, over jurisdiction. Homeland Security has had an eye on the Hmong mercenaries since they arrived in the United States, and didn't inform the FBI about them, but the FBI found out on their own anyway. The upshot is that they think they have traced the corporate aircraft with the kidnap victims to the airport in Wichita, and a particular remote hangar. That was based on an anonymous tip that came into the FBI about six hours ago.

"Homeland Security wants to take charge because they want to capture, and question the kidnappers for national security reasons. They have a paramilitary, strike team already on site in Wichita, and ready to assault the hangar," explained Lloyd. "I think they are pretty hyped up as this will be the first operation this specially trained strike team has executed since their inception. The whole idea was a special project of Director Morris who you can see is running the show down there."

"I think we have indulged Mrs. Largent long enough," said Director Morris of Homeland Security. He nodded to one of his agents who reached over and closed the laptop cutting Mai off in mid-sentence as she tried once more to protest what was about to happen in Wichita.

Mai switched gears, and Catherine's cell phone buzzed almost immediately. "Catherine get the FBI Agent in Charge sitting at the table, and take him to the communications room so I can talk to him," she said. "Tell him I have some important information for him."

Catherine got up and circled the table to whisper in the FBI AIC's ear as a large screen lowered from the ceiling, and a video feed of the Wichita hangar was projected onto it. The AIC looked up at her, and then got up and followed her to the communications room where they joined Kelly who had rushed Audrey out of the room before they arrived.

Catherine handed her cell phone to the AIC, and Mai continued, "Agent Carter, what I am about to tell you must be guarded with the utmost secrecy. There is a locator chip embedded in my daughter's shoulder that can be accessed by any police radio at the given frequency. It will report as a beeping sound. We know it works well because we have thoroughly tested it. Don't you think you could at least try that to be sure they're in there before assaulting the hangar in Wichita? I am afraid it is a trap, and a lot of those men might get killed. Can we at least check that first?" she pleaded.

"Yes, of course, Mrs. Largent," he replied. "What is the frequency?"

But as Mai was relaying the frequency they heard someone from the conference room yell, "There they go!" And then, moments later, a loud roar went up from the conference room as on the video screen the hangar exploded consuming everything in a bright flash that gradually turned into an inferno. Without a doubt, many of the assault team were killed instantly.

"I don't understand," said the stunned FBI AIC, displaying more honesty than perhaps he intended to reveal. He watched with the rest of them in horror as the flames spread out, and burned with abandon. He handed the phone back to Catherine and left to join his agents in the conference room.

Catherine told Mai on the phone what had happened and then closed the call saying she would call back later. She hugged Kelly for a few minutes momentarily stunned by the worst possible outcome of the assault in Wichita. Then Catherine returned to the conference room and sat down in silence at one end of the conference table. Through distant eyes, she watched the agents with stone-faced antipathy as the room turned again into the chaos it had been most of the night. She reigned over them as a foreboding dark and silent icon reminding them of their ineptitude and failure.

It was as if by appearing busy, they thought they could somehow save face. But then at the end of the table there sat Catherine, unsmiling, silent, staring through them and condemning them for playing with human lives like it was a video game. On the large screen in front of them, fire trucks surrounded the building and directed streams of water onto the raging fire. Suddenly, the link with Wichita was broken, and the view they had of the burning hangar went away.

All of the Federal agents in the conference room were left with the unsettling belief that the kidnapping, and follow-up assault had ended with the tragic loss of the kidnap victims and their specially trained assault team. The directors were the first to leave, hurriedly, acting as if something urgent and more important was calling them away. As Catherine watched in straight-faced silence, the other Federal agents began to close their briefcases, gather their things, and leave the command center one-by-one. Senior representatives of each agency awkwardly made attempts at giving Catherine condolences for her loss. They made similar pledges to investigate, and return after consulting with their colleagues. Catherine refused to acknowledge any of them and sat stone-faced, staring straight ahead. After the officials made their awkward goodbyes, it was not long before they had all departed leaving behind empty coffee cups, soda cans, and sundry trash. Thirty minutes after the explosion only Catherine and Big Ben remained in the conference room and sat in silence at opposite ends of the long conference table.

After the last of the agents departed, Kelly retrieved Audrey, and joined Catherine.

Catherine sat hands over her head with elbows rested on the table. Kelly went to her and held her from behind. She leaned over and kissed her on the cheek. "Why don't you go in and get some sleep, love," she said. "You look like you could use it. Lloyd told me to tell you that the video recorder documented everything that happened in the conference room since early yesterday afternoon as you requested. He has turned it off now."

Catherine exploded suddenly causing Kelly to jump back. "Those assholes! Those stupid, obstinate, condescending, incompetent bastards. If our kids had been in there, they would be dead right now. They led their own elite assault team into a deadly massacre because of a pissing contest between agencies!"

Ben stood up in surprise. "Wait! Miss Catherine, you mean that Charlie and Devi weren't in there?"

"No, Ben, they weren't in there. We're fairly certain they're someplace else and we are making plans with Mai to get them back. But those arrogant asses didn't know that and didn't care to hear us out or let us present any evidence in that regard," said Catherine bitterly.

"Oh, my Lord Almighty," exclaimed Ben letting out air in relief. He pulled a handkerchief out of his pocket and turned away briefly. After a moment he got up and went out into the hallway, and closed the door. The ladies stared at the closed door in silence because Ben's heartfelt sobs could be heard coming through from the other side.

Shuffling in her seat, Kelly said, "Well, yes, we can be thankful Devi and Charlie were not there. And now we can exclude those agents from our plans with good conscience, and damn them even if they try to question our decision on that after the fact! I have no doubt their grandstanding would get our kids killed under any circumstances."

Hagen came in and sat down beside Audrey around one end of the large conference table. "I was told you were confined to Audrey's apartment, Mr. Hagen," said Catherine, sending some of her remaining anger toward him.

"I sent for him," said Kelly. "He might have some insight as things play out. It is time we use him, Cat, and ignore, for the moment, how he came to be here."

Catherine looked at Hagen, and they had a staring contest until Hagen looked away.

A few minutes later, Mai who was in the air on her way to Munich, Germany was transferred to the speakerphone and brought up to speed on their recent conversation. On her flight, she had twenty of her best security people including Ramadi and Fetu. Their equipment, including two helicopters, was coming by a cargo plane piloted by Daniel Vega. Her computer team was back at Siem Kulea working on tracing different facets of the kidnapping in an attempt to pinpoint the whereabouts of Devi and Charlie.

"I agree with Kelly," said Mai. "Mr. Hagen may be of value to us. A case in point is what you are just about to see. I cannot get the video feed from my team at Siem Kulea on this part of my journey so you will have to interpret it for me from there."

My team is right now sending you a feed of the video surveillance from the airport at O'Hare when the crates holding Devi and Charlie were being loaded. We were able to pinpoint the correct hangar because Mr. Hagen identified the hangar where he delivered them.

I am told we have found something significant," she continued. "The remote hangar area surveillance was shut down, but they didn't get the private security camera at a building nearby that had one of its cameras pointed at what we think is the hangar in question. I am told the video is a bit fuzzy since the hangar we want is only in the background."

They watched the video that was transferred from the computer by projection to the large screen in the conference room. It showed mostly an airport tarmac outside of the hangar where the video was shot. But in the distance, you could see a very large airport hangar as a white van pulled up. Catherine was talking softly to Mai narrating what she saw on the video. The large hangar door opened slowly, and inside was a Boeing cargo plane. The van pulled up to it, and three Asians, two men, and one woman advanced toward it.

"Lloyd, do we have this downloaded? Can you back it up and freeze it when I tell you?" Catherine asked.

"Yes, Catherine," he said slowly playing the sequence backward.

"There!" said Catherine. "Stop! Can you enhance that and enlarge it a bit?" she asked.

"Just a moment," said the technician.

In a moment a closer version of the three Asian people appeared on the screen. "That's Su Ling," said Kelly.

"Well at least now we have no doubt," said Catherine. "Mai, it was Su Ling who took them. We have visual proof," she said.

"My team says the plane in the hangar is not the same model that was in that destroyed hangar in Wichita," said Mai." They say the one in the hangar is a much larger model. Do you agree?" asked Mai.

"Yes, I have to say that aircraft in Wichita was one-third the size of this one in the surveillance footage. This one is a huge Boeing cargo jet, maybe a 747. The one in Wichita, which had the transponder they were tracking, was a corporate jet. They were definitely not the same, Mai," said Catherine.

They watched the sad scene unfold before them as the casket-crates were loaded onto the cargo plane. The white van left. The kidnappers quickly boarded the plane, all but Su Ling who walked to the edge of the hangar door and looked around in several directions. She threw her head up proudly then turned and boarded the aircraft.

"I wonder if she knew we would be watching," questioned Kelly, with pure hate.

"Probably, it looks like it, anyway," said Catherine. "Mr. Hagen, do you have anything to add. I assume that was you in the white van."

"Yes, I am afraid so. They paid funds to my account before I released the locks on the crates. I gave the remote to the lady you call Su Ling. She is a piece of work. When I opened the casket holding Devi, I thought she was going to spit on her. She had a look of contempt on her face, which I was glad was not pointed toward me. I have to say, I was surprised by her expression, and it occurred to me that this wasn't just a kidnapping for ransom purposes."

There was silence for a moment as everyone thought about what they had seen. Mai was taking the time to consider some information Catherine had given her as her team identified the tail number of the aircraft used by the kidnappers. As they started to speak Mai said, "Please wait a minute, I am tracking something…no talk please."

Catherine turned off the microphone on their end while monitoring the speaker.

The kitchen staff arrived with two carts. They cleaned up the room and a complete breakfast was served just as Lieutenant Haleran came through the door.

"Good timing, Lieutenant," said Kelly. "We are waiting for Mai who is doing something on the other end of the line. I took the opportunity to get some food in here."

As they ate Kelly filled Haleran in on the raid in Wichita, and their decision to exclude the Feds on what they were doing. "I made that same decision last night," said Haleran. "I have had two major operations fucked up...sorry, excuse my language...I have had two major operations screwed up by the Feds."

Suddenly, Catherine said, "Hold on, Mai, let me put the speakerphone back on."

"I think I have something," said Mai. "They wanted us to believe they headed west toward Wichita, and they knew the feds would be following the transponder information they had. It was a possibility even I considered at first, but now with the correct tail number we can be positive they have gone in the opposite direction entirely. I will explain."

"With the remote security camera video we were able to enhance the image, and identify the tail number on the aircraft, and trace its information. We have the correct transponder number and it corroborates Mr. Hagen's information. But we also have another source with more detailed information. The aircraft involved is a Boeing 747 cargo plane with Pratt and Whitney engines. The engines of a modern commercial aircraft are the most expensive parts and are registered as a part of the airplane. They can cost $5 million or more each. Those on the 747 are the PW4000 series that have digital monitoring technology. These engines have a very distinct signal that is monitored by satellite. By monitoring the engines in flight, they can keep up with necessary maintenance and prevent a malfunction.

"I have been able to find and track the engines of that aircraft using the satellite data. They indicate that aircraft headed in the opposite direction and East toward Europe. That would put them over England about now.

"You will recall the FBI was tracking the transponder they thought was the correct one, and that signal ended up apparently in that hangar in Wichita. So, we have two aircraft leaving at approximately the same time but one designed to throw us off the path. Do we know how the FBI arrived at their conclusion that the aircraft in Wichita was the one the kidnappers used?" asked Mai. "If you will recall, that was the last thing I asked Director Morris before he cut me off."

"Yes, I asked him that earlier when they first informed me they found the aircraft," said Catherine. "It was an anonymous tip, Mai. That makes sense now that we have the whole story. But you can't blame them too much. They were desperate for a lead, and it did check out all the way to that remote hangar in Wichita. They just should have waited to be sure."

"Well, Catherine, I told you last night Mr. Hagen gave us a huge lead that gave us a jump on that, and now with your heads-up about the engine maintenance monitoring, we could prove it is true. That was good information and proved out when we followed up on it. Was that from a story you did once?" asked Mai.

"Huh? Oh actually no, Mai. Earlier in the night when the FBI was talking about tracking the transponders, Ward, who works for me, overheard us talking, and just mentioned that on many of the large jets they now can digitally monitor the engines in flight. He should get the accol…"

"What's wrong?" asked Mai. "Did you think of something?"

"Only that we discovered later that night that Ward was the mole inside NearNorth Productions, Mai. Do you think his suggestion of that tip has any significance?"

"I don't think so, Catherine, especially since we confirmed it was true through Hagen. He was probably trying to add to his credibility. I mean why would he want us to know where they took Charlie and Devi?"

"Well, that's the other thing, Mai. We didn't know it was a 747 at the time. Everyone here thought it was the corporate jet. It was only later that through Mr. Hagen we determined it was a 747 with those special engines."

"Did he inform you of anything else that you can think of?" asked Mai.

Catherine thought a moment and then said, "When Kelly and I were discussing how to intercept a plane before it got out of Chicago, he was serving coffee and mentioned the airports have lots of surveillance cameras particularly in the cargo areas."

"That's all very interesting, Cat, but I'm not sure it amounts to much. We have pretty much nailed down where they are going and it just happens to be where I suspected all along.

"Let me explain," continued Mai. "For the last three years, we have been watching the Asian World Investments group in Salzburg, Austria. This has become their nexus for entry into Europe. For Yameda it is kind of a reverse Colonialism with Asian entities scheming to control European corporations.

They chose Austria instead of other European countries like Germany because their banks are not as regulated. They purchased a bank and several viable industries there.

"They also opened a clinic there specializing in brain disorders. They get a lot of wealthy clients, and overtly it looks legitimate. For me, it always seemed out of context, which is why I had my team watching them. They have a large facility with several hangars at the Salzburg Mozart airport that can service several aircraft at once. I think they went there.

"OK, we will get our act together, and meet you where?" asked Catherine.

"Wait, I am not done. Catherine, you will never guess who is head of security at that clinic," continued Mai. "This proves the symmetry of the universe in my view."

"I can't imagine, Mai. You have an operative inside the clinic?" asked Catherine. "Why am I not surprised?"

"We have Eddie inside that clinic, Catherine. I just beeped him, and I am sure I will be hearing from him soon," said Mai.

"Eddie Martinez, the man you outed in our security, but later revealed he was turned and working for you?" Catherine grew a big smile on her face slowly as she thought about it. "Yes, I see what you mean. How perfect. Let me know when you hear from him, please. Where are you staying in Munich, or are you going all the way to Salzburg?" she asked.

"Kelly has that information. My assistant sent our itinerary," Mai said, as Kelly held up a sheaf of papers to show Catherine.

Catherine looked over the papers quickly. "We are moving as fast as we can on this end. Apparently, my jet was due for maintenance, but they are now hustling to get it up and ready to go, and we can get a police escort out to the airport, Mai. I see you are planning on staying at the Ludendorff Hotel. That's the place you visited with me when NNP did that story on the German economy and the new chancellor. We will meet you there soonest."

"Yes, Cat. Check in as a member of my party. I have reserved an entire floor for us. See you then," Mai said, hanging up.

As the line went dead, Catherine took charge and looked around the table at the others who were just finishing their breakfasts. As she had done on so many video story productions, she began giving orders. "If any of you are tired, you can sleep on the plane. In my view, the kidnappers are not aware that we know where they are. So we need to move fast. Audrey, if you still want to help as you indicated to me earlier, check with Kelly who is working on your passport so you can work the part of the plan we have in mind. I assume Mr. Hagen that you would like to go with us to help plan things. Your experience might come in handy."

"OK, hold on, Ms. Marsh. Slow down," said Hagen. "Moving fast without proper planning can get people killed. Besides that, what are you talking about? Audrey is not going to be a part of anything," said Hagen.

"Let me explain, Mr. Hagen," she replied. "Mai's daughter, Princess Devi, has a GPS chip embedded in her shoulder that will allow us to pinpoint her location. Unfortunately, its range is limited to about fifty miles. As you heard we think we know where she is being taken. We plan to have Audrey pose as a tourist, and carry a tracking device with her in a backpack. When it activates we will know for sure they are there, and we can advance our plan for extricating them safely. That's all we intend to have her do as part of the plan."

"No way. That is not going to happen," insisted Hagen. "Audrey is my daughter, and you are not going to risk her life on such a dangerous mission. You are risking my daughter to save your son."

"But father, I want to do it. I want to help. It was my idea to go, and I convinced Catherine to let me help. "

She won't be in danger, Mr. Hagen," said Catherine. "We will have escorts posing as her husband, and brother. She will be safe the entire time. No one will ever suspect her."

"When did you plan all this, and what are you talking about, two men posing as your husband and brother? I want to see them," he said. "And I want to hear this plan. All of it."

Kelly left, and in a few minutes returned with two of their security men, Cal and Greg. "Mr. Hagen, meet Cal and Greg. They would be going with Audrey to Austria. Cal will be her husband, and Greg will be posing as her brother. They are both military trained, and served in the first Gulf War."

"And they are just going to show up, and act like tourists. That's your plan?" asked Hagen sarcastically. "I could pick these two out of a crowded stadium as phonies. Has either of you done field work before?"

They both looked at him with blank faces, and neither one of them answered.

"I thought so. You have got to be kidding. No way my little girl is going into that ring of hell with these two. This is not going to happen," he said.

"I agree with your point about a plan, but I still think we have to move quickly, Mr. Hagen," said Catherine. "Otherwise we will lose our advantage.

As it is, we will be in Salzburg almost as soon as they are. They will never suspect we know where they are holding Charlie and Devi. Besides I'm not sure we can trust your opinion on any of this. I mean we really don't know that you're an expert at anything other than hacking on a computer. You say you're this international, criminal person that everyone is looking for but why should we believe you? I will not take any chances where the lives of my children are involved. You saw how horribly wrong that has already gone for those dead agents in Wichita."

Hagen let go of Audrey's hand, sat forward in his chair, and pointed his finger at Catherine. "Down that hallway are six doors. The first opens up into the main area of your condo that is about five thousand square feet. There are four bedrooms all with large king size beds, two are more feminine, one is masculine, Charlie's, I presume, and one is generic. You have a panic room off of the main bedroom where you and your partner, Kelly, sleep. There are three safes in the house, and I can right now open two of them. The third would take me a day, or so, to prepare for. You are said to be worth twenty billion dollars, but lately, you have been giving much of your wealth to charity, and that is being administered by your partner, Kelly whom you love with your whole heart, but you have a secret…"

"That's enough," broke in Catherine. "How did you get all of that information so quickly and while on the run as a fugitive?"

"I didn't. I entered your condo three years ago as part of my research when I was first offered the job to kidnap your son. I did the same for your corporate headquarters. I had complete plans on each provided by another operative AWI had working in here, but they were worthless for my purposes. In any case, I did not find either location acceptable for what I wanted to do.

"There is a safe in this conference room. Can you open it?" she asked.

Hagen got up and stood in front of the bookshelf that made up one wall of the conference room. He pulled a book out, and a door opened revealing a hidden safe with a two by two foot-door with a digital key on the front. He punched in seven numbers, and the silent room all heard an audible 'click' sound as the door unlocked. He didn't bother opening it but sat back down again.

"So, have you hacked into my personal computer too?" Catherine asked.

"And Miss Ryan's," he affirmed, "and I am telling you there is no way I am letting Audrey go on a dangerous mission with these two. Look, you're giving me the same treatment the Feds were giving you earlier. You are making a mistake by excluding me from your plans. I am the most experienced one sitting at this table right now."

"Well, do you have an alternative? What's your idea then?" asked Kelly, showing her frustration.

"I'll go," he said. "Leave her here, and send me instead."

"They know you," said Catherine. "You did that last operation with them."

"They planned it, and it was destined to fail from the beginning. I made it perfect. I coordinated my end of it. But they never saw me, especially as I am now. Even Audrey didn't know me when she first saw me. I am an expert at this. I'll go, and find them."

"We'll both go," said Audrey. "That's the perfect disguise. Father and daughter, who would ever suspect we were on a mission? That's unprecedented."

Catherine thought a moment. "She has a point, Mr. Hagen."

Hagen looked at Audrey while he considered her idea. "You really want to do this?"

"Yes, father, and I want to do it with you."

"Will you promise to do everything I say exactly as I say? No moonlighting, or varying from my orders?"

"Yes, of course. I'm not stupid, father. I have your brains after all," she said, smiling.

Hagen thought for another minute. "Can I have my backpack?" he asked Lieutenant Haleran.

Haleran handed him his black backpack, and Hagen opened a pocket hidden in the bottom. He pulled out a leather folder and spread it out on the desk. What kind of passport did you make up for her?" he asked.

"We have her on an American passport," said Kelly. She has a driver's license, and credit cards too. They look pretty good.

"How long will it take your people to put her on these instead. I already have the credit cards, but I want you to put her on this blank Canadian passport so she will correspond to mine." He handed them a passport he was going to use. He showed them the stamps to duplicate as if they were on former trips together. Then he suggested stamps for their jaunt through Europe. He also suggested hotels that would falsify records for a few dollars. "They're seven hours ahead over there so you can arrange it now. Better yet, let me set it up. You get the passports done, and they better be good. I don't want to get caught holding my...well they better be good."

"Then we're doing it? We're going together, daddy?" she asked with glee.

"Yeah, it really is a great cover, but only if you stop calling me 'daddy'. You're too old for that, and I'm not young enough," he said, hugging her with one arm, and kissing her on the forehead.

"OK, let's regroup, and make sure we have everything we need," said Kelly. "Cal, you look about the same size as Mr. Hagen. Maybe he can borrow from your wardrobe."

"I will accept a few things, so I have a couple of changes of clothes," said Hagen. "But we are flying into Munich. I know some great shops there. I will get all I need there, and it will give me an opportunity to get our characters grounded.

"How do we know you won't just take Audrey, and disappear on us," said Kelly.

"Trust me. I could have already done that if that was my intention," he said. "My commitment is much deeper than that. I hope you believe that. I will have your kids back here in a week. Be ready to move when I say. I will need six of your best men...ex-military is mandatory, guys who follow orders to the letter, and aren't afraid of a firefight. Move them, and have them in position, so they are ready to helicopter in with fifteen minutes notice."

Catherine looked at Kelly and then said, "I trust him. I am still angry with him for what he did, but I trust his sincerity in wanting to help us get them back. I will leave it up to you, Mr. Hagen, to plan your strategy, but please think this through thoroughly. We have been outthought by these people during this whole situation."

"You were outthought by me, not them. I pulled off that kidnapping I'm sorry to say. I believe I am the best at this, and for the first time I am really feeling good about what I'm doing."

Catherine nodded. "I think you two need to go with Kelly to be sure you approve of the passport stamps," she said.

Chapter 42

June 2005   On the way to Munich

Exasperated best described Mai's mood when she picked up the phone. "Jack, where have you been?" she asked, from the cabin of her private jet just as they were leaving New Delhi on her way to Munich. "I have been trying to get hold of you for the last twenty-four hours.

"I'm at Ramstein Air Base now, Mai. It has been a crazy day getting here. They took Jasmine direct on a Medevac, but Marty and I got bumped at the last minute and had to catch a shuttle. We were incommunicado for a bit. I just checked on Jasmine, and she is doing fine. It really is an amazing facility, and they're fawning over her like she was a rock star. What's up?" asked Jack

"Jack, Devi, and Charlie were kidnapped in Chicago. We are certain it was Yameda along with Su Ling who took them," said Mai.

"Oh my god, Mai!" said Jack, surprised. "I will get a flight back to Chicago as soon as I can."

"No, Jack, stay there. You're in Frankfurt, right? Ramstein is near Frankfurt? You need to get to the Ludendorff Hotel in Munich. We have booked an entire floor, and will be working out of there," said Mai. "We believe they are holding them in Europe. I am flying there right now. Can I reach you at this two-five-five-number?" she asked.

"Uh, no…this is a base phone. I told you my cell phone was destroyed during the firefight," he reminded her.

"OK, Jack get to Munich ASAP. For god's sake, get a satellite phone, or at least a cell phone, and call me when you do. I will be in the air for about ten more hours but keep trying to call me. I still have one more refueling stop, probably about four hours from now. Just keep trying until we make contact. We have a plan in place to get them back, but you know what they want."

"Give them whatever they want, Mai, if it means getting our kids back," said Jack. "Nothing else matters. You know that."

"Yes, I know. Where is the piece of the handle right now that you and Marty found?" she asked.

"Amir has it wherever he is by now. We got separated because Marty and I were trying to get the first flights we could to get here to be with Jasmine. We were on the same flight with her originally until they bumped us when they filled up with wounded. Then we were at the mercy of base ops. They put us on a shuttle, and it took us a little longer to get here. Amir is traveling straight to Ramstein on a CIA junket and is supposed to be following us after putting his kids on a civilian flight to the US," said Jack. "The artifact is protected in a large Halliburton case, and we all decided that the CIA junket was the best bet for transporting it safely, and keeping it secure."

"OK, be sure you follow up on that. I assume he will come to the hospital to link up with you two?"

"Yeah, that's the plan, Mai. Marty and Jasmine will be here to wait for him, and I will move on to Munich. Marty and I only got on the shuttle because we had no luggage. I am getting pretty ripe. Fair warning. You said the Ludendorff, right? Do you suppose someone can get some clothes for me by the time I arrive."

"Yeah, Jack…got to go…you are breaking up. I love you, Jack Largent. See you soon," said Mai, as the line went dead.

"I love you too," he said, to an empty line.

Jack hung up the telephone and rushed back to Jasmine's room where he found her and Marty talking. Marty was holding her hand. Jasmine was sitting up in her bed looking quite normal while a nurse took her temperature.

Jack waited for the nurse to leave, and then brought both of them up to date. Jasmine threw off the covers and started to get up.

"Whoa," said Marty, pulling her back into bed. "Where do you think you're going?"

"I am going with Jack to Munich, Marty, what do you think?" she told him.

"You are not going anywhere," said Jack, as he pushed her back. "You need to rest now and get back your strength. You were shot, for god's sake."

"You're not leaving me here. I feel fine, Jack. It was a through and through, and it's only my shoulder. You said yourself they did a great job on me here. I can be of more help with you involved in getting them back, instead of sitting here on my ass," she protested.

"No, you stay, and that's an order from Mai. Someone has to be here when Amir arrives anyway. If you feel up to it, then you can come to join us in Munich at the Ludendorff. Please, Jasmine, do as you're told. I have lots to do, and can't deal with loose ends well right now," said Jack. He was a bit flustered as the realization of the news of the kidnapping was starting to have an impact on him.

"Don't worry, Jack. I will stay with her, and wait for Amir. You go get Devi back," Marty said.

"I will call you as soon as I get a new phone," he said. "Oh, but you need to get a new phone yourself. Listen, I will be at the Ludendorff Hotel in Munich. Get a phone, and call me first chance you get, or whenever you can. I have to run. I have to get going and figure this out," he said, heading for the door.

"Do you know where you can catch a quick flight to Munich?" asked Jasmine? "There is a charter service out of base ops. I have used it during my training. It will be the fastest way to get to Munich," suggested Jasmine, with growing concern for the way he was acting. Jasmine did not want to leave Jack alone with the news that Devi and Charlie had been kidnapped. She knew him better than almost anyone. In her view, he was not himself and was going to need some serious counseling while he processed that information.

"Thanks, I will go there first then," said Jack, nodding his head.

"See, you do need me," she said, getting up, and moving to the closet to retrieve her clothes.

Jack looked concerned and unsure what to do as he watched her sort her clothes. He put his hand on her shoulder.

"I'm fine," she insisted. "This through and through is bothersome, that's all, and I am not even on morphine. It is important we work together on this. Come on, boss. You know you want me to go with you, don't you?" She unabashedly got dressed in front of them. Her shoulder hurt like the dickens, but she wasn't going to let them know that.

Marty showed his disappointment, "OK, I will wait for Amir to join me here, and then follow you two to Munich. Go get Devi back."

Jasmine turned and kissed him, meaningfully holding his head in both her hands firmly as she did and leaving no doubt as to her feelings. They rushed out the door leaving Marty looking at their backs with some regret.

Chapter 43

June 2005 Munich Germany

Hagen and Audrey arrived in Munich first and separate from the rest of the Chicago group by twelve hours. When they discovered that Mai was just checking in with her entourage, they decided to avoid any connection with them, and keep to themselves in case Mai was being watched.

They were already outfitted in new clothes that Hagen had chosen for them to be sure they did not stand out in a crowd. They decided to catch up on a busy first day with a late lunch in the hotel dining room. Audrey thoroughly enjoyed spending time with her long-lost father, and the more she found out about him, the more intrigued she became. She had his genes and was more of an adventurer and chance-taker herself. As he told her some of his stories, she could see it was in his blood, and she wondered how he was going to fare giving it all up.

"I think we should spend the night over in Salzburg," he suggested. "Now that we are properly outfitted, there is no reason to stay here, and the sooner we get a lay of the land, the better. So, are you up for more travel today?"

"Sure," she replied. "I'm anxious to get Devi back. In a short time, she has become a very special friend to me. We can't let anything happen to her, dad."

"Yeah, or either of them," he replied "Audrey, listen to me. One thing concerns me. When we get into Salzburg, you do everything I say, just the way I say to do it. Don't freelance, don't be flippant. This is very serious stuff. These people are the worst of the worst and trust me, I am speaking from experience."

"I have to say the shooting range this morning did a lot for my confidence, but it also drove home the gravity of what we are doing," said Audrey.

"Good, because it can't get more dangerous than this."

"But you best these kinds of people all the time, don't you?" she asked him.

"Yes, but this one is different, and I usually have more time to consider all of my options. I can still picture Devi lying in that casket. That image will haunt me to my grave if I do not save her, and darling you have to know that I will step in front of a bullet if I have to for her. I must make things right. My world is out of kilter right now, especially since those two victims have become real after meeting you, and their families."

"We can do this together," said Audrey. "I'm proud of you, dad, really proud that you are helping to get them back. It means a lot to me. I needed to believe in you as the white knight I always dreamed you to be."

Hagen laughed. "White knight, huh? I'll do my best to live up to that. Let's pay this bill, and get out of here. We have lots to do before we get to sleep tonight."

Audrey watched as two people, a man, and a woman entered the restaurant and were shown seats on the opposite side of the dining room.

"Hey, dad," she said, "I bet that's Jack Largent. Oh, and I bet that's Jasmine. I wonder why her arm is in a sling," said Audrey.

"Come on, baby. What makes you think that's Jack Largent? Those two could be perfect strangers," he challenged her.

"Well, Devi told me when he goes on location, he always wears a photo vest that her mom would have loved to have thrown away years ago. That man is wearing a photo vest, and frankly, that is the first one I've ever seen. Then he shows up with an Asian woman who is too young to be Queen Mai, so it makes sense it might be his assistant Jasmine."

"If you're right then we better be on our way right now," he said.

"Why? Don't you think we should introduce ourselves?" she asked.

"And just how would you introduce me?" he asked.

"Oh, I see what you mean. But you will have to meet him sometime during this operation. We had better run that by Kelly before things get awkward," she said.

She got up and added, "I'm ready…let's get our things, and get on to Salzburg."

By the following morning, the entire group had assembled in Munich, Germany, and were ensconced in rooms on the top floor of the Ludendorff Hotel. They were eager to put a plan in place and were approximately seventy miles from Salzburg across the border in Austria. Besides the luxury suites and rooms, making up that floor, there was also a conference room that became their operations center. It was a facility that Catherine had used before when NearNorth Production projects took them to Germany.

Daniel Vega was flying in two helicopters on large transports along with other equipment that might be needed. He set up at an airport hangar in the nearby town of Wasserberg, not far from the Austrian border and Salzburg. Ramadi had twenty of his men bivouacked there waiting for them.

They had their second meeting early on Tuesday morning. With everyone having had time to prepare, they got down to business. Catherine's production crew had gathered maps, aerial views, and photographs of the clinic.

A careful study of the layout of the clinic showed that even a minor defense on the part of the kidnappers might prove fatal for a lot of people including the two kidnap victims. The buildings of the clinic complex were positioned like a fortress when you observed them with that perspective. No assault plan promised a lack of wounded or even fatalities.

"Have you heard anything from Martinez?" Catherine asked Mai.

"No. Cell phone reception here seems to be more sporadic, and I can't make contact with him. My calls can't get through," Mai told her.

"Yeah, I got the same thing. They might be running interference from there blocking all calls and communications. I want you to consider something," she said. "You may not get any help from Eddie."

"No, you don't understand. He would do anything for me," Mai said. "I'm sure of it."

"Having set up a lot of involved and tricky productions in my profession, I know a warning of trouble when I see it," explained Catherine. "We already have evidence that these people are illusive and deceptive, and there just may be something going on here we aren't seeing. Until we know differently, you have to consider that they have discovered he is your operative. They may have killed or disabled him in some way, and not allowed him to contact you. We will have to plan as if he's not there to help us.

Mai disagreed. "We still have Hagen, and the deceptive part of the kidnapping was his idea, not theirs. I don't think they are tricky beyond hiding where they are. Hagen told me after doing some reconnaissance, he has a pretty good idea of where they are being kept," she said.

"Who is Hagen?" asked Jack.

Catherine looked at Mai, and asked, "Didn't you tell him about Hagen?"

"You know I am not good at that," said Mai. "But now is as good a time as any. Let's get it over with."

"Jack, if I can handle it, you can," said Catherine. "Hagen is one of the kidnappers who surrendered himself to us. He has helped us find where they took Devi and Charlie and is now in Salzburg planning a way to get them back."

"Oh my god!" said Jack. "Do you mean we are all here sitting around this table waiting for one of the original kidnappers to come up with a plan to get them back? Does that really sound reasonable to any of you?"

Mai stood up, and said, in a voice that dared anyone to disobey her, "Jack, Jasmine, and Kelly come with me into the next room for a conversation. Now!"

From the conference room, they heard some yelling back and forth as the conversation ensued. But soon it died down to normal, and in few minutes they all returned and sat around the conference table.

Mai said, "Jack has been fully briefed, understands our motives, and is on board with our strategy. Let's get on with it, shall we?"

"The first thing we need to do is to determine if Devi and Charlie are in there. Since they are blocking communications, it might be difficult to do, but Hagen and Audrey are working on that right now," said Catherine.

"What can I do?" asked Jasmine, "Please, let me help."

Catherine answered, "I have collected as much information on that clinic as I can find according to Hagen's request. I think we have done a thorough job, and we have information he might need such as to the location of electrical panels, and underground sewers, ventilation, etc. We need someone to get that to him, so Jasmine that might be a job for you to take care of. OK?"

"Sure, I'm ready when you are," she said.

That afternoon three agents from Homeland Security showed up unexpectedly at the door of Catherine's suite in Munich. She was stunned as they said they were there to arrest her and escort her back to the United States on charges of obstructing justice. The agent doing all of the talking was one of the ones who assisted the Director of Homeland Security two nights ago in the Command Center in Chicago. He seemed to be unsure at first, but then gained more confidence as their conversation continued over a table in her suite. That is, until Catherine said, "Get your boss, Hammond Morris on the phone right now."

Simultaneously, Big Ben entered the suite with three other members of Catherine's security. Moments earlier, Kelly had seen the Homeland Security agents arrive, and she alerted Big Ben who she now followed into the room.

"I am not sure I can get hold of him," the agent said, nervously. "We have a warrant for your arrest if you care to look."

Catherine read over the long legal document, and then looked up at him. "This has no legal status here, and trust me, I have more pull with the local authorities than you do. I am not moving until you get your director on the line, and we have a conversation. Tell your men to get out of my suite, and wait in the hallway, or I will have all three of you thrown out of this hotel. Understood?" she demanded, angrily.

The agent grudgingly motioned for the two men to leave, and Big Ben's men escorted them out. The agent then got on his cell phone and made a call. Much to his relief, his boss, Homeland Security Director Hammond Morris, was waiting for a status call from him and answered almost immediately. After a moment he handed the cell phone to Catherine.

"You want to explain why you would put out an arrest warrant on me, Director Morris?" she began.

"I have it on good, and reliable information that you have found one of the supposed victims, a miss Audrey Goodnight, and kept her hidden from us while we were downstairs at the same time risking our lives trying to save her. That's called obstruction of justice, and you are going to have to answer for it, Ms. Marsh. Your failure to report her presence may have cost the lives of eight of my men. We will have answers, and you had better not try anything cute, or you will spend a long time behind bars for this fiasco," he warned her ominously.

"I am going to put you on speaker phone, Director Morris so you can hear what I tell my production crew. Kelly, get Lloyd, Verna, and Max in here. We have a story that needs covering. By the way, Director, the Chicago police department was completely informed of our actions, and we held our information close because we possessed information that there was a mole within my organization thus necessitating our secrecy."

"Don't try to play me, Ms. Marsh. You don't have the balls, and I own the ballpark. I have a very strong case against you," claimed the director.

"Director Morris, such language! I should have warned you that all of my calls are recorded as a matter of routine procedure," said Catherine.

"That could never be used in court," he replied.

"Well, that depends on what court you are referring to, Director. I happen to regularly plead my cases in the court of public opinion, which usually trumps any other court," said Catherine.

"You will be ruined, Ms. Marsh. I will see to it," he asserted.

Catherine ignored him. "Lloyd, you still have the video recording of the meeting in the command center that night correct? OK, we will start with the part where they ended up in Wichita based on an anonymous tip. They walked into a trap based on an anonymous tip. How smart was that? Mai told the Director over and over that something wasn't right and all but begged him to use caution, and not send his men into that hangar, which later blew up in their faces. I think she even told him that the aircraft inside that hangar was not the right aircraft and that the transponder reading was weird. That was before he cut off any further of her protests of his hasty actions by summarily closing the laptop link that allowed us to communicate with her. Oh, and be sure to note that I was out of the room at the moment of the assault talking with the FBI Agent in Charge, and Mai who was giving him further evidence that the Director of Homeland Security was ignoring. Hey, we can run two screens simultaneously showing Director Morris giving the orders, and Mai informing the FBI AIC of important evidence to further consider before sending men into that hangar to be slaughtered. Let's spend a good long time going over the aftermath. That will be pretty moving footage. Better yet, Verna, get all of that footage out to the major news agencies immediately for breaking news on the inside story of the disaster in Wichita.

"You can't do…"

"You bet I can, Director Morris and you can bet your days as a director of anything are done. You will be lucky to be directing an ice cream truck after everyone sees how you bungled this," said Catherine. "You mess with my people and me, and I will end your career so completely that no one will ever want to talk to you in Washington, or anywhere ever again. How dare you try to put the failure resulting from your own narrow-minded, condescending incompetence on me, the grieving mother of one of the kidnap victims. I am going to hand the phone back to your agent here. If he is not gone in five minutes, this story goes international in the next five minutes after that with complete video footage of everything you did wrong that night, you stupid little man."

"Well, I was…"

Catherine interrupted him again, "And if I even see the hint of a Federal agent around me or my people in the next two weeks, this story is going out, guaranteed. Do you understand me, Director?"

"Yes, I guess I do. You are threatening the Director of Homeland Security," he said, trying to gain some advantage with his own threat.

"No, I am trying to save you from becoming a bigger fool than you already are, Director. Put your smug, arrogant ego away, and listen to someone who really is trying to help you just as you didn't listen the other night. You killed those men. You might as well have pushed the plunger on that bomb yourself. What's it going to be, Director?" she asked him, finally.

There was a momentary pause after which Director Morris said, "Please take me off speaker phone, and put me back on with my agent."

Catherine punched off the speaker and handed the cell phone back to the agent who surprisingly had a pleasant smile on his face. "Yes, sir. I understand. Yes, sir. Right away, sir," he said, and closed the cell phone.

The agent looked over at Catherine, and said, "Thank you, Ms. Marsh. That was refreshing. Frankly, I am a fan and did not look forward to arresting you. Have a nice day. My team and I will be leaving back for the United States now."

He turned and left the room as everyone present exchanged high-fives but Catherine. "Can you imagine what they would do if they knew we had Hagen here?" said Kelly.

Catherine shook her head. "Either way it is not a time to be celebrating. Let's get to work. I want to be sure there is nothing that we've missed, and we need to find out who is at the clinic right now. Who is working on that?" asked Catherine.

Chapter 44

June 2005   Salzburg, Austria

A udrey heard a knock at her door and answered with a pleasant smile on her face when she saw her father. He was dressed like an American tourist in tan slacks, long sleeve shirt, light tan jacket, and a floppy fedora. He even had a set of binoculars around his neck and carried a backpack.

"I chose jeans, and a heavier jacket to wear," she said, turning around for him to check. "It looks like it might get frosty later on."

"That's fine," he said. "You pass. How's your room?" he asked.

She turned back, and said, "Kind of funny in a way. This whole place is like a fairytale. Look at the bed, dad, seven feet long, and three feet wide. But the Eiderdown quilt is a foot thick! I feel like Alice, or Snow White or something…and look out the window. What do you see?" she asked.

Hagen went over to the second story window and looked out. The street was very narrow and charming with little shops lined up on either side that added to the Disneyland main street look of the place.

"Hah! Of course, a toy shop. What could be more perfect!" he said.

"Exactly!" she affirmed. "We have driven into a fairytale."

Indeed parts of Salzburg did look like it was imagined in a fairytale. It is a small compact city with narrow streets dominated by a tenth-century castle. Most of it looked like it had been untouched for centuries, and just beyond, the Alps raised up to heavenly heights. But over the previous thirty years, big hotels and new buildings had come to turn the familiar sleepy town of Mozart fame into more of a modern metropolis nestled at the foot of the mountains.

"What's the plan?" she asked.

"First, just like yesterday, you be alert at all times. Got your weapon?" he asked.

Audrey took out her Beretta 9mm, loaded the clip, chambered a round and checked the safety. On the private charter over from the United States, Hagen had drilled her on the use of the small firearm. At first she seemed a bit wary, but he had to admit that now, after spending two hours on a Munich private shooting range, she looked like she knew how to handle herself. He hoped he never had to find out if her training would pay off.

"OK," he said. "Be a tourist, smile a lot, and have fun, but look for inconsistencies too. We don't know if they are aware we're here, and it is always better to see them first. I think we will tour the castle today, and from there we can check for the chip. Ready?"

Audrey nodded yes, and then hugged him tightly, and gave him a kiss on the cheek. "I'm a little nervous."

"That's good. Focus," he said, wondering where the plans for the clinic were that Catherine had promised him. He noted earlier that morning when he drove alone by the clinic that there seemed to be some sort of interference around the complex, and that concerned him. He wondered if that interference would stop them from accessing the chip in Devi's shoulder.

Two hours later, they stood at the topmost parapet of the tenth-century castle that overlooked Salzburg and gazed at the surrounding green hills, and glorious Alpine mountains beyond. They were alone, as the tour they were taking had moved on without them.

In the distance toward the south, they could see a modern two-story building complex with front and back buildings separated. All of this was surrounded by a high wall and was nestled on a road with similar modern buildings toward the outskirts of town. The wall was formidable and had a guarded gate for an entrance. There was only one tastefully small sign near the entrance indicating the name of the facility. The front buildings seemed to be somewhat occupied, and busy, while the ones toward the back seemed deserted. An oversized parking lot by the back buildings contained only two vehicles both large black vans. But the front building had several cars, and a white ambulance parked nearby.

Hagen looked at Audrey who was working with something in her backpack on the stone floor of the castle turret. "Are you getting a signal?" he asked.

She nodded folding the flap over again closing it. "She's there alright." She got up to look over the sides of the rock tower out at the bright storybook countryside of Southern Austria beyond the sprawling city. "That white two-story building is the clinic, right?" she asked.

"Yes, I drove by there this morning before I came to get you, and there was interference of some kind coming from there. I was hoping it did not block the reception from the chip in her shoulder. Let's go over to the other visage and talk," he suggested, leading her to the North side of the tower.

Two more couples joined them on the parapet and were looking out at the countryside with snow-capped mountains beyond. One couple was Asian, and they began posing for pictures of each other right away. The other looked American, and they appeared to be tourists in their late fifties or early sixties.

The woman said eagerly, "Honey, look! I think that's the house they used for the movie Sound of Music. I don't see the Gazebo behind it though, but there is one behind the house next to it. Hey, you know what? I bet they used the back of the next house for the Gazebo scenes. Come on, let's see if we can actually go there, and see it up close," she suggested, pulling him back to the stairs.

Hagen and Audrey were on the opposite side of the parapet and talking softly to each other. "I have to tell you I am actually surprised you were able to get the signal. I would have thought the interference would have blocked that too. Wait a minute," Hagen said, as he began checking something on his cell phone.

"Yeah, the interference is gone. Interesting. I wonder what the implications of that are. We need to think about that, Audrey. Whatever the reason our equipment should be able to monitor that facility a lot better now."

Opposite them, the American couple were paused collecting themselves, while the Asian couple was already descending the stairs.

The man was still bent down with his hands on his knees after climbing the many stairs to the top of the castle overlooking Salzburg. "Wait just a minute, Charlotte. Let me catch my breath. We don't want to call another ambulance for me, do we? None of that stuff is going away anytime soon," he protested.

He turned toward Hagen and saw he and Audrey were watching them. He said smiling, "Hello, we are Burt and Charlotte Holmes from Indianapolis. Are you Americans by any chance?"

"Why, yes," Hagen answered. "I'm Fred Hanley, and this is my daughter, Audrey. We are from Chicago. Beautiful country isn't it? Did I hear you say you called an ambulance?"

"Nothing major, I just got light headed the other night over some Wiener Schnitzel and sauerkraut."

"You passed out and were on the floor, Burt," protested Charlotte.

"Well, it was nothing. The wonderful air around here seems to be doing wonders for me. This is the prettiest view we've seen so far, and we have been in Europe driving around for three weeks now," Burt said.

Charlotte continued, "We are thinking of driving up to Berchtesgaden tomorrow. Hey, Burt, maybe they would like to join us."

"Yes! Would you like to join us and tour Berchtesgaden? I hear it is a beautiful trip, and the views are supposed to be spectacular." Burt said.

"Oh, dad, that sounds wonderful," said Audrey.

"Well, we can't, pumpkin," said Hagen. "We have a Mozart tour we have scheduled from Chicago. I'm a big fan, and I hate to miss that. We are going to see "The Magic Flute" tonight at the opera house."

"Oh well, it was a shot in the dark. Perhaps we can tie up the next day, and do something. What do you think?" suggested Burt.

"Sure. We will still be around. We are staying at that small hotel downtown across from the toy store; the Hohenberg," Hagen said. "But speaking of tours we have to run. We have another tour starting soon. It was nice meeting you," he said, as he led Audrey from the parapet, and down the stone stairs.

"Whew! That was close," she said.

"Yes, but I figured out how I am going to get into that clinic. Did you notice anything unusual up there?" Hagen asked.

"Huh? No," she said. "We got the signal from the clinic, that's all."

"Those Asian tourists were taking lots of photos. Every time they posed we were in the background of their photos," he said. "They did not get a good photo of me, but they will have your face on their walls by tonight I'm sure," he said.

"Oh my God! Dad, I have a lot to learn, don't I."

Hagen looked concerned for a moment, and Audrey asked, "What is it?"

"Something just occurred to me, and if I'm right, we need to make our move very soon. Audrey, I think we had better get into that clinic, and right away."

An hour later, Audrey and Hagen were sitting in their car parked opposite a Salzburg hospital where several ambulances were parked. Hagen was focused on a delivery bay outside of the emergency room.

"This is going to be tricky," he said. "What time is it?"

She checked her watch. "Almost one o'clock, dad. What's your plan?"

In the next moment, another ambulance pulled into the bay, and two EMTs got out and walked toward the hospital.

"Keep your eye on that ambulance," he said. "I will be right back, and if I get in it, and drive it away, you follow. Got it?'

"What? Sure, but what...?" Her question was broken off as Hagen abruptly got out of their car. He raced to the emergency entrance and entered not long behind the two EMTs.

He followed the EMTs down the hall and got into an elevator with them. He followed them down one floor, and into a large cafeteria area where there was a celebration of some kind going on during lunch. They went right to a table with other EMTs in uniform and made a quick greeting before getting into a long line for food. He turned and quickly left the hospital once more.

As soon as he exited the building, he went right to the ambulance that had just driven up with the two EMTs who were now down in the hospital cafeteria. He quickly checked and found the keys inside as he suspected. He got in and drove it out of the hospital emergency area without incident, or anyone paying any attention. Audrey already had her rental started, and followed him close behind. Several streets over they found a secluded area to park their rental car, and Audrey joined him as she got into the driver's seat of the ambulance. He was wearing a local EMT jacket, and he had one for her. She put it on, adjusted the seat, and said, "Ready."

They drove off with Hagen directing her until they were near the clinic.

"OK, as we come over this next hill, park on the right of the road overlooking the clinic, so we can see what we're up against," he said.

After they had parked, he noticed Audrey seemed apprehensive. "I suspect we will only need to get by the guard at the gate, and then we can drive and park by that back building. But you never know with these things. I usually don't do stuff like this without having every detail figured out." Hagen paused to think for a moment. "Be flexible, Audrey, and be ready for anything. Follow my lead. Got it?

"Sure, dad. I'm OK."

Chapter 45

June 2005 Salzburg, Austria

Eddie Martinez was performing brilliantly as the Direktor of Operations-von Salzburg clinic. But in the last twenty-four hours, things had changed dramatically reminding him that his world was one with menacing horizons, and it did not do well for him to ignore them. He was making a final inspection of the clinic for the night, and desperately in need of a few hours sleep after a very long and stressful day. He had not slept in the last twenty-four hours due to the unexpected arrival of the sedated kidnap victims Charlie Marsh, and Devearney Largent. The stress was beginning to play on his paranoia especially since he had not been forewarned of their coming, or been able to call Queen Maisong about it since.

He was stunned when he first saw them secretly delivered and wheeled in unconscious the previous day. They came with exact orders from Su Ling, and he directed them to the two most private suites in the rear of the back building called the Anhang as instructed. He had seen the news of the kidnapping in the morning paper, but never dreamed they would end up in his facility. There had been others before that arrived for a time at the Anhang for whatever useful purpose Yameda and Su Ling needed of them. But it was not until twenty-four hours after the kidnapping on the streets of Chicago that these two kidnap victims showed up at the clinic with the world thinking they must be somewhere, anywhere, but in that fairytale setting.

They arrived with a nurse to see to their medication and a contingent of Asian mercenaries housed in the barracks above. He had carefully read over the detailed instructions from Su Ling concerning their confinement and care while at the facility, which he was expected to follow to the letter.

Almost immediately, he tried to contact Queen Maisong, and was surprised when he could not get a connection with his cell phone. He had been trying ever since with no success. He knew he had to let her know where they were, and beyond that, he had to figure a way to save them from what was most certainly a dire fate. Landlines were out of the question because he knew that Yameda's men monitored and spied on their own people at the clinic, and monitoring of landlines was performed as a matter of routine. He had no doubt his large apartment just beyond the facility was thoroughly bugged. He decided to go into Salzburg soon and find a phone. He couldn't put it off any longer. Whether due to a lack of sleep, or the situation in general, he was becoming very nervous. His old survival-sensing gut was working overtime.

As was his procedure he checked the upstairs facility of the Anhang expecting to see the mercenaries on his way through the long corridor of rooms. Instead, he found the area deserted, and assumed they had gone into Salzburg for some diversion. He was positive Su Ling would tell him soon enough about their mission, and how he could assist them. He would deal with that when the time came.

The only break from the routine of the clinic beyond the arrival of the two kidnap victims had been a surprise visit by a pair of electricians who were updating the electrical service for new equipment due to be installed in the Anhang. He tried to put them off, but they had a work order authorized by Yameda that came with orders to expedite immediately. The electrical space was situated between Charlie and Devi's rooms in the Anhang, and their proximity to the kidnap victims had Martinez on edge most of the day. They had finished their work early in the afternoon and departed after getting a signature from the attending nurse. As he walked by Charlie Marsh's room, he came to the door of the electrical room and realized he had not inspected their work that day.

Acting as a hospital administrator, Martinez took his responsibilities seriously. He set the rules for the operational safety of the clinic, and he felt that every function of the clinic's activities was within his purview. He stopped, keyed open the door, and went in. There was a newer larger electrical panel positioned next to the old one, but it was obvious that the installation was only half finished. He remembered the men mentioning something about returning when the final power requirements for the new equipment were confirmed. He gave a nod to an apparently incomplete job well done thus far. As he left he noticed a small one-inch blue wire segment on the clean polished floor of the electrical room. He picked it up, twirled it in his fingertips, turned off the light, and closed the door.

As he passed Devi's room, he looked in once more to check on her. She was sleeping soundly. There was no good reason why they had taken her. He was convinced of that. He vowed that no harm would come to her. She was under his protection now. He left her door open as he walked out. He had gone half-way down the hallway when it suddenly occurred to him that the wire segment he found on the floor of the electrical room was too thin for an electrical panel. It was more suited for a toy, or something more ominous. His gut contracted, and, purely on a hunch, he grabbed a Phillips screwdriver from a toolbox kept in a closet by the nurse's station, and hurried back to enter the electrical room.

He had not been a survivor by ignoring his instincts, and right now a little voice was telling him something was wrong. He worked out the screws on one side of the new electrical panel and pulled back the metal casing a bit to look inside.

What he saw stunned him, and he jumped back in surprise. He careful-ly pulled back the panel a bit more and confirmed his worst fears. There was enough C-4 explosive within the panel to blow that area of the building to bits, killing everyone in it. He finished unscrewing the rest of the screws, and care-fully removed the panel. He had seen enough bombs in his time to know that this one could be set off by a telephone call to the cell phone wired to its deto-nator. That could happen at any time. He was not sure what to do, and had no experience with wiring, or diffusing bombs. The one thing he could not let hap-pen was that any harm would come to Princess Devi. He left the room quickly.

The other disturbing thought was that they had not told him about the bomb. It was now conceivable that they were aware he had changed sides, and one only had to look at the C4 to find evidence supporting that theory.

He went outside toward the back of the Anhang just to get some fresh air, and think more clearly about what to do. He decided to try to contact Queen Maisong once more. He punched in the number and was surprised to hear it connecting. She answered the call almost immediately. "Eddie, we have been trying to call you. Are you OK?" she asked, with some concern.

"Yes, my lady, I have been trying to call you all day, but have not been able to get through for some reason. I have to tell you Devi and Charlie are here in the clinic, and we must get them out right away. There is a bomb that can be activated by cell phone, and it could go off any time. We must hurry," he said frantically.

"Eddie, we have an operative who is nearby. His name is Hagen. Wait. Eddie, did you say a cell phone could activate the bomb?"

"Yes, my lady. I saw the mechanism," he explained.

"Eddie, don't you think it odd that you can suddenly call out again by cell phone when you have not been able to all day? Get them out of there right now, Eddie. Hurry!" she ordered him. "I am sending a helicopter right away."

"Yes, my lady," he said closing his cell phone abruptly and running back toward the back door of the Anhang.

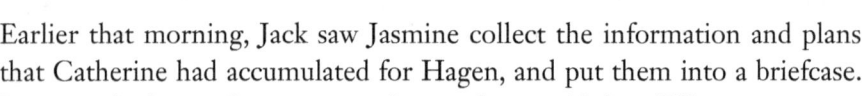

Earlier that morning, Jack saw Jasmine collect the information and plans that Catherine had accumulated for Hagen, and put them into a briefcase. Just outside the conference room, he caught up with her. "Want some company?" he asked.

"Sure, boss. The more, the merrier. Why? You gettin' an itch to see Salzburg?"

"I'm getting an itch about a lot of things, Jas. I would feel a lot better if we had more control over things. Maybe you and I can at least get a look at that clinic while we are there to put things into more of a perspective."

Later that same day, they were disappointed at the hotel when they were told that Mr. Hanley, Hagen's alias, and Audrey were out. Jack had hoped to meet Hagen, but not to beat the crap out of the guy for kidnapping Devi as everyone thought. He just wanted to know his plan for getting them back since no one else seemed to have any idea. He passed over the briefcase with all the blueprints and papers gathered by Catherine's people to the desk clerk with instructions to give them to Mr. Hanley when he returned. Having accomplished nothing thus far, they settled for taking a drive and to eyeball the clinic where everyone thought Devi and Charlie were held prisoner.

As they exited the hotel, Jack mentioned that he wished they were armed, and Jasmine without a word opened the trunk of the black Mercedes S-Class she was driving revealing her arsenal of weapons. "Holy crap, Jas, he said, "I am going to miss you as my assistant. Where did you get all of this around here?"

"Ramadi brought a lot, even RPG's, and I'm not going anywhere that I know of, boss," she said.

"Now you're lying to me. We both know where you are going and his name is Marty."

"Yep," she said, "at least I hope so, but that said, I still don't know if I am going anywhere. I'm missing him right now."

She handed him a 9-millimeter and put one in the back of her pants under her coat. "Feels like Mosul all over again, boss. How 'bout you?"

Jack nodded, and hoped she was wrong.

Armed and ready, their drive to the clinic took them about twenty minutes because they took a more roundabout route, and approached it from the other direction. It turned out to be a beautiful drive in the afternoon, which they did with the windows open. The air was clean and crisp, so by the time they arrived in the vicinity, they both felt invigorated. As they crested the hill overlooking the location of the clinic, they stopped to look.

"It doesn't look like a criminal enterprise," commented Jasmine.

"No, but you want to bet my little girl is in that back building? What do you think?" he asked.

"Well, from what I can see, if we can get by that gate, and over to the side of the first building we pretty much have cover until the space between the front, and back buildings. It really doesn't look like a difficult thing to do, but there may be surveillance we don't know about. Are you thinking of going in?" she asked.

"I wasn't when we started out, Jas. But now I really want to go get her. What do you think?" he asked. "Am I being stupid?"

"I tell you what. Let's drive up to the front gate, and check it out. We can pull the lost tourist routine. At least we will have a better idea of their security," she said.

Jack nodded and she pulled the black Mercedes away from the curve, and down the hill toward the entrance. Parked on the right side of the road was a white ambulance with two EMTs inside talking. As they turned into the gate, they found it open without a guard on duty. They stopped for a moment and waited, but no one approached them. Then on an impulse, Jasmine drove right in, and slowly made her way to the back building and parked.

They looked at each other as if both were wondering if they should go any further. Jack said, "I think we should at least take a look. You game?"

They got out quietly while looking around. Not seeing anyone they moved on, and as they neared the door leading to the back building, they pulled their weapons.

Hagen and Audrey watched the big Mercedes pull up the gate, pause, and then drive in.

"Who do you think that is?" she asked.

Hagen was scanning the clinic with his binoculars and didn't see anyone in the clinic anywhere.

"Not sure, but it doesn't matter," said Hagen. "What does matter is that no one questioned them at the front gate. There is no guard on duty in that guard shack. Come on, that's our cue. Let's head in there," he said, still looking through his binoculars.

But then he thought he caught a glimpse of something. He scanned back again and waited a moment. Suddenly, he saw a man peer out from around the first building as the Mercedes parked.

"Crap!" he said. Then he saw the man and woman from the hotel get out of the Mercedes. "Jack Largent and Jasmine," he said aloud.

"Huh? You mean they're there?" asked Audrey.

"Yeah, looks like an ambush though. I think it's a setup. Audrey, get out right now. I'm going in there, and it's going to get very dangerous for you."

Audrey replied by pulling away from the curb and heading for the entrance to the clinic.

Jack opened the door, and he and Jasmine quickly slid into the back building where they found a long dimly lit hallway. At the other end they could see lights on, but otherwise, that floor of the building appeared deserted and quiet.

Silently, they made their way down the corridor and stopped suddenly. They ducked for cover in a doorway recess when a nurse came into view, and walked further down the hallway and entered a room.

Jasmine signaled Jack to wait as she stealthily moved down the corridor and entered the same room. In a moment, she came back out and signaled eagerly for Jack to come. He followed her, and when he entered the room, he saw Devi in the hospital bed asleep. On the floor next to the bed was the nurse who Jasmine had incapacitated.

He hurried to Devi, bent over, and kissed her forehead.

"She's OK, just drugged I think," said Jasmine. She has cuffs on. Try to get them off with this," she said, handing him a scalpel she found on the counter. "I am going to see if there is anyone else lurking about."

As Martinez passed the nurse's station coming from the rear of the Anhang, he did not see the nurse and wondered if she was checking on her patients. The Anhang was separate from the clinic itself, and it was shut down except for the area holding the two kidnap victims on the first floor. This made it perfect, and there were no guards present on the first floor because they weren't necessary under the circumstances. Both victims were sedated and locked to their beds in hand cuffs on the right wrist of each of them.

He went to Devi's room and noticed the door he had left open was now closed. He silently opened it expecting to see the nurse checking her vitals. In his mind he made up a story to get her out of the building for a while so he could get the two kidnap victims safely away. Instead in the dim light of the small room he saw the nurse on the floor by the window unconscious. A man was working on the handcuffs holding Princess Devi to the bed. Thinking it might be Hagen, the man that Queen Maisong had mentioned, Martinez cautiously drew his gun as he moved into the room.

The man worked so intently on the lock, he didn't notice Martinez enter.

"Who are you?" asked Martinez in English.

The man jumped in surprise. He looked at Martinez, and replied, "I'm Jack Largent. I'm this girl's father, and I'm getting her out of here. You'll have to kill me to stop me."

Martinez moved in closer and looked intently at his face. "Of course it is you," he said, putting away his gun. "Hurry, we must move her out of here, and then get the other one. There is a bomb concealed in the next room ready to go off, I think. Hurry!"

Jack was momentarily confused by the man's reaction, and then surprised by what he said. Nevertheless, he processed it all quickly, and said, "I need to get these cuffs off of her first."

Martinez threw him the keys to the handcuffs and then began removing the IV linked to her arm when Jasmine came into the room and aimed her gun at Martinez.

"Sorry, Jack," she said. "I guess I missed this one. He must have been in one of the rooms."

Jack waved her off. "Jasmine, he's OK. He's helping us. Come on, we have to wheel Devi and Charlie out of here. There is a bomb!"

"Where is it?" said Hagen, arriving at that moment in the doorway of the room.

"It's in the room next door in the electrical panel. Who are you?" asked Martinez.

"Never mind that," said Hagen. "It appears we are all here for the same purpose. Where's Charlie?"

But before he could answer Audrey came through the door, saw Devi, and ran to her bedside. "Devi, Devi," she called out holding her hand. When she didn't answer, she asked, "Is she OK?"

"Dammit, Audrey, I told you to stay in the ambulance," said Hagen.

Jack, answering her question, said, "Yes, she's OK, but we have to get both of them out of here before that bomb goes off. Hurry! I will go with Jasmine and get Charlie. You get her out of here. Hurry," he urged them.

"Yes, out the back is the best way," said Martinez. "Quickly!"

"Wait! I need to tell you I think this is a setup," said Hagen. "From the road, I spotted at least one mercenary hiding behind this building with what looked like an AK."

"What should we do?" asked Jack.

"The plan hasn't changed. Let's get them out of here. Just keep in mind we might be ambushed," said Hagen. "Are you armed?"

Everyone replied in unison, "Yes!"

"OK," said Hagen, surprised. "Then let's get to it."

Jasmine followed Jack to Charlie's room. They disconnected him as was done with Devi, and they wheeled him out behind the other gurney. Martinez pointed to a small but modern prefab building fifty yards across the large, and empty, parking lot.

"That was the construction office when they built this place. It has never been removed, and is used for storage now," explained Martinez. "Let's take them there. It should be empty."

They rolled them across the lot, and Martinez unlocked the door to the building. They wheeled the two gurneys inside. Jasmine pulled the blinds closed, and quickly checked the Anhang to see if they had attracted any attention. Satisfied things were still quiet, she nodded positively to the others.

"Queen Maisong told me there is a helicopter coming for us right now," said Martinez. "I called her just before I came into the room, and found you."

Jack nodded and said," I don't know who all of you are, and I don't care. I don't even know how to thank you, but thank you, anyway."

"I am Audrey Goodnight, Mr. Largent," said Audrey, "and this is my father, Hagen."

Jack looked sharply at the man called Hagen for a moment and then nodded.

"I am Martinez. After fifteen, or so, years you do not recognize me, Jack Largent?" he asked. "We met on the trail at Siem Kulea. It was my duty at the time to deliver you to the work farm for my queen. I was happy to obey her, but I confess I was sad for you."

Jack looked at him with new clarity, but he was barely able to find the face he remembered on the well-groomed man across from him. "Martinez? I swore I would kill you the next time I saw you, but right now I think I would rather kiss you, my friend. Mai told me you were working with her now. Man, you look really different!"

"Yes, I am different in a lot of ways, Mr. Largent.

"That is Jasmine, she works with me," Jack said, pointing to his assistant standing by the window.

Jasmine was watching the sky outside, and listening for the helicopter. The Anhang opposite them was ominously deserted, and quiet. If there were mercenaries, why didn't they attack? She turned to the group, and said quietly, "You can jaw all you want when we get out of here, but for now if we can, we need to get Devi and Charlie dressed in something other than these hospital gowns. Look around for some uniforms or something."

"There is a supply closet at the end of the hallway," suggested Martinez pointing. "There will be uniforms of some kind in there."

"OK, but remember to keep down just in case that bomb goes off," Hagen warned.

As they were getting them dressed in hospital scrubs, Charlie and Devi began to wake up. Audrey was dressing Devi when she suddenly awoke and looked startled at her surroundings. She saw Audrey, hugged her in relief, and said, "Where are we?" Audrey briefly reassured her and gave her a comforting hug.

Charlie opened his eyes, saw Jack, and said, "Dad, how did you get here? Wait. Where am I?"

Jack looked at the handsome, fit young man and was surprised because he had never called him 'Dad' before. In fact, Jack had never been able to acknowledge he was his father as part of his friendly agreement with Catherine and Kelly. He hugged him warmly, and said, "I'm happy you're OK. I was very worried about you, son."

Just then Martinez's cell phone rang, and he quickly answered. "Eddie, this is Ramadi, we are almost there. Bring them out to the parking lot. Be careful."

"It's the helicopter. They're almost here," reported Martinez.

Hagen grabbed the cell phone from Martinez, and said, "There is a bomb set to go off in the back building of the clinic. Set down as far away from it as you can. We are in the building across the parking lot from the rear most building. We will be near there when you land. Be alert. We think this is a set-up, an ambush. I repeat, watch out for an ambush. I saw a mercenary hiding on the other side of the back building," he warned Ramadi before disconnecting.

"Martinez, how many men do they have here?" asked Jack, as they helped Devi and Charlie get to their feet.

"There are at least eight staying in the guest apartments above the clinic," Martinez said. "They're waiting for a mission of some kind, and I suspect they work directly for Mr. Yameda," he said, showing some concern.

Jack nodded. "I think we're their mission. Everyone check your weapons. This could get real crazy real soon."

They began to hear the helicopter coming in the distance. "Come on, let's go!" Hagen said.

The helicopter was just landing near their building when they went outside. Six of Ramadi's security team jumped off and quickly formed a perimeter on the clinic side of the helicopter searching with their MP5's for targets. Ramadi standing by the helicopter was surprised to see Jack, but then signaled to bring Devi and Charlie on board quickly by a wave of his hand. Martinez and Hagen took up a defensive position on the clinic side of the helicopter standing with Ramadi's men keeping steady eyes on the clinic. No doubt the mercenaries knew they were there, and would be coming to stop them very soon.

Charlie and Devi were standing, but their latent weakness showed, and Audrey helped Devi get to the helicopter while Jack and Ramadi helped Charlie. Once they were aboard, the guards began to back up toward the helicopter.

Suddenly, the Anhang exploded violently with a force that rocked the large helicopter over causing the spinning blades to almost hit ground on the opposite side before it settled back again on its tires. The area was engulfed in smoke as the clinic building, which had been ripped apart on one side, burned freely. Debris and chunks of brick covered the lot between the helicopter and the building. But the helicopter only suffered a few minor holes and appeared still airworthy. The blades spun normally in spite of the fire, and smoke swirled about like a tornado fueled by their rotation. A few of Ramadi's men had been knocked to the ground by the explosion, and were doing their best to recover and shake it off. If they had been closer to the Anhang when it exploded, they would all be dead.

Just then, around a corner from the back of the clinic came four men with AK-47s firing with focused determination. From the other end of the Anhang came four more. Their bullets pinged around the guards and helicopter.

Two of Ramadi's men were immediately hit and went down wounded. Martinez was hit in the left shoulder and went down beside them. But enraged, he got back up again cursing. He picked up an MP-5 dropped by one of Ramadi's fallen men that lay beside him and angrily advanced on the four men in front of him like a madman. He kept up a determined fire, and hit one of them, and then another as the last two remaining mercenaries on that side retreated for cover. As Jack got aboard, he yelled for Martinez to come, but Martinez was intent on keeping the remaining men from that side pinned down and waved him off.

Hagen with four of Ramadi's men, and with their aim so very accurate, made the other four mercenaries on the front side retreat. Their barrage eliminated two more mercenaries. Ramadi joined them and began laying down a focused barrage of bullets from his MP5. They killed another mercenary, and another in quick succession, and the opposing fire tapered off.

Ramadi and his men backed once again toward the helicopter to make their escape. Martinez kept advancing on the remaining two men in the rear of the Anhang who returned his fire intermittently while hiding behind some of the fallen debris from the explosion. Jack joined him urging Martinez to retreat to the helicopter. Martinez shot one of the remaining mercenaries, but then he got hit once more in the chest, and almost immediately again was wounded in the leg. He fell to the ground on his back with his arms out.

Jack bent over Martinez determined to help him get back to the helicopter.

The last mercenary stood to take a careful aim at Jack as he was bending over Martinez. But Hagen shot him before he could take a shot at Jack.

Jack said, "Come on, Martinez. You can't die. You have a date with queen Mai. Help me get him back to the helicopter," he urged Hagen.

Jasmine arrived beside them, and said, "Come on, boss, we have to get out of here, and now!"

"Jack, tell my queen I saved you. Tell her. I need her to know," Martinez said before laying his head over, and his eyes closed.

"Shit," said Jack.

Hagen pulled Jack up, and said, "Come on, man, three more mercenaries are coming around the corner, and one of them has an RPG, I think. Let's get out of here."

Jack finally gave up. He could see that he, Jasmine, and Hagen rushing toward the helicopter were the last ones left out in the open. Audrey stood by the helicopter waiting for them. The newly arriving mercenaries began firing at them, and the one with the RPG took aim at the helicopter. Bullets pinged around them. But when they nicked Audrey in the arm, Hagen turned on them angrily. He aimed and killed one man. Then he shot the man with the RPG just as he fired, spinning him around as he fired into the ground backwards. The effect blew the man airborne against the destroyed wall of the clinic in another violent explosion.

But the remaining mercenary fired at Hagen and hit him in the chest. As he went to the ground wounded, Audrey who was beside him now, made a grip like her father had shown her, took a practiced aim, and fired three times at the mercenary missing twice, but killing him with the third shot. She dropped the gun and bent down to help Hagen who was sprawled out on the pavement.

Audrey looked toward the helicopter about to take off, and yelled, "Help us!"

Quickly, Jack and Jasmine ran to Hagan. They grabbed him up between them and got him back into the helicopter. Jack lifted Audrey on board, and he jumped on board too at the same time the helicopter began lifting off.

Audrey yelled to the pilot that there was smoke coming from the engine. The pilot focused on his instruments as the helicopter took off quickly. By that time, the clinic was an inferno just across the parking lot. Police cars and fire trucks rapidly approached along the road toward the clinic as the helicopter pulled up and away toward Germany.

Chapter 46

June 2005 Wasserberg Airport, Germany

A s soon as the helicopter was in the air, and heading back to Germany, they got word to Catherine, and she, along with her corporate lawyer, contacted the German state department and informed them of what they had done. Moments later, she called the Austrian state department with the same message, and that was followed by a telephone call to the American Consulate in Munich. She informed all of them the rescue group would surrender themselves at the small airport in Wasserberg near the Austrian border in twenty minutes. Mai on advice from Catherine had ordered one of Ramadi's men to video the rescue at the clinic for legal reasons.

Catherine also arranged for three ambulances to be on the tarmac, so they could quickly get the injured to the local Wasserberg hospital. Three of Ramadi's men were wounded, one more critically than the rest. Their superior firepower, body armor, and intensive training proved to be the difference in the exchange of bullets and explosions that left the back of the clinic looking like a war zone.

Catherine, Kelly, Mai, their lawyers, and two officials from the United States State Department were waiting on the tarmac by the passenger terminal when the German officials arrived. Catherine had already received a stern lecture from the local consulate bureaucrat that felt it was his duty to reprimand her. She played good this time fully aware that his lecture carried no weight.

Soon, the helicopter arrived from Salzburg and set down with its engine smoking. A German GSG-9 Swat team unit immediately surrounded it. The injured were gently lifted off, and their vitals were checked within the next few minutes. Hagen with severe wounds was hurried away to Wasserberg hospital with Audrey who was getting her wounded arm treated. Devi and Charlie spent a few moments being greeted and kissed by their loved ones before they too were taken away escorted by Jack and Kelly. Ramadi's three wounded guards were put in the last ambulance after being thoroughly searched and checked for weapons. They went to the hospital with a police escort.

Ramadi and his remaining men peacefully surrendered to the German police. They lined them up lying on the tarmac with their hands behind their heads. Six German GSG-9s searched them and then relaxed finding them not to be a threat. They were allowed to sit in the shade by the airport terminal guarded by the GSG-9 team. Another twenty minutes passed as a German investigator interviewed Ramadi and went through their passports and papers.

This was all expected, but what was not expected was the arrival of Hans Frieh, the German Chancellor who had been visiting nearby in Munich. He arrived by another helicopter that sat down not far from where Catherine and the German authorities were gathered in conversation. Only the previous year Catherine had conducted a very positive interview with the chancellor and spent a week with him in Berlin. She smiled as he deplaned and greeted her with a warm and friendly hug. "I got a call from your Mr. Finn Collins from the United States asking if I could provide any assistance. Fortunately, I was nearby in Munich when he called," the German Chancellor explained.

"I cannot tell you how happy I am to see you, Hans," she said. "I am afraid we have created an international incident while in the act of rescuing our kids. The local U.S. Consul has already expressed his extreme disapproval of our actions. He tells me he has contacted the state department to inform them of our misdeeds. He further affirmed there would be severe consequences for me over this. His words. We may need your experience and advice for managing this situation," Catherine said, gesturing toward the US consul official who rocked on his feet and listened with focused interest to their conversation.

"Catherine, you chose this small airport wisely," the chancellor answered in English. "Its remote location has allowed me and my Austrian counterpart to decide to ignore the entire affair. That is to say, there was no international incident as far as you are concerned. This whole thing never happened. Based on the huge amount of intelligence and supporting information you sent us on Asian World Investments, and their criminal activity in the area, the Austrian police have arrested those working at the clinic in an entirely local, and heroic operation that they conducted this very afternoon, and with no loss of life. They had suspected the clinic, and several related local industries to be criminal enterprises, and money-laundering facilities in conjunction with a local bank purchased by the same organization. Together with the information, and documentation you have supplied us they now have a very solid case against them, and no doubt, their activity in the area will end. My people are already taking steps to seize their assets including holdings in European corporations and to freeze their bank accounts as part of our anti-terrorist program. So, it is with the appreciation of the German and Austrian governments that we are going to pretend your part in this incident did not happen. I have already informed the American ambassador at the state department of our perspective on this situation, and he has promised me complete cooperation."

"I don't know what to say. Thank you, Hans," she replied, holding his hand warmly. "May I introduce you to my dear friend Queen Mai Sambath Largent from Cambodia," she said, "and this is the US local consulate representative."

The Chancellor took Mai's hand and said, "Queen Maisong I have heard so much about you, and I must say it is an honor to meet you in person. But I won't hold you up. I know you are both anxious to get to the hospital and attend to your loved ones who I am happy to hear are OK," said the Chancellor.

Mai shook the chancellor's hand, and said, "You are most gracious. Perhaps you can visit Cambodia sometime. I would be honored to show you my valley."

"Indeed, I just may take you up on that, Queen Maisong," said Chancellor Frieh. "But off with you now. I don't think you want to spend any more time out here.

"Catherine, I am asking one thing in return for this favor," he continued. "That is that you get everyone to the Munich airport, and on a plane back to the United States by no later than noon tomorrow. A timely departure away from any press will benefit us both I think."

"What about my men?" Mai said.

The local police chief who was standing by the chancellor said, "We have confiscated all of the weapons, and equipment. That is our policy. I am informed there is another helicopter and other equipment nearby. I strongly suggest that you transport all of that out of the country tonight or sooner if possible. But with that, your men are free to go. What they do after that is up to you, but please, no more military operations in my country."

The chancellor then surprised them as he turned to the United States consulate official who stood with a face of disapproval next to them. He said to him, "Sir, I am not sure why you are here, or in what capacity, but I suggest a communication with your superiors in Washington will reveal that you have acted hastily, and have exceeded your authority in presuming to reprimand Ms. Marsh. I will personally be reporting my views on your conduct to your ambassador. Please rest assured that as far as everyone that matters is concerned, nothing of interest to you, or your country happened here. You may go, as there is nothing for you to do further here," he said, before he turned abruptly to leave not waiting for an answer.

Mai smiled as she watched the Chancellor climb back up to his helicopter, and wave to them. "Wow, Cat, you sure know a lot of handy people to have around in difficult situations."

"Hey, I'm as surprised as you are, Mai. It was fortuitous that he was nearby. I bet our local consul was surprised the most," she said, watching the man get back into his car and speed away without saying goodbye.

"But if you think about it, that is all German in context. Efficient to the max. It never happened. What could be a more simple answer? Come on; let's get to the hospital. I have a youngin' to hug."

The next morning Audrey with a bandaged arm over a surface wound was still at the hospital where her father was in intensive care. They were lucky that the bullet that hit his chest had missed everything vital. They monitored him closely, but the reports on him were positive. They would be more certain of his recovery in a couple of days.

The surprise was Martinez. Everyone thought he died protecting their escape from the clinic in Salzburg. Jack had already related his dying declaration to Mai. But in fact, Austrian doctors at a nearby hospital had saved him.

It was the same hospital where they stole the ambulance. He was still listed in critical condition, and his prognosis was uncertain. If he lived he would possibly become a showpiece for the case against Asian World Investments, so they were doing everything they could to save him. Even so, it was still possible he would spend the rest of his life in prison. Mai had already talked to the Austrian Chancellor that morning and explained the situation. She pleaded his innocence, and tried to make a deal for his release. The final decision on his status would wait to see if he recovered from his many wounds but the Austrian chancellor seemed amenable to her wishes.

Mai insisted on visiting him, and with two bodyguards and Jack, she made the trip to the hospital early that morning. She first talked to the chief hospital administrator, and made a very large donation to the hospital in Martinez's name, paid for the damaged emergency vehicle, and assumed all expenses related to his care. She asked that no expense be spared during his stay and that he be accorded every courtesy.

Afterward, she was escorted to his room. He was hooked up to so many wires and beeping machines it made her cry. She held his hand and told him she would be forever grateful to him for his sacrifice on her behalf, but he was comatose, and she doubted he could even hear her, or know what she was saying.

But then she remembered. She put her hand on his head, and entered his thoughts. After a moment she smiled. He was dreaming he was on a trail at Siem Kulea coming down from the mountains laughing jocularly with a few other men. But she was surprised to see herself ride up on a horse dressed in riding pants and halter as she often wore during the time with Colonel Minh. She walked the horse over to Martinez who seemed mesmerized by her presence. All of the other mercenaries were on the ground kneeling. She beckoned him forward, leaned over, and kissed him three times on the lips. Then she turned the magnificent animal and glided away effortlessly. Mai saw herself through his eyes. That he adored her, there was no doubt. She loved him for that.

She pulled her hands away from his head lying in his hospital bed unconscious and kissed him on the lips. To her surprise he smiled, so she kissed him again, and she told she had one more if he got better, and came back to her. She did not doubt that he would.

Later that morning, they all gathered with bags packed for one last meeting before departure. They sat around the conference table in the large penthouse suite at the Ludendorff Hotel in Munich, Germany. Devi and Charlie already retrieved from an overnight stay at the hospital sat on an adjacent couch on either side of Jack. Devi sat snuggled close to her father who had his arm around her shoulder protectively.

Mai, Catherine, Kelly, Jasmine, Ramadi, Fetu, and Daniel sat around the table. They had just finished a huge breakfast and were feeling boisterous after the successful mission the day before.

"You will be interested to know," began Catherine, "that two hotel employees were arrested last night as a result of interrogations during the joint German-Austrian operations against AWI. They were spies for Yameda, and they knew our every move. They knew when we were coming."

"We barely made it out of there," said Jasmine. "That was a narrow escape! All of that training that Ramadi put his men through proved fortuitous. Those mercenaries didn't expect that, I bet," she said proudly.

"It was like the good old days when you and mom beat down Colonel Minh, wasn't it, pop?" Devi commented.

Jack was very happy but not in a mood to celebrate another close escape. He just squeezed her shoulder in response and gave the required smile. The thought of what might have happened still consumed him.

But Mai aimed another friendly comment toward Jack. "Darling, what were you thinking? You are no spring chicken anymore, and baby, I am sorry to inform you, but you still don't have any commando skills. What are we going to do with you?" she asked, with a twisted smile. "We Largent ladies have a GI Joe wannabe as our protector." Mai threw him a proud kiss from across the room.

That brought Jack back to the conversation, and not about to hide his exasperation. "That's just the thing. It wasn't a bit about brains or brawn, and all about frustration. I wasn't thinking at all. Didn't care. Everybody was just sitting around, and after two days of waiting, I didn't know the last thing you and Hagen had planned or even if there was a plan. I decided that no one would pay any attention if I rode along with Jasmine to deliver those documents Catherine collected for Hagen in Salzburg. Hagen wasn't around so with nothing better to do we decided to go have a look at this clinic we heard so much about. We didn't plan to actually go in, but when we got there no one was at the front gate, and the place looked deserted, so we just went for a look around. I was trying to get the cuffs off of Devi when I ran into Martinez and then Hagen."

"Yeah, we had just talked to Martinez," said Mai. "But, Jack, we had no clue that Hagen was going to go in at about the same time you did. He picked up on the cell phone interference being on, and then off, and from his own experience he thought of the bomb angle," said Mai."

"We got lucky, I think," said Catherine. I am just glad to have our kids back. It's funny in a way. With all our planning and strategizing, Jack and Jasmine just walk in and get them."

"Yeah, Cat," said Mai. "But don't you see? The cell phone interference ends, and the front gate is unguarded. They wanted us to come in. We go in to get the kids, and the place blows up. They wanted to hurt us, to hurt me. I think they were waiting for the helicopter. If the helicopter had been parked closer to the back building everyone might have been killed. It was a setup. They lured us there to kill as many of us as they could. I'm sure of it."

"It was a diabolical scheme, Mai," said Catherine. "Su Ling and Yameda are pure evil, and they play out their operations like chess masters always prepared for the next move. But we got lucky and outsmarted them this time."

Ceva came in from Mai's adjoining suite, and informed them, "There is a telephone call for Queen Maisong. A Lieutenant Haleran is on the phone from Chicago. He says it's important."

Catherine looked at Mai and pushed the button for the speakerphone on the table. "Hello, Lieutenant," said Catherine. "This is Catherine speaking. We're all here and have you on speakerphone. You will be happy to know we have gotten the young'ns back," she said.

"Happy to hear it, Catherine. But I have been going over this whole operation in my head trying to make sense of it, and I have come to the conclusion you may have a problem we need to discuss," he said.

They were all silent still sharing the group euphoria from the success of their mission, and collectively thinking *"what now?"* Catherine replied, "What problem would that be, Lieutenant?"

"You have not received any demands from the kidnappers, have you?" he asked.

"Well, no, but it was just a matter of time. Let me tell you what they tried to do. They planted a bomb next to their rooms. Mai thinks they wanted to lure us here to kill as many of us as they could."

"Well, that's just it…no demands. They had your kids and made no demands of you to get them back. I seem to remember Mai mentioning that his kidnapping was about something they wanted from her. You need to tell me what exactly it was they wanted from you, Mai. I think it's very important. What were they after?" he asked.

"Now that we have Charlie and Devi back I can't see why that's important anymore," argued Mai.

"Please, just humor me. What did they want?" he persisted.

"They were after information I have, but specifically a key in the form of a door handle that was in three parts," said Mai. "They wanted my part, but it wouldn't have done them any good anyway. They needed the other two. I know that Yameda stole one of the parts from an ancient site the Chinese were investigating, but we still have the other two…." Mai said pausing for thought.

"Jack," said Mai. "Where is the part of the door handle now, that you found at Nineveh?"

"I told you before, Mai. I left Marty waiting for Colonel Amir at Ramstein airbase. Amir was to travel separately to Ramstein from Incirlik airbase, Turkey, when Marty and I went on the shuttle following Jasmine on the Medevac. He should be there by now. I haven't talked to him since he got his new cell phone and called me. I will give Marty a call," he said picking up the phone. "I know they were coming here after Colonel Amir arrived."

"So, if I get this right, there are three parts to this thing, this door handle. Where is this door they want to access?" he asked.

"It is in Siem Kulea," said Mai.

"Uh-huh," Haleran said. "Where does this door lead to?" he asked.

"It is an ancient door that might have untold treasure and power behind it," said Mai. "No one knows for sure. But if the legend is to be believed it could be very dangerous for anyone to open it. It is a very old portal, and legends about it are too numerous to count."

As they watched, Jack's face turned white, and he sat up straight in his chair. "Hold on, Marty, I am patching you on speaker phone with another call. We are all gathered around a table in the conference room here at the hotel. OK, go ahead," Jack told him after joining the two calls, and making sure they were both connected.

"As I said," Marty began, "Colonel Amir called me less than ten minutes before you called, Jack. He was returning my many calls and messages left for him. He was himself in the hospital at Incirlik Air Base recovering from a bullet wound.

"It happened a few days ago. He saw Sadie and Martin off on a plane to the US. Afterward, when he returned to the TDY barracks where we were staying, he caught Hakim in his room in the act of stealing the artifact that was in the Halliburton case. He tried to stop him. There was a struggle, and Hakim shot him. Before he became unconscious, he asked Hakim why he had betrayed him; why he did it? Hakim said he was being paid a handsome fee, which would change his life forever. Amir passed out and lost a lot of blood before they found him, and got him to the hospital. He has been unconscious for three days. I'm sorry, Jack. I don't know what to say. I am just about to board a plane to Munich myself right now, and was going to call you when you called me," Marty explained.

The table sat in shocked silence for a moment following Mai's lead.

"Did I hear right?" asked Haleran from the speakerphone on the table. "This man Hakim was working for your adversaries, and stole that part of the door handle, and now they have two parts to the puzzle?"

But before they could answer he asked another question, "Where is the third part of the handle that you have, Mai?"

Mai looked quickly at Jack, and then Jasmine. "It's hidden at Siem Kulea," explained Mai.

"Does anyone but you have access to this missing piece," asked Haleran.

"I am not sure for certain, Lieutenant, but possibly my former assistant, Su Ling" replied Mai, as her world began to spin.

"Is this Su Ling there with you?" asked Haleran.

"No," said Mai. "She is with Hinsu Yameda, our adversary, as you call him. Oh my God!" she exclaimed, as she got up, and began to pace rapidly.

"Here is what I think," said Haleran. "They have outsmarted you. Correct me if I'm wrong, but you are all in Munich, Germany, right now, and you have your best security people with you. I think the kidnapping was not to make a demand. I think it was a diversion to get you away from Siem Kulea and leave it unprotected and without leadership. The prize is at Siem Kulea, and it is wide open for them, right?"

There was silence as everyone contemplated the obvious conclusion he had reached. Their elation turned to a worried silence.

"Mai, contact Siem Kulea!" said Catherine.

But Mai was already ahead of her working her cell phone with rapid fingers. After a tense minute, she said, "I can't get through. I bet it is blocked. I...I haven't called them for any reason in the last twenty-four hours. I was focused on this."

"Let me try," said Jack. "I have Neru's cell, his house is to the North of the valley."

After a moment he looked up and said, "Nope. It just keeps ringing with no answer."

Catherine asked, "How fast can we get there?"

"Sixteen to twenty hours," said Mai thinking.

"They will have killed everyone by then," said Kelly.

"No," replied Mai sharply. "Yameda will not harm my people. He will go in quietly with Su Ling. I bet very few in the valley even know they're around. Su Ling may still have loyal followers there. She will use them to act as a front. They want the door, that's all. They will go to access the door before we can get back. I don't see how we can prevent them from doing that," she said.

Ramadi said, "Yes, my lady, we left only a small crew to protect the palace. This mission was everyone's priority. If they were efficient, they probably control the valley now, and its defenses. With respect, Su Ling was very skilled, and she helped devise our defensive plan when we were rebuilding the valley. I doubt we will be able to use helicopters to enter the valley. They will no doubt be shot down."

"Is there any way to get into the valley without them?" Catherine asked.

"The trails in will be blocked," said Fetu.

"How can you be so sure we cannot helicopter in, or use those trails," protested Catherine.

"Because that is what I would do," said Mai. "We have to assume they hold the valley, and it is well defended. We were prepared to turn back a full helicopter assault like the ones the Vietnamese used against Colonel Minh. We also have to assume they have all three parts for that door. They can keep us out long enough to do whatever they have in mind," she said.

"I know a way in," said Daniel.

Everyone looked over at Daniel who sat at the other end of the table close to Jack and Devi. "All of these years there was always a secret way in, which Martinez and I used back in the old days. I don't think many people knew about it. It starts halfway up the mountain on the west side where there is a cave that works its way through to a hidden exit in the jungle not far from the Palace.

"Ramadi, don't you remember it? There used to be a connection under the palace I think," said Daniel.

"Yes, I do remember," said Ramadi sitting up in his seat. Mai spread out a map of Siem Kulea in front of her and Ramadi got up to look over her shoulder. Daniel joined them on the other side of Mai.

"I think the entrance on the west side is about here, my lady," he said pointing to the map. "I only heard rumors about it, but I never actually went through it."

"No, it is up a bit higher actually," put in Daniel. "If we can gain access to it, we could get into the Palace, and stop them before they even know we are there," he said.

"How long will this take from start to finish?" Mai asked.

Daniel remembered his many times working his way through the cave. "Going up the mountain at the beginning will be the hardest, Mai. That will take five, or six hours. Once we gain the cave entrance, it will take another four to five hours to get to the other side. So about eleven hours for the entire journey," he said.

Mai didn't bother asking for volunteers. Not one of them sitting at the table would have stayed behind. "If we go in at dusk, we can be there by dawn," she said. "We will need arms, and supplies for such a raid."

"My lady, there is a civilian armory we have kept fully stocked for the militia just down the mountain from there," said Fetu. "They will have all we need, and it will give us a chance to alert the militia at the same time."

Mai stood up with her hands on the table, and ordered, "Devi, you go back to Chicago with Catherine, Charlie, and Kelly. Jack and I, Jasmine, Ramadi, Fetu and our men are leaving immediately for Siem Kulea. Leave anything you don't absolutely need for this operation. Daniel, you come with us. We will need you to get us from Bangkok into Siem Kulea. We can plan, and make arrangements on the way. Right now let's all get to the airport. I want to leave within the hour. Does anyone have anything to add?"

No one answered, so she said, "Let's get started. Catherine, please call for transportation...a police escort would be nice if you can arrange it. I would appreciate it if you gather our things for us to retrieve later."

Catherine nodded, and picked up the phone.

Kelly took Mai's arm, and led her aside so she could speak privately with her. "My lady, is it possible you can Mindspeak with someone in the valley, and find out what is going on?"

Mai looked at her and shook her head. "Kelly that is an excellent idea, but the only one in the valley trained with that skill is Lady Chu, and although that was always my ultimate goal, we have not trained for great distances yet. Maybe, when we get closer I can give it a try."

Catherine gave a confirmation of transportation arriving downstairs. They all quickly grabbed their things and headed out.

Chapter 47

June 2005 Siem Kulea

There are contingencies even when you have your own jet transportation, and they did not get back in the vicinity of Siem Kulea for over twenty-fours after their final meeting in Munich. However, they did not waste time. Marty joined them at the airport in Munich trading one aircraft for another in an exercise of perfect timing and Jasmine prompting him on her cell phone.

Mai was being unreasonable and very upset by this time, so Jack insisted she go into the private quarters in the back of the airplane, and meditate with Queen Po while they formulated a plan to take back the valley. Jack working with Daniel, Ramadi, and Fetu organized every facet of the plan while considering all the possible deceptions, and counter moves on the part of Yameda and Su Ling to thwart them. This was no easy task because they were faced with the fact that Hinsu Yameda had outsmarted them in a very complicated scheme that took years to play out. Perhaps most unnerving for them was that in spite of appearances, he had been in control the entire time. They had come up against a formidable opponent unlike any other.

When Mai returned several hours later, she had collected her thoughts, arrested her emotions, and was eager to help. She immediately, and objectively, simplified their plan allowing for only a few possible contingencies. Speed was their driving theme now. They had to get back to the valley as soon as was physically possible if they hoped to stop Yameda from what they could not even imagine.

Their one advantage was the secret entrance through the cave in the west mountains to the vicinity of the Palace. Mai thought hard and was convinced Su Ling was not aware of it because she had not known about it during her time with Colonel Minh. None of their group, most of whom were there during construction as part of the original security team assembled by Ramadi and Fetu, could remember Su Ling knowing of the secret cave. Added to their confidence was Daniel's recollection that there might be an additional exit from the cave leading to the basement of the temple now being used as a communication center for the Palace. They moved forward with their plan.

They landed in three helicopters at a farm that lay at the foothills of the mountain that was on the opposite side of the Siem Kulea valley. They arrived at dusk, and they moved stealthily just in case there were lookouts in the mountains. As soon as they landed the owners of the farm who were loyal Champa people became excited by the presence of their queen. She instructed them to gather the militia, arm them, and prepare to follow them through the tunnel in the mountain. Quickly, by coordinated radio when possible, and if not, by a runner from farm to farm the word went out with the Champa code black, meaning only Champas were to be told of the militia assembly that night. This secretive assembly is rehearsed twice a year as part of their militia exercises.

With that plan in place, Daniel led their group and their very skilled security force of two-dozen men up the mountain. It was going to be a long and arduous climb, but at night it would be cooler, and they could not risk getting any closer with helicopters.

Six hours later, and with few stops to rest they arrived at the cave entrance. It would have been invisible even in the daylight because it was well hidden, covered with brush, and behind a boulder. Daniel went right to it even after fifteen years. The cave looked like no one had been in it for at least that long. It was cool inside, and Mai who was beginning to feel some exhaustion after the long climb welcomed the cool air. Ramadi called a halt for his men to rest for a few minutes, and to eat something.

Mai wanted to push on, her anxiety steadily growing, but Ramadi for once overruled his queen. "My lady, with respect, my men and I need to rest for a moment, or we will not be of any use on the other end of this cave."

"I'm sorry, Ramadi. Yes, of course, let's take a break. We are making good progress," she said, and sat down on a rock nearby actually grateful for the respite. Drinks and rations were passed around as the men talked quietly.

"Daniel, your mercenary days have proved valuable this night," said Jack. "I'm amazed you remembered that trail and the entrance of this cave."

"It is how I used to sneak back into the valley, Jack, when I wanted to avoid the guards on the roads. In spite of the old proverb, there is no honor among thieves, and particularly among Colonel Minh's mercenaries. They were known to rob you blind on the trail, and Colonel Minh would interpret any complaint as a sign of weakness. I had a girlfriend where we just came from in the foothills. This was usually the path I took to see her. I knew it like the back of my hand. I do not think, however, Colonel Minh would have approved of me using his secret escape tunnel to further my love life," he explained.

"Escape tunnel? You never said it was an escape tunnel," noted Jack.

"Yes, well, that is why I am almost positive there is another exit leading under the palace and I do know of one place where the tunnel splits."

They ate a few rations and then headed out again. The cave was narrow in places, but these proved not to be impediments for even the largest of them. Two hours later they came to a fork in the tunnel. Daniel told them one way went to the exit in the jungle near the village. He was familiar with that one. The other one he only knew about from rumors and was not positive it exited under the temple. But he thought it was a secret escape tunnel for Colonel Minh. He told them he was not sure either of them were still open and frankly they could count their luck that they had gotten as far as they had.

Mai made the decision. She ordered Fetu to take the village tunnel. He was to alert the village militia and bring them to assault whoever Yameda had placed as guards near the palace. Then she brushed by them and led the way down the tunnel hopefully leading to the basement under the communications center.

It was an hour later when they came to an abrupt stop before a boarded-up door. The wood was worn, and old, and it was evident this part of the tunnel had not been used for many years. Not wanting to risk any noise Ramadi used a pry bar and worked one of the boards off. He aimed his flashlight through the hole.

"It is some kind of chamber, like a basement," he told them after he looked inside.

He worked more boards off until even he could squeeze through, and soon most of them were assembled in the subterranean chamber beyond. As they stood not far from where they had exited the tunnel, the problem became readily apparent because as they showed their lights around on all sides, there was no exit from the chamber. It appeared to be a dead end. Mai took Ramadi's light, and aimed it over each wall. Having done so with no success, she carefully trailed her light along the ceiling above, and also found nothing. She was worried that all of their efforts had been wasted.

She looked at Jack with a worried face and expressed her feelings. "Jack? What do we do?"

She sat down on the ground exhausted with the realization this might be the end of her effort to save her valley and people. She concentrated on her thoughts hoping that Queen Po may have an answer but then she remembered what Kelly had asked her before. She focused on contacting Lady Chu and was surprised when her thoughts were answered in kind.

"My lady, are you in the Palace? We are ready to help. What do you need us to do?" Chu asked.

"Lady Chu, I am relieved to hear your thoughts. We are in a tunnel making our way toward the valley. What is the situation there? Has my valley been attacked by outsiders? Are you OK? Are my people OK?" Mai asked her.

"Yes, Your Majesty, we were attacked yesterday. We are mostly OK now, but a few were killed resisting when the invaders first arrived in four helicopters. Their mercenaries were well armed, and I ordered everyone to stand down, and not resist. They held some of the children and it was not the time for resistance in my view, my lady. I hope I did the right thing," said Chu. "Maybe Ramadi and Fetu would have reacted differently."

"You acted perfectly, Lady Chu," said Mai. "What is the situation there? Can you tell us where their men are?"

"We are in the kitchen, and guarded by one of their men," said Lady Chu. When you are ready to bring your assault, we can easily kill him. Two of my best cooks are Xua Xamthin mamas, and they are very capable and ready to dispose of that man. They have been unusually cheerful this morning in anticipation of that I am sure.

"My lady, Su Ling and a man named Hinsu Yameda are here leading these men. There are about thirty of them in all, and they are mostly guarding the corridors. In bringing them refreshments from the kitchen I have seen many of them in the communications center, and guarding the corridor from there to the basement areas," said Lady Chu.

"We seem to be at an impasse here, Lady Chu. We expected to come up under the temple in what was formerly an escape tunnel prepared by Colonel Minh. Do you know anything about it?"

"I have lived in this valley all my life, my lady. When I was a child, we used to play in the tunnels that we found under the ruins of the Palace. Most of them are non-existent anymore. But I believe the one you are referring to comes up beneath the old Hindu temple, which you now use for your communications center," she said. "You can tell, because during the conversion of the temple to a communications center, the old temple artifacts were put down in the basement below. You should see many temple artifacts, and Hindu statues down there."

"We seem stuck right now, Lady Chu," said Mai. "We have arrived in a room with no other way out. We may have come to the end of this tunnel," she said.

"There is always an exit, my lady. As kids, we used to hide them so that we could have our own secret places. Tell your men to feel around for a hidden door or something."

Mai told a few of Ramadi's men gathered in the chamber to bang around with their hands looking for a hidden door. Almost immediately, one was found in the floor in a corner not far from where Mai stood. A guard began brushing away the dirt and dust at his feet with his bare hands to reveal an old wooden hatch. More of the men excitedly joined his effort, and soon a trap door about three feet by two feet long was visible.

Ramadi pried it open revealing another tunnel below. He jumped down into it and searched about with his light going down the passageway for a bit. When he returned, he said, "Yes, there is a tunnel that continues on." Jack and Daniel jumped down to join him, and Ramadi held out his arms to help Queen Mai down into the tunnel.

"We have found it, Lady Chu," said Mai. "Stay focused, and be conscious of me."

When everyone was finally within the tunnel, they continued on their way. In a hundred yards, they again encountered a closed passage, but this did not appear to be a door. Ramadi pushed on it and was surprised to find it seemed to be holding firmly in place. But he continued to probe the surface with his hands, and when he pushed on the left side, it began moving away grudgingly. He put all of his strength behind his effort opening up a passage wide enough for him to put his head through. Once he did, he observed he was pushing on the back of a set of shelves. At the same time, as he pushed the shelf out farther, he deftly caught a piece of pottery that teetered and fell from one of the upper ledges. Mai squeezed around him impatiently through the thin opening. She looked about with her flashlight and turned around to Ramadi smiling broadly.

"This is the basement of the temple. My communication center is above. The door and stairs are over there," she said pointing positively. "We are here. We have made it!" she said, smiling joyously.

But in her thoughts, Lady Chu was telling her to stop, and be cautious. Mai ordered everyone to stop for a moment, and be silent while she considered their situation.

Lady Chu continued to speak in her thoughts. "Most of the guards are in the communications center, and in the adjacent corridor that leads to the main basement beneath the Palace. It would not be a good idea to come up from the basement into the communication center. No doubt they will be ready to defend themselves well."

"What are we to do, Lady Chu?" asked Mai. "We have to get to that chamber below the main basement quickly. Our time may have already run out."

"My lady, the temple basement is actually connected with the Palace through the kitchen basement. If you are in the temple basement you should see all of the artifacts, and objects from the temple stacked on one side."

"Yes, I see them. I think a lot of them are gold," said Mai.

"Yes, but behind all of those objects should be another door that leads toward the kitchen basement. We have not used that connection in years, but I am fairly certain it is still there," said Lady Chu. "If you can get to us, we can come at the mercenaries from the other side through the kitchen where they will not expect us, and then you can quickly access the basement where Su Ling and Hinsu Yameda have gone. They went quickly down there after arriving."

Mai ordered the men to clear away some of the objects until they found the door and cleared a path to it. They opened the door, and entered a cool dark corridor. Ramadi and his men went first.

"We are coming, Lady Chu. Secure the kitchen," ordered Mai, following behind with Jack and the rest.

They came to another door, and within was the kitchen basement. They moved quickly to the stairs, and before they took a step ascending to the kitchen, the door to the kitchen opened, and Lady Chu declared, "All Clear, my lady."

Lady Chu briefed them on the disposition of Yameda's mercenaries. Ramadi organized his men, and sent them out to combat Yameda's men. He told them to move stealthily, and to keep it quiet for as long as they could. At the same time, the rest would head for the main basement.

"They came into the valley yesterday, my lady," explained Lady Chu. "We were overwhelmed, and surprised by their sudden presence. As I said, a few who resisted were killed, but then Yameda's men rounded up the village children, took them away, and threatened to kill them if anyone resisted further. I ordered the valley to stand down, my lady. I hoped you would return, and lead us, but I could think of no other solution. The children were my concern. I hope I have not acted foolishly," she said.

"Where are they keeping the children, Lady Chu?" Mai asked.

"They are reported to be held at the work farm, my lady," she replied.

"Where are my people right now, Lady Chu," Mai asked.

"Those that could have moved to their designated militia marshaling areas," my lady. "They are awaiting my orders to strike."

Mai looked at her watch. It was 5 a.m., and there was no time to lose.

"Very well, Lady Chu," said Mai. "Take the Xua Xamthin, and the Hui Hoa teams, and secure the children. When you have done so, give the signal, and retake our valley," ordered Mai, looking to Ramadi and finding his approval. "Do not wait for further orders from me. Take back our valley, Lady Chu."

Mai stood up and smiled at Jack. She said, "The militia is well, and organized. They are about to strike. Let's get to the door leading downstairs, and see what they have done."

Ramadi took up the lead once again, and cautiously opened the door to the corridor leading to the main palace. One-by-one they silently slipped through the partly open door with Ramadi in the lead once more.

The palace was deserted, and mostly dark with the sun not having come up yet. They quietly made their way down the access corridor from the kitchen. Ramadi was surprisingly agile and moved stealthily belying his size using only hand signals now and then with his men. He came to a corner and peeked around quickly. He turned back and signaled his men. There were two of Yameda's men dressed in dark green fatigue uniforms around the corner on guard about ten feet from the corner.

Ramadi's men were all carrying nine-millimeter Sigs with silencers. He counted to three, and they came around the corner, and quickly killed the two men with shots to the head. They ducked down, and waited, listening for the sound of any movement. There was none.

The entrance to the basement of the palace was further down the same corridor, and around another corner. The corridor was lit by one overhead light every twenty feet.

They moved down the corridor staying close to the wall, not sure where other guards might be. Ramadi's well-trained men took the lead. As they turned the next corner, Ramadi could see the entrance to the stairs leading down to the basement. Beyond were the queen's chambers and the family quarters. Off to the right was the corridor leading to the front of the Palace. Everything was quiet. Ramadi sent four of his men to the front of the Palace, four to deal with the men in the communication center, and four more to go outside through the door on the left at the rear of the palace. Their orders were to kill any of Yameda's men they came upon but to act with caution as he whispered a reminder that Fetu had taken the other cave route, and would be trying to alert the valley militia quietly.

Ramadi turned to Mai who took a deep breath and nodded. They descended into the basement leaving four men to guard the doorway to the stairs.

There was no one in the basement, and the shelf covering the deeper chamber was pulled back leaving it open. Moving to it quickly, Ramadi started down with the last four of his men followed by the rest of the group.

As they came to the bottom of the stairs, they moved quickly and quietly across the chamber to the open portal of the next room. Ramadi peered around and could see the large stone sculpture had been pulled all the way from the wall. The massive golden door to the chamber of the ancients stood wide open with the door opening inward. It seemed very bright beyond that doorway. Three guards were standing with their backs to Ramadi and were peering into the doorway. Ramadi signaled to the group to be very quiet, and he and two of his men slowly moved toward the unsuspecting guards. In a moment they were upon them and ordered them to drop their guns and raise their hands. Two of the guards reflexively brought their weapons to bear and were quickly shot by Ramadi, and his men. The third did as he was told, and looked very afraid as Ramadi frisked him, and pushed him to the ground.

Mai stood before him, and demanded, "Where are Yameda and Su Ling?" At first, the guard did not understand. She tried several languages before she found one he could speak.

The guard shook his head saying, "I do not know. They went through that doorway over an hour ago, and we have not seen them since. We were told to wait here."

Mai walked over to the doorway and peered in. Jack put his arms around Mai from behind holding her as they looked inside. The chamber beyond the door appeared to be a series of rooms that seemed like the inside of an aircraft, functional in purpose and advanced in style. The sides were smooth and rounded to the ceiling. Furniture was built into the walls, and the décor and color resembled that of a sterile environment much like a modern hospital. But beyond they could see a bright glowing area through another door.

Ramadi suggested, "I should go in, and make sure it is safe for you, my lady."

Mai looked directly at him as if his words were written on his face, and then she looked at Jack. "Your call, my love," he said. "You are the only expert among us. You have warned us about entering that chamber for several months now. We could just close this door, and be done with it."

She nodded to Jack and then turned to face Ramadi. "No, Ramadi. This place is not for humans, I think. My ancestors are screaming at me to close this door, but I must be sure of what has become of Yameda and Su Ling," she said.

"Mai, you cannot enter there alone," said Jack. "Jasmine and I will go with you."

She turned around to him still nestled in his arms, and said, "No, Jack. I must do this alone. You may not be safe in there. I will return in a few minutes."

Jasmine stepped forward, and said, "Your Majesty, surely…"

But Mai cut her off with a shake of her head.

But Jasmine insisted. "My lady, at least carry my 9 millimeter for protection. You cannot go in there unarmed. I assure you Yameda and Su Ling will have weapons."

Mai nodded and accepted the gun from Jasmine.

"Mai, we are coming after you in two minutes," said Jack. "We will not be able to wait any longer. I don't like this one bit," he said, kissing her gently.

Chapter 48

June 2005 Siem Kulea

"It is a weapon of some sort. I'm sure of it. But I confess I am hesitant to try it within the confines of this chamber," Yameda said to Su Ling. He had an oval hand-held device with three buttons on it in his hand. He held out the device, pointed it toward one wall and pressed a button. A bright ray of light flared out for an instant and part of the wall disintegrated before their eyes leaving a large whole into the next chamber. "One can only imagine the power of the rest of those weapons in the armory."

They exited the large armory and returned to the main chamber of the alien habitation. While Su Ling watched, Yameda put down the alien weapon he brought with him and stood with his hands on his hips as he studied the instruments on a panel dominating one wall of the unusual chamber. He retrieved and paged through a logbook he found on the floor shortly after they entered the chamber. "Yes," he commented, "It is very much as I imagined it would be. This logbook is the key to everything.

"I believe this to be a device to control the weather and, after I study a bit and can learn to interpret the language in this logbook, I am sure I can figure out how it works in due time. Many of the words and symbols printed here are somewhat familiar to me. This logbook along with the armory of the ancient people's advanced weaponry we discovered will make us invulnerable. I think the next thing we need to do is arm our mercenaries with the advanced weapons to be sure we can repel any counterattack."

"Oh, my darling, I am most happy for you," said Su Ling, hugging him from the side as he continued to peruse the panel and logbook. "There is no doubt now that you will realize all your dreams. You will be the most powerful man in the world, and wealthy beyond imagination."

Yameda turned to her, and said, "Su Ling, my lovely genius, ultimately it was your plan that allowed us to gain access to this chamber. You will have anything you want. No one can deny us now. With this technology, we can crush any opposition. You and I will rule the world."

As intelligent as Yameda was, it happened that it was Su Ling's elaborate ruse, and sophisticated, diabolical plan that made the Siem Kulea valley vulnerable to them. It was always her nature to look for the weak point in an opponent, and exploit that. She had done that perfectly with Queen Maisong, and now they both relished their victory.

"Everything in this chamber seems in perfect condition, remarkably so. I just wish I could talk with one of my ancestors to clear up some of the confusion I still have about the function of some of these instruments. I believe they used Earth's magnetic fields in some manner to alter the weather. I would love to ask them a few questions. Without that, it will take some time ascertaining how to adapt this technology for our purposes."

Just then, as if on cue several of the gauges before them began spinning, and lights on the panel began to get brighter. To their right was a large oval disk about seven feet in diameter that backed up to the wall. It was surrounded by lights embedded in the metal of which it was made, and these began to light up one-by-one. As they watched in amazement, the center of the disk began to glow, slightly at first and then much brighter filling with a white fog. This was all followed by a sound of wind as if in a tunnel, and the room began to shake slightly.

Peering around Yameda toward the bright disk, Su Ling said, "Darling, what is happening? Did you do this? Did you make this happen?"

Yameda seemed mesmerized as he stared in wonder at the glowing disk. He moved slowly toward the disk as if it were an invitation to him. But then, he jumped back as a man and a woman stepped out of the disk and stood before him. They had similar but slightly distorted features and very fair skin, and they were dressed in light green body suits. The man stepped forward and spoke harshly to them in a strange language. When they did not move, he put out his right hand, which released a force that forced them backward, throwing them to the ground suddenly.

"Wait, please," pleaded Yameda with one hand out toward them. "I am Hinsu, and I am your son. I am your ancestor. I am descended from you."

The creatures looked at each other in silence and then back toward Yameda and Su Ling lying in fear on the floor of the chamber. Ironically, the aliens were dressed in almost identical jumpsuits as Yameda and Su Ling who wore hunter green versions for the invasion of the valley.

The creatures were silent at first as they looked at each other, and gestured toward the two on the ground before them. Yameda noted their heads were slightly larger than human, and their brainpans seemed distorted, so the shape was of an extended sphere. Otherwise, in appearance, they were very similar. The woman was staring at the man in silence for an extended moment. Then she smiled as the man turned back toward them and said, "I am Ngocan, and this is my wife, Delane," he said.

"Yes, you are Ferrens. I am descended from you," repeated Yameda as he got up slowly. "I am Hinsu, and this is Su Ling."

Ngocan looked surprised as he said, "How is it that Champas can speak? The last Champas I saw could only make guttural sounds. Your language is very sophisticated but not one I am familiar with," he said.

"But you are speaking it very well," said Yameda.

"We have the ability to transpose and communicate in any language. We are in fact thinking our language but you hear yours and our minds translate your language in the reverse. We adapted once we heard the strange dialect you speak. Where is our daughter, Anh? She was here when we left," he said.

Yameda seemed bewildered by his question, but then he understood. "No, wait, you are confused I think," replied Yameda. "I believe you were here last over ten thousand years ago, maybe even more.

"Ten thousand years? But I only left a few minutes ago. Delane, my wife, was so upset when Anh did not come with us, she insisted on returning to convince her to change her mind," explained Ngocan. "I thought...I thought... Oh, of course. In all the confusion I did not consider and make adjustments for the space-time continuum before returning."

"Yes, I have heard that time in space and time on Earth are different. That must be the truth of it," said Yameda. "While you were gone but minutes, thousands of years passed here on Earth. We call it time dilation."

"Yes, that is so," said Ngocan wearily. "In my haste, I forgot to set certain parameters that might have prevented our error. Those exact settings will now be lost, and all but impossible to retrieve. It has made our situation impossible, and I can feel Delane is already stressing over it. It appears we have seen the last of our daughter. Ah, I see you have found my logbook. That is something else we came back here to retrieve." he said, holding out his hand for it.

Hinsu, still in awe of the alien creatures handed it to him.

After a moment of more silence, Ngocan focused, and said, "So, you are descended from us. You seem very intelligent. I am surprised the Champas survived this foreboding planet. When we left it appeared ready to be frozen over."

"Yes, we as a race we call humans have survived, and a few like myself and Su Ling, my wife, are working to secure the prosperity of our people. I was hoping I could adapt some of your technology to help those on our world to survive far into the future. Perhaps you can teach us how to use the technology that exists here in this chamber."

Delane turned, looked at Yameda sharply, and then at Su ling. After a moment of more silence, she stared at Ngocan again and then turned back toward Yameda.

"We can help in that effort," said Ngocan, "and I am proud to do so. We have developed a technology for this world that will secure a bright, and prosperous future for your race."

Just then, Mai entered the chamber, and everyone turned toward her in surprise. Ngocan saw that she carried a weapon.

At the same time, both Su Ling and Yameda drew their guns and pointed them at Mai.

Ngocan stepped forward blocking Su Ling and Yameda from Mai. "Who is this?" asked Ngocan.

"This is a traitor from our world who seeks to use your technology to rule, control, and enslave everyone. She is evil, and she must be stopped," declared Su Ling.

Delane looked fearful and looked to Ngocan.

Ngocan put out his hand, and Mai was thrown to the floor like a rag doll with the gun she held landing across the room. Mai tried to get up, but she couldn't as Delane stared at her intensely. Exasperated, she settled back against the floor.

"She will not bother you anymore," said Ngocan. "We must hurry. This portal is very spotty as it nears the end of its cycle. We cannot stay here, so we are inviting you to join us on our planet where you can learn our technology, and then you may return here to help your planet and people live prosperously into the future.

"Put your weapons and anything you possess that is metallic over there on the table," Ngocan instructed. "Metal may not be transported through the portal," he explained. "It will not resolve properly on the other side, and may bring disastrous results for you."

Su Ling and Yameda took off their holsters and placed them with their guns on the table nearby with their watches and jewelry.

"Come," said Ngocan. "We must hurry," he said urgently.

Su Ling and Yameda stood in front of the large bright disk. "What do we do?" asked Su Ling.

"Simply step into the portal," explained Ngocan. "You will soon be in our world as welcome emissaries from this one. Do not be concerned. We have marked this date and time and can accelerate the portal, something I neglected to do before our return. Thus you may return to your own time after you learn the knowledge that you need to ensure the continued prosperity of your fellow humans. Hurry, we will be right behind you."

Su Ling took Yameda's hand, and they stepped into the portal together. As soon as they disappeared Delane turned and ran to Mai who still lay on the floor. She bent down and put her hand to Mai's head. "You may open your eyes now. They are gone, my child," she said gently.

As Mai opened her eyes, she was confused and bewildered before the two aliens who stood over her.

"Are you hurt?" asked Delane. "I am sorry we had to do that, but it seemed the best way to remove the...problem."

"No, I'm OK. I understood your Mindspeak thought communication with me. I knew to just lay there, and pretend I was unconscious but that force you used to knock me down was pretty strong," said Mai.

As Mai got up, she continued, "It seemed like you believed them. When I entered I was stunned when I saw the situation, and I wanted to explain myself, but I was unable to speak, and then you used the force to throw me down. It was all so fast. How did you know to trust me?"

Ngocan reached over and gave Mai a warm hug. Then he held her back at arm's length. "You look almost exactly like our daughter, Anh. We had no doubt as to who to protect."

"Your timing was perfect," said Ngocan. "Delane had just told me using our method of thought transference that the other two were lying to us. She examined their minds, and discovered their evil intentions."

"Yes, in fact, I thought you were Anh when you first came in," said Delane. "But then Ngocan reminded me that thousands of years had passed, and that was impossible. It was then I noted the small difference in your features from us."

"What will happen to Yameda and Su Ling?" asked Mai.

"They are already disintegrated," said Ngocan. "I am afraid it was necessary to deceive those two for our own protection. As it is, metal will easily transport through the portal but corporal beings will disintegrate as a result of the process. You must wear one of these collars to travel by means of the portal," he said rubbing the thin metal collar around his neck. "Otherwise you cannot resolve on the other end and will instead disintegrate into the ether of the universe. It is a necessary means we have for protecting our world."

"I sense your name is Maisong. Yes?" Delane asked. "Ours are Ngocan and Delane. Do you mind if we regard you as our daughter? You seem just like her, and right now I find that comforting."

Mai nodded with a big smile. She liked these two very much, and she took their hands as she spoke. "But I am your daughter in a way. I am directly descended from you through Anh. She was our first mother."

"Yes, of course. That explains why you look so much like her," commented Delane.

"Do you also wish to make use of this technology?" Ngocan asked.

"No," Mai said. "Quite the opposite. The politics of this world make it impossible. I want to close this chamber, and never open it again. I wish there were a way to be sure that no one could access, or use this technology."

"There is, and I would have done it before had I not been so upset when we left. That said, I think I still hoped that Anh would follow us," said Ngocan. "But to be certain that this portal is closed forever, it is best if you do it because of the possible time differential."

"Yes, of course. What do I need to do?" asked Mai.

"You will know when we leave," he said. "When you pull that lever it will first shut off any power within the chamber lest there be an atomic explosion. That will also disable any weapons remaining within this chamber for the same reason. But I must warn you, that when you set the device, it will affect all of our sites around the world. They will all dissolve mirroring the elements of their surrounding environment erasing our technology forever from this planet. When the chamber goes dark, you have about thirty minutes to get out."

At that moment Jack, Jasmine, and Marty followed by Ramadi entered and stopped abruptly behind Mai.

Mai turned quickly toward them with her hands palms-out facing them. "Stop! Put your weapons on the ground over there," she commanded them. "Do it now. These are our friends. Hurry!" she urged them.

When they were done disarming themselves and standing with her again, Mai took Jack's hand and led him forward proudly. "This is my husband, Jack."

Ngocan shook his offered hand. He held it for an extended moment, and then touched his hand to Jack's head.

"I can see Maisong has chosen well," he said. "You are to be commended for your support of Maisong."

"I love her very much," Jack said, as Mai leaned into him.

Ngocan looked at Jasmine who was all the way down with her head on the floor in a worshipping position.

Mai explained, "This is Jasmine, one of my loyal Champa people. Since the beginning of my people, the Champas, they have worshipped you, and believe you to be Gods. They worship me in kind because I am descended from you. It is our way, and faith. I am certain you understand, and respect that. It is real, fervent and it brings purpose and wellbeing to their lives. I do not know for sure, but I suspect that was inbred in their DNA by you and the ancient ones."

Ngocan nodded. "Exactly. It was a necessary process for our survival when we could no longer live on the planet's surface. We needed a means to control them and make them devoted to us. The Champas served us well, and it appears they continue to do so loyally." Ngocan called Delane to join him, and they stood before Jasmine. Delane commanded Jasmine to stand. After she did as commanded, Delane touched her head for a moment and smiled. "You have served us well, Jasmine, and for that we are grateful."

Ngocan held out his hand for Marty who joined them. He put his other hand to Marty's head for a moment, and then taking Jasmine's hand, he joined their hands together. "Take this man, Marty, and join with him. He is a good man, and you two are suitably matched."

Jasmine kept her eyes averted humbly but showed her surprise as she asked, "How did you know of our love for each other?"

Delane smiled at her, "You are both glowing. There is a joyous aura about the two of you. Can you not see it? That is the way we determined those Champas suitably matched for breeding."

Jasmine looked at Marty who wore a big smile. He chuckled, and said, "How about that. We glow!"

Jasmine glanced over at Mai a bit concerned, but she was also smiling at them in approval.

Ngocan was still carrying his logbook. He held it up for them to see, and then he handed it to Marty. "I think this meeting was meant to be. After accessing you, I am now aware that you are the keeper of the log and will get the most use out of this," he said. "As you record the history of my daughter's people, you may find this logbook of some use. It will give you a perspective from our view, and I believe our history on this planet is relevant to your record." He rested his hand on Marty's head for a moment. "That may help a bit in your effort."

Marty did not understand at first, but when he looked at the cover of the book that Ngocan handed him he was stunned to realize he could read it perfectly. As he thumbed quickly through it, he found every page was easy for him to read. It seemed a miracle, but Marty understood it was only science even if he couldn't understand yet what had just happened.

Mai stepped forward, gave Delane a big hug, and spoke directly to her. "I have someone who wants to go with you back to your world," she said. "That is, if it is OK. She has been with me for many years, and she wants to go home. I think it is time for her to do so although I will miss her a great deal."

Ngocan and Delane both looked at Mai curiously. Mai held out her hands toward Delane who took them in hers. A moment passed in silence, and Delane developed a curious expression on her face. Mai removed the ring on her finger and put it on the index finger of Delane's hand. It fit perfectly.

Suddenly Delane's face brightened, and her eyes began to water with great joy. "Ngocan it is Anh! Anh our daughter is with me, and she has many stories she wants to tell me. She is here. I swear it is true. Give me your hand."

She took Ngocan's hand and held it tightly as he began to smile with her. He looked at Mai smiling broadly. "How is this possible?" he asked.

"I knew her as Queen Dau Tê Po," said Mai. "She was a legend to our people. I suspect your daughter, my ancestor Anh, was in spirit with all of we Champa queens since the beginning. It is probably the one thing that preserved and protected our people to this day. Now her work is done, and she is ready to return home with you."

Ngocan and Delane were beside themselves with happiness. They gave cheerful hugs to everyone even awkwardly with Ramadi who towered over them.

"I am afraid we must go now," said Ngocan. "Please know that we love you very much and our spirit and thoughts will always be with you."

Delane went to Jack and gave him a prolonged hug. She said something to him and then joined Ngocan before the portal. Ngocan and Delane looked back and threw Mai a final kiss, and joined hands. They stepped through the portal, and as bright as the portal had been, in the next moment it was gone leaving the room in a quiet, dim light.

Mai walked forward, put her hand on the edge of the portal, and held it there as they watched her. When she turned around, she was crying, and Jack rushed to her and held her in his arms warmly as they others waited patiently. After a few minutes in silence she broke away from his embrace, and as Jasmine handed her a clean tissue, she sheepishly wiped the tears away while smiling with Jack.

"That was pretty amazing, Mai," he said.

She took a deep breath and nodded to him.

"No one will ever believe this," he said.

"You cannot ever tell anyone of this, Jack. Nor you, Marty, Ramadi, or Jasmine," she said. "This secret must be kept between us," she said looking at each of them, and ending with Jasmine who nodded and bowed her head.

Marty, that logbook stays here in Siem Kulea with the other papers in the archive that you will study. It was given to you, but it is not yours. Do you understand?" she asked. "It belongs to my people."

"Of course, Mai. You should know by now that all I want is to record the narrative of the Champa people. Their story deserves to be written, and I will write it. Whether it is ever shared with the rest of the world, I will leave that decision up to you, I promise," he said, smiling.

She nodded to him and smiled in return. "Come let us get out of here. Once I activate the device there is no turning back," she said, moving to a bank of instruments by the portal. She pressed a series of buttons and pulled a lever that was no longer a mystery to her.

"Come, everyone, I think we have approximately thirty minutes," she told them.

They went back upstairs where Daniel and Lady Chu were waiting for them.

"We did not find any sign of Yameda and Su Ling. Were they below?" he asked.

Mai nodded solemnly. "They went through the portal of the ancients and were disintegrated," she said. "They are gone forever. Their ambition has finally destroyed them."

Lady Chu said, "We have retaken the valley, Your Majesty. The militia collective has disarmed a force of about one thousand men and holds them prisoner beyond the east mountains. They brought a dozen Cambodian army officers who led the invasion of the valley here and they are just outside awaiting your review. My lady, one of them is General Rhee Sonh."

Mai considered this as she stood in thought for a moment and then commanded, "Ramadi, take these officers downstairs and put them in the chamber."

In a few minutes, Ramadi returned with the prisoners. He and his men hurried the prisoners down to the lower basement, and prodded them into the chamber. They held guns on them as they left them kneeling inside the door.

As Mai and the rest joined them she saw General Rhee through the portal on his knees crying and begging for mercy. The chamber suddenly turned dark as all power within shut down. But Mai only stood impassively and watched as Ramadi pulled the massive door closed. It seemed to take forever to move its massive weight into a closed position. When it finally came to rest seamlessly in its frame with a loud THUNK, there was a sense of finality to its closing. Then he turned the ornate handle, and they heard it audibly lock with a series of movements within the door itself.

"Pull it out, Ramadi. Pull out the handle once more," Mai commanded.

Ramadi took hold of the handle and pulled with all his strength, and after giving some resistance, it slowly began to move out from the door. Then it all came out at once in his hands, and he turned around for Mai to see it.

"Drop it on the floor," she commanded.

He did so, and it landed firmly, separating into three pieces once more.

Jasmine was standing closest to the door, but suddenly she jumped away from it. "Your Majesty!" she exclaimed. "Look!"

Before their eyes, the snakeheads melted, and dissolved into the door turning the sculpture into a hideous distortion of what it had been a moment before. Everyone backed away shaken by what they saw. On the floor, the door handle melted and began to fuse into the stone. Even Ramadi stood stiffly with huge eyes stunned by what was happening.

Mai exclaimed, "Ramadi, evacuate everyone out of the palace, and into the far fields. Hurry! The chamber behind this door is going to fuse into solid rock, and I am not sure, but that might topple the palace."

Ramadi and his men hurried off, and in ten minutes everyone was assembled in the field looking back toward the Palace. Jack had his arm around Mai's shoulder, and as she looked around, she realized that most of the people in the valley had joined them.

They waited for some time before anything happened. But then there came a slight rumbling beneath the Earth. Suddenly, a glowing array of dancing lights appeared over the palace. The loyal Champa people knelt as a sign of their faith, but Mai only looked at her finger where the ring she had worn for so long was gone forever. In spite of the joy she had brought to her ancestors and the spirit she had known as Queen Dau Te Po, she was going to miss them, and that saddened her greatly.

Chapter 49

2006 Chicago

"He's Guilty!" read the headline in the Chicago Herald. The sub-headline continued, **"Senator Grimes found guilty of murdering his wife, heiress Pamela Thorne Grimes."**

Chicago. A Federal jury today convicted Senator Earl Beacham Grimes of murder in the death of his wife six years ago. The jury deliberated less than five hours before deciding on a guilty verdict on all counts. Senator Grimes will be sentenced tomorrow in Part 21 of the Federal Court in downtown Chicago.

Senator Grimes claimed his wife drowned after she was found floating dead two days after he declared her missing because of a boating accident on Lake Michigan.

A television investigation of the story last year by Catherine Marsh on her popular Newsworthy cable news program broke the story open when they showed an aerial photograph of Senator Grimes drowning his wife in the lake. Consequent investigations by Federal Agents produced evidence of a history of Senator Grime's severe gambling debts.

Senator Grimes is expected to appeal the verdict, but most experts say he will likely get life imprisonment with no chance of parole. Senator Grimes was unavailable for comment.

Catherine read the headlines in the morning paper with great satisfaction as she dined for breakfast with Kelly and Charlie. She looked over at her partner, and they shared a triumphant smile.

"Mom, can I have the sports section?" asked Charlie, sitting across from them.

Kelly gave him a look, and said, "Really?"

"Huh…what?" Charlie asked, seriously.

"That's all you have to say when the news in this paper is like getting an Academy Award for your mom? I'll have you know young man the headline in that paper is getting framed, and mounted in Catherine's office. You should be really proud of your mom."

"Oh, come on, of course, I am. But really, that's old news. You two have been talking about it for over a year. The Bears are playing the Packers today for the league title, and I want to see if Marcus Means is going to be healthy enough to play. That's what's important this day," he quipped, smiling.

"Mean Marcus, and the Chicago Bears are all you care about lately," Kelly said. "This is your sophomore year, and you have to keep those grades up if you want to get into a good law school."

She turned her attention back to Catherine. "I had ten copies of the paper brought directly from the Herald in pristine condition. I want to take one to Mai when we go over there next month," she said.

Charlie ignored Kelly's reprimand and was lost in the sports section reading about the Bears-Packers game.

Catherine smiled at him, knowing full well he had already congratulated her about the headlines in the paper that morning before Kelly came to the table. She picked up the phone that was ringing demands to answer nearby. It was Audrey returning Catherine's call after she had left a message earlier that morning.

"Yes I saw the paper," answered Catherine, to Audrey's first question. "You should be very proud. I was on the phone with the AG just yesterday after the verdict came in. He said that once they reopened the case, evidence came to them like the animals to Noah during the flood. But he also said that none of it would have happened without our persistence and the breakthrough image that we discovered. I told him that evidence was found by the newest, and brightest young talent on my team. He told me I should be proud of your work, and I am. It was a perfect crime until you showed up."

"Thank you, Catherine. I think a lot of it was luck, but I will gladly accept the accolades for a job well done. It's like getting paid!

"But, Catherine, I am really glad you called. I have been feeling guilty about being away especially since you have been so nice to me. It was really above-and-beyond that you let me take a month off to get my dad situated. I plan to be back in the office on Wednesday now that he is recovered and settled in his new place in Wisconsin," Audrey said. "I hope you still have a place for me. I really miss the office and, well, the both of you."

"I have to say I have been considering your position with us for a while now, Audrey. Your particular perspective and approach while working on the Grimes investigation and subsequent trial was consistently unique, professional and superior to your peers. I think you will be pleased to know I am giving you your own group. Think you can handle it?" Catherine asked.

"Oh my God! Yes, Catherine. But maybe I'm just too dumb to know that I cannot. Wow! Really? This is exciting."

"You deserve it, and I can't think of a better way to express my gratitude. Actually, you are very much like me at your age with one big exception. You have people who support and believe in you. You are going to be our young perspective on major issues. Your stories will be focused on issues important to young adults, and teens. I think you are particularly suited to that. But I also want you to start writing your own perspective on major news stories as part of an ongoing series in our editorial department. Sound OK?"

"Yes, of course. I'm really excited, and I won't let you down. I admit I feel like I am on a roller coaster at times. You seem always to be calm and collected," Audrey said.

"That's Kelly, not me," said Catherine. I don't know what I would do without her. Have you decided on an apartment yet?"

"No…OK, look. I've been holding off on that because I really don't want to move out. I really love being with you, and Kelly. I enjoyed starting the days with you two at breakfast, and then our dinner rotations became something I looked forward to. You have made me feel welcome and like family from the first day. I love you guys for it."

"Then don't!" said Catherine.

"Really?"

"Yes. Moving out was your idea. We were kind of bummed, you wanted to move out. We love having you around," said Catherine. "In a short time, you've become like family to us. You keep us young.

"How is Hagen doing?" Catherine asked.

"Dad is as good as new, I think. He would never admit if he was hurting anyway. He bought a nice place on Lake Michigan that allows him to pursue the things he likes to do. He and Lieutenant Haleran have become close friends. Can you believe that? He just bought a sailboat and has been teaching me how to sail. Lieutenant Haleran goes sailing with him often. They're both planning on going to Siem Kulea in late January with us," she said. "I can't wait, I have heard so much about it!"

"Tell him he needs to come talk to me when he's ready. I need to use his talents on some of our projects," said Catherine.

"Hah, you two are a matched pair. He told me he wanted to work with you and was looking forward to presenting an idea for a working relationship of some sort. I guess you know he has to keep his hand in somehow. He surely doesn't need the money. The excitement is in his blood, maybe my blood too. I was really digging it when we were in Salzburg taking on those bad guys last year," she said.

"Well forget that stuff. Your job does not require carrying a nine-millimeter. A lot of our work walks a tightrope along the letter of the law, Audrey. But I cannot condone breaking the law, in spite of your experience with that whole operation in Austria. We have to answer to Uncle Sam just like everyone else. If you or he decides to do anything illegal, I cannot protect you," she said.

"I know, and I am sure he does too. But I worry some times that will not stop him from getting up to his old tricks," Audrey said.

"Yes, I know," Catherine said. *"I'm counting on it,"* she thought.

Chapter 50

2008 Siem Kulea

Exactly three years to the day since parting with her ancient ancestors Ngocan and Delane in the chamber below the palace, Jack took Mai out to the garden just off of the queen's quarters. He led her to the bench they loved to sit in together and gaze at the stars at night. Siem Kulea was in a part of the world, and at an elevation that afforded an unusually clear view of the heavens.

Mai commented. "The stars are really clear tonight. Look at the depth. I love that, and it never gets old for me. It almost takes your breath away."

"Did you know it has been exactly three years, one-thousand ninety-five days, Mai, since that night when your ancestors departed?" he asked.

Mai took a deep breath and sighed heavily because she still felt a loss from that moment when they left. "Yes, I would have liked to have known them better, and spend some time with them. Do you suppose they are out there somewhere looking out at the stars, and wishing the same thing?"

"Of that, I have no doubt," he said.

"Mai," he continued, "I have something to tell you, which I think is important. The fact is I really don't know why. I just know to do it exactly this way."

"You goof, what are you talking about now?" she said, chuckling at him. But then, she saw he was very serious.

"That last night just before they went through the portal Delane hugged me, remember? When she did, she touched my cheek and looked right into my eyes. She gave me something to hold and give to you when the time was right. I put it in my pocket and kept it hidden because I knew I was supposed to do that and wait for the right time. Mai, this is the right time."

He pulled a necklace from his pocket. It was an intricately intertwined chain of gold, and hanging from it was a relatively large rectangular jewel of astounding color and depth that reminded her of the ring she used to have on her finger. Jack clasped it around her neck, and she held it up to look at it.

"You are supposed to take the stone, and hold it up to the stars, so you are looking through it," he told her. "Once again, I don't know how I know that. I just do."

This was one of those moments like the first time he saw her in Catherine's condo that he would never forget. She took the necklace, and grasping the stone, held it up to look through it at the stars.

"Oh, Jack! Oh my goodness! I see one star in particular. It is very bright," she said excitedly. "Do you think that might be them?"

As she held the jewel up to her face to study it, he saw the stone glow like her ring often did, and it reflected in her dark eyes. The stars in the sky were magically projected across her face through the physics of the jewel. She was as a goddess in that visage and though he already knew her better than anyone else he was still awed by that vision.

In the next instant, she turned to him smiling, and said, "I love you, Jack Largent. Do you know what this is?" she asked him.

"I cannot imagine, Mai," he replied. "Please, tell me."

"I suspect for a moment the stars were aligned perfectly just now, and I sensed her presence. I felt Delane saying "hello" to me.

"Jack, this magnificent stone is a vessel for her spirit. Delane and Anh will join with me as Queen Po has done when her spirit finally leaves her world. The three of us will travel the universe together. In a sense, I got my wish. I will have time to spend with her, and get to know her." She began to cry with happiness as he held her close in a warm moment.

As they held hands and looked up once more at the stars, Jack said softly, "I wish I could climb into one of those jewels. I have no doubt it is going to be a grand ride."

"Well, fasten your seatbelt, my love," said Mai. "We are destined to never be apart."

ABOUT THE AUTHOR

William Diebold is currently a retired teacher living in Southern California. He did three tours in Vietnam, spending two years and three months there as a photographer from 1969 to 1971. Following that he attended ArtCenter College of Design in Los Angeles. Upon graduation, he was hired by Leo Burnett Inc. to manage a studio in Chicago. After one year he went out on his own, eventually spending twenty-five years as an advertising photographer with studios in Chicago and Dallas. He was fortunate to enjoy success during those years, with many major clients such as Kellogg's, Little Caesars, Pillsbury, Bud Light, Quaker, Sam Adams, and Pepsi.

Diebold was an advertising photographer in Chicago at a time during the 1980s when the industry was at the dawn of major changes brought on by the revolution of personal computers, digital media, and the Internet. It was an exciting, portentous time, and he is still of the opinion that Chicago and its wonderful people are the best-kept secrets in the country.

As a father with two sons, a wonderful daughter-in-law, and two amazing grandchildren, he very much looks forward to what tomorrow may bring.

William Diebold's website can be found at www.debold.com (note the different spelling of his name). There you will find many Vietnam photographs that mirror some of the chapters in the story. You will also see some of his professional advertising work and many examples of his former students' work from his digital imaging classes.

He welcomes your comments. Please feel free to send him a note to
wdiebold2102@roadrunner.com

The website for his books 'Valley of the Queen" and "Palace Secret" is
http://www.valleyofthequeen.com

The cover photographs and graphics are by William Diebold © 2018

There are Facebook pages for each of his books. You are invited to go there
and add your comments.

You are invited to write your personal review on Amazon.com book page
for each title.